THE
BORGIA
RING

MICHAEL WHITE

arrow books

First published by Arrow Books 2009

6 8 10 9 7

Copyright © Michael White 2009

The right of Michael White to be identified as the author of this work has
been asserted by him in accordance with the Copyright, Designs and
Patents Act, 1988

The Borgia Ring is a work of fiction. Any resemblance between these
fictional characters and actual persons, living or dead, is purely
coincidental

This book is sold subject to the condition that it shall not, by way of trade
or otherwise, be lent, resold, hired out, or otherwise circulated without the
publisher's prior consent in any form of binding or cover other than that in
which it is published and without a similar condition including this
condition being imposed on the subsequent purchaser

Arrow Books
The Random House Group Limited
20 Vauxhall Bridge Road, London, SW1V 2SA

www.rbooks.co.uk

Addresses for companies within The Random House Group Limited can
be found at: www.randomhouse.co.uk/offices.htm

The Random House Group Limited Reg. No. 954009

A CIP catalogue record for this book
is available from the British Library

ISBN 9780099536291

The Random House Group Limited supports The Forest Stewardship
Council® (FSC®), the leading international forest-certification organisation.
Our books carrying the FSC label are printed on FSC®-certified paper.
FSC is the only forest-certification scheme supported by the leading
environmental organisations, including Greenpeace. Our
paper procurement policy can be found at
www.randomhouse.co.uk/environment

Typeset by SX Composing DTP, Rayleigh, Essex
Printed and bound in Great Britain by
Clays Ltd, St Ives plc

THE
BORGIA
RING

Laois County Library
Leabharlann Chontae Laoise

Acc No. 15/1946

Class No. ....

Inv. 13063

WITHDRAWN

OUT OF STOCK

Prologue

Rome, August 1503

Pope Alexander VI had a head like a huge scrotum. Grease dribbled down his chin and his usually mean black pupils dilated as he contemplated the mountainous sweet pudding placed before him. His daughter Lucrezia Borgia looked at him and felt vomit rise in her throat. She had been only twelve when her father first introduced her to his sexual proclivities. She had been forced to masturbate with a crucifix while she watched him sodomise a nine-year-old servant boy. When the bloated old man came he had grunted like a spiked boar.

Next to her father sat her brother, Cesare. Once, after he had kept her awake all night with his insatiable lust, he had boasted about killing dozens of men, and of how one day he would slaughter their father and have his own chance at the papal throne. But now Cesare Borgia was ill. It was the French disease. Everyone knew it. His face was covered with running sores and there was a madness in his eyes worse than anything she had seen in them before.

To Lucrezia's left sat the boy alchemist, Cornelius Agrippa. A tender sixteen-year-old with dark, piercing eyes, he was both her lover and a fellow traveller on the road to occult knowledge. Agrippa had taught her a great many things: ways to retain her youthful beauty, ways to make every man adore her. Most importantly, he had taught her new ways to kill. Together they had produced murderous potions that brought death with thrilling speed and left no trace.

The last figure to fall under her gaze was Domenico Gonzaga, youngest son of Francesco II, Marquis of Mantua. Domenico's handsome face was just beginning to show the signs of too much good living. He and Cesare had, she knew, played together as children, but now the two men despised each other. It was her father, the Pope, who had arranged for the Marquis's son to visit, the latest in a long line of suitors for Lucrezia's hand. Of course, Cesare had hated them all.

By the end of the meal Alexander was so drunk he could barely stand, but Lucrezia could tell he still had energy left for his favourite pastime. The way he looked at the two black slaves as they helped him from his chair was unmistakable: a look she had seen many, many times. He had once confided in her that the negro boys he had brought into the Vatican could satisfy him in ways nothing and no one else could. It was strange, she reflected, how the men in her life wanted to share with her their most intimate secrets. She relished the sense of power that gave her.

Soon, she found herself alone with Domenico. They were seated close together on a low couch. He ran a finger along her cheek.

'I'm really not so bad,' he slurred, breath rancid, lips and teeth stained red by the wine.

'Whoever said you were, my lord?'

'You refused to catch my eye at table.'

'It would have been unseemly.'

Domenico roared with laughter, but his face fell when he saw that Lucrezia was straight-faced and composed. 'Forgive me, my lady.' He coughed and tugged at his jerkin.

'My father arranged this visit, Domenico, not I,' she said quietly. 'Your father is wealthy and mine extremely avaricious.'

'It is true my father is a very rich man and I am heir to his lands. But I would like to think there is more substance to me than mere money and possessions.' He moved towards her, breath warm on her neck. He turned her face roughly to his and kissed her hard on the mouth. She could smell the animal taint of his sweat. Before she could stop him, he had his hand up her dress.

Lucrezia made a perfect show of trying to pull away. She was an accomplished actress who knew she could better any player on the Roman stage. She felt a sudden surge of pride. She was in the position of power here, even if this lumbering fool believed he was. She had known her own power since childhood, before the flowering of her sexual maturity. And now, in her twenty-fourth year, she was in full bloom and revelled in the knowledge that she could outperform any cheap whore from the ghetto.

'My brother will slit your throat and rub his cock with your blood,' she whispered as Domenico managed to worm his fingers into her under-garments. She felt him freeze for a second.

'Your father would not allow it,' he said hesitantly.

'My father is not the master of Cesare, my lord.'

'But Cesare is not here.'

Lucrezia felt herself slowly melting like thawing ice as Domenico squeezed himself between her legs. He had freed himself from his hose and she could feel his flesh parting her. She threw back her head and groaned.

4

'You believe you dominate me,' she said thickly, her black eyes holding his.

'It is no mere belief, Lucrezia, my love,' Domenico gasped. The beginnings of a cruel smile flickered across his face.

'But you are sadly mistaken, my lord. You impale me. But I too can impale you.'

Domenico felt a searing pain in the back of his neck. He looked down. Lucrezia Borgia was climaxing, her eyes huge, her groin thrusting back at him. He screamed and tried to pull away from her but felt sapped of energy; he could not move a muscle. Lucrezia kept grinding herself on to him, her face sharp-contoured in ecstasy, her eyes now clamped tight. Then, with her back arched, she froze, shuddered and opened her eyes: the gaze of a falcon ready for the kill.

She pushed him away and he fell back on to the sofa like a mannequin, his erection waving uselessly. He tried to move, but could not. And the pain . . . the pain was like nothing he had ever experienced. It spread down his neck to his chest. He could not draw breath. Then he felt the liquid erupt from his mouth, a red plume that engulfed his face, reaching his eyes, blinding him. He tried to lift a hand but not a single finger would move. His stomach heaved again and he spewed more blood along with partially digested chunks of pork, chicken and sweetmeats.

Lucrezia was leaning over him. With a cloth, she wiped the blood and vomit from his face so that he could see her. She was holding up one finger. Upon it he could see a large gold ring set with a round-cut emerald. The stone had been levered up and in the opening beneath he could just make out a tiny metal spike coated in red.

Lucrezia smiled sweetly and turned away as Domenico Gonzaga, youngest son of Francesco II, Marquis of Mantua, shuddered his last, and died.

Chapter 1

Stepney, Saturday 4 June, 2.16 a.m.

It was still very humid. Almost hot enough for a Bombay night, Amal Karim thought as he made his way across the construction site. The ground was hard. It hadn't rained for weeks. Most of England had sweltered for a straight run of thirteen days and that afternoon the thermometer had nudged 38 degrees, almost hot enough for the union to shut down the site.

After leaving his jacket in the works hut, he was in a short-sleeved shirt but still sweating profusely. It was very dark, though by now his eyes had adjusted and he could just make out the shapes of heavy plant and mounds of earth all around the site. He took a deep breath of hot, still air and gazed around him. He was standing beside a pit perhaps thirty metres wide and ten deep, its mud walls shored up with steel beams. Wooden planks criss-crossed the hole, supported on scaffolding and liberally coated with dried mud and concrete. On each side of the excavated footings stood construction machinery: a powerful digger, a pile-driver, and two massive trucks with two-metre-high tyres caked in mud. He could just see a truck bearing the black and silver logo of Bridgeport Construction. Lighting a cigarette, he discarded the match.

There was a sound behind him. He spun round and waved his torch towards the dark pit. He was just feeling jumpy, he told himself. Taking a few steps along a plank to his right, he drew hard on his cigarette. Standing still for a moment, he probed the darkness below with the beam of his torch, watching the cigarette smoke dance in its light. At the base of a small depression in the bottom of the pit a grey tarpaulin was stretched. Underneath it, he knew, lay an ancient skeleton.

He had been on the other side of the site when his fellow construction workers had uncovered the bones the previous afternoon. But, like the rest of the crew, he was soon aware of the find. He had run over in time to see the site manager, Tony Ketteridge, and one of the architects, Tim Middleton, leaning over the remains. Middleton had been taking pictures with his mobile while Ketteridge had seemed to be deeply disturbed by what had just been revealed. The man had been under severe pressure for weeks, the build

8

already way behind schedule. The last thing they needed was bureaucratic delay caused by the finding of human remains.

Karim left the plank and dropped the stub of his cigarette on to the hard mud beside the pit, stamping it out. Then, with his torch slicing through the darkness, he walked slowly down the slope integrated into one side of the excavation, to where the skeleton lay. He carefully removed the tarpaulin and shone the beam towards the ground. The skeleton lay on its back, just as it had earlier. By the look of them, the remains were those of a tall, slightly built man. The front of the skull was shattered above one eye and a fissure ran along one side above where the ear would have been. The bones were almost black and looked to be extremely old. There was nothing to be seen around the skeleton apart from a few fragments of broken clay and some large pieces of granite.

Karim thought back to the previous afternoon. There had been a row then about what should be done with the bones. Ketteridge wanted them removed instantly and for the workforce to pretend nothing had been found. But some of the construction workers had objected. Then two of them had turned over the skeleton, and they had all seen the ring. It was gold with a flat, round top made from a green stone, perhaps an emerald.

After that there had been no more arguments. The area was already covered by security cameras, but Ketteridge had asked for a volunteer to patrol the site throughout the night. Karim remembered how he had jumped at the chance of double time, feeling no qualms about the job in the daylight hours.

Now, he crouched down to look more closely at the skeleton and his eye was drawn to the ring. It was on the smallest finger of the skeleton's right hand. It looked to be extremely valuable, he mused, and for a fleeting moment imagined stealing it and simply vanishing. He would leave his family behind, start a new life somewhere no one could find him.

There was that noise again.

It was closer this time, a scraping sound, a scattering of pebbles. He made to stand up, but as he rose he felt an arm slide around his neck, pulling back his head. He reacted quickly, bunching his fist and slamming his elbow backwards, winding the man behind him. Karim fell forward as his assailant loosened his grip. He felt a sharp pain in his right knee as he landed awkwardly on the hard clay. His attacker let fly with a kick aimed at his abdomen. Karim dodged it, but then, as he scrambled backwards, tripped over the edge of the tarpaulin and tumbled into a pile of dried mud. Turning his head, he saw there were two men with him in the pit. His attacker was the shorter of the two. They were both wearing balaclavas, dark T-shirts, black trousers and gloves. The taller man was standing back a few paces, looking around nervously. The other, the man who had attacked Karim, was now no more than a couple of feet away. Through the holes in the balaclava, Karim could see the man's dark eyes ringed with sweat.

He backed away from his assailant, just managing to gain some purchase on the dry mud. On the other side of the mound, a line of planks led towards the sloping path up to ground level. The man who had grabbed him moved quickly around the mound where the ground was harder, cutting off Karim's escape route. The workman lashed out, landing a glancing blow on his attacker's shoulder. The man gasped and made a grab for Karim, catching the lapel of his shirt. His fist landed squarely on the workman's nose and a stream of blood poured from his nostrils into his mouth. Karim kicked him, a move that did little except anger his assailant. But although the Indian was much smaller, he was no pushover. He feinted with one hand. Bringing up the other, he went for the man's eyes but succeeded only in grasping the balaclava. The other man recoiled and the mask slid up his face as far as his forehead.

It was very dark, but Karim had seen his

assailant's face. Startled, he almost lost his footing on the uneven compacted earth. But as the other man scrabbled to pull down his balaclava, Karim quickly recovered. He swerved to one side and ran up the slope as fast as he could.

By the time he reached the top he was out of breath. The pain in his face was agonising. As he ran, he touched his nose and felt the wetness of blood. The front of his shirt was flecked with red. He glanced back and could see the two masked men charging up the incline behind him. He ran on, ignoring the stabbing pain in his side. It was lighter up here, though shadowed where the streetlights encountered piles of earth and hulking machinery. To his right stood the site hut; beyond that the perimeter fence topped with a concertina of barbed wire.

Karim reached the metal fence at the point where it cut across a corner of land immediately in front of a row of shops with flats on the upper floors that fronted the Mile End Road. There was a gate in the mesh secured with a large padlocked chain. As he ran he rifled his pockets for the key. Karim stabbed at the padlock, repeatedly missing the keyhole. Blood dripped from his nose on to the lock. His face hurt terribly. The two men were fast approaching him. They rounded a pile of earth no more than ten metres away. He saw one of them bend down. When he straightened up again, he was holding a length of metal pipe in his right hand.

Karim found the keyhole and twisted the key. The padlock snapped open and he yanked the chain away, slipped out of the gate and slammed it shut behind him. He tried desperately to lock it again but they were there. One of them grabbed the chain. Karim let it go and ran.

He charged down a narrow passageway behind the row of shops. Ahead of him loomed a blank brick wall. He could see an open wooden gate to one side and sped towards it, tripping on a step and landing spread-eagled in a small courtyard. He cursed loudly and picked himself up. Two paces ahead stood a short stairway leading up to a flat roof. He hesitated for a moment. The last thing he wanted was to be trapped up there with no way out. But it was too late. The men were already in the passageway, he could hear their footsteps. They would be on him in a second.

He dashed up the stairs. It was a large roof with two metal flues reaching to about waist-height and pointing at the sky. And, immediately, his worst fear was confirmed. There was only one way off this roof – the way he had come. Turning, he saw the two men burst into the courtyard. The one in front was slapping the metal pipe against his open palm.

Karim backed towards the nearest flue. He peered down into it – blackness. Then, before he could make another move, the two men rushed him. He managed to duck away from the first swing and the pipe hit the flue, producing a low, hollow thud. He ran round the other side, but the second man was waiting for him there. He grabbed Karim's arms and held them behind his back. Twisting away, he managed to land a kick in the taller man's groin and make a run for it, but the short man with the pipe was ready for him. He brought the length of metal up hard under Karim's chin, smashing his windpipe. He hit the floor face first with an audible crunch as bones broke and cartilage shattered. The shorter man brought the pipe down full force on the back of Karim's skull. The sound of the impact was like a coconut being shattered with a hammer. Karim sighed once and was dead.

Blood had run down the side of the victim's face and pooled on the concrete. The taller man was panting and his hands were shaking. He stood staring at the body on the ground. With his hands pressed to his head, he kept repeating the same words: 'Oh, fuck!'

The other man kicked Karim's body to ensure the job was done. 'Grab his feet,' he said.

'What?'

'Are you deaf? His feet!'

Moving like an automaton, his accomplice did as he was told. Together they turned the dead man over. He stared up at them through sightless eyes filmed with blood, his hair a matted red flecked with grey. The taller man let out a groan.

'Don't you dare fucking gag!' the other man growled, resting the length of pipe across Karim's chest.

They half-dragged, half-carried the body the few feet back to the flue. Then the murderer snatched up the pipe again. They lifted Karim's body almost upright and leaned him against the flue. His head lolled forward. Spots of blood splattered the taller man's shirt.

'Okay . . . on three,' the murderer hissed. 'One . . . two . . . three!'

They lifted Karim off the ground, using the flue for support, and levered him over the edge. With a final effort they rammed his body inside the narrow opening and it tumbled down into blackness.

Chapter 2

Stepney, Saturday 4 June, 2.21 a.m.

'ROCK DA HOUSE! . . . I SAID . . . EVERYBODY . . .
ROCK DA HOUSE!'

MC Jumbo, a one-hundred-and-fifty-kilo sweaty
man mountain in an orange boiler suit, was screaming into the microphone as he flipped a turquoise
twelve-inch and slotted it with expert precision on to
one of the turntables. With his other hand he fingered
a second piece of vinyl on his deck. His real name
was Nigel Turnbull and he was a second-year student
at Queen Mary College just down the road.

MC Jumbo went into an indecipherable rant about
the greatness of the next track, but Kath and Deb
Wilson, twins and fellow students at Queen Mary,
took no notice. They were happy simply to dance,
trance-like, and to let the tab of E they had taken
fifteen minutes earlier do its stuff.

The room was a heaving mass of over-heated

bodies, all pulsating to the incredibly loud bass-driven music pounding from an over-sized PA system. Little more than a concrete cube fitted out with some very expensive lights and a powerful sound system, The Love Shack was an acquired taste. With bare breeze-block walls and rough cement floor, it was a completely windowless semi-basement ventilated via ducted air-con. So, even though the music was played at a ridiculous volume, very little noise leaked out. In spite of its bland appearance, for many of the students at Queen Mary, situated a hundred yards away along Mile End Road, The Love Shack was the coolest venue in the world on a Friday night. As an unlicensed club, attendance there came with a frisson of danger, and for those in the know, it was *the* place to score any pharmaceutical under the sun.

Kath and Deb had been coming here for most of the past academic year. This afternoon they had sat their final exam. It was time to de-stress. Letting the sound flow through them, it was easy to let go. As the track segued smoothly into the next, Kath gestured to Deb that she was going to get another bottle of water. Her twin nodded a 'Me too, please'. Pointless to try to speak when Jumbo was on a roll. Everything had to be communicated via sign language and facial gestures.

A few minutes later Kath was back. She handed her twin an ice-cold bottle of Evian and together they moved towards the centre of the dance-floor. Neither of them heard the rumbling sound that came from the ceiling just a few feet overhead, it was completely drowned out by the music. Unheeded by anyone, it grew louder. There was a flurry of scraping and rattling sounds, the grinding of metal against stone.

Kath barely felt the liquid splatter her face, but Deb was staring straight at her and saw a red circle appear on her forehead. It ran down the side of her nose and Kath flicked a finger at it, mistaking it for sweat. Suddenly Deb stopped dancing and watched in horror as three more red marks appeared on her sister's cheek. Kath froze and stood dabbing at her face.

They both looked up at the same moment.

Three metres above the dance-floor, a large air-vent cover started to come away from its fixings. First, one screw moved a millimetre. The metal slot into which it fitted yielded a fraction. Another screw began to loosen. The cover yawed open, sheared away from the support bracket and spiralled towards the dance-floor.

One edge hit a dancer, knocking him to the ground with a fractured shoulder. He collided with a couple close by. They too were sent sprawling. Then a large, soft object slid through the hole in the ceiling and

18

plunged into the fetid air of the club. It landed on the floor with a dull thud that no one heard.

A dozen people screamed simultaneously, but over the thumping beat and the sizzling computer-generated melody no one could hear the sound. Everyone stopped moving. Hands went to faces, features froze . . . a dozen Edvard Munchs.

Kath and Deb were just a few feet away from where the object landed. They saw a blurred shape falling through the air and hitting the ground. More liquid splashed across their faces. Deb touched her cheek and stared uncomprehendingly at her red fingertips. Then, as though a power switch had been tripped, the music stopped. MC Jumbo lurched away from his deck and wobbled down on to the eerily silent dance-floor.

Deb had started to shake, her fingers held up in front of her terror-stricken face.

With remarkable calm, Jumbo crouched down and rolled over the huddled object. They could all see its smashed face, the hair matted with dried blood, the white of one eye. Then, as the DJ pulled himself quickly to his feet, another object tumbled from the air-vent and landed next to the body. Jumbo jumped back instinctively, as though nudged by a cattle-prod. Kath screamed. A muddied workman's boot lay on the floor beside the dead man.

Chapter 3

Chief Inspector Jack Pendragon grabbed for the receiver, missed and knocked the phone to the floor along with a glass of water and his alarm clock. He could faintly hear the voice at the other end of the line as he scrambled in the dark to locate the receiver.

'Pendragon,' he said, trying to sound as together as possible.

'Inspector Grant. I'm sorry to call you so early, sir. Something's come up.'

Pendragon rubbed his right eye and switched the phone to his free hand as he inched back up the bed. He glanced at the clock on the floor. The red letters told him it was 3.05 a.m.

'What's up?'

'Best see for yourself, guv. I'm . . .' there was a pause '. . . four minutes from the crime scene.'

'Can you be a bit more precise?'

'A body in a club. Don't know much else.'

'Where?'

'Mile End Road. Some sort of bunker behind a jewellery shop called Jangles.'

'Okay. I'll find it.'

He ran the shower and waited for the water to warm up. He had only arrived at Brick Lane Police Station the previous evening. His commanding officer, Superintendent Jill Hughes, had shown him around and then gone through the team's files with him. He had two inspectors under his command: Rob Grant, twenty-six, hard-working, hard-nosed and tough, a high-flier; and Kenneth Towers, thirty-one, not terribly ambitious, a bit of a plodder. Then there was Jez Turner, one of three sergeants under him and the one assigned as his 'principal sergeant'. Jez was twenty-two, keen, a bit of a lad, but a promising young cop who would, in theory at least, follow him round like a loyal puppy. But, like all the staff at the station, Sergeant Turner had in fact greeted Pendragon's arrival with a blend of outward respect and barely disguised scepticism. He knew the score when it came to new arrivals without promotion. They were seen as having failed in their last posting and consequently had to prove themselves in a new one. Pendragon also came with baggage, personal issues that had probably been discussed and dissected before he arrived to fill the role of number two at the station, answerable directly to the Super.

And that brought Jill Hughes back to mind: a career cop, confident, almost androgynous except for the softness of her face and the shapely figure her uniform could not disguise. Her large brown eyes were attractive but betrayed no hint of sensuality. Superintendent Hughes was, Pendragon knew, a very tough, very strong-willed woman and an exceptional officer. At thirty-two, she was perhaps the youngest Super in the country, but she had little practical experience. Like himself twenty years earlier, she had been a top graduate from Sulhampstead Police College. Her team at Brick Lane had grown to respect her razor-sharp mind; but there was no denying the fact, Jack reflected, that she would be relying on him and on the case experience he could offer.

He gargled some mouthwash as he did up his tie and rubbed his hand over the just-acceptable stubble on his chin. At forty-six, allowing for a slight paunch, he had kept his athletic build, and although his hair was now more white than black, the flesh on his face was still taut. In a good light, he could just about pass for early-forties.

He had been looking forward to a weekend spent revisiting his old stamping ground. Pendragon had been born within half a mile of the station and had lived in the heart of the East End of London for the first eighteen years of his life. There had been a few trips back after going up to Magdalen, Oxford, but when his parents died in the late-80s he'd felt no further inclination to return. Until, that is . . . He picked up his keys and made for the stairs.

The front desk was unmanned as Pendragon crossed the hotel foyer and exited on to the street. The hotel was close to Moorgate tube station in the City, a five-minute drive from Mile End Road at this time of day. The streets were aglow with reflected neon. Pendragon followed his nose. He knew his way around London by simple instinct. The roads and the buildings might, on the surface, have changed during the decades since he had left, but the inner structure was immutable, the underlying topography intact. He could follow these roads as though they were leylines. London was ingrained into the very fabric of his being.

And some things had not been tarmacked over or given a radical facelift. Most of the shops were now owned by Indian and Bangladeshi tradespeople, but some of the long-established family businesses remained. And although most of the old pubs had taken on new, trendy names and been made over, the landmarks of his youth still jumped out at him. Passing the Grave Maurice public house and the Blind Beggar, he remembered that they had once been favourite haunts of the Kray twins. The gangsters had been more powerful than God in this area when he was a boy.

As he approached Jangles, an ambulance pulled away from the kerb and sped past him towards the London Hospital a few hundred yards down the road. Pendragon could see two police cars parked outside the shop, their blue lights splashing brightness across the drab brick and discoloured concrete surroundings. The shop window had been emptied before closing, anything precious safely locked away. The glass was masked with inch-thick steel bars. A scratched and scuffed blue-painted door set to the side of the shop stood ajar. Sergeant Jez Turner emerged from it and approached Pendragon's car as he pulled up at the kerb.

Turner was slim and rangy, his hair gelled back retro matinée-idol style. He had large dark eyes and a long narrow nose. His suit, a Hugo Boss he had found in a designer discount sale on Kensington High Street, was too good for the job. He knew it and the thought pleased him.

'What's the story?' Pendragon asked, coming round the back of the car.

Turner went ahead of him along a narrow corridor. It took them through the building and into a small courtyard. A short staircase led on to the flat roof of

24

a concrete extension taking up most of the back garden of the property. Another door from the passage opened on to a short staircase leading downward.

'Packed dance-floor, lots of E, I expect,' Turner said. 'Then . . . a body drops from the ceiling. SPLAT!' He turned to Pendragon with a mischievous grin and started to sing. ' "I believe I can fly . . ." '

Pendragon ignored him and Turner ushered the Chief Inspector down into the large semi-basement. It stank of sweat and was unbearably hot. Two men stood in the centre of the room: a middle-aged constable and a morbidly obese man dressed in an orange boiler suit. Close by, a pathologist in green plastic forensic gear over his civvies was crouching beside the body of a man who lay twisted to one side, his neck clearly snapped. The victim was a man of colour, perhaps Indian, but his face was now dark and discoloured from internal bleeding. His black hair was matted with blood and grey matter. He was wearing a light-coloured short-sleeved shirt. Just visible were the words *Bridgeport Construction* printed on the fabric.

Pendragon crouched down to take a closer look. 'Time of death?' he asked the pathologist. The man stared blankly at him and then at Turner before realising who Pendragon was.

'Sometime between one-thirty and two-thirty a.m. And it's Dr Neil Jones.'

'Thanks, Dr Jones.' Pendragon straightened up, turned to the constable and nodded at the figure in the orange boiler suit. 'Who's this?'

The constable glanced at his pad. 'Nigel Turnbull, sir. Aka MC . . . er, Jumbo.' He intoned the words with some distaste. 'A second-year student at Queen Mary College. He made the call.'

Pendragon eyed the youth. 'Can you tell me what happened?'

Turnbull was calm and concise. He recounted events from just before the body appeared, the panic that then ensued and how he had called for an ambulance and notified the police. He omitted to mention first texting a friend to get over ASAP to take care of two hundred tabs of E.

'And the time?'

'Just before two-thirty. I remember looking at my watch a few minutes before . . . before this happened.' He waved towards the corpse.

'A miracle only one person was injured. I suppose there's no point asking you for names.'

Jumbo looked at him blankly. 'I know a few of the regulars, but we don't use membership cards.'

'Well, Nigel, perhaps a trip to the station will help jog your memory.'

Turnbull's face dropped. 'Look, I'm only a DJ here. I have no probs with giving you a few names, but they're just students, same as me.'

'Excellent. Sergeant Turner here has a sharpened pencil at the ready.'

Pendragon turned back to the constable. 'Where's Inspector Grant?'

'Upstairs, sir. He's talking to the owner of the building.'

Dr Jones stepped forward and caught Pendragon's eye. The pathologist was a short, solidly built man, with a thick greying beard and a shock of curls; an over-sized Tolkien dwarf. 'I'd like to get the body to the lab, if it's all the same to you,' he said. 'Forensics will go over every inch of this place.'

'Fine. And . . . you're sure of the time of death?'

'You know I can't give you the minute and second, but as I said – definitely between one-thirty and two-thirty.'

Jez Turner placed a cup of vending-machine coffee on the desk beside Pendragon's elbow.

'Thanks,' said the Chief Inspector, and took a sip. 'Bloody hell!'

Turner held his hands up. 'Don't blame me.'

'But this is . . .'

'. . . perfectly adequate.' It was Superintendent Jill

Hughes at the door to his office. Jack made to get up, but at a signal from Hughes sat back again.

'You're perfectly welcome to bring in your own blend if you prefer, Chief Inspector.'

'Don't worry, I will,' he said, and handed the cup back to Turner. 'Dispose of this . . . please.'

Hughes smiled and perched on the corner of his desk. 'So, what've we got?'

'The man could have been killed just before he gatecrashed the rave, ma'am, and certainly no earlier than one-thirty according to Jones.'

'But how on earth did he end up there?'

'Sheer fluke. Inspector Grant interviewed the owner of The Love Shack. He's being very co-operative, of course. A couple of my boys have been all over the house and the outbuilding. The club, if you want to call it that, was originally an air-raid shelter. It was extended in the seventies and used as a storeroom. A couple of years back, the owner was talked into converting it into a music venue. Got in some cowboys by the look of it . . . an old chimney has been widened and connected up as two air-vents. Whoever pushed the body into the opening on the roof probably thought it was a disposal chute. They could never have dreamt the corpse would end up in the middle of a packed dance-floor.'

'So . . .'

'So I'm heading over to Pathology, to see what Dr Jones has come up with.' Pendragon was pulling on his jacket and following Hughes to the door. At the end of the corridor they could see Turner with two constables. The sergeant was doing a passable impersonation of Pendragon refusing the machine coffee. They were all wearing big grins. Turner glanced around, saw Pendragon and Hughes and immediately straightened up. The uniforms slipped away. Superintendent Hughes turned to Pendragon with a barely discernible smile. 'Not a bad mimic really, is he?'

Chapter 4

By 9.15 the streets were aglow with orange light. It was obvious the day was going to be another hot one. The thermometer hadn't moved below 25 degrees all night and now it felt like a summer morning in the south of France. Even the usually grey surroundings of Mile End Road sparkled today. Amazing what a bit of sunshine could do, Pendragon thought as they pulled out of the station and turned on to the main road.

Turner drove and they sat in silence. Pendragon watched the sun-bleached shop fronts and the stained, graffiti-covered walls, metal garage shutters and broken guttering flash by. He thought how odd it all looked; as if London had suddenly been shifted a couple of thousand miles south. The strains of 'Summertime' played in his head. Traffic was light. Within a few minutes they were passing through a narrow entrance into a car park. A rectangular sign on the wall of a squat brick building read 'Milward

30

Street Pathology Unit' under the Metropolitan Police crest, blue on white.

They found Dr Jones outside the front entrance. He was drawing hungrily on a cigarette, the ash falling into his fulsome beard. He barely reached Pendragon's shoulder.

'Banned from my own building,' he said as the two policemen strode up to the doorway.

'Quite right too,' Pendragon responded. 'Funny. I would have thought opening up corpses all day would have put you off the fags.'

Jones gave a dry laugh then coughed. 'Fuck, Pendragon! It's precisely because I cut open dead people that I don't give a toss. You end up in a place like this either way. Come on, I've been here since before dawn with this one.' He squashed the cigarette underfoot and shouldered open the door.

The pathology lab was like any other, anywhere. There were two rooms. The smaller one was the morgue. It was lined with steel drawers from floor to shoulder-height. The other had blinds at the windows, workbenches arranged in an L-shape along two walls, racks of test tubes and sundry pieces of chemical equipment. Two stainless-steel dissection tables with drain-off trenches and power hoses stood along the back wall. Between the tables were two trolleys. On top of these, a set of shiny steel dishes.

Overhead, a stark fluorescent strip. The concrete floor was a scrubbed gun-metal grey. The whole place stank of cleaning agent and viscera.

Dr Neil Jones was pulling on latex gloves as he approached one of the dissection tables. The dead man lay on the table with his torso cut open. His head was raised slightly on a stabilising block. Pendragon noticed a card tied to the big toe of the victim's left foot. The card was covered in spindly black writing. In one of the steel dishes beside the table lay a liver. In the other, the contents of the man's stomach. Turner, notebook in hand, seemed fascinated by it all.

'So, do you have anything for us?' Pendragon asked, and kicked his sergeant lightly on the shin.

'No ID. Male. Late-thirties. Indian, or perhaps Bangladeshi. Five-five and overweight. A heavy smoker by the look of his lungs.' He nudged a mass of grey tissue with a scalpel. Pendragon looked away for a moment; he could never get used to the clinical dismissiveness of people like Jones.

'Oh, please! Don't tell me you're squeamish, Chief Inspector?' Jones chortled.

Pendragon ignored him and glared at Turner who had stopped scribbling. 'Go on.'

'You'll notice extensive bruising . . . here and here . . . on the upper arms. Also, his jaw is fractured and his windpipe has been shattered.' He pointed to the side of the man's face and under his chin. The flesh was black and broken, split like torn leather. 'He suffered two particularly vicious blows to the head. Either one would have killed him.' Jones rolled the victim's head to one side and they could see a large occlusion on the back of his skull. 'Blunt-force trauma. Hit by a heavy object, here and under the chin – the blow that smashed his windpipe. I've measured the opening in the skull and would guess the weapon was cylindrical – a metal pipe or tubing; heavy-duty torch perhaps. There's no blood under the fingernails, no hair or skin traces. But from the fractures and bruising, I would imagine there was definitely a struggle.'

Jones turned to another table close by and lifted up a boot. 'Workboots, size seven, caked in mud. Shirt with a company name – *Bridgeport Construction*. Our man was obviously a labourer or at least working on a building site. Should help.'

Pendragon was about to reply when Turner's phone rang. 'Yep,' he replied chirpily. 'Yep, cool . . . *ciao*.'

Pendragon gave a heavy sigh and raised his eyebrows.

'The station, sir. The murdered man is Amal Karim. Indian. Worked for Bridgeport Construction,

33

who just happen to have a building site down the street from Jangles, on Frimley Way.'

'Great.'

'There's more. Forensics have something they want you to see. Wouldn't elaborate.'

The locus – the immediate vicinity in which the body was found – in The Love Shack – was abuzz with figures in green plastic suits, scene-of-crime officers from local forensics. Yellow police crime-scene tape had been stretched across the door leading down into the club from the short passageway alongside the shop, and as Pendragon pulled himself under it two SOCOs turned to see who had invaded their space. Neither of them knew Pendragon, but one of the investigators nodded to Turner as he followed the DCI under the tape.

A woman approached them. She was dressed in a regulation plastic suit over a shirt and jeans. 'DCI Pendragon, I presume,' she said. 'Dr Colette Newman, Head of Forensics.' Her voice was clipped, a hint of BBC circa 1960. Not something you heard much any more.

Pendragon started to put out his hand then withdrew it. Dr Newman smiled. She looked to be about thirty-five, he guessed: fine features, high cheekbones, huge blue eyes. She had to keep tucking strands of blonde fringe behind her right ear.

'You have something for me?' he said.

'Yes. If you'd like to follow me.'

Dr Newman took them back out into the small enclosed concrete courtyard. Some stairs to one side led up to the roof of the club. It was flat and featureless with two metal flues rising about three feet above roof level. The cover of one of the flues had been removed. It lay on the floor a few metres away, a SOCO dusting the metal edge with a large floppy brush. Pendragon could see blood smeared across the bright metal.

'We've found plenty to go on up here.' She pointed to a large pool of congealed blood. It had dried at the edges and some had seeped into the concrete. A trail of mud and blood ended at the flue and all around were flecks of red. 'From a first look at the blood-spray pattern, I'd say the victim was hit at least twice.'

Pendragon nodded. 'The pathologist said the same thing.'

'I think the attacker came on to the roof from the stairs.' She led the way to the edge of the roof and they looked down on to the courtyard they had just crossed. From here they could see into the neighbouring properties. To the right, three shops fronted the main road, each with flats above and small gardens behind. To the left stood a high wall. Just visible behind that stood a single, derelict property taking up the corner with Globe Road. Immediately behind Jangles, on the corner of Frimley Way, was a construction site.

'So the murder took place up here?' Turner said.

'Definitely. Follow me.'

She took them back down the stairs, across the yard and through a gate. The alleyway beyond had been cordoned off. They could see a row of green council refuse bins, a dry mud path, brambles and weeds. A random line of red flags snaked its way through an opening ahead. The flags were numbered and had been stuck into the parched soil. In some of these locations they could see smears of blood, black against the mud. The opening led on to a narrow lane. At the end of this stood a tall mesh fence with barbed wire running along the top. A gate opened on to the construction site. It was unlocked, the chain and padlock hanging limp.

'As you can see, we've found traces all along this path. Plenty of blood, hair, flakes of skin. But as it's a building site, you'd expect at least the last two of these. No footprints, though, the ground is too hard. We're still looking for fingerprints, but nothing so far.'

She picked a route across the hardened mud

avoiding the flags and the ground close to them. A few steps on, they had reached the edge of a vast, roughly hewn pit criss-crossed with dirty planks supported by a framework of scaffolding. More red flags could be seen where the ground fell away. They followed her down a slope into the pit and along three planks, sidestepping more flags, until they reached the edge of a trench cut into the bottom of the pit. Piles of freshly turned earth lay all around. A cluster of flags had been stuck into the ground here.

Two SOCOs were hard at work. One was photographing the bottom of the trench; the other was on his knees, poking at the soil with a small trowel. The officer with the camera stopped work as they approached and Dr Newman stepped into his place, waving over Pendragon and Turner to see something.

The crouching figure straightened up and stepped aside as the Head of Forensics squatted down.

'This is the beginning of the trail, DCI Pendragon. There are several signs of a struggle – crumbled soil and scrapes.' She pointed to one side of the trench. 'And then there's this.' Turning, she pointed to the ground.

They could see a small white object. Pendragon crouched down to take a closer look.

'It's a metatarsal, a finger bone, from the fourth or fifth on the right hand, I believe.'

Chapter 5

The Venerable English College, Rome,
January 1589

My name is Father John William Allen and my
story begins in January, the Year of Our Lord,
1589.

History records many troubled eras. But for
one such as I, a man of deep faith, these, I am
sure, are times as bad as any in human reckon-
ing. As I write, war rages between Catholics and
Protestants, a war that has its roots in a schism
created by the demon Luther and the Devil's
vassal, Henry VIII, over half a century ago.

Throughout Europe, men fight to uphold
their vision of God. But the One True Faith, the
faith of St Peter, the faith of Christ Himself, will,
I know, prevail. Blood has been spilled, plenty
of blood. But there is the blood of the faithful,
and there is the blood of the heretic, and only

the first of these is pure. Only the spilling of this blood is a sin.

I had been a student at the Venerable English College in Rome for five years, training to be a Jesuit missionary, when, late in May 1588, we received news from Paris that the good Catholic people of the city had risen up against that vile Protestant appeaser King Henri III. He fled and the governing of the city fell to a group of noblemen, the Council of Sixteen. Within days that great French Catholic the Duc de Guise was welcomed back into Paris from exile.

For a time there was peace there; indeed, Europe enjoyed a calm not experienced for many long years. Then, a few days after Christmas, news reached us that, on 23 December, the Duc de Guise and his brother, Cardinal de Guise, had been tricked by the treacherous Henri and slaughtered by the King's henchmen – stabbed through the heart in the council chambers of the Château de Blois, where they had been summoned to a meeting.

When I heard this news I knew immediately that my time had come, that I would soon be rewarded for my devotions and offered the chance of martyrdom. For five years I had been imbued with the teachings of the One True

Faith and been taught how to teach in my turn, trained to express my heartfelt and soul-deep zeal, so as to convert the waverers and restore stray Catholics to the fold. I was ready.

I remember the gathering in the great chamber of the college at which the head of my order, Superior General Acquaviva, addressed us all and imparted the news of My Lord Guise's murder. I remember the hush, the stillness, and how I could feel anger and the bitterness all around me, actually taste these things in my mouth.

That night any true rest evaded me, and when I did tumble into the oblivion of sleep I could not be sure I was dreaming or simply remembering. For in the dark hours before the dawn unspeakable shadows haunted the corners of my cell and I could no longer separate dreams from the waking world.

The same images kept returning to torment me. Tyburn Village, to the west of London. A windswept, rain-drenched morning in April five years earlier. The execution of a Jesuit missionary, Henry Wittingham.

It began with a commotion from the crowd seated in the wooden stands to one side of Tyburn Tree, the three-poster gallows that had

40

been a place of death for so many men and women over the years. The crowd murmurs, and then, as the cart comes into view, some of them begin to cheer and shout. The procession enters the square with the prisoner bound to a hurdle, naked but for a blood-stained loincloth. His face scrapes along the ground. As he is lifted from the dirt, the crowd can see Wittingham's bloodied, swollen and blackened face. Gusts of rain sweep the scene. The executioner helps the condemned man stand upright on the cart parked beneath the scaffold. A noose is placed over the man's head and the cart quickly drawn away.

He dangles and kicks. The crowd scream with excitement. A woman and two men run out to tug at Wittingham's legs, trying to speed his end, but they are quickly spotted and dragged away by four burly wardens. The gasping man is cut loose and lowered to the ground. Then he is carried to a wooden platform where he is bound at wrist and ankle.

A hush. Even the sounds of Nature seem to recede; the wind drops, the rain slows. The prisoner's face is awash with watery blood, his mouth agape. Most of his teeth are smashed. A gag is knotted across his open mouth and the loincloth yanked away and tossed into the mud below the platform. The executioner grabs Wittingham's genitals and, with a single slice, castrates him. Blood fountains into the air, drenching the executioner's leather jerkin. Wittingham's body spasms, his back arches, and even through the gag, his screams sound like metal grinding against metal. Tossing the severed flesh into a basket, the executioner bends forward, grabs Wittingham's hair for leverage and draws his blade the length of the man's naked torso.

Wittingham has stopped moving, paralysed by shock. But he is still alive. The executioner reaches into the gaping hole and removes a handful of slimy, grey viscera. He tugs and cuts, holding aloft lengths of intestine before tossing them into the basket. Then he sets to work removing the prisoner's heart. He cuts around the organ and severs arteries and veins. Only the executioner can tell when the heart has stopped beating. The prisoner's legs and arms still twitch as the vital organ is raised into the air. The executioner adds it to the growing pile of flesh in the tumbril. The leaden silence all around is broken only by the flapping of wings as a crow lands on the edge of the basket and hungrily eyes the grey and red tangle of human remains.

A voice enquired: 'Father John?' There was a knock at the door. 'Father John? The Superior General wishes to see you.'

My eyes snapped open and the horrors of the night vanished. I was once more in my tiny stone-walled room. The voice, Brother Giovanni's, was coming from the other side of an oak door a few feet beyond the end of my narrow bed. I leapt up and strode over to it, feeling a tight knot of excitement in the pit of my stomach.

Giovanni was holding a candle. Its flame flickered wildly in the draught and cast streaks of light and dark across his benign, round face. The priest turned and I followed him. The passageway was black apart from the puddle of light cast by the bare candle but, of course, after five years at the college, I knew my way well. And in the dark, walking behind the good Father Giovanni, I finally shook myself awake, aware now that my dream had not been mere fancy, but a memory. What I had witnessed in the rain of Tyburn had led me here, to this moment. I had seen for myself how the Royal Whore, Elizabeth, treated her citizens. That experience had been the turning point which called me to Rome and the great cause. But, when I left England, I had turned my back on many things. My family in Suffolk were good Catholics, but they had never been militant. They had naively wished for nothing but peace between all faiths. In coming here to Rome, I had been forced to sever all family ties. I would never see my parents or my two younger brothers again.

The corridor opened on to a wide hallway. Father Giovanni extinguished the candle and placed it on a shelf, then beckoned me to follow him. The corridor was wide and carpeted, a red strip of expensive wool laid over white marble. Huge portraits hung on the walls, a succession of Popes dating back many centuries. Through the windows, I could see it was still dark outside. The place was enveloped in a silence so absolute I could hear my own breathing. At the end of the passageway were double doors of heavy oak. Guards in Vatican livery stood to either side of them. They stared ahead, ignoring us as Father Giovanni rapped on the oak. The doors swung open.

I had been in this room only once before; on the day a year earlier when, after completing my training, I was received into the Jesuit

Order. This was the inner sanctum of the Head of the College, the Superior General, Claudius Acquaviva, fifth leader of the Jesuits. The Order was created almost sixty years earlier by the saintly Ignatius of Loyola who had taught us that the Jesuits were God's chosen missionaries, our role to serve the great and mysterious purposes of the Lord God Almighty. Our Order had many jobs to perform, I was told, but none more important than the task of returning heretics to the One True Faith.

The Superior General was, a diminutive figure, seated at a massive desk in the centre of a vast room, studying some papers. He wore a simple black robe, a black cap on his head. A tall, slender man in priest's robes stood in front of the desk, head lowered, hands clasped in front of him. I knew that back.

Brother Giovanni slipped out and I walked slowly towards the desk. It was only when I stood alongside the other robed figure that I could steal a glance at the man. He did not return my stare, but I could see his strong profile in the dim light, his straight, long nose, the soft curve of his shaven skull. It was Sebastian – Father Sebastian Mountjoy – my closest friend at the college, a man who had been ordained on the same day as

I. Sebastian, I knew, was aflame with the same religious fervour as I was, a fervour that consumed our waking thoughts and permeated our dreams. We had spent many hours together in spiritual contemplation and debate. Sebastian was three years my senior and came from a very wealthy Herefordshire family, committed Catholics who had long been engaged in their own clandestine work against the English Queen. But although our backgrounds were very different, we were spiritual twins.

Superior General Acquaviva looked up from his papers. He was a gaunt, pale man and naturally bald. The skin of his high forehead was smooth, almost baby-like. It caught the light from the huge candles set on either side of his desk. He had very light brown eyes; soft, kindly eyes. He seemed to be about to speak when there was a movement behind his chair. A hooded figure emerged from the deep gloom, startling both Sebastian and me. The man approached the desk. The Superior General glanced up and the man pulled back his hood to reveal a hard face: high cheekbones, narrow black eyes, cropped silver hair.

I fell to my knees. The figure extended one hand and flicked his fingers.

'My sons,' the Superior General interposed. 'It was Father Bellarmino who called you here this morning.'

I was terrified. Bellarmino was perhaps the most powerful man in the Church. Many believed he was more powerful even than Pope Sixtus himself. As both the Pope's personal theologian and Spiritual Father of the Jesuit College, his influence reached into every corner of the Vatican. But Father Bellarmino was a great purifier with a fearsome reputation across Europe. He had brought many heretics back to the Faith at the point of a sword or through the purification of fire.

'I will let the good Father explain,' the Superior General concluded.

Bellarmino's voice was higher-pitched than I'd expected, but his delivery was that of a man who had long since lost any shred of self-doubt. A man who expected those he addressed to obey immediately, never to question him or to show anything but obsequiousness and sycophantism.

'You are good and honest priests, and I know from your records and from the personal recommendations of the Superior General that you are dedicated to the notion of martyrdom,' he began. 'You came from England to be trained here and returned to your country, so that you may spread the Word of the One True Faith, act as missionaries and save souls.'

I hardly dared blink and could sense Sebastian's fear too in the rigid set of his body. In the candlelight, the black eyes of the Spiritual Father of the College were fathomless pools.

'A missionary's cause is a noble one. You are aware, as we all are, that many worthy men have been lost fighting this good fight. If you are recognised upon your return to England, you will be arrested immediately as traitors and may well meet a traitor's death. But I know you are not afraid of this prospect. Rather, you relish the thought of laying down your life in the Lord's work.

'But some of us have concluded we might do more for England; that we might do more, much more, to save the souls of your compatriots. Some here have concluded that too many good men have died as martyrs, pouring more blood into the hands of the English whore who sits illegally on the throne. And so, we have decided to remove the evil . . . at its source.'

And in that moment, I began to understand why we had been brought here. I quickly glanced at Sebastian, but did not catch his eye. Bellarmino was speaking again.

'Your mission will be the most dangerous of any undertaken by the Order. From the moment you leave this building you will be spied upon, for enemies of the Church are everywhere. You will make for the tiny town of Créteil, a few miles south of Paris. You will find there a small tavern called Le Lapin Noir, close to the centre of the town. Seek out the landlord and tell him you are looking for Monsieur Gappair. Both the landlord and Gappair may be trusted. For the moment, you will assume the identity of English traders. We have prepared your papers and passports.'

He paused for a moment and fixed us both with those unreadable black eyes. 'There is one more thing.' He removed a small box from inside his robe and opened the lid. Inside lay a gold ring topped with a large, round emerald. 'You will need this,' he said, and handed it to me.

Chapter 6

Stepney, Saturday 4 June, 10.00 a.m.

Pendragon and Turner had reached ground level and were picking their way between rusty girders and piles of sand when an old Toyota Camry pulled on to the site and stopped a few metres away. A short, heavily built man, the dome of his huge head covered in grey stubble, stepped out of the driver's seat. He carried a yellow hard hat in one hand.

'I came as soon as I heard,' he told them, extending his free hand.

'Mr Ketteridge?'

'Tony.'

'DCI Pendragon. Sergeant Turner. You're the site manager here, is that correct?'

Beads of sweat had appeared on the man's forehead. He had dark rings under his eyes. 'Yes.'

'What exactly have you been told?'

'About Amal? He's dead. Dreadful. Do you know anything more?'

'It seems clear the man was attacked and killed in a neighbouring property.'

'Christ!' Ketteridge looked skyward.

'Had Mr Karim been a security guard here for long?'

'Well, he wasn't really a guard as such, just one of the construction team. Volunteered for a bit of overtime.' Ketteridge wiped away the sweat that was now trickling down his cheeks. 'We usually just rely on the security cameras, but it was the skeleton . . .'

'Skeleton?' Pendragon snapped.

'You haven't been down there yet then?'

'Yes, we have, but there was no skeleton.' Pendragon turned to Turner who simply shrugged his shoulders.

Ketteridge donned his hard hat and stepped between the two policemen, taking the sloping path down into the pit. From several metres away it seemed he could tell something was wrong and began to pick up pace. By the time Pendragon and Turner had reached him, he was crouching down close to the cluster of flags.

'This is crazy!' he said, standing up and turning to face Pendragon.

'I think you'd better start at the beginning,' the DCI told him.

They were in the site hut, a Portakabin fifty metres or so from the pit. Inside, the walls were covered with charts and plans and a calendar featuring an improbably endowed model resplendent in hard hat and nothing else. Ketteridge's desk was strewn with papers, a calculator, empty mugs and chocolate wrappers. A computer surrounded by more papers stood on a separate desk close by. Beside it stood a printer and an A3 flatbed scanner.

Pendragon paced around the room looking at the charts before going behind the desk and surveying the muddle on top of it. Ketteridge looked uncomfortable, standing with hands in pockets.

'Okay, talk us through it,' Pendragon ordered, and tapped at the keyboard of the computer to snap it out of sleep mode. Wallpaper of a tropical paradise appeared, speckled with at least fifty file names.

'We were getting ready to close down for the day – must have been getting on for five – when one of the men called me over. He'd cleared some soil away at the bottom of the excavation and there were hip and thigh bones protruding from the mud. We dug away carefully and there it was – a full skeleton. It was very old.'

Pendragon came back round the desk and began to pace again, then stopped a few feet away from Ketteridge. 'And you didn't report it?'

The site manager looked sheepish. 'Believe me, I was going to. I called my boss straight away. He was in a meeting.'

'Who was with you?' Pendragon asked, pulling a box file from a shelf and walking towards the desk with it. He perched on the edge and flicked through the file.

'There're sixteen men on the job. Only three were with me in the pit at the time. Oh, and Tim Middleton.'

'Who is?'

'Partner in the architect's firm responsible for the design.'

Turner was taking all this down.

'We'll need a full list of names and addresses,' Pendragon said. 'Go on.'

'I wasn't sure what to do, and it was getting on. The guys were all exhausted . . . bastard of a week it's been. Stifling. So I thought, well, the skeleton wasn't going anywhere. Karim volunteered to do one shift guarding it, and one of the others said he would take over in the early-morning.'

'I see.' Pendragon closed the file and appraised the man before him.

'There's one other thing . . . there was a ring.'

'A ring?'

'On the skeleton's right hand.'

Pendragon stared at the man in disbelief. 'And you just left it there? With one security guard to cover the whole site?'

'I didn't know what else to do. I needed to talk to my boss. Besides, we have CCTV.'

'Oh, jolly good.'

'I thought . . .'

'No, Mr Ketteridge. You didn't *think* at all.'

There was a brief silence, the only sound the buzzing of a fly banging against the window.

Ketteridge went behind his desk and opened a drawer. 'You may find these useful,' he said, and handed Pendragon a set of half a dozen photographs. 'Tim Middleton took some snaps of the skeleton and e-mailed them over as soon as he got back to his office. I printed them out before I left the site last night. Then I checked on Amal Karim to see if he was still okay about pulling the night shift. He seemed fine . . . poor sod. I dunno, I got the feeling he was doing it out of a sense of duty, respect for the dead or something.' He laughed suddenly. 'I must admit, we were all a bit freaked out by it.'

Pendragon studied the pictures. They were postcard-sized and taken from several different angles. The earth above the skeleton had been carefully removed and the area around it cut away, exposing the remains. The skeleton looked forlorn against the mud, a remnant from a different time, alien to this world. In one of the pictures a large gold ring topped with a green stone could clearly be seen on the little finger of the right hand.

'Okay,' Pendragon said, and shuffled the photographs together to take with him. Turning to Turner, he said. 'Get the CCTV recordings and meet me at the car. And, Mr Ketteridge, keep your mobile charged. We'll be in touch again . . . very soon.'

Chapter 7

The wall clock read 11.30 a.m. as Pendragon stepped up to a whiteboard at the open end of a horseshoe arrangement of desks. The briefing room was small and hot; an electric fan on a spindly stand whirred away in the far corner, but it was almost completely ineffectual. The entire team had gathered in the room. Sergeants Rosalind Mackleby, Jimmy Thatcher and Terry Vickers sat to one side, Inspectors Rob Grant and Ken Towers to the other. Directly in front of Pendragon, Jez Turner was perched on a desk. At the back of the room, close to the door, stood Superintendent Jill Hughes, arms folded across her chest.

'Okay, a quick summary,' Pendragon began, surveying the room. He showed no signs of the anxiety he felt inside. 'You all know about the body found in the club. Identified as Amal Karim, an Indian labourer who was employed by Bridgeport Construction.' He tapped a photograph of the man, a passport picture from a few years back, copied and enlarged. Next to this were photographs of the crime scene, the body sprawled on a concrete floor, one side of the face a mass of black and red. 'Karim was struck twice, once to the throat and then to the skull. Both blows came from a heavy, blunt object, probably a piece of metal pipe.' He indicated the injuries on the photograph as he spoke. 'His body was dumped in a ventilation duct. Time of death between one-thirty and two-thirty this morning.

'Sergeant Turner and I have just returned from the crime scene. Karim was involved in a struggle on a building site a short distance from the club. He was killed on the roof there, his body dumped in the duct. He'd been on night duty as a security guard at the site.'

Inspector Grant's hand went up. 'Any idea of motive, guv? Anything valuable taken from the site?'

'I was just coming to that. Dr Newman's team have found a human bone close to where they think Karim was originally attacked.'

'A bone?'

'A finger bone, apparently. Very old.'

'But that could be a coincidence, couldn't it?' Sergeant Mackleby asked. She was taller than half the men in the room, thin, with long auburn hair pulled back in a tight bun. Her pencil skirt and crisp white blouse accentuated her slender figure and also an impression of severity.

'Fair question,' Pendragon replied. 'There's a massive hole there, at least ten metres deep. Never know what might get dug up when you go that far down, but it's nothing so simple in this case. We had a word with the site manager, Tony Ketteridge. Turns out they unearthed a skeleton there last night. That's why Karim was keeping watch.'

There was a stunned silence. Superintendent Hughes walked round the desks to where Pendragon was standing. 'And all that's left of it is this finger bone?' She gave him an incredulous stare.

'It would seem so,' Pendragon replied, and handed her the photos Ketteridge had given him. 'When the skeleton was dug up, one of the architects for the project was there, a . . .' he glanced at a notebook in his hand '. . . Tim Middleton of Rainer and Partner. He took these pictures with his phone.'

She studied them without a word, turning them round in her hands before passing them on to Jimmy Thatcher who was closest to her. 'And they didn't report it?' she said.

'No.'

'So you think this guy Karim was killed because of the skeleton?' It was Jimmy Thatcher who was talking. He had just passed the photos on to

Mackleby. Terry Vickers was leaning over her shoulder to get a look.

'I didn't say that,' Pendragon retorted. 'Far too early to jump to conclusions.'

'But it's an odd coincidence,' Hughes said, walking over to take a close look at the photograph of the security guard's body. 'Did this Tony Ketteridge give a valid reason for not reporting the find immediately? Does he realise he's broken the law?'

Pendragon shrugged. 'Said he'd tried and failed to contact his boss. Thought it best to sleep on it first.'

'Terrific!'

'He kept reiterating the point that the skeleton was really old, ma'am,' Turner interjected.

'Oh, so that excuses him,' Hughes said, rather louder than she had intended. Jimmy Thatcher straightened involuntarily. Grant coughed and crossed his arms over his chest.

'Well, whatever his reasons, it was a bloody silly thing to do. Puts him right in the frame,' she added.

'Yes, but there's no evidence. We can bring him in on a technicality, but I think the man would be more useful to us if we let his oversight go; played it softly with him. At least at first,' said Pendragon.

'And what's this?' Mackleby had the pictures again and was pointing at the ring on the skeleton's hand.

59

'It's what it looks like. A ring,' the DCI replied.

'So, a motive then?' Terry Vickers said.

'Possibly.'

Outside the briefing room, Pendragon told Turner to take a good look at the CCTV disks he had brought back from the construction site. Turning to Thatcher and Vickers he instructed them to lead a search team to sweep the area within a two-hundred-metre radius of the site.

Superintendent Hughes tapped him on the shoulder. 'Got a minute?' She ushered him into her office and closed the door. 'Quite a first morning.'

'Nothing like going in at the deep end,' he agreed and sat facing her across a remarkably neat desk. There was a Mac to one side; a silver-framed picture of a younger Superintendent Hughes in black gown and mortarboard sandwiched between beaming parents.

'Any initial thoughts you'd like to share?' she asked.

He was silent for a moment as he glanced around the room. It was almost obsessively neat, not a scrap of paper or mote of dust visible; even the waste bin was empty and pristine.

'I think Amal Karim was simply in the wrong place at the wrong time,' he said.

'And this skeleton business?'

'Is the key, as far as I can tell.'

'So what now?'

'I've got Sergeant Turner on to the surveillance recordings and I'm going to see if Dr Jones has anything on the finger bone. Then I'll interview the construction team, maybe the vic's family.'

Hughes was nodding. 'You going to bring Ketteridge in?'

'Later. Thought I'd let him stew a bit. If he's involved, the more he mulls it over, the worse he'll feel.'

Superintendent Hughes put her fingers to her chin thoughtfully. 'Fine. Well, you know my door is always open, Jack.'

Back in his own office, Pendragon spent some time familiarising himself with his new surroundings, especially the computer system he was networked to. It was obvious from the off this was going to be a complex case; they had both a fresh corpse and a missing skeleton on their hands, and it was only day one.

An hour flew by as he wrote up a report of what he had done so far, which he saved in a newly created file named KARIM. Then he dropped in on Turner.

'Disks aren't working properly,' the sergeant said

despondently. He had a cup of murky grey liquid in his hand.

'Looks nice,' Pendragon deadpanned, nodding towards the cup.

Turner smiled. 'Sorry about earlier, guv.'

Pendragon waved it away. 'So what's up with the disks?'

'One of the tech guys is on to it. Data drop-outs or something, he reckons. Might be the heat. He says he can transfer the images to a DVD, but it'll take a few hours.'

'Okay. I'm going to see Jones. While I'm out, get on to a local historian. There might be someone at Queen Mary. Or else King's on the Strand have a great history department, I seem to remember. Oh, and do your own bit on Google. I've made copies of Ketteridge's pictures. They're on my desk. I want to know everything there is to know about that ring.'

He took a car from the pool. It had been parked facing the sun and was boiling hot. Police cars didn't come with air conditioning as standard, so he wound down the windows. The novelty of this heatwave was wearing off. A big part of him wished the aquamarine sky would cloud over.

As he emerged into Saturday afternoon traffic on Whitechapel Road, he glanced at the photos of the skeleton where they lay on the passenger seat. At a red light, he had a moment to flick through them for a couple of seconds. This whole thing smelt bad, he thought. Ketteridge was caught in the middle, by the look of it. They were probably all under pressure: the construction firm, the architects, the investors. Everyone always was, especially in high-stakes games like property development. The land alone was worth millions, and every day lost meant more money wasted on plant hire, labour, interest payments. It was easy to see why the site manager hadn't reported anything. But then, who was to say he hadn't planned to once he'd got the all-clear from his higher-ups?

There were two cars parked close to the doors to the path lab, both jalopies, a rusty Nissan and an ancient Ford Capri with leopardskin seat covers and furry dice dangling from the rear-view mirror.

'Classy,' Pendragon murmured to himself as he strode towards the entrance.

It was refreshingly cool inside, but the stink of the place was all-pervading. He was about to enter the suite of rooms that constituted Jones's domain when a door swung towards him. It was held open by the pathologist. There was a group of half a dozen people coming along the passageway. Amal Karim's family here to identify the body, Pendragon guessed. An elderly woman and a young man led the way followed by younger visitors, siblings or close relatives of the dead man, perhaps. The old woman was wearing a dark silk sari; her face was moist with tears. A young man in a cheap brown suit was supporting her with one arm around her shoulders. His own eyes were filled to brimming. Pendragon watched the group leave the building.

Jones tapped him on the shoulder and nodded towards his lab. 'Always the worst part of the job,' he said. 'The dead are dead, but the relatives . . . Anyway, I suppose you've come about the bone.'

'Bit optimistic, I know.'

'Too bloody right . . . What do you expect?'

'Anything. Hunches?'

'DCI Pendragon, I've had a corpse to deal with, and the corpse's family . . . and it's still only frigging . . .' he looked at his watch '. . . twelve-forty and I'm starving!' He looked down at the ground sheepishly then at Pendragon. 'It's old – extremely old. The very lovely Dr Newman is right, it's a metatarsal, fifth finger of the right hand, the little finger. You can tell by the size and curvature of the bone. It's been freshly separated from the other bones of the same finger. You can see that from patches of discoloration to either end of the bone.'

'Makes sense.'

'How so?'

'A few hours before this bone was found, an entire human skeleton lay in the same spot at the bottom of a dirty great hole on a construction site. The skeleton went walkies sometime last night. But whoever performed the disappearing act was obviously a little careless.'

Back at the station, the afternoon was allocated to a succession of interviews. First on the list was Terry Disher, the man who had unearthed the skeleton the previous afternoon.

'Am I a suspect?' he asked as soon as he sat down opposite Pendragon. They were at a steel table in Interview Room 2. He had declined the offer of tea. Pendragon had a cup in front of him, and took a sip before responding.

'Just routine, Mr Disher. This is a murder inquiry.'

'Do I need a solicitor?'

'No. But if you feel . . .'

The builder was shaking his head. He was a big man, at least six foot four and two hundred and fifty pounds. Not much fat on him. He had whitish-blond hair and intense blue eyes. Pendragon had read the report on him. Disher was twenty-six. Went to school in Bromley. Worked abroad on construction sites in

Germany for a few years then came back to London. Married a year ago, one son. He lived on the local estate.

'All right. Fire away,' he said. 'Dunno if I can help, but I'd like to see the bastard who did it put behind bars.'

'You were a friend of Mr Karim's?'

He reflected for a moment. 'Yes and no. As much as anyone could be, I guess. He kept himself to himself. That lot all do.'

'"That lot" meaning the Indian workmen?'

'All the ethnics. The East Europeans, the black guys. There's not a lot of . . . what do they call it now? . . . multiculturalism in the building trade.'

Pendragon produced a half-smile. 'No, I don't imagine there is.' He took another sip of tea. 'Do you know if Mr Karim had any enemies? Did anyone in the company dislike the man?'

Disher shrugged. 'As I said, he kept himself to himself. I don't think he had any friends or enemies.'

'Okay. So tell me about the skeleton.'

He didn't look surprised. 'What do you wanna know?'

'You found it, yes?'

'Me and two others. Ricky Southall and Nudge . . . Norman . . . Norman West.'

'Tony Ketteridge was there?'

66

'I called him over straight away. Dunno why I bothered, though.'

Pendragon gave him a quizzical look. 'Meaning?'

'Nothin'.'

Pendragon took a sip of tea. Returning the cup to the saucer, he placed his hands, palm down, to either side of it. The silence quickly became oppressive. 'I'm sure you can do better than that,' he said finally.

'Yeah, sure, and get me P45. What d'ya take me for?'

'This is a murder investigation, Mr Disher. Surely I don't need to remind you again?'

'I thought I wasn't a suspect. Just routine questions, you said.'

Pendragon sighed and pushed back his chair. 'Okay, you're free to go, but if I find you're withholding vital information, I'll bring you in so fast you won't know what hit you.' He started to get up.

'Okay, okay.' Disher shook his head. 'Can't fucking win, can I?'

Pendragon stared at him, saying nothing.

'We had a row.'

'Who?'

'Me and Ketteridge.'

'Over the find?'

'We've never been bosom buddies, but . . . well . . . I didn't like his attitude after we dug up the bones.'

'Which was?'

'That we should get rid of them ASAP.'

Pendragon raised an eyebrow.

'I know the skeleton was old. But, I dunno . . . it didn't seem right somehow.'

'You took a stand over it?'

'He wouldn't budge and I walked off.'

'The architect was there, wasn't he?'

Disher nodded. 'Slimy bastard. He agreed with Ketteridge, of course. Big surprise.'

'So what happened?'

'According to Ricky and Nudge, Ketteridge bottled.'

'And Karim volunteered to watch over things?' Pendragon said quietly. 'You noticed the ring too?'

'Couldn't bloody miss it. Big emerald, by the look of it. I think that made all the difference.'

'What do you mean?' Pendragon drained his cup, eyeing the builder over the rim.

'Well, there were five of us there. Ketteridge would hardly want to bury the skeleton, ring and all. And he couldn't take the ring off without looking distinctly dodgy, now could he?'

'So why didn't he report it?'

Disher gave another shrug. 'Wanted to buy some time probably. Talk to the higher-ups, pass the buck . . . Wouldn't you?'

*

Tim Middleton did indeed come across as a slimy bastard. Precious and self-important, he looked distinctly uncomfortable as he too declined the offer of tea and tried to get comfortable in the plastic seat across the table from the DCI.

Pendragon had done some research. Rainer and Partner were a small-to-middling local firm of architects. Frimley Way was one of their bigger projects: a block of six apartments, high-spec yuppy hutches for the noughties. Middleton was thirty-six, made a partner a year ago, unmarried, hailed from Leicestershire. He had graduated from Oxford Brookes and then worked for a large company in Harrow for three years before joining Max Rainer, who had been a friend of his late father.

'Did you know the murdered man, Mr Middleton?'

'Not personally,' Middleton replied, crossing his legs and flicking away a speck of dust only he could see. 'We're deeply shocked and saddened.'

'Is that the royal "we"?' Pendragon asked, his expression blank.

Middleton smiled faintly. 'We, Rainer and Partner, sent our condolences to the family.'

'That's nice.'

'Sorry, Chief Inspector, but was there a particular line of questioning you had in mind?'

Pendragon took his time studying some papers on the table. He pulled a photograph of the skeleton from the pile and placed it in front of Middleton. 'All your own work, I understand.'

'Yes. The whole thing was quite bizarre.'

'Particularly since the skeleton has since vanished.'

Middleton looked appropriately shocked.

Before he could recover, Pendragon said: 'I understand you were all for getting rid of it . . . what with the job slipping behind schedule, and all.'

'Now hold on.' Middleton had uncrossed his legs and pulled his chair towards the table. He looked genuinely alarmed. 'I had no idea . . .'

'But you did support Mr Ketteridge's suggestion that the skeleton should be dumped somewhere? The whole thing hushed up?'

'No, I did not!'

'Oh?'

Middleton glanced at the ceiling then straight at Pendragon. 'It was actually my idea to leave a security guard there overnight. It was too late on a Friday to do much else.'

'You didn't think to call the police?'

'The skeleton is . . . was . . . ancient. You could tell that straight away.'

'So everyone keeps telling me. Makes no difference.'

Middleton sighed and held his hands up, shoulders raised. 'It wasn't my call, Chief Inspector. You know that.'

'So tell me about the project. Are you indeed behind schedule?'

Middleton held Pendragon's gaze. 'We're always behind schedule. The client can never have things done fast enough. It's a given, Chief Inspector.'

'And the client is always right.'

'Precisely.'

'Okay, Mr Middleton, thank you for your time.' Pendragon was already getting up. Middleton looked surprised it was all over so quickly. But then, as the DCI pushed his chair under the table, he said: 'Incidentally, Mr Middleton, can you account for your whereabouts between one and three o'clock this morning?'

Middleton leaned against the back of his chair, a smirk on his face. 'Er . . . well, I was asleep.'

'Alone? At home?'

'Sadly, yes.'

'Thank you,' Pendragon said quietly. Pursing his lips, he nodded as if this information slotted neatly into some secret agenda.

*

Sergeant Turner was about to knock on the interview-room door when it swung open and he saw Pendragon leading Tim Middleton out.

'Do you have a minute, sir?'

Pendragon nodded, escorted Middleton to the front desk and returned to the interview room. 'Anything interesting?' he asked as he closed the door behind him.

'Not really,' Turner replied. He slotted a DVD into a machine and stabbed at the play button then stood back beside the table. Pendragon resumed his seat.

The screen was black apart from a digital time display that started at 02.14.24. The seconds clicked forward and images took shape. At 02.14.47 they caught a fleeting glimpse of a featureless shape moving behind the piles of earth. In the blink of an eye it was gone. 'I've tried to enhance that,' Turner said as the film moved on. 'But it's nothing more than a blob of grey. Someone was there, for sure, but the camera is poor quality and the image just pixellates like mad if I try to enlarge it or enhance it.' Then, as he spoke, a blurred image appeared, a hunched figure in dark clothes and balaclava. A gloved hand smothered the lens and the screen turned to static.

'Same on all four cameras,' Turner said gloomily.

Pendragon was sitting with his legs crossed

studying his interwoven fingers, perched on one raised knee. 'Predictable, really,' he said wearily, and stifled a yawn. 'Okay, let's open it up. Get on to Central Monitoring. There must be at least half a dozen cameras within a few hundred metres of that building site. They couldn't all be vandalised. And if they have been, someone must have seen it being done, even at that time of the morning. By the way, anything from the search team?'

'Got a call from Vickers just now. Zilch. They're winding down for the day. Plan to start again first thing in the morning.'

Pendragon's third meeting of the afternoon came as something of a relief; a fact-gathering exercise rather than a verbal sparring match with a suspect.

'Professor Stokes, thank you for sparing the time on a weekend.'

'Not at all. Pleased to help,' Stokes replied. He was a tall, thin man, bald except for a tuft of grey hair to each side of his head. He had a long narrow nose and small dark eyes. Pendragon had learned from Google that Professor Geoffrey Stokes was fifty-six, had held a professorship at Grenoble before moving to Queen Mary College, and was considered one of the foremost authorities on the history of London.

Pendragon showed him the photographs of the skeleton, laying them out in a row on the table.

Stokes tugged at the spectacles dangling from a delicate chain round his neck and perched them on the bridge of his nose. He bent closer to study the photos. 'Extraordinary! Your sergeant told me on the phone that these came from the construction site on Frimley Way.'

'That's right.'

'I took the liberty of stopping by there on the way in. Your forensics people were about. A very nice woman showed me where the skeleton had lain.'

'Collette Newman?'

'Yes.' Stokes looked up and adjusted his glasses. 'How exactly may I help you, Chief Inspector?'

'This skeleton was unearthed yesterday afternoon. It's clearly very old. Far too old to identify. But we have reason to believe it is somehow linked to a recent murder. I'm not at liberty to go into detail at this time, but if there is anything you can tell us from these photographs we'd be extremely grateful.'

'May I not see the skeleton itself?'

'Unfortunately that's not possible at the moment.'

Stokes shrugged. 'Well, there's only so much . . . We'd have to make some broad assumptions.'

'Such as?'

'Well, most importantly, that the skeleton hasn't been moved since it was first placed where it was found. Assuming that is the case, then I can hazard a guess at its age. The soil here is blue clay; what used to be called bungam. Very common in East London. Below this is a layer of peat, which would have been exposed during the Bronze Age. If our skeleton had been found in the peat, I would have dated it to around 2,000 BC, but in the bungam stratum, well . . . certainly less than a thousand years old.'

'Can you be any more precise?'

'I noticed a few things at the site. The skeleton was found in the mid-bungam which places it between four hundred and seven hundred years ago. I also spotted a few fragments of wall at the same depth. The stones are the type used to construct primitive drains. That narrows the timeline to the fifteenth or sixteenth century.'

'Amazing. So, do you have any idea what could have been built on this spot? Someone's home?'

'No.' Stokes smiled and shook his head, his eyes bright. 'We have very good records of all the buildings in this part of London. I know this site well. It's in my own backyard . . . almost literally.' And he produced a crooked smile. 'The house the builders have just demolished was Victorian, a rare one to miss any serious bomb damage during the Blitz. But, oddly enough, it wasn't listed. Before that a much smaller Georgian house stood on the site. It was the first private residence there. Before that it was an inn, the Grey Traveller. In one form or another, it had stood there since the late-fifteenth century. That's as far back as the records go for the area.'

'So, it's quite possible the tavern was there when our man died?'

'It's more than likely. Indeed, I would think the drain led from the tavern. Not many private houses were linked to drains in those days. An inn was more likely to have such a thing, a pipe that led from the building to a septic tank.'

Pendragon picked up the photos again and looked at the top one. He handed them to Stokes. 'The ring,' he said. 'What do you make of that?'

Stokes lifted the top picture close to his face. 'It's difficult to see clearly . . .'

'Here.' Pendragon came round the desk and handed the professor a magnifying glass.

'It's ancient. Gold, obviously, and with a large jewel, maybe an emerald. I'd have to do some close analysis. We have some useful computer-enhancement software in college.'

'They're yours,' Pendragon said as he stood up. 'And, thank you, Professor.'

Chapter 8

France, February 1589

When I bring to mind the journey from the Venerable English College in Rome to the city of Paris, the overriding memory is of my bones being chilled to the very marrow, for it was the coldest winter anyone could remember. Sebastian Mountjoy, three servants and I took ship at Civitavecchia, a short ride from the Vatican, making Genoa through high swells and two terrible storms four days later.

When we reached good solid land, it felt like God's blessing on us. I had been ravaged by seasickness almost before we left port. But although we had exchanged water for land, there was no respite from the cold. The southern part of France is renowned for its mild winters and comforting coastal breezes, but the exceptionally harsh weather had spread far.

Indeed, we witnessed snow in the town of Nice.

Of course, the weather worsened as we travelled north, so that by early-February, when our party reached Lyon, we were unable to make any headway at all. Luckily, Sebastian found us comfortable rooms in a small guest house close to the city wall. The town was packed with other stranded travellers, some of whom were fretting about the enforced delay, while others simply accepted it as God's will. Sebastian and I were definitely in the latter category and those three days and nights we were forced to stay put in the good town of Lyon proved a welcome diversion. Our mission was of the utmost seriousness and we knew we were walking into danger, but these facts only added to our desire to take advantage of the respite. I recall with fondness playing dominoes before a roaring fire, eating good venison and sampling the local hops. I'm sorry to say that, in truth, these things constitute the last good memories I can now draw upon.

On the fourth morning after our arrival in Lyon, we managed to return to the road heading north, but it was very hard going and slow. Fourteen freezing days and nights we spent on that road. The landscape had changed and was rarely more than a white carpet, punctured occasionally by the outline of a church spire or a city wall. Sometimes a purple rope of smoke ascending to the chilled heavens broke the monotony.

It was close to dusk on the eighteenth day of February when we finally reached Créteil. An early and unexpected thaw had turned the snow to slush. For a month Paris and all the towns around it had been entombed in snow. Hundreds had died. Theirs had been cold deaths, so very different from the reaper's tally during summer when plague-ravaged bodies bobbed in the Seine. With the thaw came water and mud, whole streets where the sludge ran knee-deep.

From a high point on the road, just outside Créteil, and sitting straight in the saddle, I could just make out the outline of Paris, solemnly shrouded in brown. My back ached and my limbs were sore. I was filthy, hungry and exhausted. I also felt an undeniable sense of disappointment, for this view of Europe's largest, grandest city was nothing like the one I had hoped for. Paris looked like an amorphous thing, decrepit, the colour of ditchwater.

'Not far now, my friend,' Sebastian said from his own mount to my left.

'And not a moment too soon,' I replied, digging my heels into my horse's sides and flicking the reins to urge on the exhausted beast through the mud weighing down her tired legs.

Le Lapin Noir was popular: warm and dark. The servants stabled the horses and had them fed and I followed Sebastian into the main room of the inn. It was a wide, low-ceilinged room, with just one window looking out on to the dark road. Most of the locals were gathered around the huge fireplace in the far wall. The air was thick with smoke from the damp wood and the whole place stank of embers and sweat. The regulars eyed us suspiciously as we entered. A young boy led us to a back room which we had to ourselves. There, a meaner fire burned in the grate, but it threw out a good heat. A rough wooden table and a pair of chairs took up most of the floor space, and we threw ourselves into the chairs.

I could see the inn-keeper in the main room but he was busy with his regular customers. It was only as a servant brought over our food that I caught the inn-keeper's eye. He came over to us and studied me warily.

'Good landlord,' I said as cheerily as I could manage, 'we are in search of a gentleman named Gappair. Do you know if he is here this evening?'

The man had a weather-beaten face and no more than two teeth in his head. 'No idea, sir,' he lisped. 'Never 'eard of him.' And without another word he walked off, back to the hubbub of the main room. I glanced at Sebastian who looked as lost as I felt.

We concentrated on our food for a while. We were famished. Sebastian was first to finish and rose from the table to relieve himself. I was left alone to study the figures in the other room. Sebastian was still out in the back yard when there was a commotion at the door to the inn. A figure in a black cape, his face shrouded from view, was being turned away by the inn-keeper. Two of the publican's friends, big, burly farmers by the look of them, came up behind the inn-keeper, ready with their support. In a moment, the cloaked man was gone and the room had settled down again. I turned back to the table and saw a folded piece of paper next to my empty bowl.

I was opening it when Sebastian returned. I read it as he lowered himself into his chair. It said: 'Chapelle Ste-Jeanne-d'Arc, Rue Montmartre. Midnight.'

*

We couldn't take our horses out again so soon after such a long journey, so we hired a couple of rather elderly mares from the inn-keeper. Thanks to the mud and the intense dark of a moonless night it took almost three hours for us to travel the ten miles from the inn to the Chapelle Ste-Jeanne-d'Arc. Things became a little easier as we reached the centre of Paris where the streets were cleared of old snow and drained of the worst of the slush. And our one great advantage was that Sebastian was familiar with the city from his younger days when he had spent a year studying at the Abbey of Montmartre.

He told me that, although still beautiful, the Chapelle Ste-Jeanne-d'Arc was now a mere shadow of its former glory. Half a century earlier, in the days of Francis I, it had been one of the city's finest chapels, a favourite of the Royal Family. Now the most significant thing about it, he said, was its large cemetery, still a popular final resting place for the great and the good of Paris. Sebastian had walked through the cemetery on more than one occasion in his younger days and was quick to find the main path that led through the sacred ground, threading a route between massive black slabs of marble, stone angels and crosses taller than a man. We had brought only a single lantern with us and we used it sparingly. A little light filtered through from buildings on Rue Montmartre, but I was entirely in Sebastian's hands.

The solemn grey outline of the chapel took me by surprise as it emerged suddenly from the gloom. We dismounted and tethered the horses close to the door. Sebastian relit the lantern and led the way. The ground was soft underfoot, mud covering our boots and splashing our calves.

We came to the chapel's great wooden door. It was unlocked, but the hinges were rusted and worn and it took both of us to push it inwards, the old hinges complaining as it went.

Inside, it felt unnaturally cold, far more so than the wind-swept graveyard. Shadows flickered over the walls; there were brief flashes of colour as moonlight seeped softly through the stained glass in the clerestory windows. It was absolutely silent except for the sound of our boots, loud on the flagstone floor. Then we heard a faint click, followed by a tap. We stood still in the semi-darkness, straining to hear. The sound stopped. We walked slowly up the nave.

It was so dark we could see only a few feet to either side of us. The sides of the chapel remained in shadow. A few steps on and the pulpit reared out of the gloom, an ugly stone block. Behind it stood a huge carved cross, a pale Christ hanging bloodied upon it.

The sound came again. A tap, then another. It was growing louder, coming closer. Sebastian turned with the lantern and we each caught a glimpse of a shadowy figure standing a few feet before us, a flash of long, white hair, piercing black eyes in a sallow face.

'Welcome,' the figure said in a rasping voice.

Sebastian was a step ahead of me. I saw him crumple as he was struck by a heavy object that swung out from the darkness. Stunned, I moved to catch my friend as he fell. But as I bent forward, I felt a rush of air, the sound of a heavy object whistling past my ear, and then a terrible pain shot through the side of my head. The face of an old man, his almost translucent hair flying in front of his eyes, flashed before me. Then the ground reared up, twisting and blurring before me, as my legs gave way and blackness enveloped me.

Chapter 9

The hooded figure was carrying a black metal box about the size of a large camera case. He moved rapidly along the silent, empty corridor until he reached the control panel for the university's CCTV system. After snipping the cables, he closed the cover. At the front desk and in the monitoring room in the basement of the main administration building, the surveillance monitors turned blue.

Moving swiftly on to the stairwell, the intruder took the stairs three at a time. By the fourth floor he was out of breath and stopped for a moment, bent forward, hands on knees. Then he eased open the door into another narrow corridor. A sign on the wall announced he was in the Department of Plant Biotechnology, Queen Mary College.

A door with wire mesh over its window panel was locked. Beside it was a keypad. With latex-covered fingers he punched in the code for which he had paid hard cash earlier that day. There was a satisfying click and he eased the door inwards. A sallow glow emanated from overhead safety lights. He could just make out rows of steel benches, gas taps, sinks, racks of chemicals. Along one side of the large lab stood a set of floor-to-ceiling cupboards. Next to that a gas cabinet, its thickened glass door closed and locked. On the far side was a window on to the room beyond. Inside, he could just see the outlines of many plants crammed into a tight space. Foliage pressed against the inside of the glass.

He was about to walk that way when he heard voices from the corridor beyond the lab. A square of massicot appeared at the door as someone flicked on the lights in the corridor. He ducked down out of sight at the end of a row of benches. Someone tried the door handle.

'It's locked,' a voice said.

'Good,' came the reply. 'Let's check upstairs.'

He waited a few beats before straightening up, straining to listen. Then he walked slowly towards his goal. The door into the greenhouse was opened with the same code as for the lab door. He closed it carefully behind him.

It was stifling inside, the smell of damp, and rotting soil, almost overpowering. He paced slowly along the rows of plants, neatly bedded in evenly spaced pots. He avoided brushing against the leaves and only touched a plant with his gloved fingers when it was necessary in order to get by.

He had no interest in plants, otherwise he might have appreciated the wonderful colours in the greenhouse: the rich ruby reds, sunset shades of orange, the cheeriest yellows and sombre jungle greens. Instead, his mind was focused on one thing, his objective. Passing the end of the second row and scrutinising the third, he saw them at last, a pair of small unassuming plants at either end of the row. One had narrow, murky green leaves and small red flowers, a plant that would be easy to overlook. The other had broad leaves with pale green veins spreading seemingly at random on their upper surface. The stubby plant rose from a large bulb only half-submerged in soil.

He opened the metal case. It was empty. Taking a pair of cutters from his pocket, he severed the first plant at its base and lowered it into the box, folding its leaves to fit it in. Stopping at the second plant, he cut through its stems and likewise folded them into the box. Closing the case's lid, he clipped it shut.

At the door, he listened for voices outside. Then he eased it open and slipped out into the corridor and down the stairwell. Walking casually past the desk at the entrance to the building, he emerged into the hot night and the glare of headlights on Mile End Road.

Chapter 10

'You look pleased with yourself,' commented Jack Pendragon who had just returned to his desk with a large cup of his favourite Bolivian coffee, black, no sugar.

'That's because I am,' Jez Turner replied, striding towards him while eyeing the cup. 'The CCTV disks arrived at two this morning. I couldn't resist.'

'Help yourself then,' Pendragon responded, nodding towards the cafetière.

'Cheers, guv.'

'So what have you found?'

'Best see for yourself, sir.'

The media room was three doors down the corridor. It was stuffed with electronic equipment: two large flat-screen monitors, a video mixing desk, and a wall of metal units comprising DVD players, hard drives and digital enhancers. Turner sat at the control panel and Pendragon leaned towards the monitors, letting his young sergeant deal with the technology.

'As you'd expect, there're a few cameras on Mile End Road. Working on the principle that our man would have disabled the cameras at the site almost as soon as he got there, I went back over the footage from all the CCTV in the area between one-forty-five and two-fifteen.' As he talked, Turner flicked through the seven separate camera positions along Mile End Road, Globe Road and White Horse Lane, the three major roads within a few hundred metres of the construction site.

Cars passed in and out of the area, picked up in one camera to be followed in one or more of the others, before vanishing again out-of-frame. A white van could be seen on five separate cameras as it travelled up White Horse Lane, left into Mile End Road and then next right into Globe Road. It disappeared into the night north of the monitored zone. What they really wanted was someone to approach Alderney Road, a turning off Globe Road. Then for that someone to take a right into a small side street that wound round to Frimley Way. There were no cameras on Alderney Road or Frimley Way, but they could see that anyone turning off Globe Road would just be visible from a camera set close to the

Fox's Head pub, twenty or so metres from the junction.

Turner ran his fingers over the video mixing desk and fast-forwarded the images from a set of cameras. They watched as the time display sped by. A red car flashed past, followed a few moments later by a taxi. A pedestrian appeared at the edge of the image and walked briskly towards the deserted pub and out of sight.

At 2.07.14 on the digital timer, a solitary figure in dark trousers and an open-necked shirt appeared in the first camera on White Horse Lane. He walked quickly towards Mile End Road. Turner switched cameras as the figure reached the main road and turned left. He switched again and they could see the figure approaching the camera, crossing the street and turning into Globe Road. Shifting to the camera at the Fox's Head, the two policemen now had their sharpest view of the figure so far. As it approached the pub, it happened to look around and then slightly upward, scanning the road ahead.

Turner stabbed the pause button. 'Anyone you know?' he asked and glanced up at his boss.

'Can you get that image any clearer?'

'I was just about to,' Turner said and leaned towards the rack of equipment on the right wall. He turned a dial and punched a couple of black plastic keys on a pad.

'Let's close in . . .' He stabbed more buttons and the picture changed. Lines grew sharper and at the centre of the image a short, bulky figure was caught mid-stride. The man's features were suddenly recognisable.

'Bring him in,' Pendragon said in a monotone.

Chapter 11

From their position in an anteroom on the covert side of a two-way mirror, DCI Pendragon and Sergeant Turner watched Tony Ketteridge fidgeting in his chair in Interview Room 1. Dressed in shorts and a garishly patterned shirt, he was sweating profusely. Too many buttons left undone revealed an expanse of chest hair and a gold chain. There were damp patches in the fabric of his shirt, under the arms and around his abdomen. His hair was a mess and he had a two-day-old grey-flecked beard. He reminded Pendragon of the pictures of Saddam Hussein taken after US troops had dragged him from his hideout.

'He looked even worse half an hour ago,' Turner said, as though he had read his boss's thoughts. 'Took him ten minutes to answer the door. Wife's at church, apparently.'

Pendragon led the way into the interview room next door.

'What the hell's this all about?' Ketteridge protested immediately.

The DCI had a mug of coffee in his hand. Without replying, he settled himself into a chair and switched on the digital recorder set at the end of the metal table between him and Ketteridge. He recorded the time, date and other details of the interview, then removed a sheaf of glossy prints from a clear plastic folder. He slid one of the images taken from the surveillance film across the table towards Tony Ketteridge. 'Did we catch your good side?'

The blood drained from Ketteridge's face. He looked away and heaved a heavy sigh. 'It's not what it looks like . . .'

'Oh? So what exactly is it, Mr Ketteridge?'

Ketteridge screwed up his mouth. 'I wasn't going to the site.'

'You were very close to it . . . and at a very odd time of night.'

Ketteridge bit his lip and closed his eyes. Pendragon studied the man's podgy face. He looked utterly exhausted.

'I suppose there's no bloody chance that what I say can be kept from the missus, is there?' he said finally.

Pendragon glanced at Turner who was standing a

few feet away, close to the wall. 'Well, that would depend on what you had to say.'

'Yeah, right.'

'Mr Ketteridge . . . I don't imagine I need remind you of the seriousness of the situation. Amal Karim died sometime between one-thirty and two-thirty yesterday morning. The CCTV at the site was put out of action at fourteen minutes past two that morning, and you were seen not a hundred metres from there at seven minutes past. What would you conclude from that?'

Ketteridge had his palms flat on the table, his head tilted to one side. 'I was on my way to Hannah's flat,' he said. There was a momentary flash of defiance in his eyes and then he sagged, cupping his head in his hands, elbows propped on the metal table. 'And that's my fucking marriage down the toilet!'

'Does Hannah have a surname?'

'Hannah James, flat two, sixteen Mitchell Lane. It's a little cul-de-sac off Frimley Way. She's on the game. I've been seeing her for over a year.'

Pendragon was in his office when Turner called from the car. 'The woman confirms his story.'

'Damn it,' Pendragon hissed. 'Okay, Sergeant, thanks.'

He put down the phone and stared blankly at his

computer screen. Hannah James could be lying, he thought, but there was no proof. They were back to square one.

The photographs of the skeleton lay on the desk beside his coffee mug. Such pathetic remains, he thought. Little more than an imprint of a human being. But these bones had once been encased in flesh; a human being had lived and breathed and walked the earth, a person with friends and family, lovers, children perhaps. Now all these people were long dead, as were their children and their children's children.

He snatched up the phone and called Turner back.

'Just had a thought,' he said. 'That computer-enhancement software in the media room . . . can you enhance stills as well as video?'

''Course.'

'Okay, get hold of the SIM card from Tim Middleton's mobile. There's one particular shot of the skeleton where the ring is in clear view. Do what you can with the image.'

Chapter 12

Paris, February 1589

At first, consciousness returned only fleetingly. I remember seeing a shifting pattern of light on the ceiling, feeling hot, then cold; a sensation of extreme pain, then of soporific ease. The first distinct thing that came into view was the face of a beautiful young woman. I have no idea how long I was unconscious or what had caused it, but returning to the waking world to perceive the features of what I took to be an angel smoothed the transition for me. She had large brown eyes, a slender nose and full red lips. She wore a blue kerchief but I could see a few curls of jet-black hair falling across her perfect, pale skin. When she smiled, she reminded me immediately of a Madonna of Cima da Conegliano's I had once seen in Rome.

But then she was gone and it felt as though

many hours passed before I saw anything else of substance. A hand turned my face to one side and then back. I peered upwards and the face of an old man appeared. I felt a spasm of fear, but I could barely move. He put a finger to my lips and then came around my cot to sit on the edge, close to me.

'I'm sorry I hurt you, my boy,' he said. 'But, unfortunately, it was necessary.' I could see him clearly now. He was old, very old, his skin like parchment. His eyes, though, were those of a much younger man, dark blue and with the clarity of youth. His lips were pale and narrow, nose slightly crooked. His hair was drained of all colour, like wisps of cloud.

I still could not move but managed to find my voice, albeit little more than a croak. 'Where . . . ?'

'You are in my home. You are safe here.'

'Sebastian . . .'

'Your friend is well.'

'What is this?'

'All will become clearer soon. Now you must rest.' He touched my forehead and I suddenly felt overwhelmingly tired, as though I wanted nothing but sleep.

The next time I awoke, the beautiful girl was

back. I found I could move a little. As she came close, I grabbed her wrist. Her eyes filled with fear. Some instinct made me realise that this girl was not party to what had happened to me, that she was as much subject to it as I, and I let her go. She stood up and tilted her head to one side.

'You seem much better,' she said, almost mocking me. Her voice was soft and gentle. She spoke English, but with a strong French accent. 'Here, drink.'

She lowered a cup to my lips and I allowed the cold water to trickle down the back of my throat. It was as if it awoke my senses and I suddenly became aware of my physical being. All at once I felt hungry and thirsty. My limbs seemed to come to life, my vision cleared. I could see the room properly; feel the sheet covering me, and my own nakedness under the cloth.

And then she was gone. I lifted myself up in the bed and rested my head against the wall behind me. It was a bare room. Cold, grey light came in through a small, shuttered window. I could hear nothing from outside, no sounds of man nor beast. The walls were whitewashed and blank. To one side of the room was a wooden table. On top of it stood a bowl from which steam rose. Behind it, propped against the wall, was a small mirror in a plain silver frame.

I pulled the sheet away from me and looked down at my body. I was thinner than usual but could move normally and had no visible wounds. I flexed my fingers, moved my arms and legs. Sitting upright, I ran my fingers over my head and was shocked to feel hair, something I had not known since beginning my studies at Rome. It was little more than stubble, but there nevertheless. I stood up unsteadily and the room started to spin around me. I quickly sat down again and lowered my head between my knees to ward away the sudden nausea.

I stood again, more slowly this time, and remained still, adjusting to the change. Then I noticed some clothes laid out on the bed – a tunic, hose, boots. I put them on. Slowly, I walked over to the window. Standing to one side, I peered around the edge. Outside, I saw it was very early in the morning, a poor thin light was struggling against the dark of an alley. There was the grey stone wall of a building directly opposite the window. I peered down and saw that I was on the second floor of another building. I could see flagstones, uneven and stained, directly below the window. On the ground floor of the building across the alley was a shuttered window. I looked to left and right but could see little more. There was a faint mist clinging to the walls of the buildings, slowly burning away in the mean warmth of the morning. I could just discern, far off, the sound of hooves on stone and a voice encouraging a horse. Beyond that, I could make out the cry of a grocer calling from his market stall.

I turned back to the bare room. The sheets of my bed were striped with panels of light. The sheets were clean, recently changed. I stepped over to the small table with the bowl and mirror. I touched the water with one fingertip. It was welcomingly hot. I thrust my hands into it and splashed the liquid over my face, revelling in the stinging of my skin. Then I stretched out one hand and picked up the mirror.

The shock of what I saw almost undid me. I felt my knees weaken and clutched at the table, bringing it and the bowl of hot water down on me as I slid to the stone floor. The bowl glanced against my shoulder and I felt a spasm of pain before the water cascaded across my chest and the bowl clattered across the floor.

I still had the mirror gripped in my left hand. I could not resist. I had to look into it again.

The face that peered back at me was not mine. Or, at least, it was not the face I'd once had. My cheeks were a different shape entirely. My face was altogether wider, my nose slightly longer and very different in shape. My brows were thicker and I had a full beard and moustache. I had once been fair-haired; now my hair was black, my lips thicker and paler.

I turned at a sound from the door. The girl I had seen earlier stood with her hands clasped in front of her. She looked wary. 'Sir, would you please come with me?'

I was incandescent with rage, but knew there was nothing I could do. I had the feeling this young woman was as powerless as I and would do nothing under my persuasion or even the threat of a blade at her throat, had I one to brandish. It was clear Sebastian and I were in the hands of a necromancer of great power.

As the girl led me from the room, I clutched at my crucifix and prayed. I recited the Lord's Prayer quietly and beseeched God to save me, His humble servant, in this, my darkest hour. For surely, I begged, if You need me, Lord, if

You wish me to fulfil the task You have set me, I cannot be allowed to fall at the first hurdle. I was so immersed in my devotions that I barely noticed when we arrived in another room.

It was dark save for the light spilling from the coals in a brazier set in the centre of the floor. In the gloom, I could just make out shelves covering one wall. They were heavy with glass containers and strange twisted glass tubes. Closer by, to my left, stood more shelves. In the flickering light from the fire I caught sight of a jar holding a pale yellow liquid with a solid object floating in it. I jumped as I realised the object was a human foetus.

There were three chairs set equidistant around the fire. The girl led me to one and insisted I sit. It was only then that I realised there was another man already seated in a chair identical to my own. I stared at him blankly.

'It is your friend Sebastian Mountjoy,' the girl told me.

I gazed at him in disbelief. What seemed like only hours earlier he had been as bald as I, fair-skinned, with long lashes over olive-coloured eyes, a noble Roman nose and a wide mouth – a handsome man. Now his colouring was reddish. His nose was misshapen, lips pale and narrow. He had a scar running down one cheek.

I could not suppress a sob as I looked at him, but pulled myself together, if only for Sebastian's sake. I was about to speak when the old man appeared before us. He lowered himself into the remaining chair and stared into the fire. I felt bitterness seethe within me; fury that my words with God seemed to have gone unacknowledged.

'What magic is this?' I exclaimed. 'What in the name of Our Lord have you done to us?'

The old man continued to stare into the flames, but raised one hand in acknowledgement of my questions. Then he looked up, fixing us with those black, fathomless eyes of his. 'It is not magic,' he said, his voice sounding surprisingly young for one so outwardly ancient. 'I am gifted in many magical skills, that is true, but the change in your appearance is a trifle and not permanent. I know of plants which colour the skin and hair. I know also of substances which, when placed under the skin, can transform the shape of a face.'

Sebastian was very quiet and I surmised he had been awoken more recently than I, and was still drowsy from the spells or strange substances this man was speaking of. For my part, I could still barely control my anger.

'Your fury and feelings of impotence are understandable,' the old man said, as if he could read my mind. 'And, again, my knowledge of this is not derived from magic. It is to be expected that you would feel this way. Besides, I can read the lines of your face, the posture of your body. These things tell me your mental state. It is an art that anyone may learn, given patience and time.'

'Why have you done this to us?' I asked, forcing myself to remain as calm as I could. Sebastian shifted in his seat and ran one hand across his brow.

'I am obeying the will of the Holy Father.'

I sat up in my chair and glared at the old man.

'You don't believe me,' he said. 'That too is understandable. But it is only because of the way in which I had to treat you. What else could I have done? Should I have asked you nicely if I might transform your appearance?'

'You are a deceiver,' Sebastian said. 'Why should we believe anything you say?' His voice was little more than a croak. He glanced at me for a second, taking in my new appearance.

'Because I speak the truth, my boy. I know

everything about you. You are Sebastian Mountjoy. Father Sebastian Mountjoy. And you . . .' the old man added, turning to me '. . . are Father John William Allen. You have travelled to Paris from the Jesuit College in Rome on the instructions of Roberto Bellarmino himself. He in turn is acting upon the orders of the Holy Father. You are en route to London, there to complete a most urgent and long-overdue task.'

I was shaken, but did my best not to show it. 'Your knowledge of such things does nothing to convince me that your intentions are honourable.'

The old man nodded and produced a faint smile. 'Good. That is a good answer. Then perhaps this will convince you.'

He handed me a parchment. I unrolled it and read: 'By Order of His Holiness, Sixtus V, you are instructed to aid in all and every way within your power the passage of my two servants sent to you from the Venerable English College, this tenth day of January in the Year of Our Lord Fifteen Hundred and Eighty-nine. Their purpose is of the utmost importance to Us and We grant you permission to use whatever means you deem appropriate to expedite the success of their Most Holy mission.' Beneath this was the holy papal seal.

I handed the parchment to Sebastian and turned back to the old man. 'Who are you?'

'Sometimes I barely know myself,' he replied, eyeing me closely. The light from the shifting coals seemed to set his dark blue pupils aflame. He stared deep into the fire for a moment before continuing, 'I was once named Cornelius Agrippa.'

Sebastian made a strange sound and turned to me. 'He lies. Agrippa died many years ago.'

'Yes, in a way, he did,' the old man replied. 'The person I was barely remains as part of me, but I am who I say I am. Cornelius Agrippa, alchemist, friend of noblemen and royalty, philosopher, truth-seeker, devout Catholic . . . and one hundred and three years old.'

I snorted and he smiled thinly, fixing me with those clear and youthful eyes again. I felt a shudder pass through me and turned to look at Sebastian, but he was staring at the old man.

'It matters not whether you choose to believe me,' he said in his oddly youthful voice. 'You do not need to believe that I am here to help you, nor even that the Holy Father has instructed me to do all I can to expedite your success. I will not fail my master.'

'But what help is this?' I exclaimed, finally losing control of myself. I stood up and glared at the old man who claimed he was the famed alchemist and magus Cornelius Agrippa. 'You have disfigured us. Why?'

'I should have thought that was obvious,' he replied, ignoring my fury, not even bothering to glance up at me. 'There are spies everywhere. Indeed, we are in the middle of a war of spies, if you will. Sir Francis Walsingham, Queen Elizabeth's Principal Secretary and spymaster, has dozens of servants in this city, many men and women in his pay who would denounce you in a heartbeat and collect their few pieces of silver as reward.'

'And how do we know you are not one of them?' Sebastian said. He was sitting bolt upright in his chair.

'You don't. Perhaps you should not trust me. But then, you have to trust someone. So far you've made a pig's ear of things.'

I looked at him in surprise. 'How so?'

'The inn-keeper. He is one of Walsingham's men.'

'But we were told to proceed to his inn, that he could be trusted.'

'The man has turned. I managed to get you to safety before others could intervene. In a way, I was already too late. Your faces were known. The only way I could help you was to use my skills to change your appearance.'

I let out a heavy sigh, still unable to believe him.

'Who else did Father Bellarmino say you could trust?' he went on.

'A man named Gappair.'

'Gappair?' he laughed. Sebastian glanced at me as I sank down in my seat again.

'Gappair?' He repeated. 'Hah! An anagram, my boy . . . for Agrippa.'

I sensed Sebastian sag with relief in his chair and, for my part, suddenly felt a huge weight lifted from my shoulders.

The old man rose to his feet and approached us. 'Now, perhaps we should stop wasting precious time,' he said. 'You need to learn what you must do with this.' And he held out the ring which Roberto Bellarmino had placed in our safekeeping.

Chapter 13

Stepney, Sunday 5 June, lunchtime

La Dolce Vita, an Italian restaurant on Mile End Road, was every bit the cliché its name implied. Owned by Giovanni Contadino, a former sales executive from Milan who had moved to London over a decade earlier, it was decorated with heavily patterned wallpaper and an equally strident carpet. A huge but cheap-looking chandelier hung from the centre of the ceiling, casting a surprisingly pallid light. But the food was good and the service friendly.

On this oppressively hot afternoon, all the windows of the restaurant had been flung open and a couple of portable electric fans did their best to quell the stifling heat. A storm was brewing.

By 12.45, the staff of Rainer and Partner had gathered at the bar. It was their annual get together, and, in ebullient mood, the owner of the company, Max Rainer, was buying everyone drinks. Suddenly, the storm broke. Rain came down in great torrents. The restaurant staff rushed around, slamming shut the windows.

Tim Middleton was fifteen minutes late. He pulled into the car park in his red MG, slammed shut the car door, opened an over-sized Ralph Lauren umbrella and dashed through the rain to the restaurant. He looked dapper in a beautifully tailored Ozwald Boateng suit, taupe calfskin loafers and a floral-patterned shirt. He was about to open the door when he noticed a young couple standing in the passage-way leading to the dining-room. She was slim with brown, wavy hair. Her white 1950s-style dress clung to her, accentuating large breasts and a narrow waist. Her partner was a tall man, at least twenty years her senior. He was greying at the temples and heavy-jowled. The young woman had her arm linked with his. Middleton stopped abruptly and was about to turn on his heel when the woman spotted him.

'Hello, Tim,' she said, and pressed closer to her partner.

'Sophie,' he replied evenly.

There was an uncomfortable silence for a moment. Then Middleton said, 'Well, if you'll excuse me?'

Sophie blocked his way by moving almost imperceptibly to her left. Middleton gave her a contemptuous look.

'Always were on a hair trigger, weren't you, Tim?'

The man at Sophie's side laughed. 'Ah, *that* Tim,' he said.

Middleton ignored him.

'You haven't met Marcus, have you?' Sophie said quickly. Her eyes sparkled, darting between the two men.

Middleton gave Marcus the briefest of nods. 'Charmed. Running late. Must dash.'

'Pathetic prick,' Sophie said, shaking her head.

He glared at her. 'As classy as ever, Soph.'

Marcus took a step towards him, but Sophie held him back. Middleton smirked and gave them a little wave, pulled his jacket down at the front and headed towards the Rainer and Partner table. A few of the firm's staff had already taken their seats and had been watching the scene with silent interest. Middleton did his best to ignore Giovanni Contadino, who had also witnessed the exchange. The restaurateur led Sophie and Marcus to a small private area along a narrow corridor away from the main dining-room. With strained bonhomie, Middleton dived into telling one of the secretaries a joke.

By two o'clock, most of the party were merry from copious amounts of Frascati, their hunger satisfied with some of the best pizza, gnocchi, linguine and garlic bread in London.

Since he'd become a partner four years earlier, tradition had it that at these annual lunches Tim Middleton would give a short speech, recalling in humorous fashion the highs and lows of the year, gently mocking their boss, Max Rainer, and embarrassing the junior staff. Feeling slightly the worse for wear after drinking more than his share of Frascati as well as three whiskies before leaving his flat, Tim Middleton rose to his feet and swept a hand through his long, light brown hair. Max Rainer offered a brief, jokey introduction, patted Middleton on the back and returned to his seat.

'It's always a pleasure,' he began, 'to report on the ever-upward path of Rainer and Partner. And, indeed, I have to be honest and say that much of this has been due to the aforementioned "Partner".' He paused for a moment, looking round at the strained smiles of his colleagues. 'And,' he went on, 'that upward mobility has been in spite of certain . . . shall we say . . . gaffes committed during the past twelve . . .' He stopped and closed his eyes for a moment, swaying gently on the spot.

'Someone's overdone it,' whispered one of the junior architects to a secretary on his left. She giggled. Middleton's eyes snapped open and he peered around the table, clearly struggling to focus. As discreetly as he could, he loosened his tie. It bought him a moment in which to gather his thoughts.

A low roll of thunder rumbled overhead and lightning crackled across the sky, so close by it was as though a flash bulb had gone off at the table.

'Gaffe number one,' continued Middleton, his words slightly slurred. 'Gaffo numero uno must go to . . .' He stopped again, and those who had not averted their gaze through embarrassment noticed a rivulet of sweat running down his temple. His eyes looked bloodshot suddenly. Wincing, he opened his mouth and began to form a word but nothing came out. Instead, his jaws opened and closed slightly as though controlled by concealed wires. He doubled up and grabbed at his stomach. Rocking on his heels, he clutched at the table to steady himself. One of the company's draughtsmen, sitting to Middleton's right, jumped up and put a hand out in an effort to stop his boss from falling.

Middleton took a step back. He was staring at the gathering, an expression of horror on his face. He clutched his throat, his eyes bulging. White foam appeared at the corners of his mouth. He looked down for a moment, swaying as though his sight had gone, and when he brought his head up again they could all see that his left eye had become a red disc. A rivulet of blood ran from it down his cheek. He roared and a stream of vomit and blood gushed from his mouth. It spattered the tablecloth and caught two of his colleagues across the face as they recoiled in horror.

Middleton crashed down on the table, his face connecting with a clutch of wine bottles and glasses, knocking them into laps and on to the floor. One of the women screamed and leapt up. The architect slid backwards, away from the table. As he fell, more blood and vomit gushed from his mouth.

Max Rainer dashed over to him. Middleton had stopped moving. One eye stared sightlessly at the ceiling; the other was a uniform scarlet. Rainer placed two fingers to his partner's neck then turned to the others as they clustered around, a look of disbelief on his face.

Chapter 14

Pendragon's worldly goods had been brought down from Oxford the day before and stored overnight by a removals firm. At the storage depot, it took him only twenty minutes to load the lot into his car. The hard bit was getting the stuff up to his third-floor flat. After six trips up four flights of stairs, he was exhausted. Waiting for the kettle to boil, he considered the collection of boxes and a solitary bin-liner filled with clothes, and thought, not for the first time, how little he had to show for a double first from Oxford and a quarter of a century on the force.

He poured boiling water on to a teabag and added a dribble of milk, stirred the dark brown liquid and sat down in one of the armchairs that had come with the flat. Lifting the cup to his lips, he looked around the over-lit room. The walls were covered with lining paper and had been painted caramel. It wasn't a bad colour, he thought, just worn out, a relic from the 70s. The carpet was new, but too heavily patterned for his taste. The curtains . . . well, they would have to go. Just as soon as he had time to get the place straight.

He walked over to the large bay window and looked out on to the street, a small turning off Stepney Way. The sky had darkened overhead. Storm clouds heavy with rain were bunching together ominously. Although still early-afternoon, it already looked like dusk. Just within sight at the end of the street was a mosque. On the opposite corner stood a twenty-four-hour petrol station lit up in red and blue. It looked like some exotic marine creature dredged up from the Mariana Trench.

Pendragon's building was scruffy and contained half a dozen flats, but he could see that three or four of the houses in the street had been gentrified, smartened up to become desirable homes for As and Bs. There were worse places to live, he supposed.

On the way back to the armchair, he pulled over a box and slowly removed its contents. A stack of long-playing albums: John Coltrane, Herbie Hancock, Chick Corea. A box set of Miles Davis sessions from the late-50s. Next to this was a sturdy metal container. Inside lay his most treasured possessions: an Audio Technica turntable, Guarneri Homage speakers and a 1970s Pioneer amp, each lovingly encased in bubble wrap. He lifted them gently from the crate and placed the amp and turntable on a low plastic table, hooked up the mains and the leads to the speakers and switched them on. Turning to the box of vinyl, he pulled out *A Love Supreme*, cleaned it carefully with a special cloth kept in a small plastic box in the album case, slipped it over the spindle of the turntable and moved the arm into position. The sound of immortal sax spilled from the speakers.

Coltrane always put him in an introspective mood, and he wasn't convinced this was a good thing. All the introspection in the world could do nothing to change the past and nor could it shed any light on his current problems. He turned back to the box and pulled out another album, a Stan Getz Sextet classic from 1958. Inside the clear plastic protective sleeve was the note his son, Simon, had put there just a few days earlier when he gave the album to his father as a going-away present: 'Dad, one of your favourites, I know. Enjoy, and visit soon.'

Simon was at Oxford University. A child prodigy, he had obtained his mathematics degree by the age of fifteen, and now, a month shy of his twentieth birthday, was already a research assistant close to finishing his doctorate. Socially, Simon was awkward, shy, and quite incapable of conducting a normal conversation about anything trivial, his mind constantly filled with arcane wonders, symbols and numerical relationships. Jack was just about the only person who could communicate with his son on anything like a normal level and there was a very special bond between them.

The last item in the box was a picture, framed and wrapped in plastic. He removed the covering and let the plastic fall to the floor. He cleaned the glass with his sleeve and looked at the image. His daughter Amanda, aged nine. The picture had been taken in Oxford five years earlier, a month before she disappeared. She was standing beside the cherry tree outside St Mary's Church on The High, its branches smothered with blossom, sunlight catching her golden hair. She was smiling.

The day Amanda vanished had started like any other. She had headed off on her bike to school just a few streets away. But she never arrived. The police could find nothing: no signs of a struggle; no evidence of violent abduction. As time passed, her family's grief and pain had not faded a jot. Instead, frustration, anger and bitterness were added to the mix. Pendragon had felt totally impotent. He was a detective chief inspector, his own daughter had disappeared in broad daylight, and he could do nothing.

Amanda's disappearance destroyed Jack's family.

It was not a sudden devastating collapse but came gradually, creeping up on them as the years went by and Amanda remained lost to them. Jack found that his former ambition had evaporated. He no longer cared about promotion or career progress. He did his job as well as ever, perhaps better, but had lost any drive to advance himself. At the same time, he and his wife Jean were drifting apart. A brooding feeling of mutual blame hung heavy between them. Neither of them ever rationalised it and they certainly never broached the subject, but it was there, a constant, malignant presence.

'Enough,' he said aloud as he placed the picture on the mantelpiece over the gas fire. He plucked the needle from the record and turned off the stereo. Grabbing his jacket, he locked the door, took the stairs two at a time and almost collided with a woman coming through the main door on the ground floor. She was carrying two bulging shopping bags.

'I'm so sorry,' he began.

She smiled.

'May I . . .?'

'Thanks, but I'm just down there,' she said, nodding towards the corridor. 'Number two.' She put the bags down and offered him her hand. 'Susan Latimer, Sue.'

'Jack Pendragon.'

They shook hands and he appraised her silently. She was tall and slender, her brunette hair shoulder-length. She had a pretty if tired face, soft brown eyes and fine eyebrows, a transforming smile. He guessed she was in her early-forties.

'*Chief Inspector* Jack Pendragon, I believe.'

He gave her a faint smile and looked at the bags. 'They look heavy.'

'And seem to get heavier with each step. Must be some weird Law of Nature.'

'Like toast always landing butter-side down?'

'Something like that,' she laughed.

He picked up the bags for her and followed her down the corridor.

'You must drop by for a cup of tea sometime,' she said, taking them from him again after unlocking the door.

'I'd like that.'

As he left the building it started to rain, huge drops that left dark smudges on the parched pavement. The sky was black but shot through with that almost supernatural glow that comes with electrical storms. The air felt thinner than normal, as though the oxygen was being sucked up into the higher reaches of the atmosphere. Pendragon ducked under shop canopies, dodging the downpour as best he could. A Bangladeshi grocer wished him good evening and tried to sell him some radishes. At the next corner, one of the local 'characters', a tailor, resplendent and stereotypical in pinstripe suit and with a tape measure around his neck, tried for the second time that day to persuade him to come in and be measured for a new 'whistle'.

The pub was already half-full. It still stank of cigarettes even though the public smoking ban had been in effect for years. A jukebox blared a recent chart hit and a wide-screen plasma TV was showing a football game: Arsenal versus Newcastle. At the bottom of the screen a blue strip carried news headlines. Ordering a pint, Pendragon glanced round and saw the group from the station. Jez Turner spotted him at the same moment. He stood up and beckoned his boss over.

'Afternoon, sir. The Super told me you were getting your place sorted.'

'Got thirsty.'

Pendragon glanced around the table. His two inspectors, Rob Grant and Ken Towers, were there. They nodded. Between them sat two of the sergeants, Rosalind Mackleby and Jimmy Thatcher. At that moment the third sergeant, Terry Vickers, returned from the bar carrying a tray of drinks. Noticing the chief inspector for the first time, he glanced at his pint. Pendragon shook his head. 'I'm fine thanks,

Sergeant.' Then he remembered Vickers and Thatcher had been trawling for bones around Frimley Way all morning. 'Anything turn up?' he asked.

'No, guv. We've searched the entire area. Waste bins, skips . . . nothing.'

'You going to sit down, sir?' Turner asked. 'You're making the place look untidy, as me old mum always says.'

Pendragon slipped off his jacket and sat down next to Turner, placing his beer on the rickety Formica-topped table already overcrowded with glasses and empty crisp packets.

'Your turn, I believe, Jez,' Rob Grant called over with a mocking smile. 'And, please, make it a bit tasty. Your last bloody effort was piss poor.'

Turner threw Grant a dismissive look.

'What's the game?' Pendragon asked.

'Conundrums. I set the scene and they ask me questions that I have to answer truthfully. They try to figure out how the scene came about.'

Pendragon grinned. 'God, that takes me back, I used to play this at Ox—'

For a telling moment here was silence around the table. Then Ken Towers broke in. 'It's okay, sir, no need to apologise for your education . . . I'm happy to name-drop Kennington Secondary Modern.' There was laughter around the table.

Pendragon nodded, a brief smile playing across his lips, and Jez Turner said, 'Okay. You ready? Right. John and Samantha are dead on the floor. There's a damp patch on the carpet close to the bodies and shards of glass nearby. What's happened?'

Pendragon eased back with his pint, watching the others around the table. He knew this one and had no intention of spoiling their fun.

'Anyone else in the room?'

'No.'

'Doors and windows open or closed?'

'All closed.'

'John and Samantha . . . a married couple?'

'Maybe.'

'What do you mean, maybe?' Rob Grant snapped. 'Either they're married or they're not. You can't be a bit married.'

Turner shrugged. 'They live together.'

'Are they old or young?' Mackleby asked.

'Middle-aged.'

'How did they die?'

'Suffocated.'

'They were strangled?'

'No.'

Grant turned to Inspector Towers. 'What about the glass and the water, Ken? Someone must've broken in.'

'Yeah. Broken windows?' Towers asked.

'Nope.'

Jimmy Thatcher took a long gulp of his lager and his face brightened. He peered over the glass. 'Ah!' he said as he brought his glass down on the table. 'John and Samantha . . . they ain't human, are they?'

Turner tried to look blank, but he would have made a useless poker player. 'Not human?' he bluffed.

'Nah. They're fish.' Thatcher took another drink as the others looked at him, and Turner let out a sigh. 'They're goldfish. The cat knocked the bowl off the dresser. It smashed . . . glass everywhere. John and Samantha suffocated.'

Mackleby clapped her hands together and laughed. 'Brilliant!' Thatcher bowed theatrically and Jez Turner shook his head. 'You've heard it before.'

'Nah,' Thatcher said with a smirk. 'Just a bloody genius, that's all.' And he tapped the side of his head to emphasise the point.

'Well done, smart arse,' Turner retorted. 'Your round, I believe.' The smile slid from Thatcher's face as he stood up and strode dutifully over to the bar.

'If it's any consolation,' Pendragon said quietly to Turner, 'I've already heard that one, and a tableful of Oxford undergraduates took a hell of a lot longer to get the answer.'

'Makes me feel a whole lot better, sir,' Turner said, draining his glass.

'So, did you manage to get the SIM card from Middleton?'

'I was trying his mobile all morning. He had it switched off. I finally reached him about an hour ago. He promised he'd drop it off at the station this afternoon. Said he was on his way to a company function.'

Pendragon was about to reply when his phone rang.

'Yes?' He stared off into the middle distance, expressionless. 'When? . . . Yes, I know it. I'll be there in five minutes.' He stood up and pulled on his jacket.

'Another incident,' he announced to the policemen around the table. Turning towards Mackleby and Grant, he added, 'I'll need you two with us. We've got another dead body at a place called La Dolce Vita, a restaurant a few doors down from Jangles.'

Chapter 15

Paris, February 1589

'You have doubted *my* intent,' Agrippa said. 'But it was not until I saw this ring that I knew for sure *you* were indeed who you claimed to be.'

'How so?' Sebastian asked.

'Because I have seen the ring before. I knew the one who owned it, and I know that it has been in the safekeeping of the Holy Office for almost a century since. I was a young man in the court of the Borgia Pope, Alexander VI, employed as the personal alchemist of his daughter, Lucrezia Borgia. That surprises you both?' Agrippa added with a wan smile. 'It should not. When I was young I needed patrons to survive and Lucrezia Borgia was then the most powerful woman in the world. She was also corrupt, some would say evil beyond

127

redemption, but then, so were her entire family. She was not the worst of them, but perhaps her behaviour seems more shocking simply because she was of the gentler sex.'

'But I don't understand,' I said. 'What has all this to do with our mission?'

He sighed and looked at us wearily. 'You really don't understand very much, do you?'

I bridled at that and sensed Sebastian's ire. But Agrippa merely smiled one of his knowing smiles. 'Come with me,' he said. 'I shall explain.'

He led us out of the room and down a narrow corridor with closed doors to left and right. Striding ahead, he held up a torch to light the way. Reaching the end of the corridor, we descended a narrow spiral stairwell. Shadows flickered against the walls, human outlines exaggerated by the torch's dancing flame. Our footfalls echoed on the stone stairs. We must have taken a dozen turns down them before Agrippa drew to a halt before a heavy wooden door. 'Do not be afraid of what you see behind this,' he said, his face illuminated by shifting patterns of light. 'For I am master here.'

The room stank – a horrid animal stench. I could not at first understand where the smell was coming from, and Sebastian looked equally bemused. But then, gradually, our eyes grew accustomed to the dim light and, at the same moment, I heard a low rumbling sound and the scrabbling of claws on stone. A bear, at least seven feet tall, clambered to its feet, flattening a pile of turds. It was shackled by chains at each ankle and had a thick steel collar about its neck joined to a sturdy chain that ran to a bracket on the wall. Shocked, Sebastian and I both jumped back. The bear was dark brown, with a strip of lighter fur running the length of its torso. Its eyes were darker than the fur, watery and pained. The beast was muzzled, but I could just see a red tongue lolling between broken teeth. It was a dreadful sight, and I was filled with a confusion of emotions. Fear lay uppermost, but pity and puzzlement were there also.

Agrippa stood perfectly still, torch held at head height, silently contemplating the pitiable animal.

'Fear not,' the alchemist said. 'The beast is terrified of fire, and he knows I can wound him mortally before he could possible harm us.'

'What is this all about?' I exclaimed, eyeing the bear warily. 'Why is this noble creature kept here in the dark, festering in its own filth?'

'You will soon understand,' Agrippa said. Before I could tell what he was doing, he'd stepped forward, lifting with his free hand a slender wooden pipe and blowing hard down it. Something flew from the end, catching the light from the torch as it sailed through the air. Then the bear growled. Some sort of dart, akin to the ones I used at play in my youth, was protruding from the beast's hairy belly. It looked down at it, puzzled. Slowly, the poor creature rocked to and fro before stumbling forward. It snarled and swung one huge paw directly towards me. I fell back just in time, the massive paw slicing the air an inch from my face. The chains binding the creature took the strain and he was yanked back, crashing against the wall, his eyes ablaze. It was then that the animal let out a horrible, agonised wail, a sound of fury and defeat. It shuddered and slid down the wall, legs splayed, eyes vacant.

I stood paralysed, simply staring at the poor beast as Agrippa stepped towards it. From under his cloak he produced a small glass vial.

The creature was shaking uncontrollably. Its eyes were rolling, the whites almost iridescent in the flickering torch flame. Agrippa showed no fear. He grabbed the bear's head by the fur and yanked it back. The poor thing's unfocused eyes rolled around in their sockets. The magus ran the vial across the dribbling lips of the beast, catching foam and saliva in the glass receptacle which he stoppered and returned to its place under his cloak.

'We are done,' he said, without the slightest visible sign of emotion, and made for the door. Terrified we might be locked in, Sebastian and I swiftly followed him out and watched as he slammed shut the door. Then, barely able to order our racing thoughts, we followed him up the stairs and back to the laboratory.

'What in the name of the Father did you do down there?' Sebastian exclaimed. His face was wet from his exertions and he was shaking.

'I have set you on your way, young man. That is what I have done.'

Sebastian stared at the alchemist, lost for words.

Agrippa leaned forward to stoke the fire. 'I am an alchemist, Father Mountjoy. I deal in strange substances and strange forces, just as you deal in prayers and biblical texts. Roberto Bellarmino has given you the vehicle for your task, I am to provide the substance to make it work.'

We stared at the alchemist in silence. He held the vial in some sort of metal arm and placed it into the heart of the fire. 'During my long years on this earth I have learned much,' he said. 'I have met many illustrious men and women. I have been taught well. It was the great Leonardo da Vinci himself who first discovered the power of Cantarella.'

'Cantarella?' I said. 'I know that name.'

'You do?' Agrippa replied, turning to study my face. 'Very few others have heard of it, young man. It has been kept a closely guarded secret. But perhaps shadows of the past remain to haunt certain places in Rome. Who is to say?

'Cantarella is a poison, the most deadly ever known. You need not know its constituents, and I would certainly not reveal the formula. Suffice it to say that Leonardo, and later My Lady Lucrezia Borgia, knew many merchants, many travellers, who had visited exotic parts of the world and returned to Italy with strange substances. Among other things they brought back resins from lands said to be filled with dense, lush swathes of vegetation, enormous snakes, and people with skin the colour of pitch.

'Leonardo, the consummate experimenter, discovered the formula for Cantarella when I was a child. He had no intention of producing a poison. It was a by-product of his investigations. He had been searching for a preservative for flesh, something to help him with his anatomical experiments. Later, when he worked for the Borgia family in the year 1499, he was seduced into revealing the secret to Lucrezia, then a nineteen-year-old acolyte of the Dark Arts. She realised the potential of the substance at once and was even more delighted when Leonardo let slip his theory that the potency of the poison could be increased a thousandfold if it was passed through the body of an animal and refined by the natural humours in that body.'

Agrippa paused for a moment, withdrew the vial from the flames and peered at it in the light from the fire. He seemed satisfied and laid the glass vial in a cradle placed on top of a table.

'Leonardo utterly refused to test his theory and abandoned the service of the Borgia family – an act of bravery that a lesser man would never have dared to contemplate. It mattered little, though. By then Lucrezia had learned all she needed. I was a mere boy but was drawn into her circle because I had a gift for Natural Philosophy. I like to believe I offered much to Lucrezia Borgia. I was her amanuensis, assisting in her earliest experiments to refine Cantarella. I gave her the philosophical rigour she lacked. We used cats, dogs and, on two occasions, bears, until we had perfected the technique. This,' he concluded, lifting the vial from the cradle, 'is refined Cantarella. One drop kills instantly.'

'And the ring?' I asked.

'As I said, it is the vehicle. This . . .' he eyed the liquid in the vial '. . . is the substance. It is my offering, my contribution to your mission. You are to use the ring and the poison to kill the English whore, Elizabeth Tudor.'

'But why go to such elaborate lengths? What is wrong with a simple sword? The woman bleeds, like anyone.'

'A sword is unreliable, young man. With a sword, you may injure but not kill. And believe me, Elizabeth has many enemies. Others before you have tried and failed using crude weapons. This ring and this poison are easy to conceal, and they are quite infallible. One scratch and the heretic Queen of England will be dead within seconds.'

Chapter 16

Stepney, Sunday 5 June, 2.45 p.m.

Pendragon had only ever seen so much rain once before. He was nineteen then. It was the Long Vac. His parents had expected him to spend the holiday in their narrow terrace house just off Whitechapel Road, but he had just finished his first year at Oxford and gone straight to Paris with a group of friends. They had split up in the Bois de Boulogne, agreeing to meet up in Aix, with ten francs laid on who would get there first.

After an hour spent sitting beside the road reading *The Glass Bead Game*, Pendragon was given a lift by a truck driver heading south. He hadn't realised the driver was stopping at Lyon, and so was dumped on the edge of town at 3 a.m. He'd just started walking along the central reservation of the main road when the deluge started. Taking shelter under some trees, he watched as the storm approached across the river.

Lightning like devils' fingers stabbed the water and the bass vibration of thunder thumped him in the chest.

Now Mile End Road, or what could be seen of it through the windscreen, looked like a narrow river that had burst its banks. Water lapped over the kerbs, making the road and the pavements one. Even with the wipers set to 'high', looking out through the windscreen created the illusion that they were sitting inside a waterfall.

Turner's phone beeped and he read a text from the station, passing on all the details they had. 'Call came in at eleven minutes past two, guv. The owner, a . . .' he looked closer at the screen '. . . Mr Conta . . . dino was there. Quite a few witnesses. Man collapsed at one of the tables.'

'Why involve us?'

Turner turned back to the screen as more information came in. 'Definitely doesn't sound like natural causes.' And he paused for dramatic effect. 'Might be glad they did call. The dead man is Tim Middleton.'

There were two police cars and an ambulance outside the restaurant and the pavement had been cordoned off. Two officers were putting up tape. They were drenched through. Pendragon and Turner dashed from the car. By the time they had covered the ten metres to the restaurant, Pendragon's grey suit was several shades darker and Turner's expensive suede jacket was as matt as an old chamois leather.

'Unbelievable!' he exclaimed as he peeled it off, wishing he had left it in the car. Pendragon wiped his face and watched dispassionately as drips fell to the marble floor of the entrance hall. Two ambulancemen walked past and then dived into the torrent. They had been called out but could do nothing for the dead.

Pendragon could see a dozen people in the restaurant. A woman was sobbing, the sound drowned out by the beating rain. He nudged Turner and strode past the reception desk and into the main dining-room. The dense black clouds outside cast a sombre light over the room.

The scene had been left pretty much untouched. Tim Middleton lay on his back. Blood and vomit covered his face and the front of his shirt. There were lumps of partially digested garlic bread in his hair. Dr Jones had arrived only moments before and was making a preliminary examination of the corpse. A chalk outline had already been drawn around the deceased and a police officer was videoing the scene. Middleton's colleagues and two or three other diners were standing in a group at the other side of the room. Inspector Grant and Sergeant Mackleby, who had reached the restaurant a few minutes earlier in another car, were talking to the restaurant owner and scribbling in their notebooks. Pendragon turned as a tall chunky man approached from the direction of the toilets.

'Are you in charge here?' he asked gravely. He looked to be in his mid-fifties with a careworn face, a high forehead, and sparse, greased-back black hair. He wore cream chinos, a blue polo shirt and a tweed jacket. His hand was extended. 'Max Rainer.'

'DCI Pendragon. I'm sorry for your loss.'

Rainer sighed. 'I can't quite believe it, to be honest.'

Pendragon studied the architect. He seemed self-assured, coherent, but clearly shaken by what had happened. 'Can you talk me through it?'

Rainer described the scene, including a summary of Middleton's speech and its shocking finale. 'I was first to reach him after he . . . after he collapsed. It was all horribly violent. But, even so, I didn't expect him to be . . . dead.'

'Thank you,' Pendragon said. 'We'd like a full statement from you.' He strode over to where Grant was still talking to Giovanni Contadino. Letting the inspector write a final comment in his notebook before stepping in, Pendragon addressed the restaurant owner. 'No one left the restaurant after the incident?' he asked.

'Of course not.'

'So who do we have here?'

'The party from Rainer and Partner and two other couples.' Contadino pointed them out. 'One pair were in the other room.' He nodded towards a woman in a white dress and an older man with black hair greying at the temples. 'The other couple were at the table over there.' He pointed to a spot on the other side of the room from where Middleton died.

'Can you remember what the victim ate?'

Contadino answered immediately. 'I just told your colleague – chicken pizza. He'd drunk a fair bit.'

'Any seafood?'

The man's eyes opened wide. 'You're not . . .?'

'We have to consider everything, Mr Contadino.'

'But we've never had a problem. I mean . . . besides, none of the party ordered seafood.'

'Well, thank you for your help,' Pendragon said dispassionately. He crossed the room to where Dr Jones was kneeling beside Middleton's body.

'He was definitely poisoned,' the pathologist said, without looking up. 'Notice the yellow tinge to the skin? Unless . . . do you know if he ate shellfish?'

'He didn't. No one at the table did.'

'Well, unless it was something he ate a while ago,

it can't be food poisoning. Staphylococcus takes at least an hour to present. E. coli more like eight, minimum.'

'There's nothing that works faster?'

'Well, yes, toxins, Pendragon. Allergic reaction may explain it, but that's rare. I can't imagine he would have eaten or drunk anything if he knew he'd have an allergic reaction to it.'

'But I've never seen anything like this. According to witnesses, he was relatively normal just a few seconds before he projectile-vomited blood. And then there's the eye.'

'Precisely my point,' Jones retorted. 'Can't be food poisoning.'

'No.'

'However,' and Jones looked at Pendragon now, 'if he was poisoned, which I would put money on, the dose must have been massive to cause such a rapid and violent effect. Either that or it was an incredibly powerful poison. One I've never seen or even heard of before.'

140

Chapter 17

There was a faint odour of damp in the briefing room. Pendragon noticed it as soon as he walked in with Turner. Other than this, a large brown-ringed damp patch in the ceiling was the only remaining indication that a gutter had given way under the pressure of water from the storm, causing a minor flood in this part of the station. Mackleby and Grant were already there. The sergeant was pinning a set of photographs of Tim Middleton to the board. Grant was tapping at a laptop, his eyes fixed on the screen.

'So, what have we got?' Pendragon said as Mackleby turned and walked towards the nearest desk.

She had a notebook and pen in front of her. 'The restaurant owner was keen to help.'

'He's worried we'll have Environmental Health round there.'

'Yeah, but to be fair, guv, he did well. Stopped anyone leaving, got us there sharpish.'

Pendragon nodded. 'Learn anything from his account?'

'Mr Contadino was in the kitchen when Middleton started to take a bad turn. He heard a woman scream and rushed in to see the victim hit the deck.'

'What about the others from the firm?'

'Sergeant Mackleby spoke to the women. I took statements from the men,' Inspector Grant replied, without looking up from the screen. He tapped at a button, stood up and came around the desk. 'Accounts match up. They all agree Middleton had tucked away a few. He was giving some sort of speech, a tradition in the company apparently. Then he started to slur his words and seemed disorientated. They thought he was sloshed at first, but then he spewed blood and collapsed. Rainer was the first to the body.'

'Anything different from the women, Sergeant?' Pendragon asked.

'There is one thing that might be significant. A couple of the women saw Middleton arrive. He was late and they said he had a heated exchange with a couple who got to the restaurant at about the same time. Middleton was in a foul mood by the time he reached his colleagues at the table.'

'You got the names of the couple?' Turner asked.

'Better than that. You probably saw them. They

were there earlier. I spoke to Contadino. He witnessed the incident too and told me there was almost a fight. After Middleton collapsed at his table, the woman . . . er . . .' Mackleby stopped to consult her notebook '. . . Sophie Templer, was distraught. Her boyfriend, Marcus Campbell, wanted to get her out of the restaurant, but Mr Contadino would have none of it. He . . .'

'We split them up straight away and had a chat,' Grant interrupted. 'Campbell didn't deny there had been a scene at the entrance, but insisted it was nothing serious. Apparently, until quite recently, Ms Templer and Middleton were an item.'

Pendragon raised an eyebrow. 'Their stories matched?' he asked Mackleby.

'Yes, guv. They were in a different part of the restaurant from the Rainer party. Neither of them saw Middleton between the altercation and the time he died. They heard a commotion from the table in the main room, saw Contadino rush in there. Campbell went to see what all the fuss was about and Sophie Templer came after him a couple of minutes later. She saw Middleton on the floor and went to pieces. By the time we got there she had calmed down, although she was still in shock when I spoke to her.'

Pendragon nodded and frowned, mulling over the

information. 'What about the deceased himself? Did you learn anything from his colleagues?'

'They were all in shock, of course,' Grant volunteered. 'But you know, guv, I got the feeling none of them really liked the geezer.'

Pendragon turned to Mackleby. 'Sergeant? Did you sense the same thing?'

She nodded. 'I don't think he was exactly flavour of the month at Rainer and Partner.'

'Okay. All grist for the mill. Dr Jones is moaning like hell about being "overwhelmed by the dead", as he put it, but he's sure Middleton didn't die from food poisoning. Unless it was something he ate earlier in the day. The only things other than deliberate poisoning that could act that fast would be toxins from seafood, and no one on the Rainer table had seafood.'

'How long before Dr Jones can prove it one way or the other?'

'Said he'd call within the . . .' Turner began. Pendragon's mobile rang.

'Doctor,' Pendragon said, recognising the number. 'Yes, I see. Yes . . . I understand. How long . . . No, I realise that.' He took the phone from his ear for a second and made a face at it. The others grinned. 'No, that's . . . that's excellent. Thank you.'

He snapped shut the phone and sighed.

'Preliminary tests show Middleton's blood was awash with arsenic. Enough to kill a rugby team, Jones reckons. He's getting a full toxicology report from Scotland Yard, but it'll take twenty-four hours.'

Two hours later, the restaurant looked very different. The traumatised patrons had gone, as had Middleton's body. The only people remaining were Dr Colette Newman and two of her people. The Head of Forensics was placing a fibre from the carpet into a small bottle using a pair of delicate steel tweezers.

Pendragon crouched down beside her. 'Jones thinks there's a good chance it's poisoning.'

'That's up to the tox lab to prove or disprove,' Newman commented without looking at him. 'There's precious little to go on here.'

'Oh?'

'Just a normal lunch gone wrong by the look of things. We've bagged everything on the table and one of my assistants is doing the same with the kitchen utensils. If Middleton was poisoned and it was done in the conventional way, believe me, we'll find the evidence.'

'I'm sure you will,' Pendragon replied, straightening up and pacing across the restaurant. In the kitchen, a man in a forensics suit was carefully sieving liquid from a saucepan. The entrance to the kitchen was the other side of the restaurant from the table where Middleton had died. It was hard to imagine how anyone from the Rainer party could have slipped into the kitchen unnoticed to place arsenic in the food. And if they had, how could they possibly have known Middleton would be at the receiving end and no one else? All of which still left the possibility that one of the kitchen staff was responsible. But that was almost as improbable. 'Besides,' Pendragon said to himself, 'where the hell's the motive?'

Pendragon ducked under the crime-scene tape cordoning off the pavement outside and nodded to a constable standing by the door to the restaurant. He decided there was nothing more he could do right away. He toyed with the idea of returning to the station and helping Turner, but suddenly felt overwhelmingly tired. He crossed the main road and started walking the mile to his flat. He could do with the air, he reasoned, even if it was Mile End Road air on a sticky, freakish summer evening. The traffic was light; a few families were heading back to Essex after a day in the city. The stallholders who usually lined the street across the road from the London Hospital had packed up early after suffering the deluge. They knew very few people would feel like wandering around sodden and steamy stalls; they would rather be at home watching Fox Sport.

The road and the pavements were glistening still, but the drains, dry for so long, had handled the downpour well. Steam rose from the concrete and tarmac, and Pendragon could feel the damp seeping into his bones. Soon he was lost in thought, trying to fit together the pieces of a jigsaw that would not meld. There were now two mysterious deaths linked with the construction site. The victims knew each other peripherally, but what possible links were there between them? None, as far as he could tell. None, except they were both working on the same project. But one was an Indian labourer, the other an architect. One had been beaten to death, the other . . . well, what had happened to Tim Middleton? It was possible he had died from something he had eaten, that it was no murder at all, just a bizarre coincidence. But that just didn't feel right.

Then there was the skeleton. That too was linked to the construction site on Frimley Way, but it was hundreds of years old. And yet he couldn't ignore the fact the deaths had started as soon as the thing had been dug up.

Pendragon was so lost in thought, he hardly noticed he had arrived at his building. But then he saw the front door was ajar. He crossed the threshold and heard a stifled scream from along the corridor towards Sue Latimer's flat.

He dashed along it and reached the door just as a man came crashing through from the other side. He was wearing a hoodie and an Obama mask. He was large and fit and Pendragon was caught off guard. The man's shoulder slammed into the DCI's chest, knocking him back against the doorframe. Before he could recover, the man had run almost the length of the corridor. He reached the front door and disappeared into the street.

Pendragon was about to run after him when he heard a moan from the floor. Sue was pulling herself up, one hand pressed to her face. He ran over and helped her up. Looking at her, he saw that a large bruise was blooming close to her eye and she had a cut under her right eyelid.

'He's snatched my purse,' she said, and burst into tears. Pendragon held her shoulders and let her sob into his chest.

Chapter 18

London, Monday 6 June

Sergeant Jez Turner pulled up outside the apartment block and checked his watch. It was 8.30 and the russet-coloured brickwork of the converted East India Company warehouse was awash with bright morning sunlight. Behind him rippled the dark water of the dock where once stood at anchor trade ships bringing exotic goods from far-flung places. In the distance stood the gleaming towers of Docklands dominated by Canary Wharf, testament to the social revolution that had transformed this area when he was barely out of nappies.

'Very nice too,' Turner said quietly as he looked up at the windows overlooking the water. He had studied the file on Sophie Templer: twenty-six. Graduate in Business Studies, Goldsmiths College. Now working for Woodruff & Holme, the largest PR company in Britain.

Sophie opened the door to her flat. She was dressed in a tight black skirt, cut just above the knee, neat oatmeal silk blouse and high heels. Her shoulder-length chestnut hair looked freshly washed and smelt of tropical fruits. With a brief smile and a 'Hi', she led the sergeant into a large open-plan space with a vaulted ceiling, white walls and polished concrete floor. There was an over-sized white stone kitchen counter, subtle lighting from invisible fixtures and a pair of huge grey suede sofas. An archway led to a white and grey bedroom. Next to that was a small office, the huge screen of a Mac just visible on a glass-topped table. He could smell coffee.

She indicated a stool at the kitchen counter. 'Espresso?'

'Thanks.'

Turner took out his notebook and studied the woman's neat behind while she operated the machine.

'Have you discovered anything about . . . about how Tim died?' Sophie said without turning. Her accent was studiedly middle class, Turner decided. He could detect some of the Essex vowels she had grown up with. And, for all her evident sophistication, it was not hard to imagine Soph out on the town with her girlfriends, squealing with faux-excitement at a Chippendales show or swearing like a trooper after a few vodka and tonics.

'Too early,' he replied. 'Waiting for toxicology reports.'

'But wasn't it food poisoning?'

'We're treating it as homicide.'

She gave a little gasp and handed him the espresso, a brown slurry in a minuscule white cup.

'You and Mr Middleton were an item . . . until recently?'

'Yes.' She looked him directly in the eye. The distraught young woman of the previous afternoon had been carefully concealed. 'We broke up a couple of months ago.'

'Had you been together long?'

'Two years.'

'So it was a serious relationship.'

She returned to the coffee machine to switch it off. 'I don't have casual relationships, Sergeant.'

'May I ask what went wrong?'

She looked surprised for a second but covered it well. Leaning against the counter to one side of the kitchen, she took a sip of her coffee. 'Oh, the usual. We grew apart. Wanted different things.'

'I see. And the break-up was acrimonious?'

'Look, Sergeant, what are you driving at?'

'You and your . . . friend, Marcus Campbell, had a disagreement with Tim Middleton at the restaurant.'

She shrugged and looked back at him, head tilted slightly to one side. 'Yes, it's no secret. I answered questions about it yesterday.'

'Was that the first time you'd seen Mr Middleton since your break-up?'

'Yes, it was, actually. We've deliberately tried to avoid each other,' Sophie replied. 'It's not difficult, Sergeant. It's a big city.'

'And Mr Campbell? You've known each other a long time?'

'What on earth has that got to do with anything?'

He ignored her. She sighed and drained her cup. 'Marcus is one of my clients.'

Turner glanced at his notebook. 'MD of Trevelyan Holdings.'

'Yes. They're one of the biggest in my portfolio.'

'And was Mr Campbell part of the reason you and Tim Middleton . . . grew apart?'

'No!' She was suddenly angry, the cool veneer abandoned. 'Tim has . . . had some good qualities, but he was very difficult to live with . . . Oh, for Christ's sake!'

Her eyes were ablaze and Turner decided she wasn't one of those women who looked beautiful when she was angry. He could also tell she was keeping a lot back and that he had probably blown it by antagonising her now.

'I'm sorry if you feel these questions are too personal, Ms Templer,' the sergeant replied, trying to soften his voice. 'But I'm sure you would want us to find Mr Middleton's killer.'

She seemed to sag on hearing that word. 'Yes, I'm sorry, Sergeant. I'm just not used to this yet. It seems so surreal. Look. Tim and me . . . it was great for a few months, but then . . . well, I suppose it's the same for everyone, isn't it? The initial spark goes.'

'What sort of person was he?'

'Oh, very clever. Creative. We had fun. But, as I said, we were moving in opposite directions.'

She looked very tired suddenly and made a show of studying her watch. 'Look, I'm sorry . . . I have a train to catch.'

'Sure.' Turner stepped back from the kitchen counter. Sophie Templer picked up a cream leather bag from the floor and led him back to the front door, pulling a jacket on as she went.

She took the stairs ahead of him and they emerged on to the quayside where she pulled on a pair of large Chanel sunglasses. 'I'm sorry if I haven't been that helpful, Sergeant Turner.' She was standing with her handbag held to her breasts, arms wrapped around it, head tilted to one side.

Everything she does is carefully orchestrated, Turner thought.

'The tube station is this way.' She indicated behind her, then held out her hand.

'Ms Templer,' he said, ignoring her evident desire to be away, 'do you have any idea why your friend Mr Campbell would have wanted you both out of the restaurant after Tim Middleton died? Even though the police had been called?'

With her sunglasses covering half her face, it was hard to tell what impact, if any, his remark had had. 'I imagine he was thinking of me, Sergeant. Marcus is an extremely thoughtful man. 'And,' she added with a faint smile, 'I was a complete mess, if you recall.'

'Yes, that's what I assumed,' he replied, and watched her turn and walk away.

Jez Turner had just reached the car when his phone rang.

'Anything useful?' It was Pendragon.

'Only that she's holding something back, guv.'

'All right, leave her alone for a bit. No point pushing too hard. Get back to the station and run a thorough search on Middleton. I want a complete picture of the man's past. Talk to everyone you think is relevant. And get on to Central Records.'

'No probs. Where are you, sir?'

'I've actually had a bit of luck,' Pendragon replied. 'Jones managed to call in a favour and has the tox report early.'

Chapter 19

Jack Pendragon came through the doors of the police station and flashbulbs popped. For a second, he was completely confused. Then he saw a group of journalists gathered at the top of the stairs leading to the parking bays. Two photographers continued to snap away. He decided quickly that he should not make a fuss about them. He had seen what the result of that could be when, years earlier, the *Oxford Times* had delighted in publishing the most unflattering shots of him they could find.

'DCI Pendragon,' one of the journalists shouted as he approached. 'Fred Taylor, *Gazette*. Can you fill us in? Is it true a dead body has been dug up on a building site? The same site where Amal Karim was beaten to death?'

Pendragon was speechless. He slowed his pace and the other journalists descended on him. Four of them now stood in front of him, digital recorders at the ready.

'I think you have your facts wrong,' he said dismissively. He was startled still and realised as soon as the words had left his lips that he sounded terribly pompous.

'How so, Inspector?'

'It's Detective Chief Inspector,' Pendragon retorted, letting his guard down further and immediately feeling irritated with himself. At that point he should have paused, taken a deep breath and been co-operative. Instead, he flashed the newsmen a frosty look.

'Apologies,' Fred Taylor said sarcastically. '*DCI* Pendragon. So are you saying a body wasn't uncovered on Friday afternoon at the Bridgeport Construction site on Frimley Way? Just hours before the labourer was murdered?'

'I have no further comment,' Pendragon responded and made to walk on. Without being exactly intimidating, the four men somehow managed to block his path. 'Come on, Jack,' one of the other reporters called. 'We're just trying to do our jobs. Give us something.'

The man wore a big grin on his face and had his recorder thrust directly under the DCI's nose. Pendragon glared at him and the smile dissolved. 'I told you, I have nothing to say on the matter. There will be a press conference in due course. *When* we have something concrete to report.' He pushed his way between the men and took the steps down to the car pool.

'You're new here, aren't you, *DCI* Pendragon?' Taylor called after him.

Pendragon ignored him and lowered himself into the driver's seat of the nearest patrol car.

Tim Middleton's body lay on the dissection table. There was a Y-incision running from each shoulder to the middle of his chest and then down to his navel. His ribs had been cut open and pulled back. The white ends protruded like sightless eyes in a soup of red and grey viscera. A little lower lay a section of large intestine, shockingly pale. Flaps of his scalp were folded over his eyes. Pendragon caught himself thinking the dead man had the appearance of a lop-eared rabbit.

'Ah, Pendragon,' Jones said, looking up from his computer keyboard. He finished his sentence, typing uncertainly with two fingers and peering intently at the screen, then paced over. 'We must organise a camp bed for you here.'

'What have you got?' Pendragon asked.

'As I said on the phone, an old chum of mine managed to get the tox report over PDQ, but there's something else I wanted to show you first.' He waved Pendragon over to the other side of the table. Bending over Middleton's body, Jones pointed to a fleshy spot on the man's hip. Pendragon could just make out a red pinprick.

'Puncture site,' the pathologist said. 'Explains how the poison was administered.'

Pendragon looked surprised. 'Are you suggesting a hypodermic? In a crowded restaurant?'

Jones shrugged. 'You're the detective, Pendragon.'

'It's a bit James Bond.'

'Well, it's a fresh incision, or at least it was, and I've found trace chemicals at the puncture site. Middleton certainly didn't die from ingesting anything orally. Here, take a look at this.' He handed Pendragon a printout and carried on talking as the DCI did his best to decipher the information. 'It's definitely poisoning.' Leaning in, Jones pointed to a coloured graph. 'Four different components to the poison. A huge amount of arsenic trioxide.' And he indicated a thick spike in the graph. 'But also cantharidin, abric acid and oleander. A most intriguing combination.'

'You said at the crime scene you'd never seen a poison like this.'

'I haven't. For starters, the concentration of arsenic is phenomenal. To kill a man Middleton's size quickly, you would need to use half a gram of the trioxide. Either that or it could be a much smaller amount, but with its toxicity enhanced in some way.'

'Maybe that's where the other three come in? The cantharidin, etc?' Pendragon replied.

'Well, they're certainly all deadly in themselves. But we can't escape the fact the poisoner had to administer a large dose of arsenic without being seen and without the victim noticing. There's also the fact that although arsenic used to be known as "the murderer's favourite" because it could be obtained from so many household items, nowadays it's almost impossible to get hold of. Health and Safety have done a very thorough job there.'

'Okay,' Pendragon said. 'Tell me about the other three components.'

'Cantharidin you probably know by its common name, Spanish Fly.'

'The aphrodisiac?'

'A myth,' Jones retorted. 'It's actually super-toxic, can kill in minuscule amounts almost immediately.'

'And easy to get hold of.'

'Yes and no. It *used* to be straightforward – sex shops, mail order – but strict new regulations have changed that. No problem, though, for anyone with a computer and a modem – thousands of dodgy sites are still selling the stuff illegally.'

'All right,' Pendragon said, looking back at the printout. 'Abric acid.'

'I'd never encountered it before, but a quick Google search gave me a wealth of information as only the Holy Internet can. Comes from the Paternoster Pea, scientific name *Abrus precatorius*. Commonly known as a "lucky bean". Wasn't so lucky for the poor sod over there though, was it?' Jones glanced towards the metal dissection table and gave Pendragon a wolfish grin.

'So . . . what? You can just buy it over the counter?'

'No, that's one of the big question marks for me. It's hard to get hold of, internet or no internet. Originates in Africa and Asia, a climbing plant. The abric acid is distilled from abrin which is found in the seeds.'

'And oleander?' Pendragon asked.

'Another mystery. Very exotic, very nasty. An evergreen shrub, narrow leaves, red flowers. Sometimes called Jericho Rose. Again, originates in Asia, very rare in Britain but quite popular as a houseplant in the States, apparently. The poison is distilled from all parts of the plant. According to Google, it's commonly used as a rat poison in India, Bangladesh, and parts of Burma.'

Pendragon was studying Jones's face. The

pathologist looked more animated than he had ever seen him. 'You're enjoying this, aren't you?'

Jones beamed. 'Of course I am, Pendragon. Knife wounds and smashed-in skulls can become rather tiresome.'

'So this report tallies with your findings?'

'Well, of course it does,' the pathologist replied with a nonchalant shrug. 'The first two do anyway. I think I may be forgiven for missing abric acid and oleander.'

Pendragon gave him a sceptical look.

'Still not convinced? Let me show you something.'

A row of stoppered test tubes stood in a rack on a counter behind Pendragon. Jones used a pipette to withdraw some clear yellow liquid from one of the tubes.

'As you know, I was pretty sure Middleton hadn't died of food poisoning. From what the witnesses reported, it was clear the man was fine one minute and in his death throes the next. They said he clutched his throat and then vomited blood. That immediately spoke to me of arsenic. It's just that it's so bloody unfashionable. A century ago maybe, but not these days.

'This is a sample of Middleton's urine,' the pathologist continued, and lifted the pipette to the light. He picked up a piece of plastic the size of a credit card. In the centre was a slightly raised disc. Jones allowed one drop to fall from the tip of the pipette on to the disc. It immediately turned brown. He laid the plastic card beside a strip of paper, a row of coloured discs across it. The disc on the far left was almost colourless, the next ochre, then dusty yellow, orange, and finally, on the far right, brown. 'It's a test for arsenic compounds. This result shows there's at least three parts per million of arsenic in the dead man's urine.'

'A deadly dose?'

'And then some! Arsenic is a trace element. It's in all of us. In fact, we need it to catalyse some essential biochemical processes in the body. But three parts per million is about one hundred thousand times the level you'd expect to find in a living person.'

They walked over to the dissection table. On a trolley next to one end lay a stainless-steel dish holding what looked like a pile of blackberry jelly. 'Our victim's liver,' Jones said matter-of-factly. 'Necrosis so bad it's almost liquefied. That's precisely what you'd expect from cantharidin. It's the same with his other internal organs.' Jones pointed to an identical trolley on the other side of the table. 'Kidneys and pancreas, all but wiped out.'

Jones touched Pendragon's arm and pointed to the

body with a pen. 'Genitals swollen with congealed blood. That's also the work of cantharidin. And cantharidin is another poison that causes vomiting of blood.'

Pendragon couldn't conceal his revulsion. Not much could shock or horrify him any more, but he was rather comforted by the fact that he could still find some forms of death unspeakable. 'So any one of these poisons could have killed Middleton almost instantly?' he checked.

'Many times over, Inspector. Someone wanted Tim Middleton *very* dead.'

Chapter 20

Paris, March 1589

We stayed with the alchemist for another two days and nights. He wanted to be sure his ministrations to our physical appearance had worked and that the potions he had given us, and the chemicals used to change our hair and colouring, would not quickly dissipate. There was also the fact that the weather had taken another turn for the worse.

The woman I had seen when I first regained consciousness looked after us well. Her name was Catherine and she was the great-great-niece of Cornelius Agrippa. She was a friendly and gentle young girl of, I learned, just seventeen summers. I had found her countenance most pleasing from the moment I first set eyes upon her, even if I had then been in a diminished and sickly state. But, in my fully restored sight, her beauty grew. To my mind, as befuddled as it may still have been, Catherine had the countenance of a Madonna. The way she walked, her voice, her knowing manner – it did truly seem as though she had walked out of a painting. And yet I could not reconcile this with the fact that she was her uncle's amanuensis, that she assisted him in what to me seemed to be diabolic arts.

On our last evening in Agrippa's home, I could not resist raising this subject. Sebastian was asleep in the next room and Catherine had come to deliver the draught of a potion I was required to take as part of her uncle's regimen.

'Are you not afraid for your soul?' I asked bluntly.

She looked startled for a moment and I could see she was of a mind to leave, but something made her stay. I indicated she should sit beside me on the bed.

'You do not understand, Father,' she said after a moment of hesitation. 'My uncle is not an evil man.'

'You cannot tell me the things he does are the actions of a good Christian, Catherine?'

'My uncle is a good and devout Catholic.'

'But the Black Arts and the path to the Lord are irreconcilable. You know that.'

'My uncle is not a necromancer.'

I gave her a sceptical look.

She bridled, her back ramrod straight. 'My uncle believes the pursuit of knowledge and the understanding of Nature should not be limited by the narrow vision of men.'

'The Church views alchemy as heresy.'

'It does not say in the Bible that it is wrong to concoct chemicals or to study Natural Philosophy, seeking knowledge of the world the Lord has made.'

'The Bible is not a book of infinite length even if it is one of infinite wisdom,' I retorted, growing irritated myself. 'That is why we need Church leaders and why the Lord speaks through the Holy Father in Rome. There are many things we must interpret and upon which we must make our own judgements. Not everything is laid out for us, nor would it be to our benefit if it were so.'

'Then, whether an alchemist is a heretic or not comes down to whether or not he is a true believer. It is simply a matter of motivation. My uncle is motivated by good.'

'You believe the concocting of poisons and

the committing of murder is . . .' And I stopped myself, suddenly realising what I was saying.

Catherine looked at me with a strange blend of pity and sympathy in her eyes. 'In this matter, our own Father Bellarmino has made it clear what is right and what is wrong, Father John. Bringing heretics to the One True Faith, whether by persuasion or by death when the lost soul may be given a last chance of redemption, is our duty. Killing a heretic is not murder, it is a kindness.'

'Yes,' I said after a long silence. 'Bellarmino himself guided us to you and your uncle. I apologise. It was wrong of me to cast aspersions on your uncle, to question his faith. Your uncle is a servant of the Lord, as are we, and he must use his every talent to further God's work, as must I. And if it seems to the faint-hearted that we are committing mortal sins to speed on a greater good, then so be it. On the Day of Judgement the Almighty Lord will understand . . . and he will forgive.'

I can recall little of the journey from the home of Cornelius Agrippa to the port of Calais and I have eradicated completely the memory of the sea voyage that followed. I have always feared and abhorred the sea. Since I was a child playing on the beach with my family close to our home in Suffolk, I have distrusted the primal wantonness of the waves, the viciousness and abandonment of the water.

As we approached Dover, a customs ship pulled alongside and escorted us into harbour. Although our arrival there filled me with anxiety, I cannot deny that the port of Dover was an impressive sight. The area around the port was very ancient, but the harbour had only been completed a dozen years earlier. Two great piers extended from the quayside like jaws dragging us in. It was dark by the time we docked. A few lights were just visible from the town to our north-east and there was a fire which was never allowed to go out at the end of the quay.

Four customs men boarded our vessel. They searched all over the ship and checked the cargo: a confection of spices and silks from Genoa, and a set of cages containing a score of exotic birds the captain claimed had originated in China. The customs men were much taken with these creatures for they had the most beautiful plumage in rainbow hues. And the birds were noisy – squawking and screeching and even mimicking human words as though they had been possessed by devils.

I had a vain hope the customs men would be so intrigued by the exotic birds they might overlook us entirely. As well as a crew of twenty, there was only a handful of passengers including Sebastian and myself. But, of course, we were all questioned at length and each of us was required to show our papers.

We had travelled to Paris under the guise of simple traders, silk merchants attending a trade fair in Montmartre. But as well as giving us new faces, Master Agrippa had concocted a whole new history for us. He turned us into English traders who had been in Europe to investigate the possibility of importing a substance called calamine. This material was essential for brass-making, a commercial concern just beginning to grow in importance throughout Europe. The alchemist had chosen this tale because he believed it would be suitably abstruse and save us from having to go into details of the silk trade or spice importing.

It worked. When one of the customs officers queried us on our business, it was a small matter to bore him with our enthusiasm for the technicalities of calamine. As for the ring and the poison Agrippa had distilled, I was afraid these would cause us further problems. The alchemist's advice on the matter of the ring was, however, simple. 'Brazen it out,' he had said with a crooked grin. And so I wore the ring. Its giant round emerald looked a little ostentatious, but I pulled off the deception. The poison was more troublesome. Sebastian was carrying it inside his tunic. We were subjected to the humiliation of a close search and the vial was found. Sebastian had prepared his tale carefully, however. The small glass container contained an Italian treatment for gout, extremely pungent and foul-smelling, he advised, and the customs officers let it go.

The customs men were thorough, that could not be denied, and we were perfectly aware that many of the officials at Dover doubled as spies for Walsingham. Ostensibly on the prowl for contraband, they were in direct communication with the Principal Secretary's espionage network. They were ever eager to ensnare sympathisers of Philip of Spain, and Catholic missionaries such as Sebastian and myself. This wariness on the part of the English had increased greatly during the past few months, for it was little more than six months since the

Spanish had seen their proud Armada humili-
ated by Elizabeth's navy in these very waters.

It was the middle of the night before our ship
was released to continue on its journey, and so
it was that dawn was breaking over London as
we drew alongside the north bank of the
Thames and transferred to a wherry that took
us west along the river and under London
Bridge.

I had lived in London for some years before
leaving England for Rome. But even during my
relatively short absence, the city had changed.
From the river, I could see new constructions as
well as remnants of the old, changed and
enlarged. London Bridge itself was teeming
with life. Large houses lined each side of the
bridge and some buildings had actually been
built out over the water. Not a few looked
precarious. On the banks of the Thames, too,
buildings had been constructed so close to the
water that their upper floors hung over the
river.

The wherry crossed to the south bank and the
area known as Southwark. The houses there
were also packed so closely together that, from
a few score feet away, it was hard to imagine
how people could move between them. It was

only as our little vessel docked that narrow dark streets could be discerned between the over-hanging timber houses.

I looked back to the north bank and saw the orange light of dawn bringing a new day to this grand city. Before me lay the sprawl of London. To the west, the river curved round to flow past Westminster. To my east, the Tower rose above shabby roofs. Directly ahead lay a vast con-glomeration of houses – smithies, taverns, bakers, candle-makers, tanners, cobblers and brothels – every interconnected element of human life packed into a few square miles. Above it all loomed the huge monolithic structure of St Paul's, a church that had once been the epicentre of Catholic life in the city. Now it was possessed by the new religion, usurped by heretics who called themselves believers. The building was still an awe-inspiring sight, its great square tower taller by far than any other structure in the whole of London. It would last for ever, I thought to myself as I stepped off the wherry. It would be the last thing left standing in this land and, with God's blessing, I would help return it to its true purpose, a place of worship for the One True Faith.

As Sebastian and I stepped on to dry land I felt a tremendous sense of relief. I know men must travel across the seas, but it is not for me. I like my feet well and truly planted on firm ground. Two servants found our bags among a pile at the front of the wherry and brought them on to the quayside. I gave them a farthing and saw a young woman approaching us. She looked to be of common stock, wearing a drab outfit of honest kersey, a mixture of grey and brown woollen fabric. Her black hair was mostly hidden under a dirty, dark brown head-dress. Her one striking feature were her green, intelligent eyes. She was slightly out of breath.

'I beg your forgiveness, sirs,' she began in a voice with a soft Irish lilt. 'I was detained by domestic problems.' Then, seeing our puzzled expressions, she glanced around for a second and said: 'You were expecting me, were you not? Monsieur Gappair sent me a note saying you needed lodgings. Or have your plans changed?'

Sebastian and I realised what she was talking about at the same moment. 'No, no,' he said. 'Of course not.' He tossed my bag to me and I was almost winded by it.

The girl laughed and then checked herself. 'I'm sorry, sir.'

'You need not be.' I smiled at her. 'What is your name?'

'Ann, sir. Ann Doherty.'

'Well, Ann, you'd better lead the way.'

Southwark was starting to wake up. A market stretched from the water's edge down a lane to Kent Street. Stalls lining the street were being loaded up with all manner of vegetables, fish and bread. There was a shout behind me and I just managed to avoid colliding with a young boy pushing a cart heavy with potatoes caked in dark mud. He turned off the street and disappeared down a narrow alley.

This quarter of London was renowned as perhaps the most disreputable district of the city. Although I had previously lived in the relatively poor neighbourhood of Cheapside, north of the river, my neighbours and I there had considered those forced to live in Southwark to be most unfortunate souls. The main reason for the area's poor reputation was the preponderance of brothels, alehouses and gambling dens. It was a place that was, of course, despised by the hypocrites who called themselves Puritans, the worst breed of the new religion.

As we walked along the lightening streets, I

remembered reading a pamphlet published by one such heathen who was so impervious to the joys of life he had been offended by the simplest pleasures of those living and working in Southwark. If memory serves me, he had ranted about the evils of one of the new theatres in the quarter, saying something like: 'There was dancing, music, mockery, merriment, all the things the misguided flock enjoyed but the shepherd deplored.' I too believed in propriety and moderation, but had no time for delusions such as these.

That said, I certainly would not have chosen to stay here if it had been my choice. Southwark was a dangerous and violent place where one needed constantly to be on guard against cutpurses, and where the number of vagrants outnumbered those doing an honest job to pay their rent. There was clearly good reason, I thought to myself with a smile, that so few Londoners lived this side of the Thames, but that there were no fewer than four prisons within the boundary of this small district.

Ann was walking at a goodly pace and was clearly experienced in the ways of the street. Although only a frail woman, she seemed sharp-witted and watchful enough to warn off those with any evil intent. We turned down a narrow lane and wove a route south along winding streets. Many of the houses here were in a poor state. Children in rags played under the shadows of these hovels, doing their best to avoid the turds and mossy dog bones.

After a while, I lost all sense of direction and no longer knew if we were heading further from the river or had doubled back. But Ann stayed surefooted, glancing back frequently to make sure we were still keeping up. If we had lost sight of her, I'm not sure either Sebastian or I could have found our way back to the river, and even less sure we would have escaped having our throats slit in a dark alley.

We all heard the sound before we saw its source. Ann was first to react. She obviously recognised the voices and dashed towards them down a narrow lane. We picked up speed and ran after her, emerging into a small court-yard where we were met by a most confusing sight.

Two men in the uniform of the Royal Guard, one with his sword unsheathed, were dragging a youth away from the door to one of the houses. The boy was screaming and shouting, but it was impossible to understand what he was saying.

It quickly became clear he was an imbecile or else possessed by demons.

Ann had arrived by the lad's side and was accosting one of the guards, striking his chest with her hands. The guard was stunned momentarily and let slip his hold on the boy. The youth took advantage of the opportunity and tried to dash away, but the other guard was too quick. He tripped the boy who fell face first into a muddy puddle. While he was regaining his feet, his ranting grew more crazed. I caught a few words. 'The Lord will protect me . . . you devils . . . the Holy Mother watches over me.'

The guard who was fending off the flying fists of Ann Doherty gained the upper hand. He seized her wrist as it came close to his face and twisted the girl's arm back, making her scream. I made to run forward and help her, but Sebastian held me back with a strong grip. I looked him in the eyes, feeling myself burning up with rage, but his expression was every bit as fierce. It gave me pause.

The guard who had the boy in an arm-lock suddenly shoved him back into the mud. 'Come on,' he snarled to his partner. 'The little shit's not worth it.' He kicked the boy in the stomach. The other guard slammed his fist into Ann's face and she fell back, tripping over the boy and landing heavily in a dark, muddy puddle. 'Keep the pox-ridden bastard quiet in future,' the first guard spat, and they strutted off.

I dashed over to them and helped Ann to her feet as the boy picked himself up.

'What is happening?' I asked. 'Why were those men here?'

Ann was covered with mud and filth, and a stream of blood ran from her mouth, but she was undaunted. Her eyes were ablaze with frustration and fury. She yanked her arm out of my grip and spun around.

I stopped her, pulling her back to face me. 'What is this all about?'

Tears were welling up in her eyes. 'They were coming for Anthony,' she said, between strangled sobs. 'I would die before I let him go.'

Chapter 21

Stepney, Tuesday 7 June, 12.30 p.m.

DCI Jack Pendragon was studying the screen of his computer and gingerly tapping at the keyboard. 'Damn it! Bloody thing's frozen *again*,' he hissed.

Jez Turner came round the desk. 'You're trying to save this document, yeah?'

'Trying being the operative word.'

Turner's fingers glided over the keys. 'There,' he said. 'It's like a woman . . . needs a gentle touch.'

'Oh, right, and you would know?'

The sergeant gave Pendragon a wry smile. 'I've got some info on Middleton that could prove interesting.'

'Oh?'

'I thought the first thing to check out would be the guy's finances. I hit the usual problem with the bank of course, but a couple of calls and I accessed his account. Or rather, *accounts* . . . at least a dozen of them.'

'A dozen!'

Turner took a sheaf of papers from a file and handed them across the desk. 'Nothing out of the ordinary at first glance. Quite small sums in each, just regular throughput – salary and outgoings, mortgage, car leasing bills. But then I noticed a pattern.'

Pendragon laid the papers out on the desk and glanced from one to the other. 'Yes . . . similar amounts each month from different accounts, about a grand a time.'

'And the money is distributed randomly from six of Middleton's to at least three second-party accounts. I thought it might be something legit at first.'

'No, if these were big regular outgoings, like mortgage repayments, they'd go to one account, maybe two. This has to be a private arrangement, designed to go unnoticed. Anything else?'

'Well, yeah, actually. I got on to Central Records, and our Mr Middleton has form.'

Pendragon raised his eyebrow.

'Served time in Scotland – kiddie porn and sexual assault of a minor.'

Pendragon's face was expressionless. 'A gift for a blackmailer.'

'Yep, and enough to wreck a relationship if the truth had come out.'

'You had a feeling Sophie Templer was hiding something.'

Pendragon stood up and paced about in front of his desk. 'Rob Grant made the point that the staff of Rainer and Partner didn't seem to have much of a liking for Middleton. He wasn't exactly Mr Charisma, true, but maybe they'd heard something from a little birdie.'

Turner shrugged. 'Yeah, his past could be our motive, but it doesn't help much when it comes to who did it . . . could have been anyone.'

'Agreed, but it's a start. I think it's time we popped in to see Max Rainer. Maybe he can shed some light on Tim Middleton's murky past. After all, he is a *family friend*.'

They left Pendragon's office and were walking along the corridor to the main exit when Superintendent Hughes stuck her head around her office door. 'Jack, a word?'

'See you in the car,' Turner said, and walked on.

Pendragon knew something was up when Jill Hughes did not offer him a seat. She returned to her desk and stood leaning forward on her fists. It was then that Pendragon noticed the newspaper laid out in front of her.

'I take it you haven't seen this?' the Super said, and almost threw the paper at him.

He felt the blood drain from his face. It was the local rag, the *Gazette*. Above a picture of him looking angrily into the lens, the headline screamed: LEFT . . . FOR ANOTHER WOMAN. Below this the piece began: 'Detective Chief Inspector Jack Pendragon, who arrived at Brick Lane Police Station only a few days ago, has so many skeletons in his closet he should join a travelling fun fair managing the Ghost Train. Recently booted out of Thames Valley Police, the former Oxford cop has also been given the boot by his wife of fifteen years. Jean Pendragon walked out on him last January, and is now living with her lover, Kidlington headmistress Sarah Milligan. The happy couple were unavailable for comment, but sources close to the Pendragons have described how their marriage first hit the rocks five years ago when their nine-year-old daughter Amanda disappeared on her way to school in the Headington district of Oxford. The girl was never found. According to records . . .'

He lowered the paper and looked directly at the Super. 'This is outrageous,' he began. 'How dare they?'

Jill Hughes was barely controlling her own anger. 'Jack, you're missing the point.'

'And that is?'

'Are you serious? The point is, Detective Chief Inspector, the knives are out. What the hell have you done to upset the press?'

'I haven't . . .' Then he remembered the encounter on the stairs outside the station. 'Oh, for God's sake.'

'What?'

'I had a run in with some journalists yesterday.'

'A run in?' The superintendent raised an eyebrow. She was seated now, her arms on the desk, fingers interlocked in front of her.

'I had cameras and recorders thrust in my face as I left the building. Perhaps I wasn't as polite as I should have been.'

'Obviously!'

'But this is ridiculous. What they've written is slander. I wasn't booted out . . .'

'I don't care about that, Jack. I don't care one bit about that. All I care about is not winding up the local media. They're allies, DCI Pendragon.'

He gave her a quizzical look. 'Allies? In Oxford, we . . .'

'I don't care about that either,' she interrupted, her voice raised several decibels. 'This isn't Oxford. Here, you work by my rules, and it is my wish that we keep the press on message, understand?'

Jack did not reply.

'Do you *understand*, DCI Pendragon?'

'Yes, ma'am,' he said. 'How did they know about Jean?'

She sighed and shook her head. 'I find it hard to believe anyone here would have blabbed.'

'What do you mean? How did anyone here know?'

'Jack.' Her expression softened a little. 'Nothing like that stays secret for long.'

'No, obviously,' he replied through gritted teeth. 'And it was so nice of them to raise the issue of my daughter.'

'Yes, that was below the belt.'

'Never mind though, eh? Have to be nice to the press.'

Superintendent Hughes looked down at her clenched hands. Pendragon noticed her fingertips had whitened. When she looked up her expression was carefully blank. 'I would like you to brief the press,' she said. 'I'll leave it up to you to organise the conference, but I want it done today.'

He tossed the newspaper back on to her desk and walked out.

An old lady was being helped out through the main doors by a uniformed officer as Pendragon headed towards the exit. He had just reached the door himself when the duty sergeant called after him. 'Sir?'

Pendragon stopped and took a deep breath before glancing over his shoulder. 'Sergeant.'

'Sorry to bother you, Chief Inspector. That old lady,' he nodded after her, 'reported her dog missing. A spaniel.'

Pendragon gave him an incredulous look. Sergeant Scratton caught it and went on. 'Nah, right. I wouldn't have usually . . . it's just . . . she's the third this week.'

The DCI rested an elbow on the counter and held the bridge of his nose. He suddenly felt incredibly weary. 'Okay, Sergeant. I've got to dash. Pass the details on to Inspector Towers, yes?'

Pendragon emerged into the afternoon sunshine. He could see Turner sitting in the nearest car in the lot. The air was sticky again and it was hard to ignore the smell of drains. 'So now we've got a phantom dog-snatcher,' Pendragon said under his breath. 'I think this weather is getting to everyone.'

It was a ten-minute drive to the recently renovated 1920s block on Turnmill Street in the Barbican where Max Rainer had a flat on the fourth floor. A white-walled entrance lobby lined with lush palms in black granite pots led to an original sliding-gate lift with a set of stone stairs beside it. The lift opened on to a wide corridor. The blank canvas of the walls was broken by two huge sepia photographs of the original building under construction, flat-capped labourers carrying loaded hods and pushing barrows. There were four apartments on each floor. Rainer's was number 402.

He was on the phone, laughing, when he opened the door a few inches. His face dropped when he saw the policemen. Winding up the call quickly, he clicked off the phone. 'Chief Inspector . . .'

'Pendragon.'

'Of course. To what do I owe this honour?' Rainer glanced at the DCI then ran his eyes up and down Turner.

'We were just passing. Wondered if you had ten minutes to spare.'

'Well . . .'

'Excellent.' Pendragon moved forward and Rainer could do nothing but open the door wide and allow the two men into his apartment.

It was furnished expensively. A Le Corbusier chaise stood next to large triple windows. There were antique black velvet curtains, a rosewood floor, glass shelves holding a few exquisite and exotic articles, a worn chesterfield, an Art Deco standard lamp. Rainer offered them seats. Turner sat on the other end of the chesterfield from him. Pendragon walked around slowly.

'Unfortunately, I have an appointment in twenty minutes, Chief Inspector,' Rainer said. 'As you can appreciate, Tim's death has come as a shock to us. As a result, I have a great many business and personal matters to attend to. I would like to offer you every assistance with your inquiries, naturally, so perhaps we should forego the niceties of tea and biscuits.' Rainer's usually careworn face looked more lined than usual. His brown eyes were dark-ringed and a little bloodshot. From the records, Pendragon and Turner knew he had turned fifty-six that year. Today he looked older.

Pendragon waved his hand. 'Quite understand, Mr Rainer. But I thought you would be keen to help us find Tim Middleton's murderer.'

'Murderer? Is that official?'

'Yes.'

'How may I help?' Rainer replied earnestly.

'How close were you to Tim Middleton?'

Rainer looked a little surprised by the question. 'I valued his input . . . respected him. I've known him a long time, but I wouldn't have said we were close.'

'There were family connections, though. Isn't that right?'

'I was at Cambridge with Tim's father, Greg. We

rowed together. I was best man at the Middletons'
wedding in 1976.'

'And you took on Tim as a favour to his family?'
Pendragon probed.

'Not at all,' Rainer replied. 'Tim is . . . was . . . a
very, very good architect. He worked for a highly
reputable firm for several years before joining us.'

Pendragon appeared to ignore this. Silence fell in
the room as he scrutinised the objects on the glass
shelves. At length he said, 'And what about Mr
Middleton's criminal record?'

Rainer looked suitably surprised.

'Oh, come now, Mr Rainer,' Pendragon said,
standing in front of the chesterfield. He glanced at
Jez Turner. 'Sergeant, perhaps you could jog Mr
Rainer's memory.'

Turner scanned his notebook. 'On the sixth of
June 1997 Mr Tim Middleton was arrested in
Edinburgh. On the eighteenth of October 1997 he
was sentenced to six years on two charges of Sexual
Activity with a Child and three charges of Owning
and Distributing Child Pornography. Released
early for good behaviour on the twelfth of March
2001.'

Rainer ran a hand through his sparse black hair.
'Fine. Yes, Tim had offended. Someone at
Meadhams – the firm of architects he worked for in

189

Harrow – found out about his past. He was "let go of" as they say. Tim's father, Greg, was terminally ill by then . . . liver cancer. He died soon after. I can't say I felt comfortable with Tim's . . . proclivities, but he was a fine architect. Believe me, if I'd ever suspected he had reoffended, I would have . . .'

'That's not what this is about, Mr Rainer.'

'No, no, of course. But you obviously think it's linked to his death.'

'It's too early to say, but we have to explore all avenues. Do you know anything about Mr Middleton's private life?' Pendragon pulled up a chair, placing his elbows on his knees and interlocking his fingers.

'Well, no, we were simply work colleagues. I had almost no social contact with Tim.'

'Do you know who his friends were?'

'No.'

'Did you get the feeling he was mixing in bad company? Was he in any kind of trouble?'

Rainer stood up and began to pace. 'As I said, Chief Inspector, I had almost no contact with Tim outside the office. He was a big boy. I wasn't his guardian.'

'No. Tell me, do you think anyone else in the company knew about Mr Middleton's past?'

Rainer straightened. 'I would bloody well hope

not! I certainly didn't say a word. What makes you think that?'

Pendragon let the question pass. 'And your firm is doing well?'

'Yes, we have a very healthy project list. Why?'

'Including the development at Frimley Way?'

'Yes. And, of course, I have heard about the death of the builder there. Most unfortunate.'

'Was that project one of Tim Middleton's?' Turner asked.

Rainer turned from Pendragon to the sergeant. 'It doesn't work like that. We operate as a team on all projects.'

'But with a project leader of some sort?'

Rainer conceded the point.

'And Frimley Way was one of Middleton's?' Turner pushed.

'He was the project manager for it, yes. Your point being?'

Turner met Rainer's eyes. 'Just trying to fit the pieces of the puzzle together, sir. Part of my job description.'

'Fine, Sergeant,' Rainer replied stonily. 'Then perhaps you'll excuse me? I also have a job description. It includes client liaison.' He glanced at his watch and across at Pendragon. 'Chief Inspector, I'm afraid I have an appointment.'

'What's with his attitude?' Turner said as they descended in the lift.

'Oh, I wouldn't read too much into it, Sergeant. Rainer strikes me as the highly strung sort. Besides, grief affects people in different ways.'

Reaching Brick Lane, Turner pulled into the car park and spotted the group of journalists waiting on the steps of the station before Pendragon did. 'Here we go,' he said.

Pendragon stepped from the passenger side and walked purposefully towards the steps. Ignoring the tape recorders, he pushed his way through the throng. Reaching the top of the stairs, he turned to look at the press pack. 'I would like to give you an update,' he announced, and gazed down at the gathered reporters and photographers. Cameras clicked away and a couple of the journalists checked their digital recorders were running. Pendragon spotted Fred Taylor towards the back of the group and fixed him with a hard stare.

'There have been two recent deaths associated with Bridgeport Construction's site at Frimley Way,' he began. 'A labourer named Amal Karim was beaten to death early on Saturday morning. He had been a night watchman at the site. His body was found on the dance-floor of a nearby club. Our forensics team have ascertained the attack occurred on the roof of the club and the man's body was shoved into a ventilation shaft that came out above the dance-floor.

'The second death was that of an architect from the firm of Rainer and Partner. The dead man is Tim Middleton, the "Partner" of the firm and one of the architects in charge of the development at Frimley Way. Mr Middleton died on Sunday at a local restaurant. The cause of death is presently unknown, but police pathologists are working to elucidate one. At this time, we have no evidence to link these two deaths, or indeed to say for sure whether or not Mr Middleton was murdered.' Pendragon paused for a moment and surveyed the faces in front of him.

'And the body unearthed at the site, DCI Pendragon? What can you tell us about that?' It was Fred Taylor.

Pendragon took a deep breath, buying himself time to gather his thoughts. 'I think there's been some misunderstanding, Mr Taylor,' he retorted. 'There is no body.'

'My sources tell me otherwise.'

'Ah, your sources. Yes. Well, I'm afraid your *sources* are misleading you. During the course of their examination of the murder scene, our forensics team unearthed a human bone, a metatarsal from the right hand. Would you like me to spell metatarsal for you, Mr Taylor?'

A couple of the newsmen laughed.

'A human bone?' one of the journalists asked.

'Yes. However, the bone is extremely old.'

'But from another murder victim . . . and at the same location,' Taylor insisted.

'No idea. If there is another murder victim, the crime would have occurred a very long time ago,' Pendragon retorted. 'The bone is at least a hundred years old.'

The journalists all started talking at once. After a moment, Pendragon raised his hand and they quietened down. 'I'm afraid that is all the information we have at this time. We will keep you informed of any new developments.'

'Chief Inspector, do you have anything to say about the recent spotlighting of your private life?'

'No comment,' he responded, and turned towards the doors to the police station.

'No comment, Inspector? You don't wish to respond?' Taylor pressed him.

Pendragon paused for a second and ran one hand over his brow. Pushing the door open, he strode purposefully into the station.

*

It was almost 7.30 by the time Pendragon got back to his flat. He felt exhausted, but it was not just the demands of the job that made him feel so tired. Containing his inner frustration and anger was exhausting. He had always viewed the press with suspicion. The memory of the media intrusion when his daughter had disappeared remained a bitter one. The local papers in Oxford had pointed out the irony of the fact that a senior cop could do nothing to protect his own daughter. It had been obscenely cruel and had hurt both him and his wife deeply. His marriage would have fallen apart slowly even without this added burden, but he could never forgive the press for that insult and had kept them at a distance ever since.

And now, this shit of a local journalist had regurgitated the same bile. Fine, poke fun at the fact that Jean had left him for a woman. He could deal with that. But Amanda? He could still see her so clearly in his mind. She would be a teenager now. And perhaps indeed she was. Perhaps she was living safely somewhere with someone else, and one day she would return to his life. But long ago he had decided never consciously to think these thoughts, they were too agonising, too destructive. No, the only way to maintain his sanity was to imagine his daughter dead. Long dead. At peace.

When Amanda disappeared he had thrown himself into his work, and that had been another factor in the dissolution of his marriage. Ironically, apart from offering him a much-needed distraction, his dedication to duty had done no one much good. Although he did his job well and was respected by his colleagues, he was never promoted. He had once been a high-flier, destined for great things – Chief Superintendent perhaps, maybe even Commander – but suddenly all doors had closed to him, his career had ground to a halt.

Then Jean had finally upped sticks and gone. One evening Pendragon came home extremely late to find she had removed her clothes from the wardrobe, taken a few personal items and left him a brief note. He had done his best to keep everything under wraps but naturally the story got out. Suddenly his position at Headington Police Station near Oxford was untenable. He was owed months of leave and took himself off to Ireland, losing himself in the Derry countryside, drinking Guinness in village pubs and walking twenty miles a day.

Returning to Oxford, he filed for divorce, handed in his resignation and rented out his house. Through an old friend from Police College days, he was offered the position at Brick Lane. At first, he had been a little worried about taking it on. He had grown up within shouting distance of his new station, but had barely been back since graduating from Oxford twenty-five years earlier. Part of him doubted the wisdom of returning to the place in which he had grown up. So much had changed in his life since he had last walked these streets, so much had changed in him. Indeed, he bore almost no resemblance now to the snotty-nosed young boy who had played on Mile End Road in short trousers, his knees cut and filthy from playing soldiers on waste ground left derelict by Luftwaffe bombs twenty years before he was born.

He looked around his grimy flat and sighed. He had just put Bill Evans's *Sunday at the Village Vanguard* on the turntable when he heard a soft tap at the front door. He turned the music down and went to answer it. Sue Latimer was standing in the hall outside, holding a bottle of whisky tied with a blue ribbon. 'A small token of thanks,' she said, giving it to him.

'For what?'

'Being my knight in shining armour.'

Pendragon laughed and took the bottle. 'You really didn't . . .' He saw Sue peering into the room beyond him. 'Come in.' He opened the door wide and let her through ahead of him. 'I'm sorry, it's not much to write home about. Can I get you a drink?'

'Any wine?' she asked, gazing around the room. 'I love Bill Evans.'

'You do?' Pendragon said, going to the kitchenette.

'You sound surprised.'

'Oh, it's just that, well, I didn't think many people knew about him these days. Jazz isn't exactly fashionable any more.'

'I grew up with it. I used to sing in a little band.'

'Really?'

'Oh, just amateur stuff, standards. Fun, though.'

Pendragon was smiling, holding two glasses.

'You having both of those?' Sue asked.

He handed her one. 'Cheers.' He raised his glass. 'You know, you really didn't need to buy that bottle. I'm afraid I wasn't much use.'

'Nonsense! Who knows what would have happened if you hadn't arrived at just the right moment? At least I only lost my purse.'

Pendragon shrugged. 'I got one of my sergeants to follow it up, but without seeing the thief's face, it's pretty hopeless. You cancelled the credit cards?'

'Of course, and thankfully there were only a couple of small notes in the purse. Anyway, the whisky was only partly to thank you. I thought you might need cheering up.'

He gave her a quizzical look.

'I saw the paper this morning,'

'Oh.'

'It amazes me how low tabloid journalists can stoop.'

'Yes, well. It's done. It's in print.'

They fell silent for a moment. He topped up Sue's glass and they went to sit on the sofa.

'So, my private life's been smeared all over the paper, but apart from learning that you like jazz and you can sing, I know nothing about you,' he said.

'Well, you already have the interesting bits,' she replied. 'Born in Sheffield, forty . . . something years ago.' She grinned and took a sip of her whisky. 'I'm a lecturer at Queen Mary College: psychology. I was married for twelve years, been divorced for three. No kids. There – the scintillating biography of Dr Sue Latimer.'

Pendragon shook his head and drained his glass.

'What?'

'Oh, nothing.'

She held his eye for a second.

'It's just a shame you think so little of yourself. I do the same thing. I think its collateral damage from divorce.'

She was nodding. 'Maybe. Although I have to say, I felt liberated by it at the time. Anyway, *I'm* the psychologist.' She laughed, then looked at her watch.

'You have to be somewhere?' Pendragon asked as she finished her drink.

''Fraid so. I have an evening lecture for part-time students. Poor souls have to listen to me drone on after they finish at the bank or the office.'

'There you go again.'

She smiled. 'Old habits . . .'

He led her to the door. He went to shake her hand, but Sue leaned towards him and pecked him on the cheek. 'Oh, I almost forgot,' she said as she stepped into the hallway. 'Can I tempt you to dinner at my place tomorrow night? Nothing fancy, I'm afraid. I'm no Delia Smith.'

'Very glad to hear it,' Pendragon responded. 'And, yes, I'd be delighted.'

'Eight-thirty?'

'I'll be there.'

Chapter 22

Stepney, Tuesday 7 June, 11.45 p.m.

It was a piece of waste ground popular with kids during the day and on into the dusk; now, with the sky lit only by pinpricks of stars, it was deserted.

The man wore a long, flowing dress made from rich crimson velvet. The full skirt fell away beneath a tight bodice laced at the front and pushed up and out with the aid of tissue paper and cotton wool. The synthetic threads of a black wig teased the top of the bodice and flowed over the shoulders. At the back, the wig had been plaited with great care. Gold silk threads had been woven into the hair. To finish off the costume, he had placed on his head a gold band intertwined with small white roses on slender stems. On his feet he wore gold silk slippers, a little scuffed and dirty from the dried summer mud of the field. It all clashed horribly with the white latex gloves just visible beneath frilly lace sleeves. In his right hand, the man held a carrying cage. A muzzled spaniel had been squeezed inside. It whined pathetically.

In the distance stood a row of tenements, brightly lit at this hour. On the eastern side of the field, a railway bridge could be seen silhouetted against the stars. The man came on to the waste ground through a rusted metal gate under the railway bridge. It was a hot night and the heavy velvet dress made him sweat profusely. To make things worse, the cage seemed to grow heavier with every step.

But the darkest point was not far away.

A hundred feet into the field, under the faint starlight, the man had become almost invisible, only his white, sweaty face visible beneath the black braids.

The man in the red dress lowered the cage to the ground. The dog had been whimpering through its muzzle ever since it had been taken from the boot of the car. The cage was too small for it to move around in. The poor animal just stared, terrified, looking this way and that, scraping its head against the steel mesh at the front of the container as it tried to turn.

The man opened a small leather shoulder bag and lifted out a metal tin. Inside lay two hypodermics. He removed the smaller of the two, eased the plunger in a fraction and held up the dripping needle to the faint light. The dog yelped as the needle sank into the flesh of its hindquarters, the sound stifled by the muzzle. The animal panicked and started to claw at the grille, pushing against it and trying to bite through the mesh. Then it froze, and crumpled.

The man opened the top of the cage and cautiously lifted out the spaniel, laying it on its side in the grass. The dog eyed the man. It knew instinctively that something was very wrong but could do nothing about it. Its pupils were dark and big, the look of the calf when it smells the abattoir.

The man removed the second, larger syringe. It contained an orange-brown liquid. Without hesitating, he bent down over the dog and grabbed a lump of fur and flesh just beneath its collar. The animal let out a low, almost inaudible moan as the syringe slid in up to the barrel. The man looked away, unable to meet the dog's eyes.

It began to shake. Its legs flailed the air, paws twitching. Its eyes seemed to grow impossibly large and green foam dribbled over its gums.

The man nudged the dog with the toe of his golden shoe. It was dead, rigid and staring blindly at the stars. From the metal box he withdrew a small plastic container. Inside there was a small glass dish, a pipette and a stoppered test tube. The dog's head was twisted so that its slack jaws faced the ground. With great care, the man ran the rim of the dish around the fleshy gums, gathering up the foam. Then he used the pipette to transfer this to the test tube. When his task was complete, the man swathed the stoppered test tube in bubble wrap before returning it to the metal box, along with the other equipment. This was then placed carefully in the shoulder bag.

The man looked down at the dog one last time, closed the lids over its eyes and turned back towards the gate. He retraced the path he had taken on to the waste ground, but just as he reached the perimeter there was a sound from across the street. He ducked down. A car drove past along the narrow lane beside the field, its lights sweeping the darkness.

Standing up, the man in the dress hurried across the final few feet of wet grass and mud. He did not notice the hem of his dress catching on the bottom of the metal gate that opened on to the lane, leaving behind a sliver of fabric about two inches long. Stepping on to the wet tarmac, he dashed across the lane and ducked into his car, pulling the folds of the red skirt behind him.

Chapter 23

London, Wednesday 8 June, 8.15 a.m.

The kitchen smelt of spilled milk and was filled with the sound of a chart hit on Radio 2. Julie Silver sighed heavily as she opened the door of the dishwasher and realised she had forgotten to switch it on the night before. With a curse, she slammed it shut, put the kids' breakfast bowls and cups into the sink and ran the tap over them. Leaving them to soak, she turned to the washing machine, extracted a knot of jeans and T-shirts, swung open the door to the drier and shovelled in the clothes.

There was a scratching sound at the door from the garden. Julie turned and saw Rex, the family's collie. He had something in his mouth. Switching on the drier, she crossed the kitchen and unlocked the door. She only opened it an inch but Rex pushed it back and dashed past her, leaving muddy prints on Julie's freshly cleaned floor.

'Oh, for Christ's sake!' she exclaimed. 'You little . . .'

Rex stood in the middle of the kitchen, his tail wagging, and let the object he was carrying drop from his mouth. It made a clunking sound as it hit the tiles and the dog gave a loud bark. Julie took a couple of steps towards him and Rex crouched down playfully, his tail going twenty to the dozen, saliva dripping from his jaws. Julie squatted down to take a closer look at the object. It was white and vaguely hemispherical. She could barely imagine how Rex had got his jaws around it. She nudged it with a fingertip and it rolled over. Seeing the top half of a human skull, the orbits of the eyes hollow and bleached, Julie screamed and leapt to her feet. Ten seconds later, she was calling the local police station, her hand shaking as she stabbed at the keys.

Chapter 24

Sergeant Jez Turner lived in a council flat in a cul-de-sac off Mile End Road. Even in bright sunlight the tower blocks looked grim. Turner's place was on the fourth floor of Malibu House, a seven-storey edifice built in the mid-60s. As he pushed the button for the lift, Pendragon wondered whether the town planners believed they were being funny or if that ridiculously inappropriate name had come from the genuine belief that they were constructing a future paradise. Either way, the pigeon shit and car fumes were having the last laugh.

The lift had broken down months earlier and had never been repaired so Pendragon took the stairs. Like the rest of the building, they were constructed from plain concrete blocks. The stairwell was covered with graffiti and stank of beer and urine. He could hear a baby crying and then a gruff male voice shouting something unintelligible. The sounds from several different TV channels clashed horribly.

Reaching the fourth floor, he turned on to a walkway. He counted at least half a dozen satellite dishes bolted to the ceiling, each pointing out over the car park below. A morbidly obese woman with the sad remnants of a roll-up dangling from her pursed lips was hanging some grey clothing on a makeshift washing line. The DCI gave her a friendly smile as he negotiated his way past her. She merely scowled back. A few doors on he reached 451, knocked, and turned to see the fat woman studying him suspiciously.

The door opened and Pendragon was surprised to see a woman in a wheelchair. She was extremely thin and dressed in a black shell-suit, but her eyes were bright and full of life. When she smiled her face lit up. Pendragon realised she would once have been an extremely attractive woman.

'It's all right, you've rung the right bell, love,' she said.

Pendragon glimpsed Jez Turner standing at the end of the hall behind her.

'Sorry, I . . .' Jez began.

The woman put out her hand. 'Eileen Turner. You must be DCI Pendragon. I hope you're going to come in for a cuppa.'

'Mum, we're in a hurry. The DCI's gone out of his way to pick me up,' the young sergeant said.

Pendragon smiled and glanced at Turner who looked embarrassed. Pendragon's natural inclination was to refuse politely and beat an apologetic retreat, but for some reason this time he responded differently. 'That would be lovely, thank you.'

Jez stared at him, astonished.

'Come through to the kitchen then, Chief Inspector.'

Eileen Turner wheeled herself towards her son who ducked into the kitchen before her. As Pendragon followed them, a black Labrador heaved itself up from a basket and padded over, tail wagging. He crouched down and stroked the dog's head.

'That's Beckham,' Jez said. 'He's getting on. I named him when he was a puppy and Becks first played for England. I went off the name after the incident at the 'ninety-eight World Cup, but he was soon back in favour.' He ruffled the dog's fur playfully and kissed the top of his head.

'Please sit down,' Eileen Turner said. Jez helped her with the cups. 'So, how's my boy doing, Inspector?'

'Please, call me Jack,' Pendragon answered. 'How's he doing? A credit to the force,' he declared, straight-faced.

Eileen Turner glanced at her son and beamed.

'Glad to hear it. Things haven't always been easy for us. Jez has worked hard.' She handed Pendragon a china cup and saucer. Catching his sergeant's anxious expression, he took a sip before placing the tea on the table. 'Excellent,' he said.

Beckham sat beside Pendragon and let the DCI pet him. Eileen Turner wheeled herself around the other side of the table and Jez placed her tea in front of her, retreating to the kitchen counter beside the stove to drink his.

'Jez told me about the terrible murder at the building site. Awful,' Eileen said, between sips of her tea. 'I can never understand why people do these things.'

'I don't think many people do, Mrs Turner.'

'It's only fair you call me Eileen if I'm to address you as Jack,' she told him, smiling.

'Quite right . . . Eileen. I've come to accept the fact that people find all sorts of strange reasons to kill.'

'Usually to do with money.'

'More often than not. Or at least things linked to money: drugs, gambling, power struggles.'

'So the crime of passion is a thing of the past?'

'Depends what you call passion, doesn't it?' Jez interjected. 'Money's a passion for a lot of people.'

'I didn't mean that, Jez love,' his mother replied.

'I meant the crimes of passion you see in the old movies.'

'There's nothing very romantic about murder in real life, Eileen,' Pendragon said. 'It's always repulsive and disturbing, whatever the motive or means.'

'Yes, I'm sure you're right.' She turned to her son. 'Jez, bring over the biscuits, will you, love? The chief inspector looks famished.'

Pendragon laughed. 'That's very kind of you, but we really have to get going now.'

Eileen started to protest, but Jez put a hand on her shoulder. 'Mum, we can't stay chatting, I'm afraid.' He kissed her on the cheek and she squeezed his hand.

'Take care,' she said as the front door closed behind them.

They were in the stairwell when Jez addressed his boss. 'I know what you're thinking. We hate the bloody place too. But I'll be getting us out of here within a year. I'm saving for a deposit.'

'Good for you, Sergeant.'

'You want to know what happened, don't you?'

Pendragon looked at him, surprised.

'Six years ago. Car crash. It killed me dad. Mum was left semi-paralysed.'

They reached ground level and crossed the concrete courtyard that led to the road. 'A tragic waste,' Pendragon managed to say. 'Your mum's a lovely woman, and clearly lonely.'

'I do the best I can, sir. We were on our way to getting out of this shit-hole when the accident happened.' Turner waved to indicate the grey bulk of Malibu House without looking back. He had a pained expression. Pendragon squeezed the remote for the car and the doors unlocked with a click and a flashing of lights. 'The upside is, it gave me the kick up the arse I needed. I was a bit of a tearaway before. Now look at me.' And he produced a disarming grin. 'A credit to the force!'

They had just pulled away when Pendragon's mobile rang. It was Rob Grant.

'Sir, something's come up.'

'What?'

'The skeleton has miraculously reappeared.'

'Where?'

'Close to Frimley Way. Long story.'

'Well, it had better be a good one, Inspector. I'll be there in five minutes.'

The skeleton had been found in a skip no more than fifty metres from the Frimley Way building site. Pendragon parked the car at the end of the lane and he and Turner walked towards a small group gathered around a rusty yellow skip. Forensics were there, but there was no sign of Colette Newman today. A large rectangle of plastic sheeting had been spread out on the stony ground of the lane. Two men in plastic suits stood in the skip, balancing on piles of household refuse and prising away a length of cabling that was caught around a large rusty oil drum. They laid a second sheet of plastic inside the skip and carefully manoeuvred the skeleton on to it. Then, between them, they lifted it gingerly over the edge into the waiting hands of two colleagues. Vickers and Thatcher were standing to one side, looking on. They stiffened when they saw Pendragon and Turner approaching.

'Guv,' Vickers said. He and Thatcher studiously ignored Turner who was standing slightly behind Pendragon with a smirk on his face.

'Fill me in, Sergeant.'

'Got a call from a lady at number seven Alderney Road, just over there.' He pointed to his left. 'The family's collie brought half a skull into the kitchen. Sergeant Thatcher and I had just arrived at the station and came over straight away. We made a search of the lanes and alleyways round about. Half an hour ago we found this.' He nodded towards the skip.

'And you searched this alleyway two days ago?'

'Yes, sir. The skip was here then, no skeleton.'

'You're sure of that?'

'Certain,' Thatcher said firmly. 'Oh, for Christ's sake, Turner, take that fucking smirk off your face . . .'

Pendragon turned to find his sergeant a picture of innocence. 'All right, Sergeants,' he said to Thatcher and Vickers. 'Obviously someone's playing games with us. Get back to the station and do your reports. We'll take it from here.'

Pendragon and Turner walked over to where the skeleton had been laid out. They both crouched down beside the bones.

'No ring,' the DCI noted.

'Could have been nicked by someone who saw the skeleton in the skip though, guv.'

'Possible, but unlikely.'

Pendragon straightened up and had turned towards the main road when he saw Fred Taylor approaching. The journalist was accompanied by a photographer Pendragon recognised from both his press encounters outside Brick Lane Police Station. 'Oh, wonderful!' he said under his breath.

'This must be the owner of the metatarsal,' Taylor announced as he got close. He turned to give Pendragon a cold smile. 'That's m-e-t-a-t-a-r-s-a-l.' He started to walk over to where the forensics officers were arranging the limbs and cranium of the skeleton on the sheet, but Pendragon shot out his arm, stopping Taylor in mid-stride.

'This is a crime scene, Mr Taylor. Strictly off-limits to the public.'

Taylor knew better than to push things. He turned to face off Pendragon. 'A crime scene, Chief Inspector? Well, that's really all I needed to know.' He nodded to the photographer who peeled off a dozen shots in rapid succession.

Feeling his anger rising, Pendragon took a step towards both men, then restrained himself. Thatcher and Vickers were still by the skip. 'Sergeants, would you please escort these gentlemen to their car?' he politely requested.

Chapter 25

London, Wednesday 8 June, 8.05 p.m.

Tony Ketteridge passed by the bed and glanced at his wife, Pam. There was nothing on TV so they had agreed on an early night. She was propped up against a pile of pillows reading a magazine. He could see the white lead of her iPod running down into her frilly nylon nightie. The strains of a particularly rumbustious Tom Jones track spilled from the headphones.

He had always hated this flat, hated it for the entire seven years they had lived there. He particularly despised the bedroom with its pink walls and faux-antique furniture – all Pam's choices. There was nothing of him in the room, he thought as he walked towards the bathroom. In fact, there was nothing of him in the entire flat. It was Pam's domain. He earned the money, she picked the curtains. It was an arrangement he had come to accept long ago. But he had also concluded long ago that accepting a thing was not the same as embracing it.

He closed the bathroom door behind him. At least it was cool in here. To either side of the sink stood narrow sash windows. They were open, the blinds up. They faced a neighbour's brick wall, so it was private enough. The bathroom was over-lit and painted in a different shade of pink from the bedroom. To Tony Ketteridge's eye, the colours clashed horribly, the entire ensemble looking like a pig's insides. The bath was lilac plastic and had been very fashionable in the 70s. To complement it, Pam had opted for gold-dipped, Victorian-style taps. The hand basin was white except for a pattern of lilac flowers that swept up from the pedestal and cascaded into the bowl. A gold-plated but severely tarnished waste and plug completed the look of fake faded grandeur.

Ketteridge studied his reflection in the mirror. He looked horrendous, and felt worse. Until a few days ago he was just about coping. Now . . . everything seemed to be falling apart around him. He wasn't just on the back foot – that was normal – he was tumbling into the abyss. All he could see ahead was hope-lessness, a yawning chasm into which he was being sucked.

He leaned towards his reflection, arms dangling at

his sides, and poked out his tongue. Then he realised he had forgotten to bring up a glass of water. Walking back into the bedroom, he saw that Pam was engrossed in an article about Tom Cruise's love life. There was an old picture of him in mid-leap on Oprah's studio sofa. Pam ignored her husband completely.

He padded along the hall barefoot, past the tiny living-room with its heavily patterned sofa and drawn curtains that clashed horribly with both the fabric of the sofa and the ghastly orange and red swirls of the carpet. He switched on the kitchen light and crossed the linoleum floor as the fluorescent tube juddered into life. He let the water run for a moment. It had been so hot for so long, the pipes made water from the cold tap lukewarm.

He heard a sound behind him. He turned but there was nothing. He could see his own reflection in the glass of the back door. He tested the water with his finger. Satisfied, he pushed the glass under the tap.

That sound again. It was coming from just outside the door to the yard. Maybe Minnie the cat wanted to come in. She did that sometimes though it was against Pam's strict rules. He had dutifully fed the cat and put her out only five minutes earlier. He unlocked the door and opened it a few inches.

It was quiet except for the sound of traffic passing along the main road the other side of the building. From far off, he heard a girl squeal then a peel of laughter. He was just ducking back into the kitchen when the sound came again. It was a scratching sound, like metal on metal.

'Minnie!' he called. 'You can come in for a saucer of milk but that's all. Then you're out again. Minnie!'

He saw a flash of colour and heard a swishing sound – the movement of sumptuous fabric. Then he was propelled backwards into the kitchen. Tony was a big man, but he had been taken completely by surprise. He lost his footing and crashed to the linoleum with a dull thud. A figure rushed through the doorway with astonishing speed – a bulbous crimson-and-gold blur. Tony Ketteridge registered long, black hair flying through the air and the flash of red lips. But before he could move, he felt a steel blade at his throat. Terrified, he just managed to focus on the face peering down at him.

The face was pale: lips ruby red, eyes dark discs ringed in black mascara, cheeks heavily rouged. For an instant he imagined he was looking at The Joker from *Batman*. But beneath the make-up the face was just recognisable. He felt sick suddenly. 'You!' Ketteridge managed to rasp, eyes darting from the grotesque face to the blade held in the hand hovering above his throat.

Tony Ketteridge felt a sharp pain in the soft flesh just beneath his left armpit. It was like fire, like a burning needle piercing his skin and sliding up into his shoulder. He turned his head as much as he could, but he could see no wound. His mouth fell open. Paralysis came a second later. To his horror, he had absolutely no control over his body. His vision began to go. The world started to melt into a palette of white, red and black. He wanted to scream, but instead he felt his stomach heave. He vomited blood that fountained over his chest. The face of his killer floated into view again and Ketteridge could see, in front of that painted face, the murderer's hand. It was wearing a ring, but the large green stone had been lifted and a bloodied spike rose from inside. Ketteridge tried desperately to shout a name, but nothing happened. And, all around him, the universe faded to nothing.

Chapter 26

London, March 1589

Ann Doherty's was a typical Southwark house, tall and narrow and misshapen as a hunchback. The outside was clearly in a sorry state of repair. There were ragged gaps in the plaster above the front door and the shutters on the windows were in dire need of fresh paint. But inside Ann had done her best to make it as homely as possible.

We walked into the main room straight from the street and almost immediately I felt the chill fade from my bones. It was a small place with a low ceiling. The floor was unadorned by any form of covering, just honest stone. A great fireplace took up much of one wall, with a wooden mantel above it upon which stood a line of pewter plates. A good, strong fire burned in the grate, and a kettle was boiling away on a stand above the flames. To one side of the fire-place stood a solid wooden seat, high-backed, with carved arms in the shape of lion's heads. Two other chairs stood closer to the flames. As we came in, a young servant girl bent to lift the kettle from the fire and started to pour its steaming contents into a basin beside the heath. She hurried away as we approached.

I helped Ann over to a seat beside the fire and took a closer look at her face. Her upper lip was turning black. I wetted a cloth and dabbed at the wound. She winced. The boy, Anthony, ran up and crouched beside her. 'Mistress Ann, what have they done?' he jabbered. He went to put his fingers to the woman's injured mouth. I grabbed his hand, more roughly than I'd intended. He twisted to face me, his eyes ablaze, and I let him go.

'Fear not, Anthony,' Ann said gently. 'These men are friends.'

'Friends? Friends?' he cackled. 'Is there such a thing in this cruel world, my lady?'

She smiled and stroked his hair. 'Yes, there is.'

'Those were the Queen's Guards,' I said. 'Who is this boy?' I studied him properly for the first time. He was tall and slender. Straight black hair flopped down into his eyes and he had disproportionately full lips. A faint caterpillar of hair, some way short of a full moustache, lay above the upper one. But there was still a childish softness to his features. His eyes were an unusual colour, hazel flecked with darker brown, and his eyelashes were long and dark. I guessed he was a youth of eighteen years or so, but he might have been younger.

Ann put an arm around his shoulders. 'Anthony is like a brother to me. I have looked after him for almost a year – since his parents died. He is a sweet boy and utterly harmless, but he suffers from a sickness of the mind. He is a true believer, but because of his affliction, he has no fear or caution. He believes he should preach the True Faith to all who will listen. Most of the people around here ignore him. They know he is harmless. Either someone took offence today or the guards were simply passing by and heard something they did not like.'

'I'm not happy about this,' Sebastian declared, stepping towards us. 'It's madness. This is supposed to be a safe house. This boy is attracting attention.'

I looked at Ann's shocked expression. 'Sirs,

I'm very sorry. It will not happen again. Anthony is a good soul. His heart is pure.'

'The boy's character is of little interest to me,' Sebastian snapped. 'I don't think you realise the dangers we face.'

Ann stood up. She was almost as tall as my friend. 'Sir, I have apologised. What more do you wish of me?'

Sebastian looked surprised by the girl's outspokenness. Then I could see his surprise turn to anger. He took a step towards Ann Doherty and I felt sure he was going to strike her. But she was amazingly agile. Sebastian had barely moved when she caught him off balance, grabbed his brandished fist and pushed him back against the wall. She had her fingers at his throat. 'Don't ever tell me I am ignorant of the dangers we face, sir,' she hissed. 'We face death every day. Not for us the luxury of shelter in the chambers of the Vatican, Father Sebastian. Here, we must survive by our wits.'

She released him. His face was flushed with embarrassment and he ran his fingers over his neck where Ann's strong fingers had left red marks.

I laughed to lighten the mood, which did not best please my friend. 'Come, Sebastian,' I said, and put an arm about his shoulders. 'Let's not begin this visit on the wrong foot.' Then I turned to Ann. 'Perhaps you have both over-reacted. Shall we not be friends?'

'Yes, friends, friends!' Anthony agreed gleefully, and began a little dance.

Sebastian's face was still thunderous. He straightened his tunic and ran a finger under his ruff. 'I would like to be shown my bedchamber . . . if that pleases, my lady,' he said coldly. I gave him a reproving glance, but he looked straight through me.

'I would be very happy to, Father,' Ann replied. 'I'm sure you are both exhausted after your long journey. But there is one piece of business that needs to be attended to first. If you'll excuse me.' She passed between Sebastian and me and walked to the corner of the room where there stood a small oak desk. She opened a drawer, and to my surprise removed the entire thing from the desk. Then, after taking something from the back of the drawer, she pushed it back in. In her hand was a piece of paper, folded and sealed with an amorphous blob of wax. I broke the seal, opened the paper and read: 'Our mutual friend Richard will call on you soon. He will point the way to the brothers in crime. You may trust Richard and the brothers, and heed their advice. They are all loyal. The brothers will be expecting you. Destroy this immediately after you have read it.' Beneath this was the holy papal seal. Sebastian took the note from my fingers and read it quickly. I reread it then stepped over to the fire and tossed it into the flames, watching it catch fire and turn black and crisp.

'We were told we would meet our superior, Father Richard,' I said. 'But who are the "brothers in crime"?' I looked at Sebastian and then at Ann. Anthony was making shapes with his hands, casting shadow puppets on a wall at the far side of the room.

'The brothers in crime? I don't . . .' Ann began, then smiled. 'Of course! Edmund and Edward Perch. It could be none other.'

Sebastian and I looked at the woman, bemused.

'They are local criminals. They lead a gang, the most powerful in the area, and deal in illicit goods, contraband. They are expert extortionists and each of them has murdered many men.'

'And you know where to find them?'

'Everyone knows where they are. Few wish to

approach them. But the letter was quite clear on that point: Father Richard will show you the way. Now, come. Let me take you to your bedchamber. My maid will bring you some hot water with which to wash away the grime of your long journey.'

It felt as though I had only just fallen asleep when I was awoken by Ann calling my name. I opened my eyes and found her leaning over me, holding a rush light that produced a pale and feeble glow. She placed the light on a small table beside my bier and walked around to wake Sebastian. I could see him jump up from his bed, startled as Ann touched his shoulder.

I was instantly awake and sitting up. 'What hour is it?' I asked, seeing the black sky through the mean window set high in the opposite wall.

'It is two hours past sunset, Father,' Ann replied.

'You should not have let us sleep so long,' Sebastian responded. I could see his angry expression even in the faint light from the flame at my bedside.

'You needed the rest,' she retorted. 'And you have plenty of time to prepare for Mass.'

'You have arranged a gathering?'

'Yes. Don't worry . . . not here.'

'Where?'

'We have several regular meeting places in houses around this neighbourhood. We never meet in the same place consecutively. Tonight, the Mass will be held in Swan Lane. It is not far. Now, if you would like to ready yourselves, I will show you the way.'

'Wait.' I held her arm. 'Are you sure it is safe?'

'I do not know, Father. We live in dangerous times. It is not my decision to hold this Mass tonight, but your superior's.'

'Father Richard will be there?'

'He will be taking the service.'

Ann had replaced the bowl of water and I splashed my face and ran a warm, wet cloth over the back of my neck. It was freezing in the room and I quickly pulled on my tunic and hose. In my bag, I found my coat and mittens. It was so cold our frosty breath billowed in front of our faces. I peered out of the window as Sebastian dressed. He was huffing and puffing in the chill. It was surprisingly light outside; the dirty lemon orb of a full moon lit up the frost on rooftops. I could see a few faint lights, and in the distance a ribbon of water, the Thames, silver in the moon's glow. A snowflake glided by, pirouetted and dissolved on the windowsill.

We were downstairs within a few minutes. Anthony was waiting, swathed in a tattered brown wool cloak, felt hat and gloves. He giggled inanely when he saw us. 'We look like bears,' he exclaimed, and gave a loud roar.

We saw no one as we left the house and turned straight into a dark, cobbled lane. Ann led the way, holding Anthony's hand. It was snowing in earnest now, settling on the cobbles and on the frozen soil. The lane opened on to a square. A couple of stallholders were still trading in the gloom. There was a bonfire in one corner. A group of people sat around the dancing flames, passing a bottle of amber liquid between them. One of them, a toothless old hag, laughed so loudly the sound carried right across the square. In the centre danced a jester in typical garb: yellow-and-red-striped hose, a tunic with bells attached to the hem, and a huge, multicoloured hat. He was juggling firebrands, the flames cutting red arcs through the snowfall.

We ducked into another lane beset with shadows. This was barely wider than a man's shoulders and we had to walk single file.

Directly overhead, the first floor of a shabby house hung over the lane, ending up so close to the house opposite, a bird would have found it difficult to fly between the two.

After a few minutes of quick walking I began to lose all sense of where I was, just as I had earlier that morning. This place was a veritable warren, I decided. The people who made Southwark their home knew many shortcuts and singular passageways. They knew how to avoid the beggars and the thieves, but to me it was an unnavigable maze. If I were to become separated from Ann, I would never find my way back to her house.

I was just beginning to despair and losing all feeling in my chilled fingers and toes when Ann and Anthony ducked into a doorway. As Sebastian and I came up behind them I heard Ann rap on the door, a subtle little dance of the knuckles, obviously a secret signal to those inside.

A young maid opened the door and led us into a room similar to the front parlour of Ann's house. Leading the way to the back of the room, the maid pulled a metal ring hidden at one end of a shelf full of books. There was a faint click and she slid a panel aside. In the darkness

beyond, I could just make out a narrow staircase that fell away downwards. The maid
plucked a lit reed from an alcove inside the
concealed passage and began the descent.

I was the last down and was amazed to find
myself stepping into a large, rectangular
basement. The walls were wood panelled, the
floor left as dirt. Shallow alcoves ran the length
of each of the two longer walls and in these
candles burned. At the far end, I could see an
altar. It was draped in a rich purple cloth and a
large golden cross had been placed at the
centre of the altar. Beside it I could see a
gold chalice, and next to that a plate. At each
end of the purple cloth, squat candles in simple
gold holders offered up a creamy glow. I
dropped to my knees and crossed myself,
reciting the Lord's Prayer before getting to my
feet again.

A small group of people stood close to the
altar. As I approached, they turned as one. At
the back of the gathering stood a Catholic
priest. Broad-shouldered and tall, he was
wearing a bronze-coloured robe, beautifully
embroidered in gold thread. On the front of the
robe, a large cross of silver had been stitched
into the fabric and in the centre of this was an

image of Christ, eyes directed to the heavens, one finger pointing to his heart. I recognised the priest immediately. It was Father Richard Garnet, the most senior Jesuit in England, a man who had done such wonderful work for Our Lord that in Rome his name was revered above all other Englishmen's. He stepped forward, embracing Sebastian and then me.

'It is good to see you again, my brother,' he whispered in my ear. Then he led us to the group by the altar.

There were some twenty worshippers. Father Garnet introduced us to them. The last was a narrow-faced man with a luxuriant head of silver-white hair. He had almond-shaped brown eyes and a salt-and-pepper beard.

'My friends,' Father Garnet said, addressing Sebastian and me. 'This is our guest of honour this evening, William Byrd.'

I stared at the man, astonished. The figure before me, smiling and modest, was perhaps the most respected musician in the land. But, most incredible of all, he was a favourite of the Queen's, her Court Composer no less. I knew he came from a Catholic family, but had always assumed he had surrendered his faith in order to serve the monarch.

I bowed. 'I am deeply honoured, sir.'

Byrd smiled and took my arm. 'I can understand your surprise, young man. You need have no fear of me.'

I realised this was a remarkably perceptive man, for a small part of my mind had indeed been filled with doubt the moment I heard his name. I had heard such horrible stories concerning the religious clash that had become the great dividing point of our age. Tales of brother killing brother, lovers betraying each other, and parents condemning their own children to torture in the name of their faith. In these dreadful times, it was hard to know who to trust and who to doubt.

Father Garnet led William Byrd around the altar, and six of the congregation followed them. They lined up in two rows. Byrd stood in front of them, raised his hands, and the group began to sing. With the others, I fell to my knees.

It was a beautiful sound. Immediately it transported me back to the college, my home for the past five years. I suddenly felt very homesick. But at the same time, these sounds of worship, so ingrained into my soul, lifted my spirits. The fears I harboured floated away from me as I immersed myself in the magisterial sound of the 'Kyrie'. Then suddenly . . . silence. A stillness almost unnatural in its intensity. Father Richard walked to the altar and began the Penitential Rite in Latin, in direct disobedience of the ecclesiastical laws of England: '*Fratres, agnoscamus peccata nostra, ut apti simus.*'

A prayer followed, again recited in Latin, in which Father Richard beseeched the Lord to show us, His humble servants, mercy, and to give especial grace to Sebastian and myself on our perilous mission. William Byrd and the choir regained their feet and the composer led the chant of the 'Gloria': '*Gloria in excelsis Deo et in terra pax hominibus bonae voluntatis . . .*'

I could hear Sebastian beside me, singing as though he were back in the chapel at the Jesuit College. To my right knelt Ann, her head bowed and covered with a square of black lace. She had a sweet, almost angelic voice. Looking up, I was startled to see Anthony dressed in white server's vestments over his rough and filthy tunic, handing Father Richard a small bowl. He seemed utterly calm, as though he suffered no abnormality of the mind. Indeed, his expression was one of utter serenity, his eyes bright and focused on the task.

I felt Ann press against me and realised she was getting to her feet. It was only then that I heard a discordant voice breaking through the music. The singing stopped abruptly. I turned and saw the maid who had brought us down here earlier. She was at the entrance to the underground chapel, her face ashen. 'Pursuivants!' she screamed. 'The Queen's . . .'

Before she could finish her sentence, the maid was propelled down into the room. She sprawled in the dirt as two men in leather tunics and metal breastplates barged down the stairs. One of them picked up the girl and shoved her aside while two more men descended into the chapel, each with their sword drawn.

I felt a shudder of terror pass through my guts. I felt, rather than saw, Sebastian jump to his feet beside me, and then came the rush of air as he ran past, straight towards the intruders. I yelled, but have no recollection what exactly I shouted. It was something automatic, from deep within my soul, a yell of pure terror. They were the last words I ever spoke to my dear friend. As he dashed forward, the man at the front of the group simply extended his sword arm and Sebastian ran on to it, the metal scything through his flesh and emerging, dripping, from his back.

I heard a woman scream and felt someone slam into my back. I almost lost my balance. Stumbling forward, I found myself at the altar. The choir had scattered. I caught a brief glimpse of William Byrd, his face white with terror. And then I felt a strong hand on my arm. I tried to turn to see who had grabbed me, but I was falling forward again.

In my memory, the next few seconds remain a blur, a tangled mesh of noise and colour, a burning sensation in the pit of my stomach as realisation dawned that I could die very soon. I felt the acrid taste of bile in my mouth, and almost gagged. I felt myself stumble again. I put my hands out and touched wood, the panelling of the basement wall. Then I was out of the room, crouching in a damp, confined space and the light from the chapel was extinguished. Only a narrow line of it reached us through the gap where the panels joined and the wood had split slightly.

'We're safe here,' a voice said. It was Anthony. He was panting heavily. I turned and could just make out his sharp features in the fractured darkness. He looked petrified for a second, then grinned from ear to ear before bursting into tears.

Chapter 27

Pendragon paused for a moment to gather his thoughts. He smoothed back his hair, coughed unnecessarily and pushed the doorbell. Sue Latimer opened the door. She was wearing a light blue summer dress, her hair tied back, accentuating her fine cheekbones.

'Hello. I imagine punctuality is all part of the training.'

'Sorry. Should I have been fashionably late?'

She laughed.

He held out a bottle of red wine in one hand, a bunch of tulips in the other. She looked genuinely delighted. 'Gorgeous. Thank you, Jack.'

Sue's flat was so different from Pendragon's, it was hard to believe it was in the same building. The walls were painted in warm shades, chocolate and cream and duck egg blue. The lighting was subdued.

A wall of shelves held hundreds of books and CDs. The kitchen was modern and glistened with highly polished pans hanging from hooks above an expensive-looking hob. A medley of smells came from a pan. A radio in the corner of the counter was playing some piano music he half-recognised.

'I hope you like Indian,' she said, and handed Pendragon a glass of red wine.

He felt unusually relaxed straight away. He had never been a great mixer, and often needed time to get to know people, but Sue was so open and warm, it felt natural to let the barriers down.

'I must say, you struck me as a bit of a mystery when I first met you,' she said, as she stirred the curry.

'Oh, it's a carefully cultivated act.'

She lifted a wooden ladle and handed it to Pendragon, inviting him to taste. He took a little into his mouth and nodded his approval.

'Well, the act was successful,' she replied. 'I'm intrigued.'

The music on the radio faded to silence and the host of the programme handed over to the newsdesk. Sue was reaching over to turn it off when the newsreader began: 'The homicide investigation into the deaths of two men linked with Bridgeport Construction took a new twist this afternoon . . .'

'Wait a second,' Pendragon said, and Sue took her finger from the 'off' switch.

'Sources close to the investigating team at Brick Lane Police Station have disclosed that a human skeleton, said to be several hundred years old, was unearthed at the construction site in Stepney shortly before the murder of Amal Karim early on Saturday last. The police have not released details of the find, but the skeleton disappeared the night of Karim's murder and reappeared only this morning. It was found in a skip less than a hundred metres from the building site where it was unearthed. In an official statement from Brick Lane Police Station, Superintendent Jill Hughes told reporters that police forensic scientists were studying the bones and that details would only be made public when that investigation was complete. Turning to other . . .'

'Bad news?' Sue asked, seeing Pendragon's frown.

He forced a smile. 'Oh, not really. It had to come out, I suppose.'

'Are you working on this case?'

'Yes.'

'And you only got here at the weekend.'

'A cop's life is rarely boring.'

'Obviously! So, this skeleton,' Sue said. 'It's connected to the murders?'

'We're not sure yet.'

'But the report said it was discovered just before the workman was killed.'

'That's true, but it doesn't necessarily mean the two things are connected. Could just be a coincidence.'

'So do you have a suspect . . . a motive? Oh, God, I'm sorry,' she said. 'You can't . . .'

'It's okay . . . but, no, you're right, I can't really go into details.'

Sue topped up his glass, then her own, and led him into the living-room. They sat on the couch, Sue perched on the edge, the glass held on her knee. From the kitchen came a new piece of piano music, a lilting Chopin mazurka.

'The thing is, though, if the discovery of the skeleton is a coincidence, that's one thing. If it's not, it puts a completely different complexion on the whole affair, doesn't it?' Her eyes sparkled as she studied Pendragon's face.

Protocol dictated that he should not say anything more, especially about any aspects of the case that had been deliberately held back from the public, but something indefinable told him to ditch protocol this once. 'I think you're absolutely right,' he said. 'I stopped thinking it was a coincidence, even before the second murder.'

She raised an eyebrow. 'Oh?'

'When the skeleton was first found it was wearing a ring. This was missing when the bones were rediscovered in the skip this morning.'

'You shouldn't be telling me this.'

'No, I shouldn't.'

'Well, you have your motive then, don't you?'

'Possibly.' He drank some wine.

'Was there a ritualistic aspect to the murders?'

'No, there wasn't. Why? What are you thinking?'

Sue stared into space for a moment. 'The newspapers said that the first victim, the labourer . . . Kaalim?'

'Karim.'

'Yes, Karim . . . was beaten to death. The second murdered man was poisoned. Must be transference.'

'Meaning?'

'Sorry.' She focused on Pendragon's face again. 'The ring must be the key. The killer places great importance upon it. There's no obvious ritualistic aspect to it, so it's not a cult or a religious thing. It's personal transference, or personal ritual if you like. The murderer needs the ring to carry out the killings. Well, they needed it for the second murder anyway.'

Pendragon looked puzzled. 'I've heard something about this theory before. It's pretty rare though, right?'

Sue pursed her lips and tilted her head. 'It wasn't properly understood until twenty years ago, so many older crimes were explained by different motives. I did some work on criminal psychology for my PhD. I remember one particular case study that fits the transference scenario perfectly.'

Pendragon raised an eyebrow.

'A chap called Hopper, James Hopper, a killer in the early-eighties in Devon. His wife Gina was having an affair and she deliberately let her husband know about it. She saw him as a weak, indecisive man, and had grown to despise him. She would dress up before going on a date with her lover, taunting James by showing him her stockings and fancy knickers, telling him that only her lover would get to appreciate them.'

'I'm beginning to remember this now,' Pendragon said. 'He strangled her with one of the stockings, didn't he?'

'That was the start of it. He then went on to kill three of Gina's closest friends who had been involved in the affair somehow – the woman who had introduced his wife to the lover, and two friends who had helped cover for Gina until she decided her husband should know about it and the whole taunting thing started.'

'And the stockings were used each time?'

'Yes, James Hopper had given those stockings a special significance. For him, they were all-important, the focus of his rage.'

'Yes, I can see . . .' Pendragon began, when his mobile rang. He recognised the number. 'Turner? . . . Yes, yes. All right. I'll be there in five minutes.' He closed the phone.

'Duty calls?'

Pendragon sighed heavily. 'Yes. I'm really sorry.'

Chapter 28

The first things he noticed were the crucifixes. But then, it would have been hard to miss them, they were everywhere. A line of them ran along the narrow hallway of the Ketteridges' flat, and a small side table contained three more grouped together in a Holy Trinity. He passed a small, cluttered lounge where a middle-aged woman in a pink winceyette dressing gown was being consoled by Sergeant Mackleby. A line of crosses stood on the mantel-piece, with one large crucifix, blood and all, hanging on the wall above.

A few paces along the hall, he reached the kitchen. A floodlight on a stand had been set up close to the sink. It cast an intense white glow over everything. The back door to the garden stood open and Pendragon could see a forensics officer moving around on the path between the kitchen and a brick wall covered with a trellisfull of yellow roses. Along the windowsill above the sink and draining board stood another row of crosses. Pendragon counted nine of them arranged with the largest in the centre, a smaller version of the one on the lounge wall.

'I've just arrived, Pendragon. So no, I can't give you times, dates, reasons or any other bloody thing,' Jones said as the DCI came into the room. The pathologist was standing beside Tony Ketteridge's body. The dead man lay on the floor close to a small breakfast table, his back against a dishwasher that was still going through its cycle. Ketteridge's head was twisted to one side, his chest soaked in blood and vomit, mouth wide open. Both eyes were red discs.

Pendragon looked round as Turner came in through the back door.

'Were you first here, Sergeant?'

'Yes, guv. I was just leaving the station when the call came in. I got here with Sergeant Mackleby about twenty minutes ago.'

'I take it Mrs Ketteridge reported the murder?'

'Yeah. She was hysterical, apparently. Not too surprising.'

'Had the body been touched?'

'Pretty sure it hadn't. Mrs Ketteridge could barely bring herself to open the door. Roz . . . Sergeant Mackleby's with her now in the other room.'

'Yes, I saw her as I came in.'

'When we arrived, the back door was open. Didn't

look like there was much of struggle. The table has been pushed to one side, but that's about it.' Then he added in a whisper, 'What's with all the bloody crucifixes?'

Pendragon shrugged. 'No idea. Who's outside?' He strode over to the back door with Turner in tow. A forensics officer in a plastic suit had their back to him. They turned.

'Dr Newman,' Pendragon said.

'Chief Inspector.'

'First impressions?' He looked around the narrow space. A line of paving stones stretched from the kitchen door down the side of the house into the garden, little more than a smudge of dark green in the night now. A brick wall about head-height, separating the house from the neighbouring property, ran the length of the passageway then petered out into a wire fence dividing the gardens. A cat brushed against Pendragon's calves. He bent down to stroke it. Straightening, he said, 'If only animals could talk.'

Colette Newman smiled. 'Not much to discover on the surface,' she said. 'There are some traces of mud along the path here. They look quite new. We followed them back to this side of the garden fence. Looks like our murderer came in from over there and went in through the back door of the kitchen.'

Pendragon saw movement in the garden and

noticed another SOCO in a plastic suit crouching beside the fence, dusting brush in his latex-covered right hand.

'Wouldn't the ground be too hard to carry soil through to here?' Turner queried. Pendragon and Newman spun round in unison.

'My first thought too,' the Head of Forensics said, noticing the sergeant for the first time. 'Looks like one of the Ketteridges watered the flowers earlier this evening. Ignoring the hosepipe ban, of course.'

'We'll have to charge them,' Pendragon replied darkly.

'We've taken samples anyway and two of my team are covering the kitchen and the rest of the house. The minute we know anything . . .'

'Thanks,' he replied and turned back to the kitchen. 'So, Tony Ketteridge either knew the person who killed him and let him in, or the murderer was watching the house and knew how to get in.'

'Or it was an opportunist attack.'

They walked back to the body and Pendragon crouched down beside Jones who was examining the corpse.

'Do you get a sense of *déjà vu*, Pendragon?' he asked.

'Carbon copy, by the look of it.'

'Indeed. Can't tell you where the puncture site is

yet, but I bet we'll find one. You happy for me to get the poor sod to the morgue?'

Pendragon nodded and straightened up. 'Do you mind if I come over to the lab when I've finished here?' he asked.

'Not at all. So long as you can stomach it,' Jones replied with a smirk.

Pendragon returned to the hall, pausing for a moment to look at the crucifixes on the table and the wall. They were all different shapes and sizes, some old, some looking pretty new. Most were unadorned but a few carried the image of the body of Christ. Turning into the lounge, he indicated to Mackleby that he would like to have a chat with the victim's widow. He sat down on the sofa.

Pam Ketteridge was a large woman, tall and broad-shouldered, with fat arms that filled out the winceyette. She had a wide face. Her eyes were bloodshot from crying and dark tracks ran down her cheeks where tears had washed away mascara.

'My name is DCI Jack Pendragon. I'm sorry for your loss.'

She made a snorting noise. 'You sound like you've been watching too many crappy American cop shows,' she retorted without looking at the Chief Inspector. She had a faint northern accent. 'I apologise,' she added quickly, scrutinising him. She dabbed at her right eye. Pendragon said nothing, hoping she would talk, but she looked away without adding anything.

'You found your husband's body?' he asked.

She nodded and stared across the room. 'And, no, I didn't touch anything, DCI Pendragon. I was so shocked, I thought I was going to have a heart attack. Then, I . . . I seemed to act automatically. I don't have any memory of going into the hall or making the call to the police. The next thing I knew there were two officers at the door. I haven't been back . . . back in there.'

'Had you been in here all evening?'

She looked at him, her eyes puffy, and shook her head. 'No, that's the worst thing,' she replied. 'If I had . . . I was in bed.'

'And you didn't hear anything?'

She put her hand into the pocket of her gown and pulled out an iPod. 'Tom bloody Jones.' And she burst into tears. Pendragon let her cry and gazed around the room as the woman blew her nose and tried to compose herself. The flat reminded him of his childhood, the sort of décor his parents had gone in for – no subtlety, over-patterned everything.

'If only I had paid Tony more attention,' Pam Ketteridge sighed. 'We were having an early night.

He was exhausted . . .' Then she suddenly froze. 'You don't think this has anything to do with the other . . .' She couldn't bring herself to say the word 'murders'.

'It's too early to know.'

'This is my fault,' she said suddenly, her voice trembling with emotion. 'The problems he'd had at work . . . that poor man, the workman who was killed. My husband felt terrible about it. I should have talked to Tony, should have listened.'

'Did he tell you anything about the lead-up to the death of Amal Karim?'

She stopped sobbing and looked away again. 'You mean, the skeleton? They reported it on the news tonight, just before we . . .'

'Yes,' Pendragon replied, considering the woman's face. 'Anything new could be extremely useful.' It was impossible, he realised, to know for sure how much she was keeping to herself in this state. What was she holding back? And what did she believe the police knew? Had her husband told her about being questioned at the station? He thought it unlikely because it would have led to all sorts of uncomfortable questions from Pam about what Tony had been up to on Saturday morning.

'No. Not that I . . .' She broke down again. This time she could do nothing to conceal her anguish.

Taking her hands from her face, she stared into the middle distance and let the tears run down to her chin. 'O, Lord, take me from this pain,' she cried. And to Pendragon's astonishment, she dropped from the sofa to the floor. Landing on her knees, she started to rock backwards and forwards. 'O, blessed art thou, Lord God Almighty. Show mercy upon our wretched souls. We have sinned! We have sinned!' And she threw herself on to the carpet, arms outstretched towards the line of crucifixes on the mantelpiece. Christ, suffering his own agonies, frowned down upon her.

Sergeant Turner had just walked into the room as Pam Ketteridge threw herself to the ground. He ran over and he and Pendragon began to help the woman to her feet and guide her back to the sofa. She did not resist, but kept repeating the same five words. 'He shouldn't have done it. He shouldn't have done it.'

It took a few minutes for Pam Ketteridge to calm down enough to focus on Pendragon's face and to understand that he was asking her a question.

'What do you mean, Mrs Ketteridge? Shouldn't have done what?'

She simply stared at the DCI in silence. Then she seemed to pull herself together. 'The skeleton. Tony hid the skeleton.' She glanced at Sergeant Turner who was sitting on the edge of an armchair opposite, taking notes.

Saying these few words seemed to calm her. It was as though she had confessed her sins to a priest. 'He didn't know what to do with it. They're weeks behind, see? And he thought . . . well, he thought he could just keep the whole thing quiet.'

'He told you this?' Turner asked.

She turned towards the sergeant and then back to Pendragon. 'Yes. On Sunday. I knew something was wrong with him. He was being very quiet, hardly spoke a word to me all evening. I finally dragged it out of him.'

'So, what did he say exactly? Try to remember his own words, Mrs Ketteridge.'

She frowned and ran the tips of her fingers across her brow. 'He said they had come across a skeleton . . . a complete skeleton. He was thrown by it. It was late on Friday. He didn't know what to do. A couple of his boys were spooked. When he said they should just rebury it, they balked. So he shut up shop and told them it could wait until Monday.'

'And when did he dispose of the skeleton?'

'He told me he went back a few hours later, about nine-thirty, as soon as it was dark.'

'What did he do with it?'

'He wouldn't tell me. Just said, "It's done." '

'I see.'

'I was very upset, and he knew it. I told him he had done wrong. That he had committed a terrible sin.'

'And what about this evening? After the news report about the skeleton being recovered?'

She screwed up her mouth as though she was fighting to keep the words in. 'We had a row. A huge row. He had lied to me, see? First I thought he had done a terrible thing, pretending the skeleton had never been found, but then I learned that he hadn't done that at all.'

'Did he say tonight what he had done with it?'

'He had hidden it under the site hut, then moved it to the boot of his car.'

'Then decided to make it reappear?'

'Yes.'

'Did he say why?'

'No.' Pam Ketteridge responded. 'He clammed up completely. Our last words to each other were angry ones.'

Chapter 29

'Ah, Pendragon. Just in time,' said Jones as the DCI walked into the morgue and the pathologist switched on the electric autopsy saw, a misshapen metal cylinder that nestled in the palm of his hand. 'An amazing piece of kit, this . . . the SF-4000. Weighs only a few kilos, but the blade rotates at 200 revolutions *per second*. Can cut through bone just like that . . . fantastic.'

Pendragon knew Jones was trying to intimidate him, so he ignored him and walked calmly over to the body lying on the stainless-steel table. For perhaps the tenth time this evening he asked himself why he was going to put himself through this. The answer, he knew, was two-fold. Although he trusted Dr Jones's expertise, he wanted to make sure nothing was missed. But the second reason was personal. The pathologist's comments about his squeamishness a few days earlier had hit a nerve. It was true, he had always found the chopping up of dead bodies hard to deal with. It was about time he faced up to his phobia. It was part of his job. It was never going to go away, or not at least so long as people killed each other.

As if he had read his mind, Jones put down the electric saw. 'So, why are you here exactly, Chief Inspector?'

Pendragon shrugged. 'It was that or writing up a report.'

The pathologist held his eye. 'You wouldn't be checking up on me now, would you?'

'No,' Pendragon replied emphatically.

'Then the only other reason would be that you're using me as a therapist. I charge extra for that.'

Pendragon exhaled through his nose and shook his head. 'Charge the Met. They're keen on educational courses.'

'I suppose I should be flattered,' Jones replied. 'Here, put these on,' He tossed a gown and mask to Pendragon.

Tony Ketteridge's was certainly not a beautiful corpse. Under the severe lights of the lab his skin was a bluish-white and his copious jet-black body hair merely accentuated his pallor. It gave the term 'as pale as death' a whole new meaning, Pendragon thought to himself. And then there were the red eyes.

'Not an especially fine example of *homo sapiens*,' commented Jones, removing a digital recorder from the pocket of his lab coat. Turning it on, he shifted into officialese. 'Subject: male. Anthony Frederick Ketteridge. Age: 54. Weight: 115 kilos. Height: 1.65 metres. Time of death: approximately 8 p.m., Wednesday 8 June. External examination: subject is obese, borderline morbidly obese. Small, recent laceration to the throat and fresh, superficial bruising to thoracic region. No serious contusions. No fractures or breaks. Both corneas are coated in blood; presumably from rupture of retinal vessels.' He leaned over the body and turned Ketteridge a few inches on to his right side, then lifted his left arm. 'There is a small puncture mark in the left axilla with surrounding haematoma. Appears to be a fresh wound.'

Jones placed the recorder on a side table. 'Take a look,' he said to Pendragon.

The DCI walked round to Jones's side and the pathologist handed him a magnifying glass. Pendragon looked closely at the small red hole in the soft flesh of Ketteridge's armpit.

'Exactly the same as Tim Middleton,' Jones said from behind him. 'This is looking more and more like a carbon copy of the first poisoning.' He picked up a scalpel and Pendragon returned to the other side of the table as the pathologist leaned over the corpse. 'Let's take a look inside.'

Jones sank the scalpel into the dead man's flesh. There was a thick layer of fat to cut through but the blade was exceptionally sharp and sliced through tissue, fat and blood vessels with ease. The metal made a squelching sound as the tissue parted. Blood slithered down the side of the corpse and into the run-off drains along each side of the table. It was thick and congealed, acting solely under the effects of gravity. Jones brought the blade down across Ketteridge's chest, stopping just below the breast bone. He then repeated the action, starting from the other side and meeting the end point of the first incision. To complete the procedure, he then sank the scalpel deep and made a straight vertical cut to Ketteridge's navel.

With experienced fingers, he parted the flesh, folding back skin and tissue to expose the ribs. Picking up the electric saw, he set to work, slicing through the bones at 200 revolutions per second. With the cuts made, he then buried his hands deep inside the dead man's chest and prised the ribs apart. Placing a chest clamp into position, he turned the large nut on the side of the device and, slowly, Ketteridge's body opened up like a sea clam to reveal the cluster of reddish-grey internal organs.

In less than a minute, Jones had Ketteridge's liver on a dish beside the corpse. It was black and degraded, very similar to Middleton's.

'As I expected,' Jones said, and prodded it with the scalpel. 'Severe necrosis.' He turned back to the corpse and poked around inside the abdominal cavity with a narrow stainless-steel tube. 'Pancreas all but obliterated. Spleen ditto,' he remarked. 'I'll run all the tests, of course. But it's pretty obvious what killed him. Looks like you've got yourself a serial killer, Pendragon.'

Chapter 30

Stepney, Thursday 9 June, 7.10 a.m.

Jack Pendragon was shaving when he heard his mobile ring, telling him he had a text message. He made a final sweep of the blade up his neck, washed and dried his face then walked over to the kitchen counter where he had left the phone charging. The text was from Colette Newman: 'Have findings that should interest u. Can u call in lab. Would 10 b ok?' He winced at the mangled English. He would never get used to texting shorthand and was a little surprised that someone like Dr Newman would stoop to it. Then he realised he didn't actually know how to send a reply and so he punched in Dr Newman's number instead.

Brick Lane Police Station was a hive of activity. There had been a pile-up on Whitechapel Road involving at least one reported fatality and it seemed as though half the force at the station was rushing to the scene. Pendragon found Turner in the main ops room at a computer terminal.

'I've finally got round to trying to find out something about the ring, guv. Problem is, I can't get a good impression of it from the photos. I managed to track down Tim Middleton's SIM card, but even taking the images directly from that, I can't see much.'

Pendragon leaned over his sergeant's shoulder and peered at the image on the screen. 'No, I see your problem.'

'And that's after putting it through image-enhancing software, best we have. All I can tell you is, the top is green!'

'Okay, we'll have to give up on that for the moment. I need you to get on to Bridgeport Construction. Arrange to interview the late Mr Ketteridge's immediate superiors – this morning.'

Pendragon arrived early at the Metropolitan Police Forensic Science Laboratory on Lambeth Road. It was an impressive building, renowned as the biggest and best forensics lab in the world. It was odd to be looking at it now, so grand and important. It seemed like only yesterday, Pendragon mused, that he had been reading in his *Boys' Own Book of Modern*

Science how the whole science of forensics had come about by fluke. It had been the brainchild of a simple police constable named Cyril Cuthbert who, during the 1930s, worked in his off-duty hours with a second-hand microscope he had bought for £3. The Commissioner at the time, Lord Trenchard, heard about it and visited Cuthbert and the makeshift lab he had set up in his station broom cupboard. Trenchard was so taken with what he saw, he agreed to establish a proper laboratory at Hendon Police College with a budget of £500 a year. The rest, as they say, was history.

The morning was hotting up, and according to the front page of one of the tabloids that Pendragon had glimpsed in a newsagent's on the way to his car, it was going to be the hottest day of the summer so far: 'A Real Scorcher', in fact.

Putting a police parking permit on his dashboard, he walked along the road towards the river. The rush hour was over. Workers would be at their desks and kids would be in school, longing for the break so they could get out of their stifling classrooms. He walked over Lambeth Bridge, the forbidding, angular lines of Millbank ahead of him. Leaning on the red and grey balustrade, he looked downstream and took in the magnificent vista of London glowing in the freakish heat. To his left stretched the Houses of

Parliament, its honey-coloured limestone dis-coloured by a century's worth of car fumes. Directly ahead stretched Westminster Bridge with the buildings of County Hall at its southern end. Towering above it all was the London Eye, looking like an alien spacecraft that had lost its way and landed on the South Bank.

He suddenly felt the stab of an emotion he could not easily define. It was a mixture of things: nostalgia, regret, a sense of belonging, and, yes, a touch of loss. He knew he had done the right thing returning to London, but it was going to take him time to adjust. Although this was still the London he had grown up in, it was also a foreign land in so many ways, very different from the place he'd thought he would always know.

The vista of the Thames before him opened up a treasure trove of memories. He had looked out over the river from the old Docklands when he was a kid with his dad, a lifetime ago. He remembered his father telling him then that the river was the artery of the city. How in the olden days, as he'd called them, it was the fastest way to get through the city, and how during the fourteenth century the water often froze over and people set up market stalls on the ice.

And then there were the times when Pendragon had visited London with Jean and stood with her on the Embankment, enjoying the view of the water coursing through the heart of this great city. More recent still were the times they had brought the kids up here for the day. They usually ended up on the banks of the Thames then, too, admiring the view from Waterloo Bridge, the City, or St Paul's – the building that once towered over everything but now looked like a broody hen surrounded by her postmodern chicks.

Returning to the forensics lab, he showed his pass at the reception desk and took the lift to the second floor. The receptionist had called ahead and, as he exited the lift, trying to figure out which way to go, Dr Newman appeared at the end of the hall to his left, swing doors oscillating to a stop behind her. She was wearing a pristine white lab coat. 'Chief Inspector. Thanks for coming.'

'Not at all. Your text implied some good news. I'm fond of that.'

She led him back through the swing doors and into a vast space. To one end, tall windows looked out over the road. The ceiling was high and striped with long fluorescent lights. Rows of stainless-steel benches ran across the room, crowded with glassware and equipment. At the far end, a long counter ran under the windows. A dozen or more monitors were placed a few feet apart on this, most of them responding to lab-coated staff tapping away at keyboards.

Pendragon followed Dr Newman through a sliding glass door into a smaller room beyond. It had the look of an expensive modern kitchen. A stainless-steel counter ran the length of one wall, a rectangular island bench stood in the middle of the floor, and to the left, backed against the wall, was a workstation with two computers, piles of papers and a pivot lamp.

'We're still trying to find a good DNA sample,' the Head of Forensics said as she crossed the pristine, tiled floor. 'Nothing yet, and no unusual prints.' She lowered herself on to a metal stool in front of the counter and indicated Pendragon should take the one next to her. On the counter sat a glass dish containing three clumps of dried mud. Beside this lay an A4 monochrome print. Newman handed the photograph to Pendragon who turned slightly on his stool to study the picture.

'It's an enhanced image of the footprint we found on the path running under Tony Ketteridge's kitchen window,' Dr Newman explained. 'It's only a partial, perhaps seventy-five per cent of the footprint, but it's enough to give us a clear picture of the shoes worn by whoever was on that path the evening the garden was watered.'

Pendragon looked intently at the image. 'It looks very strange.'

'It is. If it had been made by a boot it would have a much wider profile and there would be tell-tale troughs in the mud from the tread. There's no tread at all in this sample. A bare foot would be equally as obvious, and it's not that.'

'What kind of footwear leaves this sort of impression?' Pendragon asked, looking up from the photograph then peering at the mud sample in the dish.

'A rather delicate shoe, I would say.'

Pendragon was silent for a moment and looked again at the photograph, pursing his lips as he concentrated. 'So you're thinking slippers . . . something like that?'

'Yes.'

'Couldn't it have been left by Pam Ketteridge?'

'Far too big.'

'Then, Tony Ketteridge? As he watered the garden?'

'I thought the same. But I checked. Ketteridge had surprisingly small feet for such a big chap. Size seven. These prints are a size ten.'

'So, let me get this straight,' Pendragon said. 'You're saying whoever killed Tony Ketteridge was wearing size ten *slippers*? That would be a first.'

Dr Newman put her elbows on the counter, rested her chin on her interlocked fingers and looked down at the pristine metal surface. Then, tilting her head to one side, she said, 'Don't think I didn't go through all the permutations myself, Chief Inspector. I had visions of a neighbour finishing his cocoa and hopping over the fence to commit murder. Maybe it was a love triangle with the gorgeous Pam.'

Pendragon couldn't help laughing.

'But it's even odder actually because the profile of the footprint is not that of a normal slipper, the sort you'd wear at home to put your feet up. It's the shape of a fancy slipper.'

'A fancy slipper?'

'Yes, a dress shoe, something very delicate. Theatrical, really.'

Pendragon gave her a puzzled look.

'Then, using a high-resolution microscope, I found this.' Dr Newman led the DCI to the bench along the adjacent wall where a very large microscope with a huge, binocular-like appendage stood in the middle of the stainless-steel surface. 'Take a look,' she added, and showed him how to use the eyepiece.

'If I'm not mistaken,' Dr Newman continued, '*that* is gold thread. Extremely expensive, and not at all the sort of thing you find on slippers in the Summer Special bin at Tesco.'

Back at the station, the team was waiting for him. Jez Turner had put up the photographs of the latest murder scene alongside an enlarged snap of a smiling Tony Ketteridge taken earlier that summer.

Pendragon did not apologise for being late, but ploughed straight in. 'Right,' he said, surveying the room. They were all there: Towers and Grant, Sergeants Thatcher, Vickers and Roz Mackleby. Perched on the edge of the furthermost desk, was Superintendent Hughes looking distinctly unimpressed.

'Let me bring you all up to speed. As you know, Tony Ketteridge was site manager at the Frimley Way construction project. He was about to retire for an early night with his wife, Pam, when he was murdered in the kitchen of his home.' He tapped the picture. 'There seems to have been a struggle, but nothing too serious. There are bruises on the victim's back, but no skin or hair under his nails. There's a tiny cut to his throat. You can just about see it, there.

'The most interesting feature, however, is a puncture wound in Ketteridge's left armpit. It's identical to one found on Tim Middleton's body. According to Dr Jones's initial findings, Tony

Ketteridge was poisoned with the same, or very similar, blend of chemicals that killed the architect at La Dolce Vita, and it looks as though the poison was administered in precisely the same way – probably with a hypodermic.'

'But how on earth could the murderer have used a hypodermic in the restaurant?' asked Sergeant Mackleby.

'To be honest, I have no idea at this stage,' Pendragon replied.

'It's ridiculous,' Thatcher said. 'Nobody could be stuck with a needle and not know it.'

'I agree, Sergeant. It's another of your conundrums. Perhaps you should put your analytical skills to work on the puzzle.'

Turner looked over at Sergeant Vickers with a smirk.

'What have forensics found?' Superintendent Hughes asked. 'Anything useful?'

'I went to the lab in Lambeth this morning. They're still trying to find a decent DNA sample, but it looks like the murderer was extremely careful. And, of course, there are no prints.'

'Obviously.'

'But they've unearthed one very important thing.'

Two of the officers who had been contemplating their feet looked up simultaneously. Pendragon passed a USB drive to Turner and asked him to put it into a smart board to one side of the room, next to the whiteboard containing the pictures of Ketteridge. Turner slipped the tiny device into the slot and tapped at a couple of controls on the smart board before returning to his seat. A metre-square image appeared on the white surface.

Pendragon walked over to it. 'This is a partial print that Dr Newman found in some wet mud on the path close to the Ketteridge's back door. It's been so dry recently it seems an unlikely find, but it's clear our intruder got into the garden over a neighbour's fence and unwittingly put their foot into a newly watered flower bed.'

'But there's a hosepipe ban!' Jimmy Thatcher blurted out.

A couple of the policemen laughed and Jimmy's cheeks flushed.

'Bloody Brain of Stepney,' Jez Turner murmured, and jabbed the sergeant in the ribs.

Thatcher pulled a face. 'Fuck off,' he mouthed silently.

'Yes,' Pendragon said to the room at large, keeping a straight face. 'We got a lucky break there.'

'Couldn't whoever did the watering have left the print?' Ken Towers asked.

'Exactly my question to Dr Newman,' Pendragon

replied. 'But this is an imprint from a size ten shoe and Ketteridge was a seven. Furthermore, this print is not from a boot or even a regular shoe. It's from a slipper. And, even then, it's not the print of a normal slipper. The shape is long and narrow, like a ballet shoe or dress slipper.'

'But . . .' Vickers began.

Pendragon raised a hand. 'There's more. Can you flick to the next image please, Sergeant?'

Turner had the remote for the smart board in his palm. He pressed a button and the image changed to show a single wavy gold line.

'Dr Newman found this in the mud sample. It's gold thread.'

Jill Hughes was staring at the screen intently, hand on chin. 'This is a break,' she said to the room. 'That's expensive stuff. Can't be too many shoes like that. We need to check out manufacturers, retailers . . .'

'It's in hand, ma'am,' Turner interrupted. 'DCI Pendragon called me from the car on his way from the lab. I've done an internet search. The best fit for the shape Dr Newman described is a ballet shoe. There are four manufacturers in London and twenty-six retailers, ignoring the cheap places that do five quid ballet pumps for beginners. I plan to follow them up after lunch.'

'A good start, Sergeant,' Hughes replied. 'So, Chief Inspector. Any ideas about suspects?'

Pendragon shook his head. 'We've nothing concrete. No witnesses, and only this single anonymous print.'

'Well, it might not remain anonymous for long,' the Superintendent replied optimistically. 'What about the wife? We all know the stats for homicides committed by so-called loved ones.'

'Absolutely no evidence. It looks like their marriage wasn't great, but that's hardly a motive. Pam is also . . . how shall I put it . . . ?'

'Mad?' Turner interjected.

They all laughed except Pendragon and Hughes.

'This is the crucifix thing?' the Superintendent said. 'I was debriefed earlier.'

'She's a religious obsessive,' Pendragon said. 'But again, that's no . . .'

'Sounds distinctly dodgy, though, don't you think?'

'I questioned her at the house. I don't think she killed her husband, but she is involved . . . tangentially.'

'What do you mean, guv?' Inspector Grant asked, staring at Pendragon, his arms folded across his chest.

'She knew about the skeleton. According to Pam,

Tony Ketteridge did visit the construction site, but around nine-thirty or ten. At least four hours before Karim's murder. He apparently hid the skeleton under the site hut and put it in his car boot, only to dump it in the skip later. Pam Ketteridge was horrified by the thought that her husband's death could be linked with Karim's and Middleton's. She kept saying he had sinned. It was almost as though she believed Tony's murder was God's revenge.'

'As I said . . . mad,' Turner remarked.

'I think she should be brought in for questioning,' Hughes declared.

Pendragon shrugged. 'I think it's a waste of time, but okay.'

'So what's new on the skeleton?' the Superintendent asked, wishing to move things on.

'It's with Dr Newman's people at the Lambeth lab. But they've been preoccupied with the recently dead.'

'But there's obviously a link?'

'Well, yes . . .'

'And the ring? No sign of it?'

'No.'

'I see.'

The room had fallen silent.

'Okay,' Pendragon said after a few awkward moments. 'Rob, I'd like you and Sergeant Mackleby to interview Mrs Ketteridge. Go to her house, we don't need to drag her in here.' He flicked a glance at Hughes then turned to Vickers and Thatcher, as Grant and Roz Mackleby headed for the door. 'You two, start a new detailed search of the area around the skip. If the ring is there, I want it found. Ken, you get over to Bridgeport Construction. There has to be a link to them. All the victims had some affiliation with the company – two of them were employees. Jez, you work on the slippers. We'll meet back here at six. And I want some answers, yes?' He turned to the whiteboard to study the photos as the rest of the team trooped out.

'Jack, I'm . . .' Hughes was two feet behind him.

'I don't like being treated like that in front of my team.'

'I regretted it the moment the words came out.'

He stared at her stonily. 'Apology accepted.' He went back to his office without a backward glance.

Pendragon was sitting at his desk, staring into space, when Turner tapped on the door and came in. 'Bad moment?' he said.

'No. What's up?'

'I've been thinking, guv. You said Jones found four chemicals in the poison that killed Tim

Middleton, and that the poison that killed Ketteridge was the same or very similar.'

'Yes.'

'And two of the chemicals, arsenic and . . . what was it? . . . Camrinol?'

'Cantharidin.'

'Yeah . . . why do they have to make these names so bloody difficult? The arsenic and the cantharidin are both fairly easy to get your mitts on. But the other two: abric acid and . . . what was the other one?'

'Oleander.'

'Right, those two. If they're so hard to come by, Google should be able to help us find where you get hold of 'em. Can't be too many sources.'

'I see your point, Turner. But they're so obscure, I don't see how we can easily trace where they came from. It's not like the golden slippers. Someone could have brought those two chemicals into the country ten years ago and we'd never be any the wiser.'

'Okay, maybe you're right. But what about the other two then?'

'Go on.'

'You reckoned cantharidin was in some sex drug.'

'Spanish Fly.'

'Well, what about searching on the web for suppliers?'

'I think you'll find hundreds. And even if you

narrowed it down, they would probably be one-man operations working from a garage in Stoke or somewhere. But . . .' Pendragon stopped for a second '. . . actually, you may be on to something,' he admitted.

'What, guv?'

'The other component of the poison . . .'

'Arsenic?'

'Yes.'

'What of it?'

'I'm sure I've read about it recently somewhere. It's not just an old-fashioned poison.'

Turner came around Pendragon's desk and started tapping at the keyboard of his computer. 'One good way to find out.'

Pendragon sighed. 'Naturally. There's me thinking I'd have to pop to the library. I'll never get used to this,' he added, nodding towards the monitor.

'Of course you will, Granddad,' Turner laughed. In a few seconds, Google had informed him that there were over one hundred million links to the word 'arsenic'. He then typed in 'arsenic + uses'. This narrowed it down to just under forty million. He scrolled down and the fifth website listed was entitled 'Arsenic, use in Glass-making'.

'That's it!' Pendragon declared. 'Of course. Let's see if there are any glass-makers in this area.'

Turner keyed in the appropriate words and a long list of references to glass-makers in East London appeared on the screen. Almost all of them were historical or links to irrelevant websites, but the tenth on the list was for the website of Murano Glass UK, a specialist glass-maker in Commercial Road.

'Well done, Sergeant,' Pendragon said, pulling his jacket from the back of his chair. 'Get back to the search for the golden slippers. I'll see you later.'

Chapter 31

Jack was descending the steps from the station to the car park when his mobile rang.

'DCI Pendragon?'

'Yes.'

'It's Professor Stokes here. Remember, I came to see you the other day?'

'Yes, of course,' he replied.

'I was wondering, Inspector. You couldn't drop by, could you? I've managed to get some good images of the ring we discussed. I have . . . well, I've started to put together a hypothesis about it. You might be interested.'

'How soon can you see me, Professor?'

'Well . . . um . . . I'm free now. I have a lecture at two-thirty, but . . .'

'Perfect. I'll be with you in ten minutes.'

The archaeology department of Queen Mary College occupied a row of prefabs on the edge of the campus, so tucked away it would have been understandable if only the handful of students reading archaeology knew of its existence. Pendragon consulted the campus map at the main entrance to the college but failed to find his destination. He only managed to weave his way through the warren of buildings and pathways after seeking help from Main Reception. Even then, he managed to get lost twice and arrived fifteen minutes late.

'DCI Pendragon,' Professor Stokes said, hand extended as a young woman in a white lab coat showed Jack into the archaeologist's cramped little office. It was a dark, stuffy room, the only natural light coming from a small, single window half-obscured by piles of books. Stokes's desk took up the whole of one wall, and laden bookshelves covered two other walls. On the carpeted floor stood shaky towers of books and papers. 'I'm afraid there's not much room. Come with me. The lab is far more accommodating.'

They walked along a corridor lined with pictures of fossils and archaeological digs and turned left into a brightly lit, whitewashed room, the very antithesis of the professor's little box of an office.

'I know we're largely ignored here and have to put up with pre-war temporary buildings which the rest of Queen Mary hardly know exist,' Stokes admitted.

'But in here we have some state-of-the-art equipment you wouldn't find anywhere else outside MIT or Oxbridge.' He led the way across the room to a counter containing a bewildering array of electronic devices and monitors. It reminded Pendragon of something he had seen on *Star Trek* when he was flicking through channels a few years back.

'As you'll appreciate, Chief Inspector, ours is a job of two halves. Part of the time we have our heads down holes in the ground; the rest of the time we're using this sort of equipment. Of course, our detractors on the grants committee claim we have our heads somewhere entirely different most of the time, but what do they know?' He smiled at Pendragon. 'So, when we're not being Indiana Jones, we sit in here studying what we've dug up from those holes in the ground.' He pointed towards the box of tricks on the counter. 'This is a multi-faceted system incorporating several independent analytical processors all hooked up to a rather sophisticated computer system. We use it to study artefacts such as coins or pieces of pottery. We can determine the chemical composition of the artefact with a spectroscopic analyser, and study the ultra-fine structure of an object with the scanning electron microscope . . . here.' He pointed to a large box with two rubber-clad cylinders emerging from the top. It was similar to the equipment Pendragon had seen earlier that day at the forensics lab.

'Obviously, this stuff isn't much use with just a photograph to work with. But this . . .' and the professor patted another black box hooked up to a flat-screen monitor '. . . has come in very useful.'

'What is it?' Pendragon asked.

'It's a picture-enhancement system that can re-pixellate damaged or fuzzy images. But, most importantly, it can convert two-dimensional images into three-D.'

'Professor,' Pendragon said. 'I'm no technophile – in fact, I could never get my DVD player to work – but, correct me if I'm wrong, doesn't that sort of software come with most modern laptops?'

'No, Chief Inspector, you're not entirely wrong. But it's a question of degree. You can buy a picture-enhancement package on the high street very cheaply, but this machine is a thousand times more sophisticated than the most expensive domestic system. Look, I'll show you what I mean.'

He sat down at the counter and tapped on a keyboard. 'This,' he said, leaning back in the chair, 'is the print you gave me of the ring on the skeleton's finger. Pictures taken from mobile phones aren't great at the best of times, but this is actually a particularly poor example. You can see the gold band

281

and the large green stone on top, and that's about it.

'Now, I'll trim the image and apply a set of filters.' His fingers ran over the keys and the image changed. 'This is better,' he said. And it was. The ring filled the screen now and some of the fuzziness had gone, but it was still out of focus, over-exposed, and striped with shadow across half the top surface. 'A domestic software package would not be able to do much better, but I can pass this image under a scanning electron microscope. This takes the pixels one by one and passes them through a programme we developed ourselves called Illuminate – it rebuilds the image having disposed of "noise" and "interference". When we do *that*, we get *this*.'

On screen the image was transformed through a slow vertical wash starting at the top and moving down. When it was complete, the ring could be seen with amazing clarity, every chip, groove and irregularity, in superb colour and with remarkable sharpness.

'Good Lord!' Pendragon exclaimed, and peered more closely at the monitor. 'That really is something.'

'Not finished yet,' Stokes said coolly. Without even looking at the image, he tapped in new instructions. The picture on the flat screen disappeared. A horizontal line appeared at the top of the screen and moved down as it had before. Behind the moving line, a new image began to take shape, gradually filling the screen.

'Much better, wouldn't you agree?' Stokes said proudly, and looked up at Pendragon. On the screen was a 3-D image of the ring that looked so real it was easy to imagine you could reach into the monitor and pluck it out.

'I don't know what to say,' Pendragon confessed. 'The wonders of modern technology never cease to amaze me.'

'Don't worry, Chief Inspector. I still find stuff like this exciting and I work with it every day.'

'So, what do you make of the ring?'

'Let's go over here,' Stokes replied, and stood up. On a table across the room lay a large glossy print of the image from the enhancer. Written on it were a set of numbers and letters. A series of lines had been drawn in black marker across the image.

'Let's start at the beginning,' Stokes said. Pulling up a chair, he motioned to Pendragon to take a seat also. 'The ring is of gold and emerald. The stone is very high quality. You can tell that from the fact that it's almost translucent. It's a very plain design. The only ornamentation is on the band nearest the stone. See there . . . the gold mouldings? Ridges that slope up to the stone?

'Of course, it would be so much easier if we had the ring itself to examine because there might well be markings on the inside of the band as well. But, in the event, we have to manage with what we have, and the two most important aspects are the cut of the stone and the design of the setting. The cut of the stone tells us a great deal about the ring's age.'

'It does?'

'The way precious stones are shaped has developed through the ages. The oldest known cuts were simple two- or three-facet cuts, the "point cut" and the "table cut". Around the late-fourteenth century, the "single cut" was introduced. This produced a flat top with eight facets around the edge of the stone. That's the way this ring has been shaped. From the mid-sixteenth century, master jewellers found new techniques which allowed them to cut gemstones with up to forty-eight facets. Quite remarkable considering the equipment at their disposal.'

'So this ring must have been made between the late-fourteenth and mid-sixteenth centuries?'

'Yes. But with the caveat, of course, that it could have been later because a jeweller may have wanted to produce a retro-style of ring. But that's where the design of the ring comes in.'

'How so?'

'This is a classic example of a bishop ring.'

'Which is?'

'As the name would suggest. Originally it was a ring given to bishops when they were appointed. They're still made today, but their significance has been greatly devalued. You can buy them on-line for fifty pounds, fake gemstones and all. But, in centuries past, the bishop ring was a precious and rare thing. This is the real deal. Now, look closely. Do you see a faint mark on the band close to the stone?'

Pendragon peered at the print. 'A very faint mark.'

'Here, try with this.' Stokes handed Pendragon a magnifying glass. 'Even with the enhancement software at our disposal, this is still hard to see.'

Pendragon moved the magnifying glass until it was focused on the point Stokes was indicating. He lowered the glass. 'A bull?'

'Indeed.'

'So what does that mean?'

'The bull is the symbol used by the Borgias. It appears in their family crest.'

'So, you're suggesting this was once owned by Pope Alexander VI, the Borgia Pope?' Pendragon said.

'Well, that's unclear, and it might not fit with the dates. This ring is definitely Italian. You can

285

tell by those gold mouldings I pointed out. As for the date, it's most likely to be late-fourteenth or early-fifteenth century. Alexander VI was the most well-known Borgia Pope, father to Cesare and Lucrezia – the whole lot of them infamous. But Alexander's uncle, Alfonso, became Pope a generation before him, in 1455. And he was made bishop in 1429.'

'So you think this was the ring presented to Alfonso when he was made bishop?'

'It's a strong possibility. It would then have been handed down through the Borgia family so probably did end up in the hands of Pope Alexander or his children, Cesare and Lucrezia.'

'Well, this is all fascinating, Professor. But I don't think it helps much with my investigation.'

Professor Stokes nodded. 'No, I quite understand. As I said just now, if only I had something more tangible to work with.' He leaned back and rubbed his chin. 'I saw the news about the skeleton on TV last night. I imagine your forensics people at the lab in Lambeth are analysing it?'

'That's correct,' said Pendragon. 'Why?'

'I was just thinking . . . I have the greatest respect for that lab, it's probably the best in the world, but you've seen for yourself what we can do here. Is there any chance you could persuade them to loan me the ring finger? Or even just the proximal phalanx, the bone the ring rested on?'

Pendragon raised an eyebrow.

'No, I know. I'm being silly,' Stokes said quickly.

'Well, you know what, Professor? I'm a great believer in the old adage that two heads are better than one. I'll see what I can do.'

Chapter 32

London, March, 1589

There was barely room to move in the priest hole, and I was not best pleased by my proximity to Anthony who was not the most cleanly of creatures. We could hear voices, screams and shouts from the other side of the panel, and I tried not to think about what would be happening inside the chapel. I knew the powers of the Pursuivants, men employed by Walsingham to flush out seditionists and pollutants. They could arrest and restrain Catholics, but could only use their weapons in self-defence. Although it pained me to recall the fact, Sebastian had run at them. I could only hope that none of the others in the congregation met such a fate and that some might have escaped somehow.

Anthony was in a distraught state. 'My Lady

Ann,' he whimpered pathetically. Then, turning to me, 'Those devils,' he hissed, spittle flying from his mouth.

'Anthony, I understand your fears, but we must go.'

'Go where? Hither and thither?'

'Do you remember that Sebastian and I were meant to meet the Perch brothers? You know something of my task?'

'Sebastian? I don't like him. He is rude to my lady. But she bested him. Ha ha!'

I felt the pain of loss again as Anthony spoke of my dear friend. Vomit rose in my throat, and I suddenly realised how stiflingly hot it was in the priest hole. 'Do you know a way out of here?' I asked, forcing Anthony to meet my eyes. For a moment, his own seemed unusually lucid.

'I do,' he said. 'Yes. I do. Come.'

He squeezed past me and his body odour hit me anew, causing a fresh spasm of nausea. Anthony leaned into a narrow gap at the back of the priest hole and it gave way. Sliding through, he disappeared into darkness. I took a step forward and squeezed after him.

On the other side, I found myself in a damp, narrow tunnel. It stank of cold earth and mould.

I felt the touch of a hand on my arm and jumped back, cracking my head on the roof.

'This way,' said Anthony's voice.

The only light in the tunnel was a slender chink of hazy white, straight ahead. We walked towards it. Our boots crunched on whatever lay on the floor. I did not like to ponder this further and urged Anthony on. The light grew brighter and we soon found ourselves at the end of the tunnel, staring at a wall. It was wet and slimy, but there were small recesses in the stone, just large enough to accommodate clamped fingers, the toes of a boot. At the top I could see a hatch door pivoted upwards. Again, Anthony led the way, ascending the wall with the agility of an ape from distant lands. I took it a little slower and with considerably more trepidation. As I approached the last few toeholds, Anthony had reached our objective. He leaned back into the shaft and helped me out.

The hatch opened on to a small room. A single, tiny window set high on one wall was the source of the light we had seen in the tunnel. The room was empty save for an old wooden crate in one corner. Cobwebs hung from the ceiling and there was green mould around the walls at waist-height. As I emerged into the room, I noticed a closed door to my right. I walked over to it, put my ear to a narrow crack where the door met the frame and listened intently. I could hear nothing. I tried the door which opened outwards.

We were in a narrow lane. Snowflakes fell on my face and I felt the biting wind funnelled by the buildings to either side of the lane. Two paces ahead stood a brick wall. I looked to my left. The lane plunged into darkness. To my right, I could see a well-lit thoroughfare. A cart filled with people passed by. They were all merry, passing around a flagon of some sort. One of them, a cheap whore by the look of her, wearing a low-cut bodice, her hair loose and long, screamed with laughter and fell back against the rail of the cart, legs shamelessly akimbo.

I turned to Anthony. 'Which way now? You can take me to the Perch brothers, as you said?'

'I don't like them,' he said, refusing to meet my eye.

'You need not speak to them, Anthony. Just take me to them.'

'They will eat your head, Father.'

I gave him a gentle smile and placed one hand on his shoulder. 'Do not fear for me, Anthony. I must find the brothers. My mission here is of the utmost importance. It is the Lord's wish that I find the Perch brothers and seek their assistance. Do you understand?'

He nodded slowly. 'Yes, I understand, Father John,' he said. 'Our mission.' He straightened his back. 'I will do the Lord's bidding. Yes, I will. I will. The brothers will be at the theatre. Yes, that's where they'll be.'

'The theatre?'

'The Eagle. Yes, the Eagle Theatre. It's all a game, you see. My Lady Ann told me. People pretend to be other people. They sing songs there and dress up. It is very merry.' He looked at me, eyes ablaze with sudden excitement. Then, without another word, he headed for the main road at the end of the lane.

I stopped him. 'Your robe.'

He looked down at his white vestment and pulled it over his head obediently.

We could not have been more than one hundred feet from the subterranean chapel and the horrors we had just witnessed there, but as Anthony led us into the milling crowds I felt safer than at any time since we had arrived in London. I pulled my scarf over my face to add a layer of disguise and kept my head down. We were in a large square. A market dominated one half of it, with stallholders selling a bewildering array of goods. There were fish counters and stalls piled high with apples and chestnuts. Beside these I saw a counter lined with rows of wooden toys: spinning tops and brightly painted soldiers. Another stallholder was hawking wooden beads, and a few feet from him a trader was loudly beseeching prospective customers to feel the quality of the silk he had laid out on a rickety table.

We moved past the stalls quickly, avoiding eye contact with anyone, and ducked down another alley. It was powdered with untouched snow that glinted in the moonlight. Sensing that this was a hostile place, I encouraged Anthony to break into a trot before anyone could leap out on us and slit our throats.

We were soon in another busy thoroughfare. This time, though, everyone seemed to be moving in one direction – towards the river. We merged with the throng. We took a sharp turn to our left and I could see the theatre directly ahead of us. It reared up out of the shabby dwelling houses surrounding it, with the silver Thames immediately behind.

I had seen the Eagle Theatre from the north

bank of the river when I'd lived in this city five years before, but even though play houses such as this were immensely popular with Londoners of all types and classes, I had never been tempted inside one myself. The Puritans, of course, hated any form of mummery; it was all part of their dour, restrictive outlook on life. And yet I, too, did not feel very comfortable with the new craze for the theatre. It seemed to me that there were more profitable paths to pursue in life. Instead of pretending to be someone other than himself, it might befit a man more to improve that which he was. But even for one so sceptical about the theatre, my first glimpse of the Eagle at such close quarters quickened my blood.

It was like a vast drum built from flint, rising six floors above the ground and towering over all the neighbouring buildings. I noticed a red flag waving above the turret behind the stage area. This, I knew, meant the play was a 'history', and then I saw, hanging over the main entrance to the theatre, a large cloth banner carrying a picture of a Persian warrior and the title: *Tamburlaine*.

The play had already begun. We could hear the sounds of the performance: music, voices, and then a cannon blasting into the night. Around the walls of the theatre stood more stalls. These were selling refreshments, but the busy time just before the start of the performance had passed. Many of the stallholders were resting now before the rush at the end of the play. Immediately behind the stalls, I could see a line of latrines, trenches dug into the hard soil. A single customer was pulling up his hose just as the attendant dumped soil over the mess then leaned on his shovel, wiping his nose with the cuff of his filthy tunic, and sighing.

Anthony and I ducked among the stragglers around the theatre and slipped through its doors with the late arrivals. I paid the penny entrance fee for each of us. We were supposed to head straight for the pit where our penny would allow us to watch the performance among the commoners, but we were not there to be entertained. I led the way along a curving corridor that ran the circumference of the building. A few paces from the main doors, we came across a spiral staircase. Looking up, I could see it climbed to the top floor of the gallery, with openings leading off to every level before that.

I was not sure which way to go, but I knew we

had to find someone we could trust who worked here or at least knew the men who ran the theatre. Reaching the second level, I led Anthony through an opening and along the back of the gallery. It was packed with wealthier citizens seated on cushioned chairs. They had brought provisions and were drinking wine, joking and talking merrily, hardly paying attention to the play. We could see the stage from here. It was lit up with half a dozen torches and backed with a sumptuous red and gold cloth. On the stage a small group of players was gathered, each dressed in fine fabrics. At their centre stood a Persian warlord with his curved sword drawn. He had an evil face with a pointed beard and blackened eyes. He looked like the Devil incarnate. I pulled Anthony away from the spectacle and we moved quickly down the narrow passageway behind the gallery.

A few moments later we were behind the stage itself. Through a slender gap in the backdrop, I could see the audience. Many in the pit were rapt, drawn in by the drama unfolding before them. I turned away and noticed a door to our right. I nudged it open and took a step into a small, windowless room. A man was sitting at a table, his back to us. I caught a glimpse of coins and a pile of wooden boxes of the type used to collect the admission charge. The man spun round and reached for his dagger. I raised my hands and Anthony ducked under my arm.

The man glared at us. 'What do you want?' He stood up, his hand remaining close to his weapon.

'I'm sorry to disturb you,' I said. 'I . . . we are looking for Edmund and Edward Perch. I was told they would be here tonight.'

The man's eyes narrowed. 'I have no knowledge of these men.'

I knew he was lying but I was on shaky ground. The last thing I wanted was for this fellow to sound the alarm.

I bowed. 'Then I'm sorry to have troubled you,' I said, taking Anthony by the shoulders and turning him towards the door.

'Why do you seek the Perch brothers?' the man asked.

I was almost out of the door but glanced back and studied the man for the first time. He was tall and thin, almost bald on top but with long, dark hair hanging to either side of his bony face. 'It is a private business matter,' I said after a moment.

'Lucky you,' the man retorted, and fixed me suspiciously with his eyes. Then his expression softened. 'The brothers have done their business here for the night. They left but a short time ago . . . with their takings.' He was about to say something else when another man appeared at the door. He looked me up and down. I caught a glimpse of Anthony who had retreated a few paces along the passageway.

'Ah, Will,' the man in the box office said. 'These . . . gentlemen are looking for the brothers.'

The new arrival stared at me, one eyebrow raised. He was in his early-twenties and had the demeanour of an actor or entertainer of some sort. He was wearing the costume of a sailor. His face was painted and he was holding a sheaf of papers. He threw himself down into a chair beside the table and grabbed a jug of wine that had been standing close to the takings boxes. He swigged some, wiped his mouth and belched. 'They'll be at the Bear Garden,' he said. I was surprised by his voice. It was rich and resonant with a rustic accent. I guessed he had not been in the capital long, but had come from a town to the north of London. 'You a friend of theirs?'

'I wish to discuss a business arrangement with them.'

'Good luck,' he replied, echoing his friend. The two men exchanged a grim smile.

'You said they would be at the Bear Garden. I'm a visitor here. Where is that?'

'If I spat from the roof, I could reach it,' the young man replied, and nodded towards the stage. 'Just follow the stink. Best be quick, though,' he added. 'Our beloved audience flocks over there as soon as our performance is over . . . sometimes before, God curse them.'

Anthony and I reached the ground floor without meeting another soul, slipped through the main entrance and out into the night. The snow was coming down fast now, great flakes the size of thumbnails. I looked up and let them land on my face. They felt like tiny feathers that dissolved as they reached the warmth of my skin.

The young actor had been right about the smell. As we passed by the far side of the theatre we found ourselves downwind from the Bear Garden. The acrid animal stench hit us.

'I hate this place,' Anthony said, slowing his pace. 'They hurt animals. I don't want to go in.'

'Anthony, I have to find the brothers. Besides,

I cannot leave you to fend for yourself. The Pursuivants may still be searching for us.'

'But they hurt animals.'

'I know. Needs must . . .'

There was a commotion behind us. A woman screamed and I turned in time to see two men wrestling with a third wearing a shapeless brown tunic and black hose. He was struggling to break free but his two assailants were pulling him to the ground. In the struggle an elderly woman had been toppled into the snow. I recognised the man in brown from the chapel.

'Quick!' I hissed to Anthony, and pulled him none too gently away from the scene and towards the looming walls of the Bear Garden.

I tossed another couple of pennies into a wooden box at the door and we were in and merging with the crowds. A large elliptical arena occupied most of the space within the walls. A rickety-looking three-tiered stand had been built to circumvent the arena and this was packed with people yelling and screaming, the entire audience transfixed by what was happening. For a second, I became fascinated by the face of one particular spectator. His flabby cheeks were flushed, eyes wide, pupils huge. His lips were pulled back in a snarl, and a line of spittle had dribbled down from the corner of his gaping mouth and reached the bottom of his chin. Unheeded, the drool dangled there and formed a long, pale string that shook as he moved his head and shouted at the spectacle. His fists were clenched at his sides and he was punching the air with rapid, almost involuntary thrusts. I stopped staring at him and turned to see what was happening in the arena.

A bull was on its knees, roaring with pain as a mastiff gnawed at its neck. The dog's teeth, smeared with blood, flashed tarnished white, and a red spray flew up into its eyes. Two other dogs were gnashing at the bull. One sank its fangs into the animal's rump and the other attacked its flank. I heard Anthony squeal beside me and bury his face in my shoulder. I turned and led us away from the terrible sight. No one took the slightest notice of us, their minds focused entirely on the grisly entertainment.

As we reached the perimeter of the stands, a roar went up from the crowd. We didn't stop to find out what new obscenity had been committed but walked quickly along the circular passageway, low-walled and open to the falling snow. Rounding the bend, I almost collided with a huge man sitting on a stool to one side of a large door. He shot to his feet with surprising agility and blocked our way. He had a head not much smaller than the bull's in the arena, but his large, watery eyes looked almost benign. At first glance, his gigantic face had a childlike quality, but the effect was marred by a scar at least six inches long, running in a jagged red line from his left temple across his cheek to his mouth.

I looked back the way we had come and was about to retreat when Anthony took a step forward. 'Benjamin,' he said quietly.

The man ceased staring at me, peered at Anthony and broke into a gap-toothed smile. He placed a massive hand on Anthony's bony shoulder and made a low gurgling sound. It was then I noticed how slack his mouth was and realised this giant's tongue had been removed.

'He cannot speak,' Anthony said quickly, darting his gaze from me to Benjamin and back again. 'The devils cut out his tongue for criticising the new church.'

'Who is he?'

'Benjamin protects the brothers,' Anthony replied. 'He is my friend.'

'Well, why didn't you say before?' I snapped. The brute, who was still smiling at Anthony, turned to glare at me then. He took his hand from the boy's shoulder and I could see his fingers curl into a fist.

'No,' Anthony said gently, and pushed down on Benjamin's hand. 'Friend.'

'Can you take us to the brothers?' I asked, keeping a close eye on that massive fist.

Benjamin eyed me suspiciously then made one of his low, guttural sounds deep down in his throat.

'I need to speak with them. It is a matter of great urgency.'

Benjamin fixed me with those huge childlike eyes of his for a few moments. Then he shrugged, turned and opened the door into a darkened room. He nudged me to go in first. I took one step inside and was immediately grabbed about the neck by a strong arm. I felt cold steel at my throat and tried to speak, but my assailant's grip was like a vice. I brought my hands up, but the grip merely tightened. I was almost lifted off my feet and propelled across the room before being thrown to the floor. Anthony landed beside me and started to whimper.

I pulled myself up and helped the boy to his feet, putting a finger to his lips to prevent an outburst. We were in a small room, its walls draped with brightly coloured silks. A large sconce hung from the ceiling, holding a dozen or more white candles. The stone floor was covered with a sumptuous, patterned rug.

A few paces in front of us an enormously fat, bald man, dressed in purple silk, reposed on a velvet-covered couch. His ruff was lilac and he was wearing make-up like a stage performer, bright rouge on his cheeks and dark smudges beneath his small black eyes. He smiled and his whole face creased grotesquely. To either side of the man lay a pale-skinned, semi-naked young boy. But the most extraordinary thing about the fat man was the contraption he had in his mouth. It was a long slender tube with a bulb at one end. He was drawing on the narrow end and smoke was curling up from the bulbous bowl. The smell was like nothing I had ever experienced. It racked my throat, and I coughed involuntarily.

'Well, what have we here?' the man said, removing the contraption from his mouth. His voice was shrill and effeminate. He looked straight through us at the two men who had dragged Anthony and myself into the room so indecorously. Benjamin stepped between them. He made a strange sound from the bottom of his throat and the man on the couch studied us properly for the first time.

'Friends, Benjamin?' he said. 'Really? Well, what a wonderful and rare thing.' He waved one hand as he spoke, and I noticed he was wearing far too much jewellery: huge gold rings on each finger, and a thick, jewelled bracelet. 'What's your name?' he addressed me.

'I am John Allen,' I told him.

'And how may I be of assistance to you, Mr Allen?'

I heard one of the men behind us laugh. Anthony clutched my arm.

'I am looking for Edmund and Edward Perch. I was told they would be here this evening.'

'Oh? And what would be your business with those two gentlemen?'

I paused for a moment to take stock and held the fat man's eye. 'You are one of the brothers?'

'You have not answered my question . . . friend.'

'I am a trader visiting London on business. I arrived this morning with my friend, Sebastian

Mountjoy. If you are one of the brothers, you will have heard of our visit.'

'Perhaps I have,' the man said, a faint sardonic smile playing across his lips. 'Tell me, what is the nature of your business?'

'We are calamine importers.'

He nodded. 'And the whereabouts of your associate? We were told there would be two of you.'

I gave a heavy sigh and squared my shoulders. 'My friend was killed this evening,' I said quietly.

'How very unfortunate. And what of your monkey?' the man said softly, flicking his gaze towards Anthony. The two boys on the couch burst into giggles.

'If you cannot help me, then I would like to leave,' I replied.

'Bring him closer,' the fat man ordered, and I saw Anthony tugged to one side as the guards dragged me to within a few inches of the man on the couch. I could not stop myself from coughing. He rose to his feet and brought his face close to mine, blowing a plume of blueish smoke full into my face. My eyes stang and I felt my throat burning as I tried to cough away the smoke. Through the haze, I could see one of the pale-skinned boys guffawing. The fat man leaned closer and started sniffing me. Then, to my disgust, he flicked his tongue along the side of my neck, sat back down on the couch and smacked his lips.

'Mmm, I love the taste of fear,' he said, and clicked his fingers at the two guards. They let me go and I took a step back, wiping my neck with the back of one hand.

'Tell me, Friend John, what is it you want of us?'

'I was told you could help with our business venture.'

'And how do I know you are not a spy from the Queen's court, come to trap me and my brother?'

'How would a spy know the things of which I have spoken?'

'That would not be difficult. Walsingham's servants are unrelenting in their work. You know that well enough.'

'I might say the same to you, sir,' I replied with all the conviction I could muster. 'How do I know *you* are not a spy?'

The man stared at me, his face expression-less. Then he eased himself up from his couch and walked slowly towards me again. He stopped, looked down and grabbed my left hand, bringing it up to the light.

'So this is the ring,' he said. 'I was told it was a thing of beauty, but this . . . this is . . . Remove it.'

I yanked my hand away and one of the guards stepped forward. The fat man glared at him and he retreated. I saw the flash of a heavily jewelled hand and felt the touch of metal at my Adam's apple. Then a sharp pain. I gasped. Peering down, I could see an ornate dagger with a serrated edge. The tip had drawn blood that ran in a narrow stream down the blade.

'Edmund.' The voice was quiet, but sharper than the blade at my throat. The fat man turned his head lazily towards the door. I dared not move a muscle.

'Put the knife away,' the voice said.

It did not move.

'PUT IT AWAY.'

I felt the blade lift away from my throat and Edmund Perch took a step backwards, his eyes filled with malice. I turned to see a man standing beside the door. With him was Ann Doherty.

Anthony ran forward and threw his arms around her. 'My lady!' he squealed. 'My lady.'

And kissed her on each cheek. Ann hugged the boy and smiled wanly at me over his shoulder.

The man with her strode over to me. 'I apologise,' he said. 'Edmund is a little . . . theatrical. Are you not, dear brother?' Edward Perch gave his brother a contemptuous look.

I must have been in mild shock because, for a few moments, I could not put my words or thoughts in order. Instead I stared at the new arrival, barely able to imagine that he and Edmund Perch were indeed brothers. Edward was tall and well built with a full head of black hair. He might once have been handsome, but the years had ravaged his face. One of his eyelids drooped low, covering much of his left eye. His nose had been shattered at least once and a white line of scar tissue ran from septum to upper lip.

'Ann has told me all about your mission, Father,' Edward Perch told me. 'If you still seek my assistance, I'm here to offer it.'

Chapter 33

Stepney, Thursday 9 June, 3.30 p.m.

'Sorry, guv, but that thing bloody stinks,' Turner said, and opened the window on his side of the car as they swung off Mile End Road, heading south towards the river.

Pendragon gave a contemptuous shake of the head and took another bite from his baguette. 'Believe me, Sergeant, it's wonderful,' he said with his mouth full. He was starving and had been delighted to find a superb deli not a hundred metres from the station.

'What's in it? Smells like my dog's breath.'

Pendragon pulled a face and lowered the baguette to the paper wrapper on his lap. 'Charming. It's actually very fine Parma ham and Brie. I've found the ideal lunch spot.'

'You'll put on a stone in a month if you fall for that.'

'Very possibly. Tell me, what did you find out about the slippers?'

'Not much, I'm afraid. There are only two places in the country who use gold thread for their top-of-the-range dance shoe, and neither of them make men's sizes. I then took a look at makers of men's fancy slippers. Dress slippers, they call 'em. Versace sells them for over a thousand quid a pair, would you believe? Every place I tried imported them from Italy and France, but when I checked there I found they were actually manufactured in Thailand. Cheap labour. Makes you wonder what the mark-up must be, dunnit?'

'So that line of inquiry has run dry?'

'I think it has, guv. Unless you can come up with another angle? Whoever bought those slippers could have got them from a dozen places in London any time over the past thirty years. Or they could have bought them abroad. I think it's a dead end.'

'Yes, you're probably right,' Pendragon agreed. 'Do you know where you're going, by the way?'

It was the sergeant's turn to offer a contemptuous look, and Pendragon returned to the pleasures of his baguette. A few minutes later, they pulled off Commercial Road into a small industrial complex with warehouses and utilitarian low-rise brick office buildings lining a narrow access road. Murano Glass UK was one such building on the right, towards the end of the road. Its frontage consisted of closed warehouse shutters and a plain red door to one side. Pendragon rang the bell. An intercom crackled and a woman's voice said: 'Murano Glass.'

'DCI Pendragon. The station called through this morning. I've come to see the MD, Mr Sidney Gregson.'

There was a buzz and the door opened. Pendragon led the way into a brightly lit corridor. A woman's head appeared around an opening at the end and she beckoned to the two policemen. 'I've called Mr Gregson. Should be here in a moment,' she said as they came into the room. 'Please take a seat.'

Turner had just picked up a motor sports magazine from a coffee table when the door opened and Sidney Gregson came in. He was a well-dressed man in his mid-forties with a goatee and large red spectacles. He had 'moneyed bohemian' stamped all over him. 'Gentlemen,' he said with a smile. Pendragon introduced himself and the two men shook hands. Gregson turned as Jez walked over.

'Sergeant Turner.'

'Please, this way.'

They followed him out, Turner trailing behind. Glancing round, he caught the secretary giving

Gregson's retreating back a very black look. They entered a smart office and Gregson closed the door behind them. Cabinets filled with exotic glass sculptures lined one wall, a large limed oak desk filled the far end of the room, and a plush suede sofa stood to its left. Gregson threw himself into a huge leather swivel chair. He didn't offer the policemen a seat. Picking up a crystal paperweight, he tossed it casually from palm to palm.

'Thank you for seeing us at such short notice, Mr Gregson,' Pendragon said.

'The person who made the appointment mentioned that you were investigating the Stepney murders. I saw a report on TV last night. I can't imagine what you would want here, Chief Inspector.'

'Two of the victims were poisoned. Preliminary analysis indicated one of the major constituents of the poison used is arsenic.'

The MD knitted his eyebrows. 'So you immediately thought of glass-makers?' There was a sarcastic edge to his voice. Pendragon very quickly decided he didn't much like Sidney Gregson.

'Arsenic and arsenic compounds are controlled substances,' the DCI replied. 'As you would know, you can't just pop into a shop and buy some.'

'That's quite true, Inspector. So you think your poisoner works here?'

Pendragon gave Gregson a puzzled look. 'Not at all. But the arsenic had to come from somewhere. Have you had any chemicals stolen from the foundry?'

'I can give you a pretty unequivocal no on that,' Gregson replied smoothly, halting the paperweight-tossing for a second. 'But would you like me to check with the stores manager, just to make sure?'

'That would be helpful.'

'Let's go.'

They turned right out of the office, away from reception, and down a flight of stairs. A swing door opened on to the foundry floor. It was a relatively small space, but filled with activity. A group of workmen stood along one wall, grinding some sort of powder using large pestles. Beside them was a large machine that had the appearance of an enormous food processor. A furnace took up most of the centre of the floor. At its mouth stood a burly man wearing a heavy leather apron, protective gloves, and a visor pulled down over his face. In his hands he held a long metal pole. A large blob of orange-red molten glass extended from the far end of the pole. As Gregson and the two policemen passed, the glass worker leaned over and twirled the metal pole. The molten glass shifted and changed shape like melting toffee. Beside the furnace, another man in similar clothes but with his visor up over his head was stirring a brightly coloured substance in a large metal tub.

'We make top-end stemware here,' Gregson explained. 'Wine glasses primarily. But we also accept private commissions for figurines and vases. We're a boutique manufacturer, we only produce a few thousand hand-crafted pieces a year.'

'How many staff do you have?' Turner asked as they passed into a glass-sided passageway that ran the length of the foundry, well away from the dangers of the furnace.

'Fourteen,' Gregson replied. 'That includes admin staff and drivers. We have three master glass-makers. The chap you see there is Tom Kanelly – almost a celebrity in his world. And the man stirring the treacle-like stuff is Francesco Donalti. He's what's called a "hot metal man". He's one of the top colourists in the trade. Actually worked on Murano for ten years. We're very lucky to have him.'

At the end of the corridor, they came to a door with a sign that read: CHEMICAL STORE. AUTHORISED PERSONNEL ONLY. It was a small, square, window-less room lined with metal shelves, a single spartan wooden bench standing the middle. A man in white overalls was sitting at a computer terminal. He stood up as Gregson entered.

'Alec, where's Daniel?' Gregson asked him.

'Daniel Beatty is our storeman,' he added, turning back towards the two police officers. 'This is Alec who helps out here a couple of days a week.' Gregson's tone was dismissive. Then, to Alec, he said, 'This is DCI Pendragon and Sergeant Turner. They think we might have been supplying arsenic to undesirables.'

Alec was in his early-twenties. He wore thick-framed glasses and had greasy hair worn in a side-parting. 'A-a-arsenic?' he stammered. 'We d-d-d-on't use that m-m-much.'

'It doesn't take a lot to kill someone,' Pendragon retorted.

Alec flushed. 'N-n-n-o. That's r-r-right.'

'So where is Daniel?' Gregson repeated impatiently.

'He's p-p-popped out f-f-for a late l-l-lunch.'

Gregson looked at his watch and sighed. 'Okay, Alec, could you just confirm for these gentlemen that we have not mislaid any arsenic trioxide?'

'Yes. I-I-I m-m-mean, n-n-n-o.'

'See over here, Inspector,' Gregson said, pointing to a toughened glass box with a combination lock. Inside could just be seen a small collection of brown bottles. On the front of the glass box there was a sign: DANGER — CONTROLLED SUBSTANCES. EXTREME CAUTION. FOR USE BY AUTHORISED PERSONNEL

ONLY. HAZCHEM LEVEL 2. 'This is where we keep the most hazardous chemicals. Arsenic trioxide is not just a poison, it's extremely carcinogenic. Only Daniel knows the combination . . . and I myself, of course.'

'Could we take a look at your inventory?' Turner asked him.

'Oh, for goodness' sake, man!'

'It should be an easy matter, should it not, Mr Gregson? It would be computerised, surely?' Pendragon insisted.

'Yes, very well. Alec, can you pull up the files?'

The young storeman tapped at the keyboard and quickly brought up the appropriate screen. Gregson nudged him aside and took up position in front of the monitor. 'Here we are,' he said. 'We had a fifty kilo delivery of arsenic trioxide from Toulouse in March. As Alec said, we use relatively little. High-quality glass has nothing like the arsenic content of the cheap stuff. Here are the daily uses throughout April and May. We had a second delivery on May the twenty-third. Take a look. Everything's accounted for.'

Turner studied the figures for a moment and then nodded to Pendragon.

'Well, thank you, Mr Gregson. We won't trouble you any further,' said the DCI.

Gregson showed them to the main entrance to the building. 'I'm glad we couldn't be any more helpful. If you see what I mean,' he said, closing the door.

'Lovely man,' Turner remarked as they walked across a small parking area towards the car.

'DCI Pendragon?'

The two policemen turned in unison. The secretary from the glass company was striding towards them. She kept glancing over her shoulder.

'I have to be quick,' she hissed. 'I know why you're here. We *did* have a break-in – two weeks ago. *He* was away on one of his fancy holidays.'

'He being Mr Gregson?' Turner asked.

'Obviously.'

'Why didn't someone report it?'

'We did. I did. I phoned Limehouse police station on May the twenty-fifth.'

'And you felt you couldn't tell the boss?' Turner queried.

'Were you born a genius or have you had to work at it?' the secretary snapped in reply. Turner was speechless. 'Alec is my son. He's . . . well, he's very bright, but he has problems. Gregson thinks he's a retard. He only gave him the job to shut me up. Oh, don't look so shocked, Sergeant,' she said, breaking into a grin. 'Women like me learn to use every weapon in the arsenal.' She glanced behind her again.

'Dan covered for us and we all chipped in to repair the lock – it was forced open. Look, I have to go.'

Pendragon caught her by the elbow and held it gently. 'Sorry, but what's your name?'

'Lydia. Lydia Darlinghurst.'

'Lydia, I'm a little confused. You had a break-in on . . . what? . . . the twenty-fourth?'

'Yes.'

'And the only thing taken was some arsenic trioxide?'

'Yes.'

'How much went?'

'Just one small jar of a hundred grams.'

'We'll have to check with Limehouse.'

'You do that, Chief Inspector. I'm no liar.' She looked over her shoulder again, then fixed Pendragon with a hard stare. 'You will keep this quiet, won't you? You have your information. If that bastard learns . . .'

Pendragon touched his nose and let go of Lydia's elbow. Without another word she ran back to the building.

' "Oh, what a tangled web we weave",' Pendragon said, opening the door to the squad car.

The DCI arrived in the briefing room ten minutes before the others. He brought a freshly filtered cup of his preferred Bolivian blend with him and was busy reading up about the Borgia family on Wikipedia. Jez Turner was the first of the team to arrive.

'You're not supposed to download from iTunes on police time, you know, sir,' he said, seeing Pendragon at the computer.

'I'll remember that, Sergeant.'

'What you up to?'

'Taking a lead from you this morning and doing some research on the Borgias. Remember I mentioned them yesterday after I saw Professor Stokes? His theory about the bishop ring once owned by the family?'

'Yeah, I do. But, well . . . what of it?'

Pendragon sighed and sat back in his chair, holding his cup above his crossed knees. 'It wasn't owned by just any old family, Sergeant. The Borgias . . .'

Turner looked blank.

'For Christ's sake, why do I bother paying my taxes? There's no bloody education system left! The Borgias were one of history's most notorious families, at the peak of their influence in the late-fifteenth century. The head of the family, Rodrigo Borgia, became Pope Alexander VI. His son was Cesare Borgia . . . ring any bells? No? Of course not! He was what you'd call a warlord, and vicious with it. In fact, the Borgias were a sort of Renaissance

Mafia, super-rich and very, very unpleasant. And the Pope's daughter, Cesare's sister Lucrezia, was perhaps the worst of them all: spoilt, cruel, a nymphomaniac and murderess . . .'

Turner looked interested suddenly. 'What? Like a psycho Renaissance Paris Hilton?'

'Paris who?'

'You *are* joking?' Turner gave Pendragon an incredulous look.

The DCI's mobile rang.

'Detective Chief Inspector Pendragon?'

'Ah, good evening, Dr Newman . . .'

'I've just put down the phone on a Professor Stokes.'

'Ah, yes, I should have called you. I'm sorry. I forgot.'

'He claims you told him he could have samples of the skeleton?'

'I said no such thing,' Pendragon replied, pulling a face at Turner. Meanwhile Sergeant Mackleby and Inspector Rob Grant walked in and sat down.

'But he . . .'

'Dr Newman, if I may interrupt? Professor Stokes has actually been very useful to us and has some interesting ideas about the skeleton. He asked if we could loan him one of the bones. I think he called it a . . .'

'A proximal phalanx. Yes, I know.'

'Is there any particular problem with letting Stokes take a look?'

There was silence at the other end of the line.

'You do have the rest of the skeleton?' Pendragon added hopefully.

'All right, Chief Inspector,' Dr Newman said in her crispest, most official tones. Then, more gently: 'As a personal favour to you, this Professor Stokes can have the bone for twenty-four hours. Is that good enough?'

'Thank you,' Pendragon said, and frowned at the phone for a moment, puzzled, before hanging up.

The team sat in a rough semi-circle, with Pendragon in a chair in front of the smart board at its focal point. 'Would you like to go first, Rob?' he said, turning to Inspector Grant who had Roz Mackleby sitting beside him.

Grant cleared his throat. 'Can't pretend we learned much, sir. We spent over an hour with Pam Ketteridge, and I can honestly say I left knowing nothing more than I did when we got there. I hate to agree with Sergeant Turner on anything,' he added, glancing at Jez, 'but he's right. The bloody woman's as nutty as squirrel shit.'

'Sergeant, do you agree?' Pendragon glanced at Roz Mackleby.

'Well, the facts are these, sir. She was upstairs in bed when her husband was murdered. Her dabs are all over the kitchen, as you would expect. There's no DNA evidence she killed Tony. No prints of hers on him. And, most importantly, no murder weapon. That said, she is the only suspect we have, and with a good motive – plainly an unhappy marriage.'

'Yeah, but there's also the religion crap,' Vickers said.

'We've already gone over this, Terry,' Mackleby sighed. 'It's not against the law to fill your house with crucifixes.'

Vickers shook his head but said nothing in reply.

'There is also the business with the skeleton,' Ken Towers suggested.

'What about it?' growled Grant.

'Maybe she got so upset by what Tony had done with the remains . . .'

'Oh, rubbish,' snapped Grant. 'No, the only likely motive would have been if she had found out about her husband's fancy woman. The slapper . . . what's her name?'

'Hannah James,' Pendragon said quietly, staring into space. He turned to Mackleby. 'Did you raise the subject of the girlfriend?'

'I didn't want to add to the poor woman's misery. But Inspector Grant asked a few leading questions.'

Pendragon glanced at Grant.

'I asked her if she suspected her husband of having an affair at any time.'

'And how did she react?'

'She laughed.'

'Confident woman.'

'Crazy, more like.'

'Okay,' Pendragon said. 'We may have to call her in and probe a bit deeper. Maybe we'll have to tell her about Hannah. See how she reacts. Ken, what's the story with Bridgeport Construction?'

'Not much, I'm afraid, sir. I interviewed Ketteridge's boss and *his* boss. Both of them have alibis which I've checked out. They're clear. The company has over three hundred employees, and of those twenty-eight are involved with the Frimley Way project in some capacity – building, management, admin. The company has its own surveyors, structural engineers, and guys who liaise with the council over building regs and approvals. Looks like the only outside firms they employ are architects.'

'Which brings us to Rainer and Partner. But they had nothing directly to do with Karim or Ketteridge except that their company was designing the building due to go up at Frimley Way,' Pendragon said. He turned to Vickers and Thatcher, sitting together at one of the tables in the middle of the semi-circle. 'Please tell me you have something positive to report?'

''Fraid not, guv,' Sergeant Thatcher replied. 'Absolutely no trace of the ring.'

Pendragon folded his arms across his chest and looked down at the floor. 'Okay, get home,' he said with a sigh. 'Maybe we should all sleep on it.'

Leaving the briefing room last, Pendragon turned into the corridor leading to reception and the main doors. He saw Superintendent Hughes shaking hands with a tall man in top brass uniform. Pendragon immediately recognised him as the divisional head, Commander Francis Ferguson. The Super turned, head down, and walked towards Pendragon, only glancing up at him when she was a few paces away. 'Ah, just the person I wanted to see,' she said, and indicated her office.

She sashayed around her pristine desk and lowered herself into her chair. Without being asked, Pendragon took the chair on the other side of the desk. He suddenly felt dog-tired.

'That was the Commander,' she said unnecessarily.

'I noticed.'

'I'm in line for promotion. He just came by to give me some advance warning.'

'Congratulations,' Pendragon replied with as much enthusiasm as he could muster.

'Thank you. Just one problem, Jack. The Commander's getting a bit antsy about what the media have dubbed "The Mile End Murders". If you don't get this case solved pronto, I can say *au revoir* to that Chief Super's job. And I *really* don't want to do that . . . Jack.'

'I'm doing my best. We all are.'

'So, what's happening?'

He sighed and ran his fingers over his forehead. 'It seems clear the three murders are connected. The skeleton is the common link between them, but we don't have any idea exactly how it's involved. Middleton and Ketteridge were definitely murdered by the same person, but they have been extremely professional. Forensics have almost nothing to go on. There's no murder weapon, no prints, no DNA.'

Hughes sat with her fingers pressed against her chin. 'No one in the frame?' she asked.

'No.'

'What about Pam Ketteridge?'

'You seem to be fixated on the woman,' Pendragon replied coldly. 'She's a slightly demented housewife. I don't really think she could have battered Amal Karim to death.'

'But she could have poisoned the latest victims.

She was right there at the scene for the murder of Tony Ketteridge. No alibi. And if she knew about her husband's affair with the prostitute, she would have a motive.'

'Yes, ma'am, but there's absolutely no evidence. And what about Karim? There has to be a link between the three murders . . .'

There was a knock at the door then and a young constable appeared in the doorway. 'Sorry, ma'am. I saw DCI Pendragon come in just now. There's a fax for him, marked urgent.' He took a few paces into the room and handed two sheets of fax paper to the DCI.

'What is it?' Hughes asked Pendragon as the constable closed the door.

'The tox report for Ketteridge. An almost exact copy of the one for Middleton.' He handed it to her.

'Same four components: arsenic, cantharidin, abric acid, and oleander,' she said. 'Have you found out anything more about them?'

'That's one area that has opened up. At least a little. Dr Jones tells me cantharidin can be found easily on the internet even though it is legislated against. This afternoon I had a breakthrough with the arsenic. A one-hundred-gram bottle of arsenic trioxide was taken from a boutique glass-maker less than a mile from here. Enough poison to kill hundreds.'

'It was never reported?'

'Yes, to the local station, Limehouse.'

'Could the thief be an employee? The owner?'

'It's possible, although the owner himself was out of the country when the theft happened. Turner's checking it out. There was a bit of a cover-up at the glass foundry. The owner's pretty obnoxious and not very popular with the staff. They closed ranks, said nothing about the break-in to protect the son of the receptionist, a young lad who works in the storeroom.'

'That's a bit odd, isn't it?'

'Not really. If you'd met the characters involved, you'd see it makes perfect sense. The owner, Gregson, thinks he's really something. The kid who would have been blamed, and no doubt sacked, is . . . vulnerable.'

'Vulnerable?'

'Mildly autistic, I think. Has an extremely bad stutter.' As the words left Pendragon's lips, he thought of his own son, Simon. How his incredible mathematical talents were counterbalanced by an inability to communicate easily with people.

'All right. It may be worth Turner looking a little deeper into this glass company. Then we're down to the other two chemicals in the poison, oleander and abric acid. You said in your report that these both came from exotic plants. You've obviously checked Kew?'

'After we learned what killed Middleton. Turner's been on to the people there – nothing. He's also called Chelsea Physic Garden, and our local botanic garden, Queen's Park. They all say nothing like that has gone missing. Although, to be honest, ma'am, it doesn't help us much. It wouldn't be too hard for someone to slip in and steal a few leaves or seeds. Jones tells me the poison needs only tiny amounts of those substances.'

'And you've been to the Plant Biology Department at Queen Mary, of course?'

Pendragon gave her a puzzled look.

'You haven't?'

'I wasn't aware . . .'

'Well, now you are, Inspector,' Hughes retorted coolly. Pendragon got up to go. As he reached the door, the Super announced: 'You have forty-eight hours to get a result, DCI Pendragon. Then I'm taking you off the case.'

Jack Pendragon felt numb as he left the station and began the short drive to his flat off Stepney Way. What bad luck, he mused, to be in a new job less than a week and be slapped with such a complex and intractable case. It started to rain as he parked. In the time it took for him to run from the car to the front door of the house, it had really begun to pelt down. He was about to take the stairs when he thought better of it.

'Well, hello, stranger,' Sue Latimer said, opening her door wide and beckoning him in.

'I'm sorry I've been so elusive,' he replied. 'It's been . . . well . . .'

She waved her hand. 'Don't worry. You're here now. Fancy a glass of wine?'

'I'd love one.'

He walked inside her flat, peeling off his wet jacket and sat down on the sofa. Sue came over and handed him a glass of red.

'Cheers,' he said.

'So, how's it going?'

Pendragon sighed. 'Not great, actually. Sue, the other evening, you were telling me about something you called transference. The idea that the murderer needs the ring. But then I had to dash off.'

'Another murder?'

'Yes. The MO was identical. But forensics can find nothing.'

'Nothing at all?'

'You're asking that as if you already know the answer.'

'Trust me . . . I'm a psychologist.'

Pendragon laughed and took a sip of wine. Then he said, 'Sue, I have two requests.'

'Oh?'

'Would you be willing to spare half an hour to come into the station to talk to the team – tell us your ideas about transference? That way, I can get the all-clear to let you have access to information about the investigation that lies outside the public domain – you'll have an official role.'

She looked surprised. 'Well, okay. It's not really my area of expertise, but . . .'

'You sound to me like you know what you're talking about. Besides, I thought I had to trust you.'

'*Touché*. Okay, I'll do whatever I can to help. And the second thing?'

'Will you have dinner with me on Saturday night?'

Chapter 34

Stepney, Thursday 9 June, 9.05 p.m.

Max Rainer closed the document he had been working on and logged out of the network. Standing up from his desk, he paced to the other side of the office where a tan leather four-seater sofa stood against the wall. Picking up his laptop from the sofa, he slipped it into a sleek, neoprene pouch and zipped it up. Taking one final glance around the office, he flicked off the lights then closed and locked the door.

It was silent in the reception area. Along the corridor, three other smaller offices stood in darkness. The reception desk was empty. In the pale light, the words 'Rainer and Partner' could be seen on the wall behind the counter. Each letter was a foot tall and made from artfully distressed metal streaked randomly in fifty shades of iron oxide.

The terrazzo floor echoed to the click of his heels as Rainer crossed reception and passed through a pair of large smoked-glass doors. Opposite the dimly lit lobby, a single flight of stairs led to the ground floor. He turned to lock the doors and felt a sharp pain at the base of his skull. The pain seemed to shimmer over the top of his head and down his spine. He was vaguely aware of a shape behind him, reflected in the glass door. He stumbled forward. Smashed his head hard against the doors and collapsed to the floor.

Chapter 35

Stepney, Friday 10 June, 8.45 a.m.

'Oh, Christ,' Hannah James exclaimed. 'What the fuck do you want?'

Jez Turner lowered his police ID. 'Just a quick chat, Hannah.'

'You do 'ave a warrant, I take it?'

'What for? I said a chat. Of course, if you'd prefer to come down to the station . . .'

'Okay, okay. Fuck! We are a little early bird, ain't we? Bet you're all nicely tucked up in bed by nine with a glass of milk.'

'Yeah, something like that.' Turner grinned. 'So, you going to let me in or do you want to chat here on the doorstep?'

Number sixteen Mitchell Lane was a crumbling, detached Victorian building that had been converted into half a dozen tatty flats. Hannah James's was at the back of the house, on the ground floor. It was just a clutch of rooms off a dark hallway. She led Sergeant Turner through to the lounge. He caught a glimpse of a tiny kitchen, sink filled with dirty plates and saucepans, bin overflowing with McDonald's cartons and Coke bottles. Next to that, the door to the bedroom stood open. A mirror hung over one end of the bed; a bedside table had a lamp with a red shade. One wall was plastered with pictures from hard-core porn mags, and on a rail hung a collection of frilly translucent garments in red and black. The air was heavy with the stink of cigarettes and bodily fluids. Hannah kicked shut the door as she passed.

The lounge had an old TV in one corner. On the far wall there was a fireplace boarded up with slats of pine. A two-bar electric heater had been built into the panels, slightly off-centre, the thin plywood cut ineptly around it. On the mantelpiece stood a collection of cheap plaster animals: unicorns, puppies, an Ewok from *Star Wars*, and a set of Russian dolls descending in size from left to right. Above the mantelpiece hung a painting of a brown-skinned woman, naked but for skimpy leopardskin bikini bottoms. She lay along a branch, exotic ferns brushing her skin. She had huge brown eyes and ridiculously long lashes. It was the sort of painting you could pick up for two quid at the weekend market on Mile End Road, Jez thought, and about on a par with the photo of the tennis player scratching her arse. Surveying the room, he wondered what Hannah would have thought of Sophie Templer's place, only a couple of miles away but light years distant in every other respect.

Hannah threw herself into an old armchair with stuffing spilling from a gash along the top of one of the armrests. 'You're here because of Tony, of course.' Hannah lit a cigarette and blew a plume of smoke into the stuffy room.

'Yes.'

'Why do you think I can help?'

'Because you knew him well. You had been "seeing each other" for a something like a year, he told us.'

'Why do you say it like that?' Hannah asked, fixing Jez with pale blue eyes.

'Like what?' he said.

'With such contempt. I really liked Tony. He was a fuckin' idiot, of course. Christ knows what he was doing here twice a week. But then I've known a few like him, but not so long-lasting . . . if you see what I mean.'

For the first time, the sergeant studied her properly. She was twenty-three, maybe twenty-four, he thought, and pale to the point of looking ill. Her black hair had little sheen to it, and in the harsh morning light, with no make-up on, she looked really rough. Her skin was greasy from the fast food, Coke and fags, not to mention other stuff she was probably smoking or injecting. She was wearing a hideous beige needlecord dressing gown, frayed at the sleeves and stained. Not at all her usual attire when men came a-calling, he speculated.

'Do you know if Tony was into anything he shouldn't have been into?'

'What? Apart from me, you mean . . . *Sergeant*?'

Turner could tell there was pain behind her bravura. Hannah was genuinely cut up by what had happened to Tony, but she couldn't admit it. 'He was poisoned with arsenic,' the sergeant said. 'Did you know that?'

She said nothing, but held his gaze.

'A very painful death, apparently.'

'You fucker!' Hannah exclaimed, lighting another cigarette from the dying embers of the last one. 'As I said, I *really* liked Tony. Yes, he was a fat, middle-aged dreamer, but he loved me. At least, he told me he did. He certainly didn't love that fuckin' lump of lard!'

'Pam Ketteridge?'

'Who else? The lovely Pam. No clit apparently. At least that's what Tony told me.'

Turner was shaking his head and grinning. 'So,'

he said after a moment, 'did he promise to take you away from all this?'

'Of course,' Hannah said, her voice rising angrily. 'At least twice a night. As I said, a fuckin' idiot.'

'Hannah,' Jez said, and waited for her to stop staring at the ceiling and meet his eye, 'you could help us find Tony's killer, you know?'

'Yeah?'

'Yeah. We think he was involved in the other murders.'

'Tony was a teddy bear, Sergeant Turner. He couldn't have killed anyone.'

'I'm not saying he did. I said, involved. That CCTV footage of him close to the time Amal Karim was killed . . . it seems a bit of a coincidence he was coming to see you then.'

'Why? Do you think he could just pop out for a quickie straight after his fish and chips?'

'Two in the morning, though. It's an odd time, Hannah.'

'Look, I don't know what you're driving at. Whatever happened last Friday, it won't tell you who killed Tony, will it?'

'It might.'

She stared at him for several seconds then started to consider the ceiling again. A tear ran down her cheek and dripped on to the floor. She wiped it away and looked at him. 'He wasn't here. I made it up. Tony begged me to. Said it was life or death.' She laughed bitterly then and drew deeply on her cigarette.

'Did he say what "life and death" meant?'

'No.'

'Did he say where he really was?'

'NO!' Hannah snubbed out her cigarette and stood up. The dressing gown fell open to reveal a long cotton nightdress covered with kittens and baby rabbits. She quickly pulled the robe back into place and tied the belt. 'I want you to go now,' she said, her voice suddenly brittle. At the door, she added, 'I s'pose you'll be doing me for falsifying my statement, wasting police time, the whole fuckin' works, right?'

Jez gave her a compassionate look. 'Right now, we have bigger fish to fry, Hannah. I wouldn't lose any sleep over it.'

Chapter 36

Stepney, Friday 10 June, 10.00 a.m.

'This is Dr Sue Latimer,' Pendragon told the team before introducing each of them in turn. 'Sue is a psychology lecturer at Queen Mary. I've asked her in today because she has some ideas about criminal motivation that might help our thinking.' He waved to her to take over and sat down on the edge of a desk.

'The subject came up when I was talking to Jack . . . er, DCI Pendragon . . . about the idea of transference,' she began. 'I was describing it in the abstract really, but now that I've seen the case notes for this series of murders, I realise it may well be of relevance to the investigation.' She looked at the faces of the people gathered in the briefing room. The whole team was there, including the Super.

'Criminal transference is the idea that someone commits murder using some totemistic object . . .'

'Sorry, Dr Latimer, could we have that in English, please?' Inspector Towers interrupted.

Sue smiled and looked at the floor for a second. 'By "totemistic", I mean that the killer places some special significance on an object. It might be anything, but it is directly related to the means by which they commit the crime. In the case of these recent homicides, the latest two have practically identical MOs. All three murders appear to be linked to Bridgeport Construction, and all have happened since the ancient skeleton was unearthed on the construction site.'

'So you're saying the skeleton is the totemistic object?' Grant said.

'Not the skeleton itself, the ring that was originally on its hand and has since vanished.'

Grant raised his eyebrows and looked across at Pendragon. 'But how can a ring be a murder weapon? Besides, Middleton and Ketteridge were poisoned.'

Sue was unruffled by this scepticism. 'I would suggest the poison is in the ring.' A stunned silence fell over the room at this. 'In fact, a ring is a perfect totem. It's a personal object, a thing that is kept close to the body. But, most importantly, rings usually possess some form of emotional resonance. They are used in many rituals to "seal the deal" – just think of a wedding ring.'

'I'm sorry,' Towers commented, 'I'm afraid you've lost me again. The ring that was originally on the skeleton was presumably at least as old as the skeleton itself. But you're saying that somebody today, living and working somewhere near here, is using that ancient ring to poison people? It sounds . . . well . . . far-fetched to say the least.'

'I think it's the best model we have to work on,' announced Superintendent Hughes from the back of the room. All of them except Pendragon turned towards her. 'It gives us a murder weapon, of sorts. It links in with the unearthing of the skeleton, and it's at least a step along the road to a motive. It also suggests why Karim's murder doesn't fit the pattern of the later two homicides. It can't be pure coincidence that he was killed the night the skeleton was unearthed. And if Dr Latimer's theory is correct, then his murder at least was unplanned. He simply got in the way of our killer acquiring the ring.'

'But how could our contemporary murderer first of all know about the ring being discovered and then so quickly learn what to do with it – acquire four poisons, the works?' Turner asked. 'Isn't *that* too much of a coincidence?'

'I can't answer your question,' Sue responded. 'There's not enough information as yet. I have no idea what the psychological connection between the ring and the murderer might be. I can, though, offer clues to the sort of mind that would be susceptible to criminal transference.'

'Please do,' Hughes told her.

'The killer could be male or female. Indeed, women are more likely to be drawn to totems . . .'

'But if our killer is a woman, how could she have overpowered Karim and bashed his skull in?' Mackleby interrupted.

'I'm just generalising,' Sue responded. 'Obviously, each situation has to be judged separately. It's conceivable Karim was killed by a male accomplice, but I think that's extremely unlikely. Totemistic murder is a *very* personal matter. Two people never share a totem. The only way the accomplice scenario could play out is if a woman, for the sake of argument, used a man to kill Karim but went on to commit the two poisonings herself.'

'I think we're getting off the point here,' Hughes said. 'Doctor, could you go back to your profile?'

Sue took a deep breath. 'The killer is intelligent, sophisticated, well educated, possibly homosexual – though that is not a prerequisite. And they wrap up the process of murder in layers of personal ritual.'

'What does that mean exactly?' Sergeant Vickers asked. 'There hasn't been a ritualistic element to the murders.'

'Not that we've seen. We're not talking about positioning the bodies in a certain way or writing symbols on them. I said "personal ritual". The murderer goes through a process to which they adhere religiously. They'll prepare the poison under special conditions, following a formula. And they'll probably dress up when they're committing the murders.'

'Dress up?' Pendragon queried, frowning.

'Yes. I have no idea what form that could take. Every documented case I have read is different. The best-known is actually fictitious – Norman Bates in *Psycho*. His mother was his totem. He could only kill when he dressed up as her. The rest of the time he was a placid guy who ran a motel. Hitchcock went to extremes there. It's very unusual for the killer to use a person as a totem, and to *become* that totem. But, that said, the link between the murderer and the totem is always a very strong one.'

'The gold thread and the slippers,' Pendragon said suddenly, glancing around the room at the faces of his team. 'If wearing gold footwear isn't dressing up, I don't know what is.'

'I really appreciate your coming in, Sue,' Pendragon told her.

'Don't mention it.'

They were in his office with the door closed.

'At least it should get the team thinking outside the box,' she concluded.

'Well, that's right. Oh, I almost forgot.' Pendragon bent down to retrieve a plastic bag lying against the leg of his desk. 'I bought you this,' he said, removing a vinyl LP. 'Just a little thank you for sparing the time . . .'

'Jack! You didn't need to do that.'

'I hope you like it. Charlie Parker, *Jazz at Massey Hall*, his first record. This is an early pressing from 1956.'

Sue studied the cover, beaming. 'I love this album.'

There was silence for a moment. Jack tapped her arm. She looked up.

'You don't have a record player, do you?'

'No,' she said, head tilted to one side. They both laughed.

'It's the thought that counts,' she said, and kissed him on the lips.

Chapter 37

The Department of Plant Biology at Queen Mary College was on the sixth floor, one down from the top. As Pendragon ascended in the lift he remembered an old adage from his university days: engineering departments were always put in the basement so their heavy machines couldn't fall through the floor. Chemistry departments were put on the top floor so that if anything exploded it wouldn't damage anything above it. With some satisfaction, he noticed from the floor directory inside the lift that the departments were exactly where they should be – engineers in the basement, chemists on the top floor.

He was met by a tall man wearing a lab coat. Pendragon guessed he was in his mid-thirties. He was unusually handsome, with jet-black hair cut short, a narrow face and large, dark eyes. A three-day stubble gave him the look of a movie star trying to look rugged.

'DCI Pendragon,' he said. 'My name's Frampton, Adrian Frampton.' He had his hand out and shook Pendragon's hand with a firm grip before leading him into the lab.

Pendragon surveyed the large room and was struck by the fact that, to his untrained eye at least, all laboratories looked the same, with just the details changed from place to place. He had been in three laboratories during the past couple of days, and whether they were places devoted to forensics, archaeology or plant biology, they all had benches, pristine scrubbed floors, Bunsen burners, racks of test tubes, and a certain chemical smell that seemed to seep from the walls.

'So, how can I help you, Chief Inspector?' Frampton enquired. 'I imagine it's something to do with the Mile End Murders.'

Pendragon pulled a face. How he hated the way the media trivialised *everything*. 'Yes,' he said. 'It is to do with a series of crimes linked by the use of a particular poison. The police tox lab has isolated two rare chemicals in the poison that derive from rather unusual plants, not indigenous to this country.'

'What are they?'

'Abric acid and oleander.'

Adrian Frampton raised an eyebrow. 'Very exotic,' he said. 'Abric acid is from *Abrus precatorius*.'

'The Paternoster Pea.'

'That's right,' Frampton replied, a little surprised. 'The other is from the Jericho Rose. What are you hoping to discover?'

'If any lab or botanical garden has lost some plants recently.'

'We've never had either plant here.'

'Really?' Pendragon looked disappointed. 'I know they're rare, but . . .'

'There are a lot of plants in the world, Chief Inspector. Have you contacted Kew, or down the road at Queen's Park?'

'Yes, we have.'

The door to the lab swung open at that moment. Pendragon turned and saw a very large man wearing a lab coat that barely came down past his sides. It was Nigel Turnbull, aka MC Jumbo from The Love Shack. He saw Pendragon, turned and ran.

The DCI reacted with lightning speed, setting off in immediate pursuit. Turnbull was extremely overweight, but he knew his way around the college. By the time Pendragon reached the hallway beyond the lab, he had disappeared.

Pendragon ran to the top of the stairs and looked down, but there was no sign of his quarry. Surveying the hall, he noticed an Emergency Exit sign and ran towards it, pulling out his mobile as he went.

Stabbing two numbers for speed-dial, he was straight through to the station. 'Immediate back-up required,' he said, pushing through the emergency door. 'I'm in pursuit of a white male, about twenty years old, morbidly obese, bald. Last seen wearing a white lab coat over jeans and a dark top.'

He was in the emergency stairwell. Peering over the side, he saw a hand moving down a rail several floors below and heard the clatter of heavy feet taking the stairs at speed. 'Target is Nigel Turnbull,' Pendragon added as he leapt down the first flight of stairs. 'Approach with caution.' He heard the thump of a door crashing shut on the ground floor. 'Contact Sergeant Turner immediately and get a couple of cars over to Turnbull's address. It's on file. Out.'

He clipped shut the phone and swung round the landing. Then stopped. He leaned forward, hands on knees, trying to catch his breath. He was over this sort of policing, he thought to himself. Straightening, he climbed back up the stairs and emerged into the hallway on the sixth floor. Adrian Frampton was standing outside the lab with another man by his side.

'What the hell's happening?' Frampton asked.

'I'm afraid I'm going to have to close off this lab while my people go over it,' Pendragon replied.

'What? Are you mad? We're doing important . . .'

'I'm sorry, Dr Frampton.'

'But this is outrageous. You'll need a warrant. Besides, I can't authorise it.'

'Dr Frampton, this is a very serious investigation. One of your team, the young man who was just here . . .'

'Turnbull? What of him?'

'He moonlights as a DJ at a club near here where the first body was discovered less than a week ago. Now he turns up, sees me and runs. I think that's a bit suspicious, don't you?'

'But what has it got to do with us?'

'I take it Nigel Turnbull is a student here? One of yours?'

'Well, yes, but.'

'No buts . . .'

Dr Frampton glared at Pendragon, his face rigid with indignation. 'You'll have to take it up with the Dean's office,' he said coldly.

Nigel Turnbull lived at number twenty-four Northam Road a short drive from Queen Mary College. Pendragon pulled into heavy traffic on Mile End Road and made two calls. The first was to Superintendent Hughes, explaining the situation. She told him she would get on to it straight away. Forensics would be into Frampton's lab as soon as possible. The second call was to Sergeant Turner.

'Where are you?' Pendragon asked.

'Just pulling up at Nigel Turnbull's place.'

'I'll be right there.'

Turnbull occupied one of five bedsits on the ground floor of a large detached house. The landlord lived on the upper floor. Inspector Grant pulled up in a squad car at the same time as Turner arrived with Roz Mackleby. The three policemen walked up a path overgrown with weeds to a front door that looked as though the last time it saw a lick of paint, Elvis was alive. Grant rang the bell. There was no response. He leaned on it. An upper-storey window over the porch opened and a man's head appeared. His hair was a mess and he looked as though he had just woken up.

Grant flashed his ID. 'Police,' he called to the man. 'We'd like a chat.'

The head disappeared. They heard sounds from inside the house and the front door opened. A man in his late-forties stood there in a tatty dressing gown. He had a stubbly, flabby face and black rings under his eyes. He said nothing, but opened the door for the policemen to enter.

'I just got to bed. I'm on shifts,' he said wearily, and rubbed his right eye.

'Sorry, sir. It's Mr Francis, isn't it? You're the landlord?'

'It is, and yes, I am,' the man replied, suddenly awake. 'What's up?'

'You have a tenant, a student at Queen Mary College – Nigel Turnbull?'

'Yeah, they're all students there. Why?'

'Is Mr Turnbull in?'

'I should think he's at college,' Francis said. 'His room's down the hall on the right.' He took them along a dim corridor lit by a naked light bulb dangling from a frayed cord. He rapped on a door with chipped, grubby paintwork. There was no reply.

'Do you have a key?'

'Well, yeah, but I don't . . .'

'It's a serious matter, Mr Francis,' Grant said evenly. 'We have reason to believe Nigel Turnbull is a suspect in a homicide.'

Francis's eyes widened. 'Well, okay. Hang on a minute.'

He left them at the door to the bedsit and returned shortly after with a large bunch of keys. He was going through them as he paced along the hall. After a few moments, he found the key he was after and slipped it into the keyhole. As it turned, they heard a sound from inside the room. Turner jumped forward and pushed the door inwards with the side of his body. Grant and Mackleby were right behind him.

They were just in time to see a man's leg slip through the open window.

Grant ran across the room. Turner spun on his heel and dashed for the front door, almost knocking Francis off his feet. Mackleby was only a second behind him. When they were on the garden path, they saw the burly form of Nigel Turnbull running alongside the house, heading for the street. He was so large he seemed to roll along like a ball. Turner raced for the gate, turned right and almost collided with Turnbull's vast stomach. The man was pulling a pained expression and gabbling incoherently. Behind him, holding the runaway in what looked like an agonising arm lock, was DCI Pendragon.

'Ah, you got here then,' said Turner, a little out of breath.

Chapter 38

London, March 1589

I was extremely tired, but Edward Perch
insisted we talk right away and draw up plans.
He led me out of Edmund's room and I
followed him into a small office at the end of a
corridor. The room was sparsely furnished,
containing a large desk strewn with papers
and, along the far wall, a pair of old chairs. A
servant was sent to fetch wine and some bread.
It was only at the mention of food I realised
how hungry I was.

The office was at the back of the Bear Garden,
away from the stands and the noise of the
crowds. Edward was businesslike. He cleared
his desk and directed me to a chair.

'I have been aware of your mission for some
time,' he began. 'I have people working for me
in France. A lot of our business is conducted

between Paris and London, but you need not concern yourself with that.' He waved one hand dismissively. 'My people have infiltrated Walsingham's network. I'm confident that we know a great deal more about the dealings and schemes of the Principal Secretary than he knows of ours.'

'So you only heard of my work through your spies in Paris?'

'Of course not. I have also had personal correspondence with Roberto Bellarmino himself. I have helped others before you – men sent to England simply as missionaries. I am aware of the recent shift in Vatican policy, however. His Holiness has been losing too many good men. As much as I despise Francis Walsingham, his methods are extremely effective. It is clear we must pull the plant up by its roots. The Queen must die.'

There was a heavy silence, broken by a barely audible roar from the crowd around the arena in the main part of the building. Then Edward said, 'May I see the ring?'

I lifted my hand. He brought over a candle. 'How remarkable to see something that once graced the hand of Lucrezia Borgia,' he said quietly. Then he quickly returned to his chair behind the desk. 'To business. Ann has brought the poison from her house.'

He must have seen the relief on my face. 'She is a good girl,' he confirmed. 'Now, I have given much thought to how we should proceed. The Queen is at Hampton Court but will be leaving the day after tomorrow, to travel to York. If we are to strike, it must be tomorrow night. We are now some five hours from sunrise. You must lie low until sunset. I have arranged everything. This is what you must do.'

It was quiet in the little room they gave me under the now empty spectator stand of the Bear Garden. The noise of the slaughter and the braying had ceased but nothing could mask the stink. Over long years, the smell of fear and death had permeated these walls. It would hang here for ever, I thought to myself, or at least until the building was razed.

I had no idea of the time, and little sense of the passing minutes and hours. I lay on a bier, staring up at a sloping white ceiling. But gradually a small window close to the door began to take shape in the darkness and the black sky gave way to the grey wash of pre-dawn. I must have drifted off to sleep, for the next thing I was aware of was the sound of a cock crowing. I pulled myself up and rubbed the sleep from my eyes.

There came a gentle tap at the door and Ann walked in, carrying a bowl of steaming water and a length of cloth.

'This is becoming a habit,' I said as I watched her place the bowl on a side table and drape the cloth over the end of the bier.

'It is my pleasure, Father,' she answered gravely.

She turned to go, then hesitated.

'What is it, Ann? Stay, talk to me.'

She sat down on the end of the bier, hands in her lap. 'You know, you do not have to carry on with your mission,' she began. 'No one would think ill of you if you . . .'

'Maybe that is so,' I interrupted, smiling. 'But I would think ill of myself, and I know the Lord would be disappointed in me.'

'But . . .'

'But nothing, Ann. I have no fear. I know I'm doing the Lord's work. I know that if I die in my attempt, then that is God's will. That it is His plan for me.'

'But things have changed, Father. Sebastian is dead.' She crossed herself as she said it. 'And the Pursuivants . . . they have destroyed our circle. Two of my friends have been taken and Master Byrd only escaped by a miracle. Father Garnet is also in custody.'

'I heard about Father Garnet,' I replied. 'Edward told me. But I knew nothing of your friends. I'm sorry.'

'Do not be. We all know the risks.'

'Then you must also know that I am aware of the dangers I face, Ann. I've known of them since I first began training in the Vatican. I believe my purpose is to serve God in the best way I may.'

'Then I can say nothing more.'

'You could wish me luck,' I said.

She smiled. 'I will do better than that, Father John. You will be constantly in my prayers. And you will need this.' She handed me the small glass vial of poison.

'And what will you do?'

'Me? I shall continue with my own work. The Pursuivants have their suspicions, of course, but no proof. I'm sure that one day I shall be trapped or betrayed, and will suffer the consequences. But I will go to the scaffold with a clear conscience and a proud heart.'

I moved closer and held Ann's hands in mine.

'You are a brave woman,' I told her. 'May the Lord bless you and keep you.'

I looked down at her hands for a moment. When I met her gaze, I could not hide the tears brimming in my eyes.

'What is it?' she asked.

'Sebastian,' I said. 'It seems it is only now I am able to believe he is dead.'

My anxiety grew as the day wore on. For most of the time I was left to my own thoughts, with only past pain and future fears to dwell upon. Ann brought me meals, and in the late-afternoon Edward Perch arrived with a piece of paper containing a detailed plan of Hampton Court Palace.

After he had gone, I thought through the plan he had conceived and could not help slipping into self-doubt. I prayed for long hours, asking the Lord to give me the strength I needed to fulfil my task. But worse than the self-doubt were the times I questioned my faith in those helping me. How could I be sure, for instance, that Edward Perch would not betray me? He spoke of his faith, his commitment to the Holy Father in Rome, but how was I to know he was not also receiving financial reward for his work? Men like him did nothing except for gold. He would have me believe his reward was surety of Heaven, and perhaps this was true. Perhaps I was being unfair to the man. But, just as I had questioned the morals of Cornelius Agrippa, I found it hard to eradicate the doubts I felt about a man who, by all accounts, made his living from extortion, gambling and supplying prostitutes. Would he not view assassination – nay, regicide – in the same way? Simply another means of making money.

I was praying so hard, I did not notice the light fail in the room as the little window near the door framed a dark blue sky streaked with the red of sunset. I was pulling myself to my feet when the door opened and Edward Perch was revealed. 'It is time,' he said, and searched my face with the alert eyes of a man who lived each day on the fragile margins of society, relying solely upon his wits.

He handed me a small bag and some clothes: a black tunic, black hose, a dark cap. 'Put these on,' he said. 'It will help you remain concealed. In the bag is a change of clothing and a dagger. It is the only weapon we can risk you carrying en route to the palace, but it should be enough. You have prepared the ring?'

I nodded and handed him the vial Sebastian had brought from Paris. 'I shall need but one dose,' I said.

'Then it only remains for me to wish you luck.'

'I do not need luck,' I said curtly. 'I have God on my side.' Then, thinking I sounded like an ingrate, added, 'But I thank you, sir. I could not have proceeded thus far without you.' I withdrew a folded paper from my tunic. 'Here is your drawing of the palace. I have committed it to memory as best I can.'

A man in black attire was waiting for us outside the room. He was holding a torch to illuminate the corridor.

'This is Martin Fairweather,' Edward Perch told me. 'He may be trusted. He has suffered the tortures so favoured by the Principal Secretary.'

Perch then shook my hand, crossed himself and walked away.

'Follow me,' Martin Fairweather instructed.

It was a cloudy night with no moon to light the shrouded alleyways and overhung passages of Southwark. The Bear Garden stood very close to the bank of the Thames. We left through a back door as crowds began to gather at the front for the evening's entertainment. I followed

Martin Fairweather in silence down to the river, placing my trust in God.

A short flight of worn stone steps took us close to the water's edge. In the gloom, I could just make out a small boat bobbing on the swell. A man whose face was obscured by shadow helped us into the boat and indicated that we should lie down and cover ourselves with a pair of large sacks. I felt the vessel move off into the stream as it began to rain, heavy drops pelting the surface of the water and soaking the sackcloth.

Although I knew it was no more than four leagues to the Queen's palace at Hampton, it felt as though we were on the river for an eternity. The rain was unrelenting, and the knot of anxiety in the pit of my stomach made me feel nauseous. It was freezing, but I was lathered in sweat and the rough wet sacking irritated my face and hands. I could feel fleas biting me all over. At last, the little boat slowed and I heard the scrape of reeds against its hull and a dull thump as we knocked against the bank. I risked pulling the sack away from my face and peered out over the side into the blackness.

Crouching low, the boatman took the few steps back to where we lay. 'I go no further,' he whispered. Throwing our bags on to the bank, Martin Fairweather and I slipped over the side into the water. It came up to our chests and I gasped as the freezing shock cut through me. It took me several attempts to scramble up the muddy bank. I only made it thanks to a shove from Martin.

The boatman waited to ensure we were safely on dry land, and then, without a word, turned his boat for Southwark and vanished into the night. We quickly changed into fresh clothes, put our soaking wet garments into the bags, then tied these to a large stone before lowering them among the reeds. We were now dressed as guards in red hose, leather tunic and white ruff.

'We are a short distance downriver from the palace,' Martin said in a hush. 'I'll lead the way. There is a concealed iron gate in the outer wall, to the east of the main buildings. If Edward's boys have earned their keep we should find it unlocked. Once inside the perimeter we should have little difficulty in finding access to the palace itself. No one will notice two more anonymous guards.'

The terrain was rough. Snow had settled and been only partly thawed by the recent rain. The mud beneath had been frozen solid for weeks. Across a field and through an avenue of trees we saw the palace for the first time. I had marked it from the river before, but never at such close quarters. It seemed larger than life: brick walls rising from snow-powdered gardens, great rectangular chimneys rearing up into the cloud-smudged night. There were a few yellowy lights showing in the upper windows on the eastern side of the building. These, I knew from the diagram Edward Perch had given me, were the Queen's private quarters.

We kept to the shadows of trees as best we could until we reached the flint outer wall. In the gloom, it looked quite featureless but Martin led us east and soon we found the gate he had described. It looked as if it had not been used in many a year. The metalwork was a rusted lattice and the hinges groaned as Martin pushed against it. A few inches in it stuck fast, but there was just enough room for us to squeeze between the edge of the gate and the stone wall.

A long hedge ran parallel to the wall. We could see through its intertwined branches that on the other side a grass parterre stretched ahead as far as a gravel footpath. Beyond that lay a flower bed, and then the wall of the palace itself.

Martin was searching the ground beneath the hedge. Kneeling on the hard earth, he chipped away at a patch with his dagger. I heard him curse, saw him shake his head. Then I caught a glimmer of metal in the faint light. He leaned forward and chopped at the ground with renewed enthusiasm. Pulling on something just under the surface, he straightened and held up in both hands a guard's pike. He handed this to me and scrabbled away at the earth again until he found a second weapon – a sheathed sword and belt. 'The boys have done well,' he told me. 'Our uniforms are now complete. Come, this way.'

Martin slipped out from under the hedge first, beckoning me to follow. We carefully scraped away fragments of hard soil that had clung to our boots and rubbed any residue from our knees. Stepping on to the footpath, we marched with all the authority we could muster towards the first entrance into the building we could see, a heavy oak door that swung open on to a dark corridor.

We could hear voices coming from the end of the passage and a pale light spilled from a door left ajar. The rooms leading from the corridor were kitchens. Beyond them, a servants' staircase led up to the main dining hall.

We passed the kitchens at a fast walk. Running would have drawn attention to us and we had already made good time. Some drama was unfolding nearby. I could hear one of the cooks screaming at a subordinate, and then the crash of pans, curses and a yelp. A short, very plump man slammed open the door into the corridor and almost bowled me over. I managed to step to one side just in time to avoid a collision. He seemed to be almost totally oblivious to our presence and stamped off, swearing and mumbling curses.

The stairs were narrow and enclosed. We turned off at the first landing and marched along a passage that opened out on to a galleried area. The Queen's quarters were directly overhead, on the second floor, but I knew we could not risk going there yet. Instead, I took the lead and we followed the gallery round to a grand staircase on the far side. I took us down the stairs, tapping the pike against the steps as I went.

The bottom of the stairs opened on to a large hallway with doors leading off in all directions.

A footman was hurrying towards the main doors at the end. Two men in the attire of bakers were carrying what looked like heavy wicker baskets. They were accompanied by a guard who directed them to the servants' stairs. Two more guards stood at the far end of the hall. We had arrived a little earlier than planned and took up position at the foot of the stairs.

For several minutes, Martin Fairweather and I watched the comings and goings of the Royal household. It was clear the servants rarely stopped working. Dinner had been served hours earlier, and the Queen would now be in her bedchamber, but the kitchen staff were preparing for the next day and the tradesmen were doing late-night rounds so that everything would be ready for the morning.

I had just turned to glance at Martin, standing opposite me at the foot of the stairs, when the nerve-racking interlude ended. Two men in guards' uniforms crashed through the front doors. 'Fire!' one of them screamed. 'Quickly, the north tower!'

A man rushed past us from a door behind the stairs and spun round on his heel. He was clearly a senior guard, his lined face and pronounced limp evidence of long service to his

Queen. 'Come on!' he yelled at us. 'What you waiting for?'

We ran after him the length of the hall. The two guards who had been stationed at the far end had followed the men who'd raised the alarm. As we neared the end of the hall, the senior guard took the corner with surprising speed and Martin and I dived under a narrow archway, almost tripping over each other on the steep stone stairs that fell away just beyond the opening. I grabbed a handrail and Martin slammed into my back, the handle of his sword knocking into my hip making me cry out in pain.

We emerged back into the hall with Martin leading the way and came face to face with the senior guard who had yelled orders at us only a few moments earlier. He had his sword drawn. 'What in God's name is wrong with you?' he screamed. In a panic, I lowered my pike threateningly. He fell back and took up a defensive stance. Martin unsheathed his sword and took a step towards the man.

'Go!' he yelled to me.

I hesitated for a second then turned and ran towards the stairs, my heavy boots echoing on the marble floor as I picked up pace. A guard emerged from a door to my left. He looked at me and then at the scene along the hall. Without hesitating, I plunged my pike into his chest. He fell back, his face frozen in shock and terror. I yanked out the pike and ran on. At the foot of the stairs, I glanced back and saw the old guard knock Martin's sword from his hand and force him back to the wall at the tip of a dagger. I was torn between running on up the stairs and dashing back to help Martin. But my decision was made for me.

The guard kept Martin pinned against the wall with the dagger and slid his sword into my friend's abdomen, levering it up towards his heart. Martin gasped and began to choke on his own blood. Sneering, the guard leaned closer, pushing in the steel blade with all his weight behind it. But the sneer faltered, to be replaced by an expression of bewilderment. Two lines of blood rolled from the guard's nostrils and he fell back, a dagger in his chest. Martin turned his head painfully in my direction. 'Go,' he gurgled, and slid down the wall.

I took the stairs three at a time. Reaching the top, I spun to my left and ran as fast as I could along the carpeted gallery. From far off, I could hear shouts and the faint smell of burning. At the end of the gallery, a second staircase led upwards. I slowed to a stately pace and tried to proceed calmly, in spite of the fear raging through me. Marching along the gallery on the second floor, I could see ahead of me the doors into the Queen's private chambers. A guard stood to one side.

'What's happening?' he exclaimed. 'I was told to wait here. Simon said something about a fire. He's gone to find out.'

I shrugged and looked to my left suddenly as though I had just seen something strange. The guard followed my gaze and I slammed the shaft of my pike into the side of his head. He swayed, half-stunned, and before he could cry out, I plunged my dagger into his throat. Slicing it away from me, I ripped a great gash along his neck. He dropped like a stone, his blood splashing on to my leather tunic.

I opened the door and stepped inside. In the small antechamber a sumptuous Persian rug lay on the floor and the walls were covered with murals: scenes from an Athenian pageant. A door the other side of the chamber was half-open. I leaned against the wall and peered into the next room through the narrow space between the back edge of the door and its frame.

A young woman was arranging a gown over a long stool. A mirror on the wall showed the room behind her. It was otherwise empty. I slid around the door and into the second room.

The girl heard me and spun around to face me. She was probably no more than seventeen and exquisitely beautiful, with huge, doleful brown eyes and full ruby lips. Her long golden hair was artfully arranged in curls around her pretty face and two narrow plaits ran back on each side of her head and were caught up behind it. I rushed towards her, managing to get my hand to her mouth before she could make a sound. She struggled, landing a kick in my groin that sent a terrible pain up into my abdomen. One of her hands came round and she dug her nails deep into my cheek, raking them downwards, taking flesh and skin with them. I stifled a scream and thrust an arm around her neck. She bit the palm of my hand, clutched to her mouth, but I held on. I knew not what to do. I could not risk trying to knock her unconscious and tying her up. I felt possessed, fury burning in my guts, full of a crazed desire to do whatever it took to kill the Queen. I twisted the girl's neck and heard it snap. I lowered her to the floor, limp and lifeless.

The door to the Queen's chamber was closed. I eased the handle round and prayed the hinges had been well oiled. They had. The door opened silently inwards. The only light in the room came from a single large candle set in a magnificent gold holder which occupied an alcove close to a row of windows overlooking the most splendid gardens in England.

The room was dominated by a massive four-poster bed. Each of the four posts was carved out of oak. Faces of strange creatures from the depths of dreams emerged from the wood. They were accompanied by nymphs and wolves, hunters, stags and gargoyles. Hanging down beside the posts were rich, red velvet drapes. These had been drawn across three sides of the bed, but on the side closest to me, a swathe of the finest silk formed a diaphanous screen. In the bed lay the Queen of England. She was on her back, her head propped up on a pile of pillows, her arms over the sheets. She was snoring softly. She moved suddenly and I froze. She twisted on to her side, facing me, farted and turned on to her back again.

I took a step forward and parted the silk screen. I could see her face now. She looked much older than I had imagined. Her face was leathery and lined, but her eyelids were gossamer-like, lightly veined and frail. I pivoted the top of the ring and gazed at the spike that rose up as the emerald fell away. And I paused.

Time seemed to come to a halt. The silence of the room filled me with sudden dread. We were in a cocoon, isolated from the world. Nothing of reality could reach me now. I looked again at Her Royal Highness Elizabeth Tudor. She appeared completely powerless. This was not the woman who ruled a kingdom, wielded a power that awoke fear in the hearts of men, ruled by Divine Right. This was not the sovereign who had sent the Spanish Armada packing. This figure on the bed was just an old woman, flesh and blood, like any other.

I leaned forward, brought my hand over the edge of the bed, closed my eyes and thrust forward.

The first thing I noticed was the sound . . . a whoosh! A rush of air close to my arm . . . and then the pain. My eyes opened wide and I saw the blade slicing through my hand and my fingers tumbling to the bed. Blood flooded out of me, spraying across the horrified face of Queen Elizabeth who had leapt from her bed into a waking nightmare.

I could not scream. No sound would come. I sensed someone beside me. He grabbed my arm and I felt the tip of a sword press against my throat. He was about to plunge the blade into me.

'No!' the Queen shouted, her face as pale as death.

'But . . . Your Majesty!'

'I said, no, William.'

I managed to turn my head as the blade was snatched away from my throat. Standing with his sword arm stiff and straight, in line with his out-thrust chin, stood Anthony.

Newgate Prison, London, March 1589

And so now I come to the end of my confessional, for that is what this sorry tale really is, the confession of a failed assassin.

I can hear the sound of boots outside my cell and the clanking of keys as the guards arrive to take me to my place of execution.

At this moment, I feel strangely calm. Oh, do not doubt I have had many nights of terror as I have foreseen my fate. In my dreams, I have already felt the executioner's blade disembowelling me. There have been many times when I wished I would die from the torture I have received. But thanks to the skill of the Royal Physician I have been kept from Heaven's Gate . . . temporarily. And now a new hope pervades my mind. For I know that although I failed in my mission to kill the Tudor whore, still I served God with my every fibre, my entire heart, my entire soul. And I like to believe the Lord will forgive me my failure and welcome me into Heaven.

Here, in this prison, I have heard strange and terrible things. My guard has taken great pleasure in relating how Ann Doherty died, and how Edward Perch sobbed like a baby as the hangman placed the noose around his neck. His latest news was to tell me that the Queen herself will be attending my execution. Well, we shall see.

And my nemesis – what of him? Anthony is a kinsman of Walsingham. My gaoler's tittle-tattle informs me that, to perfect his role in my downfall, he took lessons from no less a figure than London's greatest thespian, Edward Alleyn. Now, even through my pain and my fury, I cannot deny the lad's skill, God curse him.

Ah, the clanking grows louder. And there

goes the door. I fear my time has drained to
nothing. What will be my final words? Shall I
scream outrage and splash bile on to the page?
No, I shall not. For I have the best of it. Soon, I
shall meet my Lord. I shall once again be with
Sebastian, with Ann, and all the other martyrs
who have died for the One True Faith. For,
Lord, Yours is the Power, and the Glory, for
ever and ever. Amen.

Chapter 39

Stepney, Friday 10 June, 6.30 p.m.

Pendragon clicked on the digital recorder in Interview Room 2 and leaned back in the chair with his fingers interlocked in his lap. 'Maybe we should start at the beginning,' he told Nigel Turnbull.

The young man was so grossly overweight, his buttocks overflowed both sides of the metal chair. Studying him closely for the first time, Pendragon realised that Turnbull looked at least ten years older than his true age. He was completely bald and there were lines under his eyes. His massive forehead was beaded with sweat.

'I was DJ-ing at The Love Shack when some dead dude came through the air duct in the ceiling. That's all I know about your investigation, DCI Pendragon.'

'You know, Nigel, for someone in as deep as you, you're being awfully cocky.'

Turnbull stared him out, arms crossed over his huge, flabby chest.

'All right then. Let's not start from the beginning. Let's start with the findings of my forensics team. Within the past few days, two rather unusual plants have been removed from the greenhouse next to the lab at Queen Mary.'

'That happens all the time.'

'Yes, but these were removed rather amateurishly. Not, I imagine, the way trained scientists like yourself would handle their valuable specimens.'

Turnbull shrugged.

'Okay, Nigel. Let me help you a little more. The two plants are rare in this country. But, most importantly to my investigation, they each produce an essential ingredient in a very complex poison which has been used to kill two people. Furthermore, those victims were each associated with the building company who were the employers of "the dead dude" who landed so indecorously on your dance-floor only a week ago.'

Turnbull looked genuinely shocked. 'I had no idea.'

'What do you mean, you had no idea, Nigel? You're involved in these murders up to your walrus neck.'

'Now, hang on.'

'What do you *mean*, hang on? You are either the murderer we are looking for or their accomplice – the expert poison-maker. It's obvious.'

Turnbull turned very pale. 'Look . . . I really don't know what you're talking about.'

'In that case, why did you run?'

'I don't know. I panicked, I guess.'

'Oh, come on. You can do better than that. I'll tell you what I think, shall I?' Pendragon didn't wait for a response. 'You're hard up, but you have a useful skill to sell. Someone made you an offer you simply couldn't refuse. A nice fat cheque in exchange for a small vial of poison. You needed some plant materials from your lab, but they're nursed like babies because they are extremely rare and valuable. So, you yanked them up to make it look like a theft.'

'If I did that, why wasn't it reported?' Turnbull responded.

'Well, that's a good question, isn't it, Nigel? Perhaps you could tell me. Or maybe we should bring Dr Frampton in? He would have been responsible for contacting the police.'

'Do what you want.'

'I tell you what I will do, Nigel. I'll give you a chance to help yourself. It's not you we're really after. You're just a stooge, a hard-up kid with some knowledge of biochemistry. Having said that, Accessory to Murder, Theft, Resisting Arrest. Well . . .' And Pendragon pretended to count on his fingers. 'I can't see you getting less than ten years, even without previous.'

Turnbull threw his head into his hands and started to sob. It was an awful sound, like a hippo with diarrhoea. His shoulders shook, which made his whole body vibrate in sympathy.

'Now, if you were able to impart some names, I might, just might, be able to pull some strings.'

Turnbull raised his head from his palms. His eyes were red, cheeks streaked with tears. 'I swear, Chief Inspector, on my mother's grave, I don't know anything about this.'

Pendragon fixed the young man with a truly spine-chilling look. 'Nigel, your mother is still alive. I've read your file. And I don't believe you. Not for one minute. Now, you can either carry on the innocent act and serve a decade in Pentonville, or you can do the sensible . . .'

There was a knock at the door. Turner came in holding a sheet of paper. He leaned close to Pendragon's ear and said quietly, 'Sir, the second report from forensics. I think you should read it straight away.' He sat down next to the DCI.

Pendragon scanned through the report, then focused on the summary and conclusion at the end.

Traces of 3-4 Methylenedioxy-Methamphetamine, or MDMA (ecstasy), found in laboratory equipment at the benches of Nigel Turnbull and Dr Adrian Frampton. Further traces found at the home of Mr Turnbull, 24, Northam Road. Weighing apparatus and a hand press to produce tablets from MDMA powder were also found on the premises. Study of the toilet bowl in Mr Turnbull's rooms revealed trace amounts of MDMA.

Pendragon lowered the sheet of paper, glanced at Turner and let out a heavy sigh. 'It seems you and Dr Frampton have been very industrious,' he said in a sorrowful tone.

Turnbull looked at his chubby fingers, clasped together in front of him. 'I don't really understand, Chief Inspector.'

Pendragon slid over the last page of the report. Turnbull's eyes darted over it.

'So that's why you ran . . . and why you didn't report the theft of the plants.'

Turnbull took a deep breath. 'I swear I know nothing about the poisonings.'

Pendragon closed his eyes for a moment, leaned his elbows on the table and ran his fingers through his hair. Then he stood up and strode towards the door. 'Charge him, Sergeant,' he said, without breaking stride. 'Then bring in Frampton and charge him too.'

Chapter 40

Pendragon was pacing along the corridor, in one of the worst moods he could remember. Questioning suspects was one of the aspects of the job he really disliked. He hated putting on the tough guy act because he had to adopt a persona that was very different from the way he saw himself, and he was always concerned that once he had taken on the role, he would not be able to shake it off. He didn't want to become the person he pretended to be in the interview room. Other cops seemed to be able to slip in and out of character as easily as changing a shirt, but he found it unnatural. Perhaps, he mused, that was one of the reasons he had never progressed beyond DCI. What made today's performance particularly bad was the fact he had been so far off-target with his hunch. Lost in thought, he didn't hear the uniformed sergeant the first time he spoke.

'Sir?' Sergeant Scratton repeated.

Pendragon snapped out of his reverie. 'Sergeant?'

'Sir, just had a call from Constable Smith. He's found the body of a dog down by the canal on South Street, about a mile from here.'

'A dog?' Pendragon looked completely confused.

'Remember on Tuesday I told you we had three reports of missing dogs? That old lady was just leaving . . .'

'Yes, yes,' Pendragon recalled. 'I remember. Her spaniel, wasn't it?'

'It was, sir. Smith says this one's a mongrel, not the old lady's dog. He told me he thinks the poor thing's been dead for less than a day. But get this – he reckons it was poisoned. There're no visible wounds, and its gums are coated in some greenish stuff. He didn't elaborate. Oh, and there was a hypodermic needle next to the body.'

Pendragon was about to say something glib, like, a hypodermic by the canal in that part of Stepney being almost de rigueur, when he stopped. Along the corridor, a door slammed, and they saw Turner emerging from Interview Room 2. Pendragon stepped towards him. 'You done with Turnbull?'

Turner nodded.

'Good.' Then, turning back to Scratton, Pendragon added, 'Sergeant, lock up the suspect, please. Turner, you come with me.'

*

'What's up?' Jez asked as they took the stairs to the car park three at a time.

'A poisoned dog.'

'A what?'

Pendragon filled him in as they got into a patrol car. The sergeant went very quiet and gazed out of the passenger window.

'What have you found out about Murano Glass UK and the charming Mr Gregson?' Pendragon asked, pulling out on to Brick Lane.

'Oh,' Turner said, facing his boss, 'nothing very helpful, guv. No real previous on anyone working there. The storeman, Daniel Beatty, did a bit of joyriding when he was a teenager, but then . . . who didn't? Both Alec Darlinghurst and his mother are clean. Not so much as a parking ticket between them. Sidney Gregson and his wife flew to Nice on May the twenty-third, the day before the break-in. There's not a speck of evidence to implicate any of them.'

'No big surprise, really,' Pendragon replied. 'Still, I'm going to get Mackleby to ask everyone involved in this investigation to submit to a voluntary DNA swab test. Nothing's giving.'

They fell silent again, and Turner watched the buildings flash by as the main road gave way to a small side street. Pendragon pulled to a stop at the end where a line of white metal pillars separated the road from a patch of worn grass. Beyond that, a narrow path of baked mud joined a concrete towpath running alongside the canal. A short walk brought them to a rusted wire fence. They could just make out the solid form of Constable Smith in his bright yellow jacket. He was standing with three other people in the middle of a patch of land covered with great chunks of concrete, piles of rusted petrol cans and the occasional tuft of long, scrubby grass.

The dog lay in a sad heap on a patch of gravel. Its eyes were open and milky-white, but there were few outward signs of decay. Its matted, brown fur was greasy, and exuded the pungent smell of urine.

'A couple of kids found the poor little bugger,' Constable Smith said as Pendragon and Turner reached the animal. 'I've bagged the hypodermic and kept anyone from contaminating the scene as much as I could, sir.'

'Good work, Smith,' Pendragon said. He crouched down and looked closely at the green stains around the dog's gums. 'Okay, I'll get someone down here to take this away. Smith, can you send these people home? God knows why they have to stand around here. Sergeant . . .' he looked at Turner. 'Sergeant?'

Jez looked up and Pendragon could see he was

very pale and tears were brimming in his eyes. 'How could anyone do this?' he said.

'Come on,' the DCI replied. 'Let's get back to the station.'

They picked their way through the detritus. Pendragon opened his mobile and speed-dialled the station.

'Get me Inspector Grant, please.'

'Guv?'

'Turner and I are heading back from the canal near South Street. I take it you've been told about the dog?'

'Yeah, Scratton just showed me the report. Smith found it, right?'

'Correct. It's pretty clear it was poisoned.'

'You sure?'

'Well, no, Inspector,' Pendragon retorted. 'But something weird is going on and it seems a bit too much of a coincidence that the first dog was reported missing before Middleton's murder.'

'What? You think the killer practised on dogs first?'

'I'm not sure what I think, Grant. There are so many unanswerable questions. This dog died only last night at the latest, so who knows?'

There was silence on the line.

'Inspector?'

'Yes, sorry, sir. Just thinking.'

'All right, listen. I want every piece of waste ground, park, canal footpath and back alley in the borough searched. Pull everyone off what they're doing. I want those other missing dogs found by the end of the day.'

'Will do. By the way, sir, something else has come up.'

'What?'

'Got a call just before you rang in. From Max Rainer.'

'Rainer?'

'Claims he was attacked leaving work last night. Smacked over the head. He spent half the night in A and E, apparently, and he's mad as hell. Wants the culprit in chains.'

'Was it a mugging? Was he robbed?'

'Apparently not. His wallet was untouched.'

They had reached the squad car. Pendragon got behind the wheel. 'Okay,' he said to Grant. 'I want to be told the minute you find anything.' He shut the phone and turned the ignition key.

Max Rainer was a great deal more welcoming than he had been on their first visit to his flat. He opened the door to them wearing a long silk dressing gown over expensive-looking pyjamas. He had a large plaster on his forehead and was holding a cold pack to his right temple with one hand and had a glass of whisky in the other. Aren't we the drama queen? Pendragon thought to himself as Rainer invited them into his sitting-room.

'I appreciate your coming over, Chief Inspector.' He gave Pendragon a weak smile and glanced at Sergeant Turner who was looking the other way at a painting on the wall. 'Please sit down. May I offer you both a drink?' And he held up his tumbler.

'Not on duty, regrettably,' Pendragon said.

'That's a shame. This is a particularly fine single malt, a thirty-year-old Macallan.'

'I'll have a glass of water, please,' Turner said merrily. Pendragon gave his sergeant a fleeting grin as Rainer strode through to the kitchen.

'So, talk us through what happened,' Pendragon said as Rainer handed Turner a small glass of tap water.

'I was leaving the office. It must have been just after nine. I had stayed on to do some work. The others had left hours before. I was locking the main door to the office – the one leading from the lobby on the first floor. I heard a sound behind me, but before I could turn, I felt this incredible pain in the back of my head and I collapsed, smacking my forehead on the door as I went.'

'So you saw no one?'

'No.'

'And you came to, when?'

'It was three minutes past twelve. I found a cab and got myself to the London Hospital. They kept me in until this morning. Concussion, of course, and I had four stitches . . . here.' He pointed to his forehead. 'And seven here, at the back.'

'Do you have any idea who could have done this?'

'I was rather hoping you could tell me that,' Rainer retorted, the old brittleness returning.

'I understand nothing was stolen? Your wallet was untouched.'

'That's correct.'

'Then it's possible you were attacked by someone with a grievance.'

Rainer was silent.

'Mr Rainer, is there no one you suspect? Do you have any enemies?'

'Not that I'm aware of.'

Pendragon glanced at Turner, who was concentrating on his notebook. 'It's just that your partner, Tim Middleton . . . .'

'Yes. All right. I know what you're going to say. Tim's not even in the ground yet and I'm attacked with no apparent motive – odd. Okay . . .' He paused for a moment, stood up and walked over to a drinks cabinet where he poured himself a generous new measure of the particularly fine Macallan. Returning, he admitted: 'I'm being blackmailed.'

Pendragon and Turner both stared at him. 'When did this start?' Pendragon asked.

'About three months ago. I have no idea who it is, or why. But they seem to know an awful lot about my past and are completely unscrupulous about how they employ that knowledge.'

'Can you elaborate, please?'

'No, I can't, Chief Inspector. It's irrelevant.'

'You think so? I would say it's entirely relevant. You see, Tim Middleton was also being blackmailed. Before he was murdered.'

Rainer blanched and took a large gulp of whisky. 'Before I qualified as an architect,' he said quickly, 'I did a bit of teaching on the side. Sixteen- and seventeen-year-olds doing their GCSEs. I . . . I had a brief relationship with one of the girls. She was seventeen, all perfectly legal.'

'What went wrong, Mr Rainer?'

He sighed and looked at the ceiling. 'She fell pregnant and I pushed her into having a backstreet abortion. She died of septicaemia. I never owned up to her family.' Rainer glared at the two policemen. 'It was thirty years ago, for God's sake! I can't imagine how *anyone* could know about it.'

'Someone obviously does,' Turner said, returning Rainer's glare.

He drained his glass. 'So, what are you going to do now?'

'Would you be willing to give a full statement and provide access to all your accounts?'

'No!' Rainer's voice was slightly slurred.

'Do you have any letters, e-mails, anything from the blackmailer?'

'No, they contacted me by phone. They've called three times. The last time was over a month ago to say they were doubling the payments.'

Pendragon stood up. 'Well, in that case, there's not a lot we can do.'

'What do you mean, there's not a lot you can do?' Rainer demanded. 'This is outrageous! Surely you have forensics, DNA people, fingerprint experts?'

'Mr Rainer, what evidence do you think we'll find at the scene of the crime? You were hit over the head from behind. You saw no one. You had the wound cleaned and stitched – quite understandably. The person who attacked you was almost certainly wearing gloves, and they would not have left DNA at the scene. We could check surveillance cameras close to your offices, but I would say the chances of seeing anything useful would be . . . well . . . zero.

The only real chance we have of getting anywhere with our inquiries would be to try to trace the blackmailer. To do that, we need to follow a paper trail beginning with your bank details and a full and thorough statement from you, giving names, dates, every detail you can about your . . . indiscretions thirty years ago.'

'I'm not willing to do that.'

'Very well,' Pendragon retorted. 'If you change your mind, you know where to reach us. We'll see ourselves out.'

Chapter 41

Pendragon looked at the photographs spread out on his desk and felt a growing sense of hatred for all humanity well up inside him. He had seen so many mangled bodies over the years, there was little shock value left for him in that sight. The only things that upset him, apart from seeing bodies in the morgue being prodded and poked by pathologists, were pictures of murdered children or abused animals. What adults did to each other was one thing, but the killing of innocents made him realise that, for all the cleverness of the human race, all the great things civilisation had created, at its core humankind was maggot-ridden.

The team had found all three of the dogs reported missing and one that had not been, which, along with the dog found near the canal, made a total of five. Here were the pictures. Five dead dogs in different stages of decay, all of them twisted, pathetic things, a rich endorsement to human depravity. Pendragon looked away and picked up two sheets of A4 stapled together – a preliminary report written by a young and enthusiastic forensic assistant named Janie Martindale, who had been sent by Collette Newman to assist the search team. He glanced at the neatly typed report, absorbing the essential facts.

The dogs died at different times during the past week.

The most recent was the dog found near South Street (designated Dog No.1 according to order of discovery). The earliest (Dog No.2), a collie, was found near a housing estate just inside the search perimeter.

Time of death determined by stage of development of the larvae of *Lucilia sericata*, a common blowfly.

Because of unusually hot weather, the larvae have developed considerably faster than at average outdoor temperatures.

No eggs found on Dog No.1. This determines time of death to be less than 18 hours before body was found.

Two dogs (Nos.3 and 4) were found to have '1st instar' larvae (1st stage of development).

This places time of death to between 18 and 38 hours before discovery of bodies.

Remaining two dogs (Nos. 2 and 5) showed presence of both '2nd instar' and '3rd instar' larvae, placing time of death to between 50 and 90 hours before discovery.

All five dogs were killed in similar ways, using a powerful poison. Preliminary analysis shows extremely high levels of arsenic.

Hypodermic needle found at Site No.1 shows traces of same poison. Also a partial strand of black, synthetic material found on barrel of hypodermic. Currently under analysis at Lambeth Road lab.

He placed the report back on the desk and ran his fingers over his forehead. What connection did the dogs have with the murders of Karim, Middleton and Ketteridge? There had to be a link. Three dead men and five dead dogs within a few square miles, and all within a week? The dogs couldn't have just been 'practice', as Inspector Grant had put it. If the murderer had experimented before turning to his first human victim, why continue killing dogs? No, that theory didn't hold water.

There was a tap at the door. He looked up to see Janie Martindale. She was small, no more than five feet tall, with cropped black hair, a boyish face and figure. 'Sir? Sorry, you looked lost in thought,' she said.

'No problem at all. I *was* lost in thought, but going nowhere with the exertion.' He gave her a smile.

'I thought you might be interested in this.' She held out a sealed plastic bag. Inside lay a piece of red fabric. He took it from her and peered through the plastic.

'It's velvet, sir. I found it on a gatepost at site number two, a piece of waste ground near the railway bridge off Sycamore Road . . . the spaniel. It's hard to tell how long the fabric has been there, but the dog died around seventy-two hours ago. This piece has kept its pigmentation integrity – sorry, its colour. Strongly coloured fabric like this fades in intense sunlight, and we've had abnormally bright sun recently. The degradation isn't noticeable to the naked eye after such a short time, but under a microscope you can tell. I would say the velvet has been on the gatepost no more than a week and quite possibly about as long as dog number two has been dead – three days. I wouldn't normally stick my neck out and say something like that. But if you put it together with the gold thread and the slipper imprint found at the scene of the Tony Ketteridge murder . . .'

Pendragon nodded. 'Someone dressing up.'

Janie Martindale shrugged her shoulders. 'It's a theory.'

'It is, Dr Martindale.'

She laughed. 'Not a doctor . . . yet, Chief Inspector! Only six months away though, hopefully.'

'Okay . . . well, good work, Ms Martindale.'

The young forensic scientist had only been gone a few minutes when there came another tap at the door and Superintendent Hughes peered in. 'You busy?' she asked.

'I was about to knock on your door actually, ma'am.' He looked at his watch. 'My time's almost up.'

She perched herself on the edge of the desk. 'That's what I wanted to see you about.'

Pendragon put his hands up. 'Okay, I've done my best. It's back to you.'

'Jack, I think perhaps I've been a little unfair on you. You look shattered. It's been a hell of a week.'

He stared at her, surprised.

'I've just had a call from the lab. They've found a tiny piece of DNA on the synthetic fibre they found on the hypodermic. It could be from someone completely unconnected with the case, but they'll do their best to find out. They told me you'd put Sergeant Mackleby on to collecting voluntary DNA swabs from everyone even vaguely linked with the case.'

'Yes.'

'Good move. If Dr Newman has any chance with that sample on the fibre, it will only be of any use if we have something on file we can match it to.'

He produced a half-smile. 'Glad to hear I've done something right.'

Hughes looked at the photos of the dogs and then up at Pendragon. 'I've also had a call from Commander Ferguson.'

'Oh.'

'He was cheerful for once. Though still very much pissed off we haven't caught the "Mile End Murderer".'

'Oh, God! Even the bloody Commander is using that ridiculous . . .'

'Commander Ferguson sees himself as "the people's copper",' Hughes interjected with a faint smile. 'And that's strictly off the record!'

Pendragon sighed. 'So, he's pissed off about the murders, but . . .?'

'But he's delighted we've caught the bastards who've been flooding the market with cheap E.'

Pendragon raised an eyebrow.

'Turnbull's given a very full confession and has named names. He and Dr Adrian Frampton were actually manufacturing the stuff, but we also have the names of half a dozen dealers. I think we can safely say we've shut down distribution for . . . oh . . . at least a month. Until, that is, some other clever little sod sets up in business.'

'So, catching Turnbull has bought me a reprieve, has it?'

'A brief one, Jack, a brief one. But you know what? I feel quietly confident we're closing in on the "Mile End Murderer".'

'I wish I could share your confidence,' Pendragon replied.

Pendragon had just turned off the light and was closing the door to his office when his phone rang. For a second he considered ignoring it, but then thought better of it, flicked the light back on and retraced his steps.

'Pendragon.'

'Chief Inspector? It's Geoffrey Stokes. I wasn't sure if you'd still be at the station.'

'How may I help you, Professor?'

'Well, I think I may be able to help *you*, Chief Inspector. I've become rather obsessed with your case, I'm afraid. I've slipped way behind schedule and my students have been ignored!' He produced an odd, whinnying laugh. 'But I think you'll consider it worth my while. Could I trouble you to pop over to the lab?'

Pendragon glanced at his watch. It was 6.32. 'Well, I . . .'

'I have some very exciting findings.'

Pendragon couldn't help thinking that, in his experience, what academics considered 'exciting' was not nearly as titillating or as useful as they thought. But then he recalled how much the professor had already discovered, from so little, and found himself agreeing to come over to Queen Mary right away.

As Pendragon passed the front desk, a young constable taking the evening shift saw him and nodded. Then he suddenly remembered something. 'Oh, sir. I was just about to pop down to your office. Just had a call from a . . .' he looked at his pad '. . . Mr Jameson. He lives on Sycamore Road. Says he saw something odd the other night.'

'Odd?'

'He reckons he saw a woman leaving the waste ground where one of the dogs was found.'

Pendragon frowned. 'When?'

'He said Tuesday, about midnight. He said the woman looked odd.'

'That word again, Constable. What does "odd" mean?'

'Apparently, he only caught a brief glimpse, but she was wearing a long flowing dress and she had long black hair. Sounds a bit dodgy, don't you think, sir? Maybe he'd had one too many.'

Pendragon nodded. 'Thanks, Constable,' he said, and strode towards the main doors. Tuesday night was around seventy-two hours ago, he mused. Dog No. 2 found on the waste ground near Sycamore Road showed evidence of '2nd instar' larvae. And the words Sue Latimer had used rang inside his head: 'They'll probably dress up . . .'

'Chief Inspector, it's good to see you again,' Stokes said warmly as he guided Pendragon through the doors of the lab where they had talked the previous day.

'So, what are these exciting findings you mentioned?'

'There's so much, I don't know where to begin.'

Pendragon looked at the professor and realised with a sudden stab of pity that this man was even more married to his job than he was to his, and he was probably even more lonely. At least, Jack remembered, he had a date tonight. He somehow doubted Professor Stokes had been out with a female since his graduation dance.

'Well,' Stokes went on, 'one thing at a time. The bone. Please thank Dr Newman for me. It's been most revealing.'

'How?'

'Well, I found a tiny, tiny trace of soft tissue on it.' He walked over to another of his futuristic-looking machines and patted it. 'And our DNA analyser is second to none. In fact, Thomas, our tech guru, modified this himself. It's more sophisticated than anything you'll find at Quantico.'

'And what did you find?'

'Our skeleton is that of a young Caucasian male, aged fifteen to twenty-five. He died between 1580 and 1595. And the cause of his death?' Stokes paused for dramatic effect and held Pendragon's gaze. 'Arsenic poisoning.'

Pendragon raised an eyebrow. 'Well, that is . . .'

'It's exciting, isn't it? But there's more, Chief Inspector. The ring. I've been studying the main image again. I've put it through various filters and enhancers, but it took a fresh eye to spot something I kept missing. Thomas . . .'

'Your tech guru?'

'Yes, the same. He took one look at the picture of the ring and pointed out the anomaly on the side of the jewel.'

'Anomaly?'

'Yes, take a look.' Stokes walked to a desk and pulled over a huge enlargement of the ring. 'There.

See that bulge? Here, take this.' He handed Pendragon a loupe.

The DCI peered at the image with the loupe at his eye. Straightening, he said, 'What is it?'

'Good question, Chief Inspector. I've given it a great deal of thought and can reach only one possible conclusion. This ring is no ordinary bishop ring. Yes, it was almost certainly owned by the Borgias, which means it wasn't ordinary to begin with. But there's even more to it than that. I believe this ring is the famous "poisoner's" ring once owned by Lucrezia Borgia.'

'Poisoner's ring?'

'Yes. You know about Lucrezia Borgia?'

'Well, I know she was the daughter of Pope Alexander. She was an infamous nymphomaniac and probably a murderer, depending on which historical account you accept.'

'Oh, make no bones about it, Chief Inspector. Lucrezia Borgia was pure evil. She is known to have murdered at least three people. And this ring . . . *this very ring* . . . was almost certainly the means by which she killed those people without ever being caught. Documents written after her death tell us that Lucrezia possessed a ring which fits the description of this one.' He tapped the photograph. 'The jewel pivoted back and a spike levered up from inside. She coated the spike with a particularly potent poison she named Cantarella. The major component of Cantarella was arsenic, but nobody knows the exact composition. According to some accounts, the recipe for the poison was inscribed inside the ring.'

Pendragon stared at the photograph. 'That tiny bulge on the side – what you call an anomaly – that's the mechanism used to open the ring?'

'Correct. When Lucrezia was about to kill, she depressed that tiny lever. The top flipped open, the spike swung up and . . . well, you can imagine.'

'So, what happened to the ring?' Pendragon asked.

'That's the really fascinating thing. It disappeared.'

'Disappeared?'

'Actually, it disappeared twice. Lucrezia died in Ferrara in June 1519, and the ring was not listed among the effects in her estate. We know that several people wanted to get their hands on it, including her third husband, Alfonso d' Este, who survived her by some fifteen years. But it's almost certain he never found it.'

'And the second time?'

'There's a story that the ring was used in an attempt to kill Elizabeth I during the late-sixteenth century.'

Pendragon looked incredulous.

'You find that hard to believe, Inspector? Well, you shouldn't. There were many attempts on the life of the Queen. You have to remember, the religious chaos her father, Henry VIII, had initiated troubled Elizabeth's entire reign, and the wrath of the Catholics was only exacerbated by the humiliation of the Spanish Armada in 1588. Jesuit missionaries were sent to England in an effort to indoctrinate the people against Elizabeth, and some were trained assassins.'

'I had no idea. So, you think the skeleton is that of a Catholic fanatic who tried to kill the Queen of England?'

'Well, I can't be certain. Almost nothing is known of the assassination attempt using the ring of Lucrezia Borgia. The ring was lost and it seems the whole affair was hushed up. But there is a strongly held view among some academics that the assassin almost succeeded.'

'And that's why it was hushed up?'

'Precisely.'

'But it doesn't make sense. If the skeleton is that of the mysterious assassin, how did he die from arsenic poisoning?'

'Sadly, Chief Inspector, I think that's something we may never learn.'

Chapter 42

Stepney, Saturday 11 June, 7 p.m.

The opening notes of Palestrina's Missa Papae Marcelli 'Kyrie' spilled out of the speakers as the man crossed the floor to the cheval glass standing in the corner. The room was lit solely by candles which cast jagged shadows around the walls and the ceiling.

He contemplated his reflection and smiled with satisfaction. He looked good, he thought, very good. The long, black hair of his wig fell around his white-pancaked neck. A new band of gold roses, designed by a master craftsman he had found in Rome, rested on his head. He had chosen a rich blue silk gown with a gold bodice. His make-up was particularly dramatic tonight, and very fetching, he thought: a red slash of lipstick, the shade of spilled blood, black eyeliner and shiny green eyeshadow, rouged cheeks and a beauty spot just above his upper lip. His eyes sparkled as he considered himself. He smiled, revealing even white teeth.

Turning, he took two paces over to the bench. Above it was a print of his favourite portrait of Lucrezia. It was the Bartolomeo Veneziano, painted around 1510, in which she is wearing a white robe and a Turkish headdress, a small posy of flowers clasped in her right hand. She looked remarkably innocent, he thought, so wonderfully deceptive. A woman of pure genius.

He picked up a test tube from the rack and raised it to the candlelight. It contained a green, viscous liquid. He tilted the test tube and watched the substance flow slowly along the glass and back again.

Next to the rack of test tubes stood the little bracket he had fashioned himself. The ring rested in the bracket, the jewel levered back, the spike protruding. Taking a slender glass wand, he unstoppered the test tube, stuck the rod inside and removed it, coated in green. Very carefully, he smeared the spike in the ring with the green liquid and pushed the jewel back into place. Plucking the ring from the bracket, he pulled it down on to the fifth finger of his left hand.

He held up his hand and gazed at the ring. His own good fortune in learning of it never ceased to amaze him. It was destiny, of course. And, in his eyes, the ring's beauty never faded. In the green depths of the jewel he could see infinite space, a trillion universes, all things, for ever. He felt his stomach churn as he remembered again how this object had once been owned by the Goddess Lucrezia herself. Her finger had slipped inside this gold band just as his now filled the space. It was a communion, a deep, deep connection between himself and the woman who had been the object of his adoration for so long.

He turned back to the mirror and rotated his hand, jewel outward, letting the candlelight catch the myriad tiny green worlds inside the emerald. He shifted his fingers, admiring the way the colour set off his eyeshadow so brilliantly.

He heard a sound and stopped. He turned the music off and concentrated on the silence. The sound came again. What was it? A swish of fabric? Something scraping? He tiptoed to the end of the room. The door was ajar. The living-room was dark, the curtains drawn, the lights off. He flicked the wall switch and the room was flooded with light. He stood motionless, his breathing stilled, eyes surveying the room. But there was nothing to see and the only sound was the traffic from the main road and the faint whirring of the fridge in the kitchen.

Returning to the small, candlelit room, he crossed back to the counter where he kept his chemicals and laboratory apparatus. There was a distillation set up: a condenser, flasks, rubber tubing. Next to this stood a Bunsen burner, a tripod and a set of crucibles. To the right of these, a mortar and pestle, an asbestos mat and metal tongs.

He moved to the end of the bench where a small pile of black-and-white photographs lay. He picked them up and walked over to a candle in a holder close to the edge of the bench. The photographs were portraits of familiar faces. He took his time studying some of them, his facial expression constantly shifting: a smile, a frown, another smile, a grimace.

'Who should it be?' he said aloud. 'Who should it be?'

Five pictures in, he stopped. 'Yes.' He pulled the photograph closer, his eyes moving around the image, taking in every detail. 'Yes. Detective Chief Inspector Jack Pendragon, MA (Oxon). Oh, yes, perfect, perfect!' He chuckled as he selected the picture and went to place it on the bench top. Then he stopped. 'Oh, but hang on . . . Oh, my!' He stared at the next image in the pile, glanced back at the photograph of Pendragon then again at the other image. 'Now that . . . that would be pure genius.' And he let out a roar of laughter. 'Pure . . . fucking . . . genius!' He plucked the picture from the pile and put it down on the counter. Staring up at him was the face of Sue Latimer.

Chapter 43

Westminster, London, March 1589

It was the greatest day of his life. As William Anthony backed out of the Queen's council chamber, bowing low, he fingered the Collar of Esses which Her Majesty had just bestowed upon him. This was the single greatest honour any man could receive from the Queen – a personal gift, as well as an official acknowledgement. The collar was solid gold and carried the badge of the Tudor rose, to signify the wearer's perpetual attachment to the Royal Family. It had once been worn by no less a figure than Sir Thomas More.

But this was not all. After the Queen had placed the chain over William's head, resting it across his shoulders, with a smile, she had presented him with a small box as well. 'We wish you to have this, Anthony,' she had told him. 'In further token of Our undying gratitude. Open it only after you leave.'

Outside the chamber, servants had escorted him along a succession of empty corridors. Unable to contain his impatience, William opened the box the Queen had given him and gazed in awe upon the ring of Lucrezia Borgia. Emerging into the light of morning and the Royal stables, he removed the ring from the box and pulled it on to his finger.

Two companions, Thomas Marchmaine and Nicholas Makepeace, were there to meet him, already on their mounts. William's white mare, Ishbel, was saddled and ready. He flicked the reins and led them out from the stable on to the mud track that wound down a gentle incline. From there they picked their way through the mud towards the path east that would take them to the City and beyond.

By the time the small party reached London Bridge, a weak sun was high in the sky. Nicholas and Thomas had trotted ahead and William saw them stop at the entrance to the bridge. William caught up with them and saw three pikes protruding from a buttress. There was a head on each. They were barely recognisable as human, let alone the remains of three people he had once known. On the first pike hung the head of Edward Perch, recognisable only from the scar that ran from his nose to his upper lip. In the centre, the head of Father John William Allen. The left side of his face was missing, the sinews black and flapping away from the bones. To the right of Allen hung the head of Ann Doherty, remnants of her black hair plastered to her face with long-dried blood. Her eyes had been pecked out, her mouth was a red hole.

'A merry threesome,' Nicholas Makepeace chortled. 'Aye, William?' He turned towards his friend. But William ignored him and simply stared at the three heads. And for the first time, the full weight of what he had done bore down upon his shoulders. Edward Perch had been a criminal for sure and a Catholic, an unforgivable combination perhaps. But Father Allen? He had been at worst misguided, controlled by forces he neither understood nor questioned. Perhaps, William Anthony mused, he and John Allen were not so different. Each of them had killed to defend their beliefs. They were soldiers fighting a war. If their roles had been reversed, they would each still have acted in the same way.

He could barely bring himself to consider

Ann, but made himself look at her, made himself study her ravaged features. This was part of his penance, for even though he was a soldier of God, he must answer for his part in bringing about such a death. Ann, sweet Ann. She had cared for him and he had deceived her. Hers was a noble soul. Her only crime was that she had worshipped the wrong God, prayed at the wrong altar. Perhaps, in a better world, William thought, he could have changed her instead of leading her to the worst of deaths. He forced his eyes away. Without a word, he removed the Collar of Esses and placed it carefully in his saddlebag. Flicking his reins, he gave Ishbel a nudge with his heel and broke into a canter along the road heading east out of London.

They passed the east gate without incident and took the road towards Essex. The snow and rain had turned the track to a slurry and then sleet began to fall, a brisk wind picking up from the north. An hour of struggling along the path exhausted the horses, and as the day started to darken, they saw a welcoming light ahead of them.

'I would pay double for a jug of ale at the Grey

Traveller this eve,' Nicholas declared, coming up between the other two.

'I would pay triple, my friend,' William replied. 'And offer my first-born for a comfortable bed.'

It was an old inn. Parts of it had been built using wattle and daub, and a few claimed it had first served travellers making the long journey between the capital and Colchester when Henry II had been King, centuries earlier. The innkeeper knew Walsingham's relative and his friends and welcomed them into the warmth, serving them soup and ale, and offering them his best rooms.

William was in celebratory mood and bought drinks for everyone in the inn. But then, after a few tankards of ale, he became morose and not such good company. Thomas and Nicholas noticed it and tried to cheer their friend with bawdy tales. When these failed, they invited over a couple of local whores they had spotted. But even this effort foundered.

'Come, William. What troubles you?' Thomas asked. 'Surely, my friend, tonight you should be the merriest fellow in all England.'

William forced a smile. 'You are right, Thomas. But I am melancholy, and on my life I cannot account for it. If you will excuse me, I think maybe I need to take the air. Perhaps that will jolt me from my ill humour.'

The inn stood on the banks of a stream, a wide wooden balcony overhanging the water to the rear of the main building. It was said that old King Henry, the Queen's father, had hunted in the fields beside this stream and had stayed at the Grey Traveller with his favourite mistresses.

William leaned against the railing and stared out across the stream. Directly ahead, he could see the drain that led to a cesspit beneath the inn. Beyond that lay black fields. He knew the source of his misery. It was Ann. He could not shake off that last glimpse of her face, ripped apart and desecrated. The hollow black spaces where her lovely green eyes had once been seemed to draw him in, dragging him into the very pits of Hell.

Throughout the ride from London, he had paid little heed to the foul road, the treacly mud or the cold. His mind had been filled with memories of dead faces. He had tried losing himself in false merriment and alcohol, but it had not worked. Over and over again he had asked himself the same question. Would God forgive him? Would God excuse the horrors he had allowed to befall someone who had trusted and loved him? He knew the three traitors had also been heretics and deserved to be doubly punished. And he knew that God forgave the killing of heretics . . . but Ann, dear Ann.

He turned and saw two men walking towards him. They were shrouded in shadow, and for a fleeting moment he thought it was Thomas and Nicholas come to try and console him once more. But it was not. As the men emerged into the faint light cast by the inn, he saw faces he did not recognise. Instinctively, he reached for his dagger.

The two men stepped up to the railing nearby. 'A chilly night,' one of them said, his voice strongly tinged with the local accent.

'It is,' William replied.

'Travelled far?' the other man asked.

William felt a spasm of anxiety in his guts. He had been born into a world of privilege, but had learned much about acting and deceit. Had he not lived by his wits, playing that duplicitous game in Southwark for an interminable year? He started to reply to the second man, to alleviate any suspicion of his own intent, and then darted quickly sideways and made for the door to the inn.

But the other men had lightning reflexes. One of them stuck out his foot and William was sent flying. Before he could right himself, the man was upon him. William twisted and rolled about, managing to unbalance his attacker and send him sprawling along the wooden boards. Propelled by sheer terror, William sprang to his feet and dodged a blow aimed straight at him by the second man. He swiftly drew his dagger, its blade glinting in the light. He brandished the dagger threateningly, slashing the air in front of him.

The man William had floored was on his feet again now. He drew his own blade and edged round behind his quarry. The other man jumped forward, and William lashed out. His elbow landed in the man's abdomen, making him groan and tumble backwards, landing heavily against the wall of the inn. William saw his chance and dashed for the end of the balcony. He could see a small door leading off it, just a few paces before the railings ended.

He grabbed the handle, but it took him only an instant to realise the door was locked. The effort had cost him dear. The man with the dagger was incredibly quick on his feet. Anticipating William's move, he sprinted to the end of the balcony. Out of the corner of his eye William could see the other man had clambered to his feet and was running towards him. He had pulled something large and heavy-looking from inside his tunic, a cosh.

William stood with his back to the door, the dagger in his right hand, his left hand close to the blade, just as he had learned on the streets of Southwark. The man with the knife took a step forward, thrusting at him with startling speed. The tip caught William's left hand, making him cry out. Before he could recover, the man with the cosh threw himself forward. William felt a sharp pain at the side of his head as the leather-covered club hit him hard. He slashed with his dagger. The man with the cosh sidestepped the blow and brought his weapon down again, hard, knocking the blade from William's hand and shattering three fingers.

It was only then, through his pain and the terror, that William remembered the ring. He fell back against the door, sweat running into his eyes. Raising his shattered hand, he flipped open the top of the ring and waved it in front of him.

For a moment, the other men seemed confused and then one of them broke into a smile. 'Oh, what new terror is this?' he mocked.

William thrust his arm forward into the face of the man with the dagger. Some strange intuition or superstition made the attacker step back. But he quickly found new courage. He glanced at his friend and they both rushed forward together. William lashed out and somehow managed to pass between the two of them without further injury. But his foot found a loose board and he lost balance. Falling badly, his arm went under him and he felt a stab of pain as the spike of the ring slid through the fabric of his hose and drove into the flesh of his thigh.

He pulled himself to his feet and backed towards the balcony's railing. The two men watched him retreat, then froze.

William had slumped against the railing. His assailants watched as he raised his injured hand slowly through the air towards his face and then stopped, paralysed. He began to shake violently. A hideous sound came from deep within his body and his mouth hung open. He convulsed, spewing a stream of blood and vomit. The force of the eruption pushed his head back and he pivoted over the railing like a wax effigy, tumbling backwards into the stream.

The two men rushed to the railing, just as Thomas Marchmaine and Nicholas Makepeace emerged from the door to the inn. In shocked silence, they watched as William Anthony hit the bank of the stream head first. He bumped along among the reeds half-submerged, his blank, white face paralysed, mouth agape, eyes staring. Then he was gone, sucked down into the drain that led under the building where the stream flushed out the cesspit of the Grey Traveller.

Chapter 44

Nellie's was a new restaurant in Bethnal Green, a kilometre or so north of Mile End Road. It had received a rave review in *Time Out* and had quickly become *the* place to eat locally. Pendragon was lucky to get a table for two on a Friday night. The owners had designed the restaurant to suit the modern and moneyed East Londoner. It reminded Pendragon of a reception space in an office building: white and grey walls, huge post-modernist paintings, stone floor, spindly chairs that looked like they would collapse if you shifted about on them too much. He hated it.

'Isn't this gorgeous?' Sue said as a very skinny and almost bald waitress dressed in black took their coats.

'Impressive,' he replied, looking around.

At their table they were given enormous menus, single pieces of thick black card with a very small block of grey writing, just off-centre. Pendragon looked at his, slightly bewildered. The restaurant resonated to the hubbub of dozens of conversations, and just audible behind this was the sound of ambient electronic music, Brian Eno or perhaps it was Moby.

Pendragon was about to ask for the wine list when, from behind his chair, he heard a male voice he recognised.

'Well, well, well,' the man said.

Pendragon turned to see Fred Taylor, the *Gazette* journalist. As usual, he had a photographer in tow. Pendragon glanced back at Sue, and sighed.

'DCI Pendragon,' said Taylor ingratiatingly. 'Well, this is cosy, isn't it? And who is your lady friend?'

Pendragon was about to speak when Sue intervened. 'I find it extraordinarily rude when someone doesn't address me directly,' she said. 'I am Dr Sue Latimer. And you are?'

Taylor looked momentarily stunned, but recovered very well. With a sickly smile, he stepped forward and offered his hand to her. 'Fred Taylor, from the *Gazette*.'

'Oh,' she said quietly. 'You wrote that tawdry little piece the other day.'

'Sue . . . it's okay,' Pendragon told her.

To their surprise, Taylor was giggling. 'You do

pick the feisty ones, don't you, Jack, old boy?' he said, eyes darting from Sue to Pendragon and back again. 'Gaz?' He turned to his photographer friend. 'Could you get a snap or two of the happy couple?'

'Now hold on!' Pendragon exclaimed. But it was too late, the flash had gone off. He took a deep breath and managed to control his mounting anger, but Sue was out of her chair and reaching for the camera slung around the photographer's neck.

'Don't touch the gear, lady,' Gaz squealed, and took a step back, colliding with the table behind him.

Taylor was laughing out loud. 'Fantastic!' he said, turning to go. 'I have the headline already, Jack. DCI OUT ON THE TOWN: KILLER STILL AT LARGE.' And with that he strode out, still chuckling to himself, Gaz trotting after him.

'Jack, you're not letting them get away with that, are you?' Sue challenged.

Pendragon was gritting his teeth and mentally counting to ten. When he spoke, he sounded so calm he surprised himself. 'Retaliating plays into their hands,' he explained. 'Believe me, getting angry makes everything ten times worse.'

'But it's not fair! You're allowed to have some time out, like everyone else.'

'Yes, but that man has had it in for me from the moment he first set eyes on me. There's nothing I could say to him that would make any difference. He's on a witch hunt. The best thing I can do is break the case. Success is the sweetest revenge.'

Sue took a deep breath. 'You're right,' she conceded, and broke into a smile. 'Forget about the stupid little man.'

'What stupid little man?' he retorted.

Despite the bad start, Jack found himself quickly relaxing. Sue seemed to have a calming effect on him. He had noticed that when he had gone for dinner at her flat a few days before. There was also the fact that he had chosen a good wine, a five-year-old Saint Emilion, and the crusty French bread served from a wicker basket was delicious.

'It's good to see you outside the police station and away from the flats,' she said. 'And I do like your tie.'

'Oh,' he said, looking down. 'Thanks. I've had it for years.'

She rearranged the napkin on her lap. 'You must be exhausted. Hardly a normal week, I imagine.'

'Never a dull moment, though. Now, you have to promise me – no police talk and no psychology. Is that a deal?'

She smiled. 'A deal.'

He gazed around the room for a second. The place wasn't actually that bad, he thought. At least it had a good ambience. Most of the tables were for two, with a few small groups and the odd solo diner. To either side of them were other couples, engrossed in conversation. Perhaps they were on first dates too. He surprised himself by the thought. He hadn't been on a date for . . . what? Twenty years? He glanced away from the couples. A few tables ahead of him a woman sat alone, her back to them, long black hair draped over the back of her chair. Nearby sat a party of four. They seemed to be a little merry already and were laughing loudly.

'Jack, excuse me a moment. I just need to powder my nose,' Sue said, snapping him out of his reverie.

'Of course.' He stood up and helped her with her chair. She looked into his eyes and smiled as she left him.

Sue was at the hand basin when the door to the Ladies opened. She took no notice as a woman with long black hair and wearing a dark blue dress came in. Sue pulled a lipstick from her clutch bag and leaned forward to apply it. The flush sounded in one of the cubicles. Sue was fishing through her bag looking for eyeliner when the black-haired woman came out and walked slowly towards the mirror. Sue looked up and glanced at the woman properly for the first time.

She was unusually big, with broad shoulders and

what looked to be thick arms under the sleeves of the dress. The woman caught Sue staring and smiled briefly before leaning forward to wash her hands at the adjacent basin. Sue put away her lipstick, checked her hair and closed the clutch bag. The woman glanced up from the basin, catching Sue's eye in the mirror, sending a shudder of anxiety through her. Turning to face her, she took a step towards Sue. She was just about to say something when the door crashed open and two women stumbled in, laughing drunkenly.

'Did you hear what he said to me?' one of them guffawed.

'Yeah, I did, Sal. Dirty bugger!'

Sue sidestepped the new arrivals and slipped out of the Ladies into the narrow corridor leading back to the dining-room.

At the table, Jack was trying to make sense of the menu once again when Sue dropped into her chair. 'If I've translated this correctly,' he said, 'I think I might go for the beef carpaccio.' He looked up at her. 'What's wrong? You look like you've seen a ghost.'

She shook her head and took a gulp of her wine. Placing the glass back on the table, she said, 'I just saw the weirdest-looking woman in the Ladies.'

Pendragon gave her a quizzical look.

'I think it was a trans-sexual. She . . . he . . . was just too big . . .'

Pendragon grabbed her wrist involuntarily. 'What exactly did they look like?'

'Well, er . . . tall. Um . . . long, black hair. And this strange dress . . .'

Pendragon was out of his chair and dodging between the tables.

'Jack!' Sue exclaimed, standing up.

Dashing into the corridor leading to the toilets, he paused for a second at the door to the Ladies, took a deep breath and pushed it open. He squinted in the glaring light and saw two women standing at the hand basins. They saw him. One of them faked a scream and the other burst out laughing.

'Sorry . . .' Pendragon said, and ducked back into the corridor.

'What the hell's going on, Jack?' Sue said as he returned to their table.

'I think you just met our killer,' he said matter-of-factly. 'I'm sorry, Sue. We have to go.'

At the front desk, he began to pay the bill while talking into his mobile tucked under his chin. 'Turner . . . I'm at Nellie's restaurant. Yes, the new one on Bethnal Green Road. I need you here pronto with back-up. I think we've had a positive sighting of our prime suspect . . . No, I can't explain now. Where are you? . . . Just leaving the station? Good. Get here ASAP.'

The girl at the front desk was making a fuss about them leaving. The manager passed by just as Pendragon started to explain. Losing patience, he whipped out his ID, tossed a few large notes on to the desk and turned to Sue. 'Come on. I need to get you home.'

'But our coats . . .'

They walked out into the car park at the rear of the building. It was badly lit and night had set in. A pale milky light from the crescent moon fell across the tarmac. Pendragon flicked his remote. Doors clicked and lights flashed. He walked to the passenger door and helped Sue in, then strode around the back of the car. As he reached the driver's door, a figure burst out of the shadows on the passenger side and dived for the door to the car. In an instant, he had it open and was reaching in. Sue recoiled in terror, banging her head on the rear-view mirror and colliding painfully with the central console.

Pendragon dashed back around the rear of the car. A pair of blazing headlights bore down on them from one side, and he heard the screech of tyres as a car skidded to a halt nearby. The dark figure at Sue's side of the car looked up, his face caught in the powerful

430

headlights. The long wig had slipped, revealing greased-back black hair in a net. Even through the pancake and eyeshadow, the man was immediately recognisable as Max Rainer.

Turner and Inspector Grant were jumping out of the police car as Pendragon darted forward. Rainer slammed shut the door of the car and swung his hand, reaching to within an inch of the DCI's face. Pendragon caught the glimmer of a jewel and a deadly-looking metal spike protruding from Rainer's fifth finger. He fell back and his attacker twisted round with remarkable agility, sliding away and bending low in front of the car bonnet. Pendragon crouched down and peered into the deep shadow just beyond the front of his car. Rainer had vanished.

'He went that way!' Pendragon yelled to Turner and Grant. 'I lost him in the shadows. Be careful, he's armed.' He yanked the door open again and saw Sue, pale and sick-looking. 'You're hurt,' he said, squatting down and turning her head towards him. She winced and clutched her side. A line of blood ran down her temple.

'I banged my head on that thing,' she said, pointing to the mirror. 'And I think I've cracked a rib.'

'Okay, just sit back. Take slow, short breaths.'

Pendragon heard a sound and spun round to see

Turner and Grant emerging from some shrubs a short distance away. They each held a torch, the beams bouncing in the gloom.

'No sign of him,' Turner called.

'Okay. Grant, I'd like you to take Dr Latimer to the London Hospital in my car. Turner, you come with me in the squad car.' He tossed his keys to Grant who ran round to the driver's door.

Crouching down again, Pendragon checked, 'You okay?'

Sue nodded. 'Never a dull moment, Jack.' She smiled and screwed up her face in agony. 'Remind me not to laugh,' she added. Then, reaching for his arm, she said: 'Take care.'

He leaned into the car and kissed her on the lips before running over to the squad car where the sergeant was waiting with the engine turning over.

Chapter 45

Turner had the siren on before they had left the car park and they made it to Rainer's apartment building in the Barbican in four minutes flat. Pendragon called the station for back-up and an armed team was sent out.

He and Turner took the lift and ran along the corridor to flat 402. Turner was brandishing a truncheon.

'Knock it in,' Pendragon ordered.

'You serious?'

'What do you think?'

'Cool.' Turner took two steps back and charged at the door. It creaked but held. Pendragon gave it two hard kicks near the lock. Turner rammed it with his shoulder again and finally it gave way. The door flew back with the wood around the lock splintered, one of the handles drooping.

Pendragon flicked on the light and a gentle halogen glow lit up the hall. Straight ahead was the sitting-room they had been in twice before. Turner stood at the entrance to the room, reached in and flicked on the lights, then slid to the other side of the door frame before slinking into the room. It was empty. The curtains were open, the neon of the Barbican Centre flooding into the room.

Turner walked slowly into the kitchen, his truncheon in front of him, while Pendragon headed for the dining-room leading off the lounge. It was in semi-darkness, the only illumination spilling in from the neighbouring room. A narrow door stood in the centre of the far wall. Light was visible under it. Pendragon crept over, turned the handle and pulled the door slowly towards him.

It was a corridor of a room, narrow and running the length of the dining-room. Along the back wall there were shelves from floor to ceiling. These were filled with an odd assortment of objects. There were rows of leather-bound books, a skull, laboratory apparatus, bottles of chemicals, jars of brightly coloured liquids. He turned and was confronted by an entire wall covered with pictures of a single woman. Some were reproductions of old portraits of Lucrezia Borgia, but some originals had obviously been produced by an unremarkable artist – probably Rainer himself, Pendragon mused. At the end of the room stood a tall mirror; beside it, a cabinet with

434

drawers overspilling with sumptuous fabrics – silks and velvets. Over the cabinet lay a red velvet skirt and bodice. On the floor immediately in front of it lay a pair of gold-coloured slippers. On hooks along the wall to the other side of the mirror hung a row of wigs – one black, another blonde – long strands of hair trailing to the floor. Next to these was a curly blonde hairpiece with a pearl-adorned headband attached.

Pendragon spun round as Turner walked in. The sergeant gazed open-mouthed as his boss paced along the narrow space, studying the contents of the shelves. Just before the mirror stood a worktop. On top of it were beakers, pipettes and distillation equipment – a mass of glass cylinders and rubber piping. Next to these lay a notebook. Pendragon picked it up and flicked through a few pages. Turner looked over his boss's shoulder. It was written in some sort of code, but the odd symbol jumped out at them: AsO_3, the chemical sign for arsenic trioxide, as well as a Latin name, *Abrus precatorius*, which Pendragon knew was the proper name for the plant from which abric acid was refined.

'Ah, I see you've found my lair.'

Pendragon and Turner looked round simultaneously. At the door stood Max Rainer, in full costume, his wig reinstated. He carried an ancient-looking dagger in one hand. 'It's like scissors-paper-stone, isn't it, Sergeant?' His voice was jaunty. 'I think a dagger beats a truncheon any day.' Then his voice hardened. 'Drop it.'

Turner glanced at Pendragon, who nodded. The sergeant let the truncheon slide to the floor.

'Kick it over.'

Turner complied.

'Excellent. I'm sorry I can't offer you a place to sit. This is my work space.'

'Mr Rainer,' Pendragon began calmly.

'Don't . . .' Rainer hissed. 'My name is Lucrezia Borgia, you snivelling nobody!' In the low light, his eyes were black, fathomless.

Pendragon was taken aback for a second, but quickly recovered. 'Don't you think the game is up? I have an armed team outside. I've told them to move in if we're not out in ten minutes. Meanwhile all I have to do to call them immediately is speed-dial with this.' He held up his mobile. 'They'll be in here in thirty seconds.'

Rainer laughed suddenly. 'Oh, just listen to yourself, you silly little man. Push your stupid speed-dial button. Bring your soldier boys up here. They'll find you already covered in your own vomit and blood.'

'All right,' Pendragon placated him. He put his hands up. 'What do you want?'

'Him!' And Rainer grabbed Sergeant Turner, spinning him round and twisting one arm up hard behind his back. Jez yelped with pain. Rainer brought the knife up to the young man's throat and drew blood. A line of red slithered along the blade.

'Okay,' Pendragon shouted. 'Let him go! *I'll* be your hostage.'

Rainer laughed again. 'I need nothing from you.' And he fixed Pendragon with a cold stare. Beads of sweat had appeared on his forehead and his make-up was beginning to run. A green streak slithered down his cheek. The pancake had started to bubble on his chin. 'Actually, that's not entirely true. I want you to *listen*. I want to make it clear to you just how *clever* I've been, how the divine Lucrezia has helped me.'

Pendragon opened his arms, palms upwards. 'Fine,' he replied evenly. 'That's fine. Just let Sergeant Turner go, okay?'

'No.'

Jez was also sweating, beads of perspiration leaking from his temples and running down his neck.

'Oh, no, no, no, DCI Pendragon. That would never do. All right, where do I start? Oh, such good fortune, such good fortune! Fate, of course. DESTINY!' Rainer exclaimed. He looked up at the ceiling for a moment before turning his black eyes back to Pendragon.

'It was Tim Middleton who opened the door for

me,' he went on. 'Tim, that sickening bastard who liked to fiddle around with little boys. Even goddesses act in mysterious ways, it seems. You see, I've always been obsessed with Lucrezia Borgia. I built this shrine to her. I studied everything I could find about her. I knew all about the fabled ring. How it was lost. How I could find it.'

'But that's a ridiculous coincidence,' Pendragon put in quietly.

Rainer paused and looked hard at him. 'Perhaps, Chief Inspector. But good fortune comes to those who help themselves, those who are best prepared. As I said, I've made a very careful study of the Borgia family and everything associated with them. I've spent more hours than I care to remember in libraries and private collections across Europe. Then Timmy boy comes to me with photographs of the skeleton. I knew immediately what I was looking at, though I could hardly believe it.

'That night we broke into the construction site. It was easy to persuade Middleton to help me. I knew a great deal about him, remember. And, yes, it was I who was blackmailing him. Tim had a tidy inheritance from his old dad. And, well, I needed to fund my research and expand my collection. Oh, and by the way, just to tidy up the loose ends, Chief Inspector, I never was being blackmailed myself and never did get a young girl pregnant years ago. I was just playing with you.' Rainer cackled. Then his face darkened. 'Unfortunately things at the construction site last Saturday did not go entirely to plan. The security guard turned up just after I had removed the ring. There was a scuffle . . . and he saw my face.'

'So you killed him?'

'Obviously. We dumped him in what we thought was a waste chute. Turned out it wasn't!' Rainer gave a sickly grin. 'Middleton, being the arsehole he was, began to panic and I was sure he was going to blab. I warned him . . .'

'And so you killed him too?'

'Will you stop fucking interrupting me!' Rainer cut Turner again. A second red line appeared on his neck.

'The ring had the recipe for Cantarella inside it. I knew it would, of course. I didn't waste a second. After all, I'd been dreaming of this day for so long. I've been making poisons here for years. I knew Cantarella was based on arsenic, but I couldn't even hazard a guess at its other components. I already had some arsenic from a local glass-maker, and when I knew what other chemicals to acquire, I broke into the Plant Biology Department at Queen Mary and produced the poison. Yes, I know what you want to ask now . . . the dogs, right?'

Pendragon gave an almost imperceptible nod.

'*This* is why I love Lucrezia so much. She was just so . . . so gorgeously cruel. You see, Cantarella is no normal poison. It is, well, for want of a better expression, "fortified". Lucrezia learned that if you gave an animal the raw poison, they would die quickly, but their body processed the poison and then you could collect the refined product from its blood or from its foaming mouth, its saliva. The dogs were the amplifiers of the poison.' And he roared in delight. 'Genius! Pure fucking genius.'

After a moment, he calmed down and suddenly seemed to become aware that time was passing quickly. 'So, yes, DCI Pendragon, I killed Timmy boy. Jabbed him with the divine Lucrezia's ring just before he was about to start his ridiculous speech. He was so drunk anyway, he didn't even notice. Then I killed Tony Ketteridge because he was the one person who could have got me into trouble after I disposed of Tim. Tony and I go way back. He knew about my interest in the Borgias. He suspected I had taken the ring, and you were putting so much pressure on him, it was inevitable he would say something incriminating, without even realising what I was doing or how.'

'And for that, you will suffer in Hell!'

The loud voice made them all jump. Pendragon

stared towards the doorway. Rainer spun round, keeping Turner close before him, the knife at his throat. Pam Ketteridge stood just inside the room, holding a revolver in her right hand. 'Let the young man go,' she ordered, her voice shaky.

The three men stared at her in shock. None of them moved.

'Are you deaf, Rainer?'

'I am Lucrezia Borgia,' he snarled, and cut Turner a third time, making him gasp.

'I said, let him go, Rainer, you ridiculous little shit! Or I swear I will blow your fucking head off.' Pam Ketteridge's eyes were ablaze, her face scarlet.

Rainer flinched.

'Now, you fuck!'

He lowered the knife.

'Toss it over there,' she said, her voice calmer.

Rainer stared at her, his eyes screwed up, muscles in his jaw twitching involuntarily. With a resigned sigh, he threw the knife to the floor. Turner yanked himself free and stepped back, clutching at his cut neck, fixing Max Rainer with a look of pure hatred.

'Mrs Ketteridge,' Pendragon said slowly, 'I must say, I'm a little surprised.'

She flicked her eyes from Rainer to him. 'Yes, I'm sure you are, Chief Inspector.'

'What's going on?'

'I'm here to take this . . . this piece of garbage to Hell,' she replied. Pendragon tilted his head and gave her a quizzical look. Rainer stood absolutely rigid, glaring at Tony Ketteridge's widow.

'I was there that night. I saw it all.'

'At the construction site?' Pendragon said.

'I followed my husband out at two o'clock. He went then, not nine-thirty like I said before. I suspected he was having an affair. I kept out of sight and saw him go on to the site. He had a bag buried under a pile of soil. Tony was about to start packing up the skeleton when *he* turned up with another man.' She twitched her head in Rainer's direction. 'We both watched him take the ring while he and another man were down there with the Indian workman. There was a fight and Amal Karim pulled Rainer's balaclava off and we all saw his face. He and Middleton, it must have been, chased Karim across the site, and my husband, God rest his soul, reappeared and took the skeleton . . .'

'Why didn't you just come to us?' Pendragon asked.

'Isn't that obvious, Chief Inspector? The whole story would have come out then and Tony would have been arrested. Besides, this is not your job, it's the Lord's work, and I am his vessel.' She took a step towards Rainer who retreated against the bookcase.

Grabbing his upper arm, she rammed the gun against his neck. Shocked, he went limp. From her pocket, Mrs Ketteridge withdrew a length of twine.

'Please tighten this around his wrists,' she instructed Turner. The sergeant hesitated for a moment, then stepped forward.

'Make it as tight as you like, young man,' Pam added.

'Look, is this really . . .'

'Shut up, Rainer!' she snapped, her voice shrill with emotion. 'Don't . . . just *don't* . . . dare say a word.' She checked the tightness of the twine about his wrists, then turned to Pendragon. 'I'm going to have to take your mobile.'

He stared at her hard.

'Please, Inspector. There's only one person here I want to hurt.'

He reached into his pocket. She took her hand from Rainer's arm for a second but pushed the gun into his neck harder, just to confirm that he should do absolutely nothing. She took Pendragon's phone and slipped it into her pocket.

'And yours.' She turned to Jez.

'Look, Mrs Ketteridge,' Pendragon pleaded. 'Can't we discuss this?'

'What's there to discuss, Chief Inspector? I tried to kill the sinner once before and failed. Now . . .'

Rainer twisted towards her. 'It was you? *You* hit me over the head?'

'The Lord guided my hand, as he does now. I thought I had killed you, but when I discovered I had just knocked you out, God made me realise something important. I can't *just* kill you, I have to take you to Our Lord first. That's why He saved you. I need to show Him I have done His work. Then I will kill you.'

'Mrs . . .'

'No, DCI Pendragon,' Pam Ketteridge hissed. 'No. Please, just leave me to do the Lord's work.' She was backing towards the door. Rainer looked desperately towards the policemen as he was dragged after her. Then, captor and captive were gone.

Turner was the first to reach the door. It wouldn't budge.

'She's probably wedged a chair against the handle,' Pendragon said. 'Here, let me.' He stepped forward and gave the door a kick. It flew open into the dining-room.

They dashed through the sitting-room and into the hall. There was no sign of Mrs Ketteridge or Rainer. A loud clanking sound came from the landing outside the door. Pendragon moved slowly along the wall of the hall with Turner beside him. They reached the door and saw three armed policemen emerge from the lift, four more appearing at the top of the stairs. Two of the cops crouched with their pistols pointed directly at the plainclothes policemen. Pendragon and Turner put their hands up instinctively. Then the cops relaxed and lowered their weapons.

'What's happening?' Pendragon snapped. Then, whirling round, he noticed an Emergency Exit sign at the end of the landing. 'They've gone down there!' he yelled to the armed unit. 'A man and a woman. The woman is Mrs Pam Ketteridge, the man Max Rainer. He's dressed as a woman. Mrs Ketteridge has a firearm and has taken him hostage. Go!' He spun round to check on Jez Turner. 'Sergeant, are you okay?'

Turner was pressing his hand to his neck. 'Just a couple of nicks.'

'Good. Let's go!'

Chapter 46

They took the stairs, racing down three at a time. Emerging through the front doors, they arrived just in time to see an old Volvo tearing towards them. It missed the kerb by a few inches and screeched away. In the streetlights and neon glow, they could see Pam Ketteridge at the wheel. Rainer was in the passenger seat, unconscious, his head lolling forward. It was raining heavily.

Climbing into the squad car, Pendragon grabbed the radio. 'All points,' he said, breathing heavily. He was silently directing Turner, waving his hand in front of him as he spoke. 'A silver Volvo 340, registration GOLF, HOTEL, ROMEO, 9, 0, 6, YANKEE. Repeat: GOLF, HOTEL, ROMEO, 9, 0, 6, YANKEE. Last seen heading south along Aldersgate Street. Two occupants, Max Rainer and Pam Ketteridge. Mrs Ketteridge is carrying a firearm. Rainer is wearing a potentially lethal ring. Approach with extreme caution. Repeat: approach with extreme caution.'

Turner spun the car on to the main road, the siren blaring. He tore down Aldersgate Street, the wipers on max, and they caught a glimpse of the Volvo ahead. It was weaving between the other cars, setting off a fanfare of car horns and a screeching of brakes. A few hundred metres along the road, Pam Ketteridge turned left, racing along London Wall. Reaching Bishopsgate, she threw the car hard left again and then immediately right. Thirty seconds later, she was on Whitechapel Road.

Turner was keeping up with the Volvo, but Pam Ketteridge was driving so fast in the heavy rain, he could not gain on her.

'Where do you think she's heading, guv?'

Pendragon shook his head. 'I just don't know. I think she has somewhere in mind, she's not just running.'

'But she's a nutter.' Turner didn't take his eyes from the road.

'Yes,' Pendragon replied. 'She's probably insane, but she has a clear purpose. She's working to an agenda.'

'Yeah, the Lord's. Hallelujah!'

Pendragon twisted in his seat. 'Right again, Sergeant. That's it! She's going to her church. What did she say at Rainer's place? She needed to take him to "Our Lord" before she killed him? The church at the end of her street is the Church of Our Lord of Bethlehem. That's where she's heading!' He snatched at the radio. 'Suspect is heading for the Church of Our Lord of Bethlehem, Manning Street. Repeat: Manning Street. We are currently two minutes away. Report status.'

A moment passed and then, one by one, five patrol cars and a helicopter called in with their positions and ETAs. 'Red Alpha 3 will be there first,' Turner said. 'The chopper should be overhead any second.' And with perfect timing, they both heard the police helicopter shoot over the car, heading directly east to the church on Manning Street.

The Volvo slowed as it hit Mile End Road, then tore out of the traffic on to the wrong side of the road. The headlights of another car raced towards it. The driver caught sight of the Volvo, slid his car to one side and screeched to a halt just in time for the Volvo to slip past and overtake two cars on its side of the road before accelerating through a red light and narrowly avoiding a side-on smash with a van. Barely slowing, Pam Ketteridge spun the car left into a narrow street off Mile End Road.

A few seconds later, Turner had made it to the narrow street just as the red tail lights of the Volvo vanished to the right. He made the corner and twisted the wheel, letting the power-steering ride. Ahead was another squad car, but no sign of the Volvo.

'She's changed her mind,' Pendragon said, thrown forward as Turner slowed. He gripped the dashboard. 'There! A turning on the right. See it? Go.'

Turner slammed his foot down and the car roared forward. Pendragon was on the radio again, giving fresh instructions. 'Red Alpha 3. Try to head her off at Lemmington Road. Blue Beta 2, get back on Mile End, heading east.'

The chopper roared low overhead again, a massive searchlight sweeping through the night. Turner swung the wheel right, then hard left. For a couple of anxious moments they lost it. Then Turner pulled on to a main road heading north and they caught sight of it again. The Volvo hit a huge puddle and sent a plume of dirty water high into the air.

A hundred metres down the road the Volvo spun 180 degrees before tearing down a side street. A car that had been behind it shuddered to a stop, but the driver behind him could not stop in time and aquaplaned straight into the back of the stationary vehicle. The crunch of metal and the screech of tyres cut through the night and the two cars stuck together, danced across the tarmac and slammed into a wall on the other side of the road.

Turner braked hard and managed to avoid

smashing into them before spinning the squad car down the side street. The rear lights of the Volvo were directly ahead and started to bounce as the car hit a roughly tarmacked lane. Turner and Pendragon hit the same stretch, and were thrown around inside the squad car. Mud splashed up the windows.

Then, suddenly, the chase was over. A short distance ahead, glaring red brake lights came on. As Turner tried to stop their car, its wheels losing purchase and sliding in the mud, the driver's door of the Volvo flew open. Pam Ketteridge emerged wearing a long, lightweight coat. It flapped around her as she ran round to the passenger side, opened the door and dragged Rainer out. She didn't even bother looking at the police car slithering to a halt along the lane. Rainer, his wrists bound, struggled to get out of the car and then fell into the mud with a pathetic squeal. With remarkable strength, Pam Ketteridge dragged him to his feet. In the headlights, Pendragon and Turner could see Rainer caked in mud, his long wig matted with brown slime.

The squad car stopped a metre behind the Volvo, but Pam Ketteridge had vanished into the shadows together with Max Rainer.

'Where've they gone?' Turner asked, exasperated.

The two policemen ran into the gloom as the

chopper appeared overhead. Its powerful beam swept across the muddy lane, picking out two figures no more than thirty metres ahead.

Pendragon and Turner ran as fast as they could. The torrential rain had soaked them through in seconds. A hundred metres along the track, they saw Pam Ketteridge veer off to the right with Rainer in tow, and it was only then that Pendragon and Turner realised they were on the banks of a river. The light from the chopper dimmed for a moment as it circled round. Then the landscape was ablaze again as it turned back towards them, its searchlights cutting away the darkness.

Pam and Rainer were on a bridge over the river. She had her captive on his knees and was standing over him, her pistol at his head. Water rushed under the bridge, sending up spray that caught in the lights of the chopper.

Pendragon looked down and saw they were next to a weir. Rain slammed into the swollen brown water. They ran on to the bridge as the chopper ascended, dispersing the floodlight, the sound of the rotors diminishing.

'Mrs Ketteridge . . . Pam!' Pendragon shouted.

She looked up, but appeared not to see him. Rainer was shaking, his face contorted as he whimpered.

'Pam,' Pendragon repeated, 'put the gun down.

We can sort this out. Rainer will spend the rest of his life in prison. Believe me.'

Pam Ketteridge turned to Pendragon again and broke into a huge, manic grin. 'Prison, Chief Inspector? Yes. Prison.' Then she turned back to Rainer. He looked up at her. Water splashed over them. His wig was lank with spray and stuck to his smeared face.

She took the gun from Rainer's head, and for a second his expression changed. Despair and terror slithered into guarded relief. Then she shifted the pistol to her left hand, reached into the pocket of her long coat with her right, and withdrew a crucifix. It was metal and at least twelve inches long. The bottom of the cross tapered to a point. With lightning speed, Pam lifted the crucifix. 'O, Lord,' she said, 'Thy will be done.' And she plunged it deep into the side of Rainer's neck, ramming it in with such force it sliced through his windpipe and emerged the other side. He fell back, legs splayed and back arched. Swivelling on to one side, he tumbled from the bridge into the crashing water.

Pendragon and Turner stood paralysed with shock. Three uniformed officers had appeared beside them. They could hear the men's heavy breathing.

Pam Ketteridge was smiling and staring up at the sky, rain falling into her eyes and running down her neck. She was covered with blood washed pink by the rain. She turned back to Pendragon and Turner, her face aglow. For a fleeting moment, she looked twenty years younger.

Then, as if in slow motion, she transferred the pistol to her right hand and shot herself in the mouth.

Chapter 47

Sue Latimer opened the door to her flat and broke into a smile. 'Jack,' she said and kissed him on the cheek. 'Ouch!' she exclaimed and stepped back, clutching her side, a pained expression on her face.

'Still hurting then,' Pendragon said and surveyed her face. She had a large plaster at her temple and her cheek was bruised.

'What have you got there?'

He looked down at the objects in each hand. 'This,' he said, handing her a small plastic cylinder, 'is some chicken soup from my favourite deli. They tell me it is just the thing for a broken rib. And this . . . well, can I come in?'

'Sorry, Jack.' She opened the door wide and he placed a large box on the kitchen counter.

'This *you* have to open.'

'What is it?' Sue said, her eyes sparkling.

'Here, let me help the invalid,' Jack said, and handed her a pair of kitchen scissors from a drawer.

She cut through the paper and peeled it away to reveal an expensive-looking turntable. She clapped her hands together in delight. 'Oh, Jack. That's so thoughtful of you.' She went to kiss him and stopped herself, then blew him a kiss. 'Thank you.'

'A pleasure,' he replied. 'I'll set it all up for you. I noticed when I was here for dinner that you have a CD player. It's easy to connect this to it and then you can hear music how it was meant to be heard – on vinyl.'

Sue looked at him doubtfully and led the way to the sofa. 'So,' she said, sitting down slowly, 'the ring has been lost . . . again?'

'Looks like it. Pam's body has been found, but there's no sign of Rainer.'

'But how on earth did he come by the ring in the first place?'

'He insisted he was guided to it by the "divine Lucrezia".'

'Yes, of course. He would.'

'In actual fact, he went about it like a professional archaeologist. We found a set of notes in his lab. Apparently, about a year ago he stumbled upon an ancient private journal in the archives of the British Library. It was written by a nobleman named Thomas Marchmaine who described how his close friend, William Anthony, had been murdered at an inn called the Grey Traveller. He had been killed the day he received a mysterious ring from Queen Elizabeth I herself; a reward for saving the Queen's life. The ring was said once to have been owned by none other than Lucrezia Borgia. Rainer then found the location of the Grey Traveller from local records. He learned an old Victorian house stood on the site and persuaded the owner to sell. Rainer was also a close friend of the CEO of Bridgeport Construction. He knew the company was looking to develop sites around Mile End Road. It was as though he had set up his own professional dig. Professor Stokes is in raptures. Can't believe the material Rainer had in his little lab.'

Sue was shaking her head. 'Classic obsessive behaviour. It's such a shame the man's dead. He would have made a fascinating case study.'

Pendragon raised an eyebrow. 'That's one way to look at it.' Then, brightening, he said, 'As you pointed out in the restaurant last night, it's not exactly been a normal week. I'm meeting the team for a little celebration. Are you feeling up to a drink at the pub?'

'You joking? I'd love to. I can't stand being housebound, broken rib or no broken rib.'

They walked the short distance to the pub. The small garden at the front was dotted with tables accommodating families, kids diving into packets of crisps while Mum and Dad enjoyed a leisurely Sunday lunchtime drink in the summer sunshine. The public room was packed, as usual, and noisy. Customers lined the bar. A small crowd had gathered around the dartboard at the far end of the room, and a rerun of Saturday's Premier League game was playing on the plasma screen. As Pendragon walked in he could hardly believe that only a week ago he had been in this bar when they'd learned of Tim Middleton's murder. The past seven days had sped by.

He caught sight of the team from the station. Jez waved them over and pointed to a couple of chairs. A cheer went up around the table as the others saw the Chief Inspector, and as he lowered himself into his seat he felt Rob Grant slap him on the back.

'Thanks,' Pendragon said and looked round at the smiling faces. 'I think we've had what they call a result.'

'So, it's your round then, guv,' Ken Towers announced.

Pendragon laughed and turned to Sue, shaking his head.

A few minutes later, he was back at the table with a large tray crowded with glasses. Roz Mackleby was trying desperately to clear a space, telling Turner to give her a hand. Jack handed Sue her drink first. When everyone had a glass, he raised his. 'Congratulations on a job well done,' he said. 'Cheers.' He sat down and took a gulp of his beer.

'Back just in time, sir,' Turner declared.

'Oh?'

'Ken reckons he has the conundrum to beat all conundrums.'

Pendragon turned to Inspector Towers as he took another sip of beer. 'Let's hear it then.'

'Not only is it the best, it's also very topical.'

'Ooooh!' three of the team around the table cooed in unison.

'Okay. A man goes to a party and drinks some of the punch. He leaves early. Everyone else at the party who drinks from the same punch bowl subsequently dies from poisoning. Why did the man not die?'

'What? I would have thought that was bloody obvious!' Jimmy Thatcher declared. 'The first guy poisoned the punch after he drank from it, and then left.'

'Oh, for Christ's sake, Jimmy! Give me a little more credit, please.'

'Oh, well, I'll just shut up,' Thatcher said, embarrassed, and took a large mouthful of beer.

The table was silent for a moment.

'So, the first guy, he's not a murderer? Remember, you have to answer truthfully, Ken,' Mackleby said.

'I know that. No, he's not.'

'Someone else put some poison in after the first guy drank from it?'

'Nope.'

'Guv? You're being awfully quiet,' Turner said suddenly. 'You heard this one at university too?'

Sue grinned and looked at Jack. He drank some more before answering. 'Actually, no. I haven't heard this one before. But I think I could have a shot at the answer.'

Everyone turned to him.

'I think the poison in the punch was actually contained in ice cubes. When the first man drank from the punch bowl, the poison wasn't able to work. But later, when the ice had melted, it got into the punch and killed the other drinkers.'

Pendragon put his glass down and all heads turned to Ken Towers who was hiding his face behind his own beer glass. Then he groaned and lowered his glass. 'I bow to you . . . o, master,' he said, and looked up as a figure approached the table behind Pendragon.

The DCI felt a tap on his shoulder and turned to see Superintendent Jill Hughes standing just behind his chair. 'Shame you can't solve real crimes so fast,' she said, grinning. 'Mine's a gin and tonic, thanks, Jack.'

The Facts Behind the Fiction

As with my first two novels, *Equinox* and *The Medici Secret*, *The Borgia Ring* is a work of fiction, but one based upon many true facts and real events. Here is a quick guide to help distinguish between the facts and the fiction.

HEINRICH CORNELIUS AGRIPPA

Heinrich Cornelius Agrippa was an alchemist and philosopher who would have been sixteen in 1503, when he appears as a teenager at the Borgia court in the Prologue to this book.

Agrippa was born in Cologne in 1486 and taught for a while at the University of Dole in France. However, he quickly clashed with the authorities there and was denounced as a heretic by the local clergy.

He led a peripatetic life, finding employment with wealthy families as a magus, court philosopher, and sometime soldier-at-arms. Although he travelled extensively throughout Italy, there is no record of Agrippa working for the Borgias, and of course no hard facts to show that he was involved in the preparation of the poison Cantarella with Lucrezia Borgia. But Agrippa was a contemporary of Lucrezia and of Leonardo da Vinci, who is said to have theorised about the production of the poison.

Agrippa wrote many books and lectured widely. His masterpiece is *Libri tres de occulta philosophia*, a perfect example of Renaissance occult thinking.

Cornelius Agrippa has been mentioned in several other works of fiction, most notably in Mary Shelley's *Frankenstein* (1818) and James Joyce's *A Portrait of the Artist as a Young Man* (1916).

ASSASSINATION ATTEMPTS ON ELIZABETH I

There were several attempts on the life of Queen Elizabeth I. Although she was generally very popular with her subjects, Elizabeth had many enemies. Indeed, when she came to the throne in 1558, she was crowned by the Bishop of Carlisle, an unimportant cleric, because none of the important churchmen in the realm would conduct the ceremony for 'a heretic' who was an illegitimate successor (Elizabeth was the bastard daughter of the hated Ann Boleyn).

Elizabeth was dedicated to the reforms her father, Henry VIII, had initiated, and her servants hunted down and executed Catholic activists. In consequence she was hated by Rome, excommunicated by the Pope in 1570, and denounced as a heretic. At the same time, Elizabeth was opposed to extreme Protestant sects who were threatening to destabilise England.

The most famous plot against her was concocted by a Catholic zealot named Anthony Babington and his cohorts, who planned to kill the Queen and replace her with the Catholic Mary Queen of Scots. This plot was exposed in 1586 by Elizabeth's dedicated and extremely effective spymaster, Francis Walsingham.

THE BEAR GARDEN

During the reign of Henry VIII (1509–47) commoners were banned from playing or watching most sports. It was believed by the ruling classes that their inferiors should work and that sports distracted them from their labours. However, wealthy people were not subject to such draconian rules and they became keen followers of football and tennis as well as such cruel pastimes as cockfighting and animal baiting.

By Elizabeth's time, such barbaric sports as bear-baiting and bull-baiting were popular with all classes of people. The Queen herself attended bear gardens, and arenas built especially for these spectator sports sprang up in every large town in England. The most famous was the Bear Garden in Southwark which appears in *The Borgia Ring*. This was built around 1540, and stood close to what is now Southwark Bridge Road. It remained open for almost a century and a half, not closing down until 1682. The sport of bear-baiting remained legal until 1835.

ROBERTO BELLARMINO

Born in 1542, Roberto Bellarmino was a cardinal, a powerful and dedicated Jesuit and a great papal adviser. In 1588, a year before this book is set, he was made Spiritual Father to the Roman College. He is seen by some Catholics as a great man who was a guide to successive Popes and an intellectual who wrote a collection of important treatises on theology.

He was canonised by Pope Pius XI in 1930. However, by many, Bellarmino is seen as an obsessive who prized the power of the Church above all else, including innocent human lives. He was known as 'Hammer of Heretics' and did his utmost to eradicate those who opposed the Church. He was instrumental in the early stages of Galileo's persecution by Rome, and masterminded the torture and execution of the philosopher Giordano Bruno who was burned at the stake in 1600.

LUCREZIA BORGIA AND THE BORGIA FAMILY

The Borgias may be thought of as Renaissance Mafiosi. Their time at the pinnacle of power was short, but they ruled over extensive papal lands across Europe. The head of the family, Rodrigo Borgia, was born in Spain and ascended to the papacy in 1492. He was a vile man who committed sodomy, bestiality and incest. He threw extravagant orgies using papal funds and meddled in the political scene of Europe without understanding anything about it. He was a murderer who stopped at nothing in his pursuit of wealth and power.

Pope Alexander's son, Cesare Borgia, was, if

anything, even more corrupt and evil than his father. He played at being a warlord, but preferred to kill his enemies via deceit and deception rather than fighting on the battlefield. He is strongly suspected of killing his own brother, Giovanni, as well as many of his sister Lucrezia's suitors. His favourite pastime was travelling into Rome in disguise with an entourage of thuggish minders. There, he would befriend some unfortunate at a bar and coerce them into insulting the Borgia family. He would then drag them into the street and chop off their hands. If the victim was lucky, Cesare or one of his henchmen would finish them off. If, however, Cesare felt particularly annoyed, he would leave his victim to wander the streets, bleeding to death.

Growing up in such a family, it is hardly surprising that Lucrezia Borgia, five years Cesare's junior, ended up as corrupt as her relatives. She was a nymphomaniac who was known to have indulged (or been forced to indulge) in incestuous relationships with her father and her brother, often at the same time.

However, Lucrezia is most famous as a murderess. She really did produce a poison called Cantarella and she did have a ring with a top that opened. I have, however, adapted this to a ring containing a spike. In reality, the ring simply contained the poison which she surreptitiously added to the food or drink of a prospective victim.

It is also true that she knew Leonardo da Vinci, who worked as a military adviser to the Borgia family for a year (1502–3). Leonardo did indeed theorise about the idea of fortifying poison by passing it through the body of an animal. However, he absolutely refused to conduct experiments to prove his ideas. It is believed that Lucrezia had no such scruples.

WILLIAM BYRD

Byrd's exact date of birth is not known, but he was aged between forty and fifty at the time in which the story of *The Borgia Ring* is set. He was greatly favoured by Queen Elizabeth and appointed her Court Composer. His works are still popular today, some four centuries after his death. William Byrd was a devout Catholic who is known to have attended many clandestine Masses, so it is perfectly possible that he would have turned up at a religious gathering in Southwark in February 1589, as described in the novel.

CANTARELLA

This is a real poison. Its formula has been lost, but its key ingredient was arsenic. The poison was indeed created by Lucrezia Borgia (almost certainly with the help of an alchemist). She is also thought to have used bears and dogs to create the fortified version of the poison.

JESUIT MISSIONARIES

Jesuit missionaries were trained in Rome with the specific task of indoctrinating non-Catholics and giving spiritual support to their brethren in England. Between 1570 and 1600 there were many Jesuit missionaries who went further than this remit and deliberately tried to subvert English society and damage the standing of the Queen. Many of them were executed as traitors. Of course, the parallel with modern-day terrorist cells in England is striking.

PURSUIVANTS

This was the name given to those employed by Francis Walsingham, the Queen's spymaster, whose job it was to hunt down and flush out Catholic activists. Supporters of the Roman Church lived in constant fear of these men, a force that might be likened to a Tudor-era Gestapo. They responded to intelligence gathered from Walsingham's spy network and raided Catholic gatherings and secret Masses, dragging off unfortunates to be tried for high treason, and, in many cases, cruelly executed.

SKELETONS UNDER LONDON

There are many of these. As London is redeveloped, more and more skeletons are being unearthed. A recent report (*Tales From Beyond the Grave*, BBC Online, 19 July 2008) described how some 17,000 skeletons have been discovered during the past thirty years in London. Many of these were victims of plague found in communal pits. However, it is relatively common for single skeletons to be unearthed by builders, as described in *The Borgia Ring*.

SOUTHWARK

This district on the south bank of the Thames is today a rather desirable and quite expensive area in which to live. However, until at least the middle of the twentieth century, it was regarded as one of the worst areas of London. In Tudor times it was home to bear gardens and theatres, brothels and gambling dens.

THE LONDON THEATRE

The theatre flourished in London during Tudor times. The Queen herself was a big fan, and the London stage was a fertile proving ground for the development of such immortal talents as William Shakespeare, Ben Jonson, John Fletcher and Christopher Marlowe.

Shakespeare's Globe Theatre was not built until 1599, a decade after the setting of this book. However, it is believed that William Shakespeare started acting in London around the time in which I have set this novel, and of course he has a brief cameo appearance in it. The theatre described in the novel, the Eagle, is fictitious, but I based it upon old descriptions of real theatres in Southwark and elsewhere.

Flags were used to tell the public what sort of play would be performed each night. A different colour was used to signify comedy, tragedy or history.

TUDOR EXECUTIONS

These were conducted pretty much as described in the book. The difference between execution for treason and high treason was immense. Those convicted of treason were either beheaded or hanged, a relatively swift end. Those unfortunate enough to be condemned for high treason were hung, drawn and quartered. The execution described towards the start of *The Borgia Ring* is closely based upon the execution of the Catholic missionary Henry Wittingham who was hung, drawn and quartered at Tyburn, by decree of Queen Elizabeth I.

FRANCIS WALSINGHAM

Sir Francis Walsingham was born into the aristocracy around 1532 (though the exact date is unknown). He was a great administrator and Queen Elizabeth's right-hand man for almost thirty years. He served as ambassador, military adviser and Principal Secretary, and was knighted in 1577. Walsingham is best remembered as the Queen's spymaster. He created the first properly organised 'secret service' and employed many innovations to further his work, including the use of ingenious codes and intelligence-gathering methods. He employed a network of thousands of spies throughout England, Scotland, Wales and Ireland, as well as on the continent of Europe. Walsingham was almost single-handedly responsible for the thwarting of at least half a dozen plots against the person of the Queen, and his spy network was invaluable in the ongoing conflicts with Spain during Elizabeth's long reign. He died a little over a year after the setting of this book, in April 1590.

ALSO AVAILABLE IN ARROW

Equinox
Michael White

**A brutal murder. A three-hundred-year-conspiracy.
A deadly secret.**

Oxford, 2006: a young woman is found brutally murdered, her
throat cut. Her heart has been removed and in its place lies an
apparently ancient gold coin. Twenty-four hours later, another
woman is found. The MO is identical, except that this time her
brain has been removed, and a silver coin lies glittering in the
bowl of her skull.

The police are baffled but when police photographer Philip
Bainbridge and his estranged lover Laura Niven become
involved, they discover that these horrific, ritualistic murders
are not confined to the here and now. And a shocking story
begins to emerge which intertwines Sir Isaac Newton, one of
seventeenth-century England's most powerful figures, with a
deadly conspiracy which echoes down the years to the present
day, as lethal now as it was then.

Before long those closest to Laura are in danger, and she finds
herself the one person who can rewrite history; the only person
who can stop the killer from striking again . . .

arrow books

ALSO AVAILABLE IN ARROW

The Medici Secret
Michael White

An ancient mystery. A conspiracy of silence.
A secret to kill for.

In the crypt of the Medici Chapel in Florence, palaeopathologist, Edie Granger, and her uncle, Carlin Mackenzie, are examining the mummified remains of one of the most powerful families in Renaissance Italy.

The embalmers have done their work well in terms of outward appearance. But under the crisp skin, the organs have shrivelled to a fraction of their original size, which means it is difficult to gather a usable DNA sample. Edie and Mackenzie both have serious doubts about the true identity of at least two of the five-hundred-year-old bodies.

And no one can explain the presence of an alien object discovered resting against Cosimo de Medici's spine.

For Carlin Mackenzie, this is the most fascinating and the most dangerous discovery of his life. For Edie, it is the beginning of an obsessive, life-threatening quest . . .

arrow books

THE POWER OF READING

Visit the Random House website and get connected with information on all our books and authors

EXTRACTS from our recently published books and selected backlist titles

COMPETITIONS AND PRIZE DRAWS Win signed books, audiobooks and more

AUTHOR EVENTS Find out which of our authors are on tour and where you can meet them

LATEST NEWS on bestsellers, awards and new publications

MINISITES with exclusive special features dedicated to our authors and their titles

READING GROUPS Reading guides, special features and all the information you need for your reading group

LISTEN to extracts from the latest audiobook publications

WATCH video clips of interviews and readings with our authors

RANDOM HOUSE INFORMATION including advice for writers, job vacancies and all your general queries answered

Come home to Random House

www.randomhouse.co.uk